HIS MAJESTY'S TRAMP

Together they'd gone down to the riverside park and were sitting on a bench under the bridge, Geebo and the tramp. Jack. Geebo had started calling him Jack; he wasn't the tramp anymore, he was Jack, this guy that Geebo knew. Geebo let him talk because it was interesting; hell, it was fascinating. Here was a guy claiming he'd come from another time and place ("a few Moments farther from Creation" was how he'd actually phrased it), a guy just going on and on about wizards and witches and a king named Agel who sat on his throne like a sack of potatoes and hardly twitched a muscle.

It was all very impressive, Jack was a talented bullshitter. Even though Geebo figured he was rehashing a bunch of four-ninety-five sword-and-sorcery novels he'd read at the men's shelter, this guy Jack was still one hell of a talented bullshitter.

A king named Agel.

A wasp called Lita.

"What," Geebo had interrupted a few minutes ago, "no unicorns?"

And Jack had shaken his head, insulted for half a second, then he'd bummed another menthol cigarette, and started talking again. Telling Geebo then about some crazy cult and its cruel high priest whose face, get *this,* was crawling with slugs. Yeah, sure.

Geebo let out his breath. "Who the hell *are* you?"

"I been *telling* you for the past hour, you just haven't been listening. Think you're so smart, think I'm crazy. I'm Jack," he said. "A Walker. His Majesty's Tramp."

OTHER BOOKS BY TOM DE HAVEN

CHRONICLES
OF THE
KING'S TRAMP
BOOK 1

WALKER OF WORLDS
TOM DE HAVEN

SPECTRA™

BANTAM BOOKS
NEW YORK · TORONTO · LONDON · SYDNEY · AUCKLAND

Special thanks to Lou Aronica, Betsy Mitchell, Alan Lynch,
David Keller, and Alice Alfonsi.

All of the characters in this book are fictitious,
and any resemblance to actual persons, living or
dead, is purely coincidental.

*This edition contains the complete text
of the original hardcover edition.*
NOT ONE WORD HAS BEEN OMITTED.

WALKER OF WORLDS

*A Bantam Spectra Book / published by arrangement with
Doubleday*

*PRINTING HISTORY
Doubleday edition published / July 1990
Bantam edition / July 1991*

FOR KATE AND JESSIE,
WHO DREAMED UP ALL THE BEST NAMES IN THE BOOK
—AND MADE SURE THAT I USED 'EM.

*"The true adventurer goes forth
aimless and uncalculating
to meet and greet unknown fate."*

—O. HENRY

WALKER OF WORLDS

A DOG'S LIFE IS BRIEF

THROUGH A SUNLESS NAR-
row alley, Black Dog hastened with a mind keenly aware of
itself. I HAVE NEVER EXISTED IN THIS WAY BEFORE, he
thought, amazed and delighted (appalled and frightened) by
the voice in his head. AND I AM LOOKING FOR SOMEONE.

He stopped to sniff at the ground, then—ears suddenly
up—he glanced behind him, down the alley to the street,
where a peddler was then passing, wheeling his cart of
rusted iron scrap. Then Black Dog continued up the alley.
Littered with broken glass, and with offal of every conceiv-
able sort, it was bordered by two clapboard buildings. In
each building were several doors, their lintels greasy.

Black Dog went to the only door that was whitewashed,
and scratched at it till his nails were nearly blunted. Finally
—through the big keyhole—a wasp came out. It was long,
about three inches in length, with a narrow waist and a
yellow-and-black banded abdomen. Its wings quivered petu-
lantly. Black Dog dropped back onto all fours.

I AM FROM MASTER SQUINTIK, he said, surprised by

his own message and with no idea who Master Squintik might be.

WHAT DOES THE MAGE WANT WITH HIS MAJESTY'S TRAMP? asked the wasp.

Black Dog could think of no response. I AM FROM MASTER SQUINTIK.

WHERE IS THE MAGE?

I CAN TAKE YOUR HOST, BUT I CANNOT TELL YOU, replied Black Dog.

Closing its wings, the wasp vanished back through the keyhole. Black Dog barked once, then retreated up the alley a short distance and sat down. Soon, the door opened and a man, stuffing his shirt into his trousers, stepped outside. On his feet were heavy walking shoes. "I am His Majesty's Tramp," he told Black Dog, "you may take me to Master Squintik."

So, guided by instinct, Black Dog led the tramp through a crowded merchants' bazaar with its clouds of midges and mosquitos and biting gnats, then into a big stone building behind the bustling square, then along a series of damp twisting corridors, to a chamber. Where Master Squintik (whose long, pale, sorrowful face, Black Dog realized suddenly, he both feared and adored) stood waiting. Squintik patted Black Dog on the head, and the canine part of his being responded warmly. "Go lie down," Squintik told him , after leading the tramp into the chamber and barring the heavy wooden door.

WHO AM I? the dog asked. DO I BELONG TO YOU?

"Go lie down," Master Squintik repeated, his voice becoming stern. Black Dog whimpered at the rebuke, but did as he'd been told, and slept.

When he came awake, the master's chamber was

empty. No, not empty. There were no *men*, both Master Squintik and His Majesty's Tramp were gone, but Black Dog sensed other intelligent lives about, curled up in the gloomy corners, scuttling across the gritty floors, slung in tiny webs.

I HAVE A HUMAN MIND, announced Black Dog. CAN ANYONE TELL ME WHAT I AM DOING WITH SUCH A FACULTY? COULD YOU MAKE YOURSELF KNOWN? COULD YOU TALK TO ME?

But no one responded.

Black Dog began to sniff around, and poked his nose toward a spider, who was crossing a web, moving quickly toward a trapped green fly.

DO YOU HAVE A HUMAN MIND?

Apparently not, or else it was refusing to communicate, rebuffing him. Was he an odious thing? Did others not like Black Dog, for some reason?

He continued his examination of the chamber, which was lit by only a few squat candles. There was the merest slit of a window in one wall, and through it was a patch of starry night. A long table, several chests of drawers, and many shelves of various-shaped bottles filled with colored vapors and fluids.

Black Dog heard a tinkling sound among some of those bottles, and, standing upon his hind legs and bracing himself against a shelf with his forepaws, he asked, MOUSE, DO YOU POSSESS A HUMAN MIND?

ALL RIGHT, YES, admitted the tiny wrinkled creature appearing from between two clear bottles. WHY ARE YOU MAKING SUCH A COMMOTION? DON'T YOU REALIZE IT'S THE MIDDLE OF THE NIGHT? SOME OF US ARE VERY BUSY.

AND OTHERS OF US, put in a voice from somewhere in the chamber, ARE RESTING.

BUT I'VE JUST GOT MY HUMAN MIND, said Black Dog, AND HAVE MANY QUESTIONS.

The mouse clicked over to the edge of the shelf. It stopped mere inches from the dog's muzzle. YOU BELONG TO MASTER SQUINTIK OF DWINDLING STREET, A COLD MAGE. THIS IS A ROOM IN THE BUREAU OF CHARMS AGAINST CHAOS. YOUR SELF-AWARENESS IS LIKELY TO BE ONLY TEMPORARY. PURSUE YOUR INSTINCTUAL LIFE AS BEST YOU CAN. IF YOU BECOME TOO HUMAN, YOU WON'T BE WORTH ANYTHING LATER ON AS A—

DOG, said the dog.

DOG, said the mouse, distastefully, then ran off.

WAIT! TELL ME, WHAT IS THE BUREAU OF CHARMS AGAINST CHAOS? said Black Dog, but right away that other voice from somewhere in the chamber, said, KEEP IT DOWN!

With another apology, Black Dog turned away from the shelf, slinked across the floor. Under the table, he walked in a tight circle three times before settling comfortably into a ball of fur. Though he wasn't tired, he slept again, and dreamed about the mouse, and the tramp he'd brought to this chamber, and of the many wagons he'd seen in the bazaar laden with gleaming fish and salted pork and honey cakes, everything covered with undulant layers of insects.

Much later (the stars were gone, the sky was pale), Black Dog snapped alert, roused by a loud noise, and saw Master Squintik at the door, jamming the crossbar into place. When he'd finished and turned into the chamber, the Cold Mage's face was blanched with panic; his eyes were open wide, his tongue flicked from side to side in his red mouth, his hands were clenched tightly. In the same instant that Black Dog absorbed his master's terror, he was intestinally aware of something dangerous coming this way down the corridors beyond the barred door, along the same gloomy corridors he'd led the tramp.

Fur bristling, a low growl in his throat, Black Dog watched Master Squintik hurry to a high chest that stood against a wall; watched him pull open a drawer, then take from it a tray containing three small cups of gray liquid. He carried the tray to his table and set it down.

Something outside struck the chamber door; wood splintered.

Black Dog urinated, and was immediately ashamed of himself.

MASTER—!

But the Cold Mage paid no attention to Black Dog: having removed a gold ring from one of the cups, a ring set with three sharp points, he slipped it over the first finger of his left hand. Then, as Black Dog watched, frantic but rapt, he clenched his fist and struck his arm downward. Scintillation burst along the arc, and faded to reveal a long, surgically neat cut in the air. Its edges moved in and out with the rhythm of labored breathing.

After taking one final glance toward the door, Master Squintik pushed a foot and leg through the slit. Seeing the mage leaving, vanishing, Black Dog leapt across the floor. He snatched hold of Squintik's cassock, clenched the hem in his teeth and pulled. DO NOT LEAVE ME!

Master Squintik plucked up the dog roughly by the scruff of the neck, and sent him tumbling backwards, to collide with a table leg, a rag of fabric in his mouth.

By the time he could recover and spring back onto his feet, Master Squintik was gone, and the tear sealed.

With a blast of panic, Black Dog swung his head around. The door was buckling in, hinges shrieked. Then wood exploded, jagged chunks of it striking the ceiling, clattering on the floor, exploding several bottles on a shelf.

Framed in the doorway stood a skeletal man dressed in high-churchman's vestments: cassock, alb and chasuble, and a precious miter. Except for his thin lips and his eyes, his face was covered with grayish-white slugs in motion. He stepped into the chamber, shoving aside pieces of broken door with his crosier. He was followed in by a dwarfish woman wearing a brown habit and veil.

Black Dog went down on his belly and nestled his face on his paws. He tried to keep the guilt and fear from his eyes, but knew that he was largely unsuccessful.

MAGE OF FOUR, MAGE OF LUCK, said a creature somewhere, and Black Dog could hear its words, and their obsequious tone, clearly in his mind. SQUINTIK HAS USED ONE OF THE SCHOOLTEACHER'S RINGS TO ESCAPE.

The woman gave a short groan of disgust, then produced a stick of lead and a wrinkled sheet of paper from her knitted bag. She wrote something down. "And Jack, a Walker?" she asked. Her voice was like sandpaper, yet very forceful.

ESCAPED IN THE SAME WAY, SISTER. BEFORE.

The Mage of Four, Mage of Luck strode across the chamber. He glanced at the tray of cups, then poked a fingertip into a spider's gossamer web and snapped it. The spider scuttled onto his polished nail.

"Who brought the tramp here?"

THAT DOG, replied the spider.

Black Dog trembled, feeling the eyes of the great mage and the eyes of the dwarf turning upon him.

"Abomination. Where did you find the tramp?" said the Mage of Four, Mage of Luck.

Shakily, Black Dog got to his feet, keeping his tail between his legs.

"Answer His Excellency," said the dwarf, threatening him with her booted foot.

IN AN ALLEY NEAR THE MARKETPLACE, said Black Dog. IT HAD A WHITE DOOR.

"Aculita," said the dwarf, addressing the great mage. "He was at the witch's house. I *told* you—"

"Lower your voice, Sister Card," said the Mage of Four, Mage of Luck. Then he glanced down at the spider for a moment before pinching it between two fingers and crushing it to a bit of matter.

Black Dog felt a twinge of nausea and despair, and slinked off to the farthest corner of the chamber. He went down again on his belly, moving his lustrous brown eyes back and forth. Sister Card had gone to the long table, and now gave another throaty groan. "The Cold Mage has traveled to Kemolo." She held up one of the cups of gray fluid.

The Mage of Four, Mage of Luck stood and considered for a few moments, then striking the floor emphatically with his crosier, he said, "Tell Eudrax, a Finder that I shall expect him at my residence for dinner this evening. Tell him to come alone. And see to it that all of Squintik's abominations are destroyed." He strode from the chamber. Black Dog could hear his footsteps receding down the corridor.

With the blade of her left hand, Sister Card—who'd spread her skirts around her and knelt down—described a seven-sided figure in the air; then, over it, she made an **X**, which she then bisected, horizontally. In the meantime, her lips were moving.

A point of light appeared where she'd gestured, then expanded. When it was the size of an apple, the light softly misted, and from the mist emerged a pale-green *thing*, vaguely toad-shaped but several times larger than any toad. It had two short legs, a sloping back, lidless eyes, a massive gullet, and a mouth full of sharp teeth.

Black Dog began to growl, his tail rising, his lips drawing back.

As the pale-green thing moved slowly toward Black Dog, it used its tongue to seize and swallow a waterbug, then a daddy longlegs. PLEASE DON'T KILL ME, said Black Dog, pulling his head between his shoulders, his fur going electric. I'VE ONLY JUST BEEN BORN.

Sister Card reverently kissed an ivory cameo that she wore on a purple ribbon around her neck, then bowed her head to meditate.

So deep was her concentration that she heard nothing whatever of the noisy kill that followed. . . .

CHAPTER 1

GEEBO

WHEN THE GUY IN THE white Corvette spotted Geebo coming off the avenue divider with a squeegee and a squirt bottle, he started wagging his head. Then he crisscrossed his arms. But since you wouldn't make a dime all night if you paid attention to signals like that, Geebo just leaned over the hood and pumped out Windex, then drew the rubber blade neatly across the windshield.

The light at the intersection of Erie Street and Avenue F stayed red for exactly one minute. Geebo finished with about twenty seconds to spare, then scooted around the front of the 'Vette to the driver's window, which was up. No big surprise.

Guy at the wheel, young guy, maybe twenty-five, twenty-six, staring straight ahead, blank-faced. Tweed overcoat, blue necktie, small perfect knot. Geebo tapped on the glass, lightly.

Nothing. The guy completely ignored him. With maybe twelve, fifteen seconds till green.

Cellular phone, Bensi Box, and a trim little attaché case, the kind guaranteed a gorilla couldn't nick. Instinctively, Geebo made a mental note of it all. He was constantly noticing little things about the cars that he "serviced"—vanity plates and witty bumper stickers, dashboard junk, titles of magazines in the footwell. It was puzzling to him: how come he did that? Yeah, how come? How come (for instance) it gave him such a kick now to spot a caddy of audio tapes on the passenger bucket (George Michaels, Prince, the original London-cast recording of *Phantom of the Opera)?* All that information was nothing to him. Stupid details. Yet: he collected them. How come? If he tried to answer that question, though, if he racked his brains and really thought about it, he'd just end up sick to his stomach and shaky all over. Then the Headache would come down.

"Hey!" said Geebo. "Little heart, my man. We live on tips down here."

That did it, made the jerk look at him, at least. And once he'd looked, he curled his lip, then peeled out, hanging a left into Avenue F and tearing south toward the Cushing River Bridge. If Geebo hadn't jumped clear, he'd've had both feet crushed. But it wasn't even close. He'd seen it coming. Sure. Nothing wrong with *his* reflexes. Yet.

As lethal traffic whizzed by on either side of him, horns blowing, Geebo zigzagged back to the divider, home base, and squatted on the cold greasy concrete, trying not to breathe much. He watched the stream of cars pass by, wondering again, as he frequently did, just how long it had been since he'd driven a car himself. He was certain that he *could* drive, that he knew *how* to drive, even though he had no license in his possession. No license? Christ, he had no *wallet* in his possession—no identification, period: just cigarettes, some change, mostly quarters, a dollar bill, and a lead sap sheathed in black rubber.

Waiting for the next red light, he shivered like crazy.

The temperature that evening—Friday, the first of December—was somewhere in the low twenties. You factor in that old wind-chill, though, and it was maybe seven, eight degrees. And Geebo was dressed the same as he'd been at summer's end—in a camouflage jacket over a long black sweatshirt, jeans, and canvas sneakers. The only thing he'd done so far to winterize was to buy a cheap pair of gloves.

Halfway up the divider, ten or so feet away, Nestor Crash and Billy Pollux were feeding hamburger sacks and beer cartons and candy wrappers, all sorts of gutter junk, anything that would burn, into a fire they had going in a big steel drum. Pollux was tall and lanky with a wedge-shaped head and long, green-dyed hair, same as the Joker in Batman comics. Nestor Crash was enormous, not only fat but tall, and bald except for a longish fringe around his ears. In his left ear, he wore a small black-enameled earring shaped like an old-fashioned A-bomb. They were a pair of strung-out badboys doing windshields till the upscale bars along Avenue A closed at four. Then they'd drift over there and make a few moves. Do some crime. "Manipulate," was how they phrased it.

The orange flames spurted in the drum, and Pollux started beating sparks from his coat collar. The fire looked good to Geebo, inviting as hell—he could almost feel himself being drawn to it, like a moth. But he resisted. It wasn't very bright to get cozy with Pollux and Crash. They were running on speed. Running on empty. And they were scary. They sure enough scared Geebo. He'd seen them turn on a Jamaican guy named Coke Cup, supposedly a good friend of theirs, and stomp him bloody. They'd broken three of his fingers, just snapped them like diner breadsticks. Two nights ago, over by the men's shelter on Woodlawn Avenue.

Next light, Geebo had his choice of a red Chevy pickup or a beige Colt with lots of coloring books in the back window. He took the Colt since there was a woman driving, and women, he'd discovered, were more apt than men to give you money. This woman was about thirty, with long wavy brown hair, a small clear mole on her cheek. A tan cashmere coat. Her husband sat beside her, a theater program—from *Cats*—tubed in his lap. The car radio was playing country-western, loud. Randy Travis segued into the Judds. Geebo duly noted.

As he backed off, he gave the driver a wink, almost flirting, and she gave him a look of pity. "Have a nice weekend," he said, pocketing fifty cents. Then, from the corner of his eye, he glimpsed somebody, a skinhead in a black leather jacket, drop off the curb at the northwest corner.

Don't let it be Johnny Stillborn.

So of course it was. Geebo cut suddenly to his right, and Johnny Stillborn screamed past him, leaping the divider and clicking a pair of barber shears. He stopped on the southwest corner, and laughed, but then his crazy grin quit suddenly when he saw Billy Pollux aim a Colt at him.

"I'll shoot off your foot, you dirtbag," said Pollux. "I truly will."

While Johnny Stillborn stared soberly down at his biker boots, Geebo tucked his squirt bottle and squeegee into his shoulder bag and started walking north on Avenue F, moving quickly, following his Immutable Law of Survival. Leave at the first name-calling.

He passed a row of Cuban funeral parlors, then a Fili-

pino travel agency with its accordion gate closed and pad-
locked, then a corner social club that had a green neon palm
tree in the window seat. Inside was some kind of party: he
could see twisted crepe and red balloons, and a crush of
people standing around holding cans of malt liquor.

Slowing down a little and hunching his shoulders
against the cold, he turned east on Vick Street, at the White
Castle. Some minutes later, he arrived at Stephen Crane
Park, entering through a big stone arch covered with flam-
boyant signature graffiti. He followed the path around. In
the playground, a few broken chains dangled from rusted
swings, and a couple of stoned hookers sat laughing on the
jungle gym. The wading pool was a busy drug bazaar.

As he topped the next hill, clouds moved away from
the moon, and the lawn below—Big Lawn—was suddenly
bathed in milky light that illuminated several dozen packing
crates, tents, and shacks built of interior doors. Broken glass
sparkled in the dirt. Fires were burning in trash cans. A
haphazard city of the homeless.

Crossing the lawn, Geebo nodded at a few people standing around a fire, heard somebody inside a nylon tent cough
up phlegm, then he stopped dead in his tracks, and cursed.

His carton was gone!

Oh man, somebody stole his carton! He couldn't believe
it. He could not friggen believe it! Somebody had literally
dragged his carton away, the beautiful water-heater carton
that he'd lugged all the way from the city dump, that he'd
written on in green Magic Marker, big capital letters: PRI-
VATE PROPERTY. DO NOT REMOVE OR INHABIT.

"If you're looking for your house, honey, some guy took
it over to the band shell."

"How long ago?"

"Couple minutes. Maybe half an hour."

"One guy? By himself?" Geebo was talking to Jere Lee, his neighbor for the past two weeks. She was ensconced inside a windbreak made of Sheetrock and half-buried under a lump of coats and blankets.

"One guy," she said. "By himself."

Geebo shook his head, then turned and looked toward the band shell, at the far end of the lawn: an oval silhouette with a railing and a peaked roof. "Did you say anything to him?"

"Don't you know you shouldn't talk to strangers?"

Geebo cursed again.

"But so why don't you squeeze in here with me?" said Jere Lee, shifting a little, making room for him. Without hesitation, he took her up on her offer. Once he'd crawled in, she let him cover himself with her blankets. He drew up his knees and leaned on them, folded his hands below his chin.

"Guy just walks away with your house," muttered Geebo.

"Finders keepers."

"Still, it's pretty stinking low. In my opinion." He shrugged. Then he asked Jere Lee what was new with her, anything?

She said, "Not much," then told him about going to the Shop-Rite on Kensington Boulevard that afternoon. She'd applied for a cashier's job. "I used to work a cash register, way back when I was first married. So I got some experience. Of course," she added with a soft chuckle, "that was a long time ago."

Geebo leaned out of the windbreak, and took another look at the band shell.

"I got married in 1962," said Jere Lee. "December the eleventh, 1962."

Geebo grunted, thinking again (he couldn't help it) that it was pretty goddamn stinking low, somebody stealing your water-heater carton—especially when it was so clearly marked private property.

"I was working the cash register at Woolworth's when John F. Kennedy was shot," Jere Lee was saying now. "I remember that I got so upset, my hands started shaking on the keys. I kept tearing Green Stamps." After a beat, she asked, "Where were you?"

"Where was I when?"

"Kennedy was shot."

Geebo tried to think, and it hurt. Where *had* he been? "I don't remember."

"Oh, come on. Everybody does."

Geebo lifted a shoulder, dropped it.

"I was eighteen," she said, "when JFK got shot. I was seventeen when I got married."

Geebo said, yeah, he knew; he remembered her telling him that just the other evening. In a short time, he'd learned a lot about Jere Lee (well, she was a big yak), all kinds of stuff—where her grown daughters were living, one out in Denver, the other up in Bangor, Maine; even where her ex-husband was living, in Cleveland. Geebo knew that she was born in August, 1945, the same week as Hiroshima, but not the exact day; that she liked to read Louis L'Amour novels and books on American history; that she was prone to kidney infections, and allergic to potatoes. That she'd lost her clerical job last April, undergone abdominal surgery in June, and that her apartment building had burned down while she was still in the hospital. That it would take her ten years to pay all her medical bills, *if* she still had a job. And that she couldn't bring herself to go to a social agency, she had too much pride.

Geebo, on the other hand, hadn't told her anything. Except about his most recent life. His life since the first Tuesday of last September. Geebo had begun to date things relative to last September fifth. Which was the date he'd spotted on a newspaper the morning he woke up on the steps of the Astor Place subway station. With blood on his hands, a blank memory, and a single word, Geebo, throbbing in his head.

Somewhere nearby, an argument had erupted; a black man and two black women, from the sound of it, everybody really agitated, screaming obscenities. Geebo couldn't figure out what it was all about, but it was sure loud and it kept getting louder.

"So where were you?" Jere Lee asked. "Really and truly. The day Kennedy was killed."

"I told you, I don't remember. And who cares?"

"How old were you? You must've been a kid."

He didn't reply.

"How old are you now?"

He shook his head.

Jere Lee fumbled around and pulled out a flashlight from behind her. It was long-barreled and aluminum with a red plastic head. She thumbed it on, and shined it in Geebo's face. Her small face was also lit. She had a gray watchcap pulled down almost to her eyebrows. Her skin was dry, lined. She had good cheekbones, though, and clear blue eyes. "Amnesia like yours," she said, "is for soap operas, kiddo. I don't believe it."

"I can't help that."

"You know what I think?" she said. "I think you just want to be a man of mystery."

Now it was Geebo's turn to laugh. Man of mystery. Right.

Jere Lee turned off the flashlight, then shifted around and suddenly kissed Geebo. He tasted butterscotch Life Savers on her breath. When she tried to kiss him again, Geebo pulled away.

A few moments later, she asked him, "You ever been to Florida?"

"I don't know."

She let that pass. "I like Fort Lauderdale. I was thinking of going there."

"You mean soon?"

"Sure, soon. Why stick around here? Want to come?"

"Me?"

"Yeah, you and me. We could find jobs. Start fresh."

"I don't know."

"What, I'm too old for you?"

"Don't be stupid. Too old. How do you know I'm not older than you?"

"Take it from me, Geebo. You're not."

"Well, my age got nothing to do with it. Or yours. I just don't want to go to Florida, is all."

"What's here to keep you?"

He didn't answer immediately. Then he just said, "I don't know."

"Well, all *I* know is, you don't freeze to death in Florida." Then she said, "Listen, Geebo, it's kind of crowded in here, huh?" All of a sudden, her tone was nasty. "You think you could find someplace else?"

"Yeah, sure," he said, ticked off. So really ticked that,

purely for spite, he picked up Jere Lee's flashlight and slipped it into his bag. She didn't notice. Or even look at him as he crawled outside and stood up. He had a sudden malign impulse to kick her shopping cart over, but didn't. He wasn't a shit.

Whoever he was.

Geebo ambled away across Big Lawn, trying to figure out what to do next, where to go. He didn't have too many great ideas. Forget the city shelter. It would've taken a blizzard to get him back in there. He'd spent three long nights at the shelter in November: he'd been slugged, robbed, and infested with lice. And he couldn't go sleep in the bus station anymore: recently the cops had started to clear everybody out at eleven. So what did that leave? A bench? But he never could fall asleep on a bench. Too exposed. He had to be indoors, or inside *something*.

Something like his water-heater carton. That carton was perfect. Almost . . . beautiful. Six feet long. Man, he could stretch out, full-length, even kind of make believe that he was camping. (He used to *go* camping; he felt that, very strongly, in a cellular way, but it just wasn't worth trying to remember specific camping trips, places camped. Companions. Nothing would come of it, except the Headache.)

If he had his carton, he could get a good night's rest. So what if it was only cardboard; so what if he was as vulnerable inside it as he would've been lying on a street corner; so what? It was a confined space, somewhere to *be*. Private. You could even close the end flaps.

And some friggen thief had stolen it!

Without planning it, or maybe he'd planned it without letting himself know, Geebo found himself, two minutes later, standing at the foot of the band shell. And there was

his A. O. Smith water-heater carton (sixty-gallon capacity)
lying up there on the plank floor. Climbing the steps, he toed
a big chunk of glass. It shot away and struck the riser. Plink.
Geebo went rigid. But then something weird happened. He
suddenly felt . . . steadier and more focused than he had
since . . . since waking up in September. It was almost a
euphoria. It was certainly a resolve. He was going to go kick
at the side of his carton—*his* carton—and he was going to
demand that this goddamn squatter, big or small, mean or
chickenshit, move his butt *out* of there.

Very slowly, and as carefully as if he were performing a
ritual, Geebo put down his shoulder bag and took out his
sap. Thinking, And if the guy doesn't come out, I'll keep on
kicking till he does. Then I'm going to bust his head.

But with that thought, a memory flashed in his brain.
Of hitting somebody with a fireplace shovel, a bald guy. He
could *see* the guy, crumpled on a blue carpet, bleeding from
his ear. Eyes open. Christ. He'd struck somebody with a fireplace shovel!

Sometime before last September fifth. . . .

Killed him?

Geebo's vision blurred, and he felt waves of nausea.

All that euphoria, or whatever it had been, was
abruptly, totally gone. And a pressure was starting at the
base of his neck, crawling slowly through his head. Branch-
ing. Geebo squeezed the bridge of his nose between two fingers, gave a groan, staggered. Felt sick at his stomach.
Grabbed for the railing, and missed.

He sat down, hard, on the top step, left hand going to
his forehead. His fingertips were cold.

Then something brushed against the back of his hand.

Something small, practically weightless, with beating wings and a prickling touch.

And whatever it was would not be shaken off.

Finally, it stung him.

CHAPTER 2

MONEY TALKS

AT FOUR IN THE MORN-
ing, Money Campbell woke in the dark, not sure where she
was. She hoped she was in her own apartment, but no, the
bed sheets and pillow case were satin—which meant she
was in the city, and that the man spooned against her, snor-
ing gently, was Eugene Boman. The realization brought a
long groan from Money, and she moved closer to the edge of
the mattress, drew her knees up, and eventually fell back to
sleep.

When she woke again, it was because the morning sun
was in her eyes. The drapes were pulled back. Framed and
hanging on the walls were several watercolor drawings by
Dr. Seuss and an original "Beetle Bailey" Sunday page. In the
building directly across Sixty-third Street, a uniformed-and-
capped maid was vacuuming the living room of a corner
apartment. The one with all the Warhol paintings.

Dressed in a gray French-made suit, Eugene Boman was
seated at the little plastic bedroom table of arty design, having coffee and paging through a collectibles catalog. He was

fat and moonfaced, and even though he wasn't yet thirty (the Boy Billionaire, the newspapers and TV still called him), he was almost completely bald. Very little hair left, only a few white-blond licks pasted across his forehead. "It's going on nine," he said, his raspy voice setting Money's teeth on edge. As usual. "You should get up."

Money nodded, then checked to see if she was wearing a nightgown. She was, a filmy black one. Boman kept a bureau full of racy negligees for her to wear. Tossing off the covers, she ran into the bathroom.

"Don't I even get a good morning?" said Boman. Christ, he was whining already.

"Good *morning,*" she said, and closed the bathroom door. First thing Money had to do, she had to brush her teeth, or she couldn't stand it. She kept a tube of her favorite brand there, the kind that tasted like Bazooka bubble gum.

A few minutes later, while she was in the shower, she remembered—with a tingle that raced up her spine and quite suddenly made her light-headed—that Peter Musik was still alive.

At least that's what Herb Dierickx had told her last night, driving her back here from a party at the art museum. "The Music Man," he said, "is still breathing."

And then he'd told her that he'd seen him, that he'd actually seen Peter with his own two eyes. Cleaning windshields. "I'd thought he was long buried in some pine swamp. But there he was, kid, cleaning windshields. A bum."

"Money, are you ever going to get out of there?" Eugene Boman had come into the bathroom, and was dispelling steam clouds with both his hands. "How can you stand to take such a hot shower?"

He slid the shower door open. Naturally, his gaze went first to her breasts, and *then* to her face. At least he didn't fondle her. "I want you out of here in fifteen minutes—okay?"

"I'll be out in a minute."

"I mean out of the *apartment.*"

"Oh, thanks a lot. Why fifteen minutes?"

"Some people are coming up," he said, sounding almost apologetic. He stepped away from the shower. "You can come back anytime after two. Or do you have classes tonight?"

"Today's Saturday."

"Oh. Right. Well—Dierickx is downstairs, if you want the car." He pronounced the driver's name Deer-ick. He did it all the time, and it really pissed Money off. He couldn't say Deer-ix? He couldn't say it right? Curtly, she closed the shower door, and turned her face directly under the spray of water. "You'll have to find something to do for a few hours," Boman said. "Think you can?"

Yeah, she thought. I can find something to do. You son of a bitch. I can go find Peter Musik.

Or try to.

It took Money half an hour to get ready, blow-drying her hair then pulling it back and clipping it with shell barrettes. No makeup. She put on jeans, a long-sleeved T-shirt, then a lightweight leather jacket. When she left, she didn't bother to say good-bye.

Boman never looked up from his catalog.

In the lobby, thirty-nine flights down, she passed four solemn-looking Japanese businessmen. She smiled at the doorman, and walked outside. It was a chilly, gray morning. She went into a coffee shop on the corner of Avenue A. Had a cheese danish and a diet Pepsi, then phoned Herb Dierickx and told him where to pick her up. While she waited, she smoked a cigarette and read the Cliffs Notes to *The House of Mirth*. It was going to be on her final exam later in the month, American Lit of the Gilded Age. . . .

Once every week, usually on a Thursday or Friday, Herb Dierickx visited a secondhand paperback store called The Trading Post. It was on Fifth Street, in a seedy neighborhood in the Bridge District, just south of Crane Park. He'd spend an hour browsing in there, then come away with a white plastic sack laden with fifteen, maybe twenty books that would cost him only three or four dollars. That's all. Three or four bucks. It was great. The place always had a lot of fifties novels, which Herb collected—at least he collected the great spicy covers. After he was done reading a novel (by Jim Thompson or Erle Stanley Gardner or Frank Yerby, those kind of guys) he'd tear off the cover and plasticize it. He kept his collection filed alphabetically in a shoebox.

Besides the fifties stuff, he'd load up on true-crime books of more recent vintage; he loved those babies, which gave you the shocking *real* stories behind last year's headlines—stories about rich murderous families, serial killers, devil cults, love triangles turned lethal. He was addicted to true-crime books, he just loved them. There were so many monsters in the human race, it was incredible.

Herb had gotten several of both kinds of books at The Trading Post just yesterday, and it was on his way back uptown afterward that he saw Peter Musik at the intersection of Erie Street and Avenue F.

Jesus God, there he was: Peter. It was Peter, all right, it

was the Music Man. He'd lost a lot of weight, and grown a tangled beard, but he was still wearing the same clothes he'd had on last Labor Day weekend.

Transfixed, and more than a little creeped, Herb had sat out the red light watching Peter Musik briskly clean the windshield of a maroon BMW.

And then all the rest of the way up to Sixty-third Street, he'd tried to figure out what to do. Should he tell somebody? Who should he tell? He couldn't mention it to Mr. Boman— could he? Well, *could* he? No, he couldn't. Nor could he tell his wife—she wouldn't understand. So who *could* he tell, then?

He'd finally told the girl with the great breasts, Money Campbell, which—when he'd thought it over, afterward— he probably shouldn't have done. But he'd had to tell somebody. Just *had* to. And besides, she'd known him. Money had known Peter Musik. Quite well, as a matter of fact. . . .

At ten of ten that Saturday morning, Herb Dierickx left the underground parking garage at Lincoln Towers, where Mr. Boman lived, to pick up Money Campbell. On the telephone, she hadn't said where she wanted to go, but he was *hoping* it was out to the college. That was always a nice ride, once you got over the bridge, and Herb wouldn't mind leaving the city for a couple of hours.

When he pulled up and double-parked in front of the coffee shop, he had an all-talk station on the car radio. He switched it off, though, when he saw Money come outside; he knew her well enough by then to know she hated phone-in shows, discussions of AIDS and current books and race relations and glasnost, all that kind of stuff. She wasn't much of a music lover, either. She didn't even like rock. Usually, when he drove her around, he left the radio off.

Yeah, he sort of knew what she liked and didn't like—superficially. She was somebody he'd got to know on the job. A co-worker, you might say.

Heads turned as Money darted across the sidewalk. Men checking out the blonde. Herb smiled to himself. It *was* a pleasure to see her. Absolutely. Although he'd be fifty-seven come next birthday, Herb was still young enough in spirit to appreciate the girl's killer good-looks. Man, when she dressed up? You could mistake her for somebody at the Academy Awards. He'd told her that once—he'd even told her that, with her face, her figure, that great hair, she could easily be an actress.

She'd thanked him for the compliment, but said she had no interest in becoming an actress.

Herb had wanted then to ask her, "So what *do* you have an interest in, kid?" but felt he had no right to ask that personal a question. He just hoped she wasn't planning to marry Eugene Boman, because it wasn't about to happen.

The boss already *had* a wife, and two small sons. They lived downstate.

"You want to find Peter?" Herb was saying now, as he nosed the long white car into traffic. All of sudden he didn't feel so good. He glanced into the rearview mirror. Money was lighting a cigarette. He wished she wouldn't smoke, but what was he going to say: Don't? He was only the driver. "Seems to me, the boss wants him lost."

"Yeah? Well, too bad. If Peter's alive, I want to find him."

"And then what?"

She leaned forward. Her cigarette smoke drifted past his nose, and he couldn't resist: he inhaled. Watch, he'd probably end up buying a pack at lunchtime. And after he'd dropped a few hundred bucks last June for Smokenders. Margie would kill him if he started smoking again. "You know how Gene thought that Peter Musik was getting information about him and Major Forell from somebody in the company? Well," said Money, "it wasn't somebody in the company, exactly. It was me."

"Oh Jesus," Herb said. "I didn't hear that."

"Yes, you did. Oh yes, you did. Because I said it."

"Why're you telling me?"

"Because I want you and me to find Peter, and then I want us all to go to the District Attorney. Or somebody like that. Or the newspaper. Or the President of the United States."

"No way, kid." Herb thinking, Holy shit. Thinking, Would you *listen* to this bimbo? Looks like a million bucks, looks like Michelle Pfeiffer, and she's talking like some nitwit sixteen-year-old. The President of the United States! "Be a little reasonable."

Hitting the directional, he turned off A into West Fifty-ninth Street. Along here were facing rows of diamond shops. Herb pulled to the curb. Money bounced forward again. "I said I wanted you to take me downtown. I want you to show me where you saw Peter."

"No." Hitching around in his seat, he looked at her. Jeez. Even without makeup, she was one very attractive young lady. "Forget it. You put me in a bad position. Me and my big fat mouth."

Money stubbed out her cigarette with such violence that she nearly pulled the ashtray off the door. "I'm going to find him."

"No, you're not. No, you're not."

"Just don't tell Gene. If you tell Gene, he'll tell that

Major guy and then I'm dead." She opened the door and jumped out.

"Hey, Money, *no!* Come back! I won't—"

He didn't chase after her. Just stood in the street and watched her run to the corner then disappear into the subway.

Thinking, Jeez, he could end up a character in somebody's true-crime book next year. In next year's true-crime *bestseller*. If things got out of hand here.

Way to go, Herb, he said to himself. Way to go.

CHAPTER 3

BREAKFAST WITH THE TRAMP

"**Y**OU SICK?" ASKED THE TRAMP, squatted down opposite Geebo. His eyes were pale blue, squinted, utterly steady. His pupils were like pindots. "I'm asking you a question: you sick?" And the skin on his face was like leather. Gray leather.

Still cradling his left hand—it was all swollen, especially around the little puncture—Geebo licked his lips. They felt dry, chapped. His mouth was slimy. He was sitting on the floor of the band shell, his legs straight out, his back against the railing. The cold sun was up. He'd been sleeping off and on, uncovered and shivering in the wind, hunched fetally, his hand throbbing in sync with the Headache.

A couple of times during the night he'd heard—or *thought* he'd heard; maybe he'd been delirious—voices inside the water-heater carton.

A man's voice and a woman's voice.

Now Geebo lifted his chin and looked at the tramp.

(Who was alone: no girlfriend.) Looked at his long ropy black hair and the wide scar above his left eyebrow, at the smaller, ragged scar on his throat. Impossible to say how old the guy was. Somewhere between thirty—twenty-five?—and forty.

Squeezing his temples between his fingertips (the torment in his head had finally receded), Geebo looked down—at the wasp, at the biggest damn wasp he'd ever seen in his *life:* on the toggle of the tramp's jacket zipper. A few moments ago it had been on the tramp's shoulder. A wasp—in December?

The tramp rubbed his eyes with the palms of both hands. Circling his left wrist was a thick bracelet—it looked like hammered copper. "You were moaning out here. You sick?"

Geebo said, "I'll be all right." Moaning? What, in his sleep? The dream. (. . . the baby.) Was still fresh in his mind: he'd been climbing a flight of decrepit stairs, he'd climbed all the way to the top, and gone through a wooden door onto a flat roof. There were two moons, one full, the other a quarter. The sky was deep dark blue. Beside a chimney pot, and striped with moonlight (moons' light) was a cradle with a, Jesus, some kind of weird mud baby (mud and straw and stones) laid in it. Geebo had watched it play with its fingers and snatch at its toes. Then it turned its head, and its eyes were like greasy eggs. He'd stumbled backwards, against the parapet. . . .

"I just had a bad dream," Geebo said now (but why tell *him?)* and got to his feet. His knees popped. The tramp remained hunkered, then turned a slow, quizzical gaze on Geebo and finally stood up himself. Geebo's eyes cut immediately back to the wasp. Still on the zipper, its membranous wings opening and closing, opening and closing.

"How much money do you have?" said the tramp. "On you?"

Geebo didn't answer right away, just inclined his head to one side. Thinking, What, I should tell you? But he said, "A few dollars."

"So let's have breakfast," said the tramp, going down the steps.

Geebo scratched at his scalp, then scratched behind one ear. "You slept in my carton," he said, gesturing foolishly toward it with his free hand, his left hand, the sore hand. "That's mine."

"Let's go," said the tramp.

Figuring what the hell, he could do with some companionship, Geebo shrugged, then picked up his shoulder bag and joined the tramp on the macadamized path.

A guy clutching hand-weights loped past; he was wearing a Coors T-shirt and red nylon track shorts, and the bunched muscles in his legs stood out like biscuits and loaves of bread. Geebo watched him disappear around the curve, and felt a momentary urge to do the same thing, go for a run. Maybe he used to be a runner? Possible. He'd been in pretty decent physical shape back in September, and he really wasn't in *bad* shape now, just a little bit starved, a little bit stiff.

Go for a run? And burn up a whole lot of calories? Screw that.

Walking alongside the tramp, Geebo said, "I only got maybe five dollars, I can spring for donuts but that's about all."

The tramp nodded, then his long gaunt face broke into

a big smile (yellow fang-teeth in dark red gums). It was so unexpected—till then, he'd kept his mouth and eyes practically expressionless—that it struck Geebo as bizarre, even scary. Maybe this character was a nutcase.

In three months, Geebo had developed an acute fear of weird street people, of old ladies in tight white slacks, of guys who wore junkshop medals and oddball caps, of anybody who smiled too much, or too suddenly: they could get real violent real quick.

"What's so funny?"

The tramp let his smile relax, then pass. "Something wrong with your head, man." A statement, not a question. "I don't know what," he said, "but something is definitely wrong with your head." Then, with a low grunt, he walked on, and Geebo warily followed, thinking, What's *he* know about something wrong with my head?

After they'd left the park and started ambling up Broadway, not talking, Geebo checked on the wasp again, but it was no longer on the tramp's jacket.

They turned at Tenth Street and headed west, walked clear across town to Avenue A, where there was a strip of fast-food places. Geebo counted up his money before going into the Dunkin' Donuts: $5.60. "How come I'm buying you breakfast?" he said, pulling open the door. "You wanna run that by me again?"

The tramp merely smiled.

Geebo recognized both girls working in the donut shop, but when he said hello to them, they just looked at him deadpan. He'd begun to realize only recently that he could engender fear and revulsion in others—that some people were afraid that *he* might be a loony tune.

Geebo and the tramp took stools at one of the horseshoe

counters and ordered coffee. The tramp wanted soup, but there wasn't any available that early (it was a little past nine), so he settled for a french cruller. Geebo had a powdered donut. He looked around; the only other customer was a bag lady sitting hunched over, reading a novena booklet.

"Please pay when served," said the Hispanic waitress, pointing to where it said just that on the menu sign.

Geebo gave her the exact amount in change, and she rang it up, then went and put a fresh basket of coffee into the Braun machine.

"You're buying me breakfast," said the tramp, "because you got stung by a wasp. Just to answer your question." Then blithely *(so* blithely that it had to be intentional, wise-guy punctuation) he reached across Geebo for the little tin milk pitcher.

"Wait a second," said Geebo.

"A wasp named Lita." The tramp pushed back his left shirt sleeve, and there it was, the wasp (named *Lita?)* splayed on the bracelet. Actually, it looked fitted into a notch.

Geebo got up to leave.

"Sit down," said the tramp. And Geebo sat. "Pass me the sugar." Geebo passed him the sugar. "Ashtray?" With a frown, Geebo reached over and got the ashtray, then put it down in front of the tramp, whose face was shining with amusement. "What's your name?"

"Geebo."

"That's all?"

"That's all."

The tramp lifted his hand to shake Geebo's. "Jack," he said. "Walker. We meet by accident."

"What?"

"You smoke?"

"Yeah," Geebo answered, suddenly cautious.

"What kind? Menthol?"

"No."

"You hate menthol?"

"I don't smoke them."

"Okay. I want you to get up and go over to that machine there and get a pack of menthol cigarettes."

Geebo took a sip of coffee. Before setting the mug down, he grabbed a napkin and put it underneath. "Get it yourself."

Jack bit on his lip, nodding. "You have a concussion lately, something like that?"

"Why?"

"You don't feel the *slightest* inclination to go buy a pack of menthol cigarettes?" He seemed a little baffled, a little amused, a little chagrined.

"No," said Geebo with a glance behind him at the cigarette machine. "Sorry."

The tramp pushed out his lips, shrugged, then finished his cruller.

"But I'm still back on the magic wasp, okay?" said Geebo. "Let's stick with that for a minute." He was starting to laugh—forcing it, maybe, but still, he was laughing.

Jack poured a bit of sugar into the palm of his hand, licked it up. Then he stood. "Thanks for breakfast."

"You going somewhere?"

Jack looked through the plate window, then back at Geebo. "Somebody hit you in the head recently? Like with a brick or something? Something like that?"

"Not that I know of."

Jack widened his eyes.

But when Geebo didn't say anything more, he nodded and walked out. Just—walked away.

After gulping the rest of his coffee, Geebo wrapped half his donut in a napkin and stuffed it into his bag. Then, on his way to the door, he stopped at the cigarette machine, ran his eyes across the brand selections. Usually, he bought cheap no-brand smokes at Foodtown, buck-twenty a pack. Two-bucks-a-pack stuff he couldn't afford.

Nevertheless, he started feeding quarters into the slot, eight altogether, and chose Salem. Salem *Lights*, for crying out loud.

He ran outside after Jack Walker, calling, "Hey, wait up. Wait *up!*"

CHAPTER 4

THE BOY BILLIONAIRE

THE BOMAN FORTUNE HAD its genesis in 1909, when Eugene Boman's grandfather Harold I. Boman—a forty-one-year-old municipal health worker—developed, during his spare time, a petroleum-based ointment for cold sores.

With a two-hundred-dollar stake borrowed from his in-laws, he began marketing the goop under the name Lip Service. After a slow start, the product caught on, and then one thing just led to another. To baby powders and sore-muscle balms, alcohol astringents and powdered antacids. To a company called Boman Pharmaceuticals, which Gene's father inherited in 1962, when H.I. died at the ripe age of ninety-four.

Though the company was still in the home-medicine-chest remedy business (and the suntan-lotion business and the surgical-dressing business), it had become, over the course of fifty years, primarily a prescription-drug company, right up there with J & J and Merck, G. D. Searle, Hoffman-

La Roche, Mead Johnson. And the huge operation was still entirely private.

An only child, Eugene had entered the family business when he was still a high school boy. He'd worked in the research department, sat in on board meetings. Though awkward around people, he was eager and bright, especially with figures and marketing strategies. In May 1979, when he was a freshman at the College of Business at Old Tappan University, he made his first commercial trip, to a Swiss subsidiary in Berne, where he was arrested one evening on suspicion of murder. But it was a mistake—really!—just a big mistake, and next morning he was released, with official apologies.

The following January, he dropped out of school and took charge of the company when his father died suddenly of a heart attack while addressing the annual convention of the American Decency League. (He'd keeled over midway through a passionate denunciation of sex education in public schools.) Eugene Boman hadn't yet turned twenty. He was profiled in *Forbes* and *People;* there were front-page articles about him in *The Wall Street Journal* and the *National Star.* He was treated as something of a cross between a captain of industry and a lottery winner. There were even a few jokes cracked about him on "Saturday Night Live." The Boy Billionaire.

Briefly, Boman lived a highly public life—he wore a tux at least twice a week, went to charity balls, political dinners. He was a guest of President Reagan's at the White House, and saw Vladimir Horowitz play. Big deal. He'd grown tired of acting gregarious. It wasn't in his nature to be outgoing, and he was about as smooth at small talk as a third-grader. He decided finally to refuse all further social invitations, and did, immersing himself totally in corporate affairs.

After 1983, just about the only time he was seen in public was at some collectibles auction, where he would bid on such things as the Stetson hat worn by Hoss Cartwright on "Bonanza," an original animation cel from *A Charlie Brown Christmas*, Alan Alda's "M*A*S*H" fatigues.

It had been at a Christie's auction in New York that Eugene Boman met Major Richard Forell and his redheaded daughter. Boman and the Major had bid against each other for the lamp used to bludgeon Dr. Kimble's wife to death in the old "Fugitive" series, though neither had gotten it.

That had been in the early fall of 1984.

Eugene had ended up marrying Edie Forell and doing sensitive business with her father.

Six years later, he was still doing business with Major Forell, who was now retired. But whether what existed between him and Edie could still be called a marriage was debatable. . . .

Shortly after eleven that Saturday morning, Eugene Boman spoke with Major Forell on the telephone. The Major was calling from downstate.

"Richard. What's up?" Boman made a little check mark in his Disneyana catalog: a musket from *Swiss Family Robinson*. One of his favorite movies, from when he was a kid.

"I was wondering if you planned on coming down here this weekend," said the Major.

"Don't think I can make it. I just had a meeting with some fellows from North America Ikona, and I still have some things that need to be done around here before lunch. And this afternoon I thought I'd—"

"You don't understand, Eugene. I *want* you to come down."

"Why? Is something—wrong?"

"Wrong? No, not wrong. Interesting."

"What?"

"See for yourself."

"You're at the farm?" Short for The Pharmacy. And safer to say over the telephone.

"Of course."

"Let me see what I can do."

"So you'll come?"

"I'll try."

"Eugene? Come."

Boman hung up, and sighed. Then he glanced back at his catalog, but his heart wasn't in it anymore. Damn. He didn't want to go down to Leesboro. He never did. And in recent months, ever since all that Peter Musik trouble, the Major, in disgust, had pretty much left him alone. Which suited Boman perfectly. So why was the son of a bitch calling him now? What was so important that he had to run downstate and see it? What was so—interesting? Dammit! Damn The Pharmacy, anyway.

And damn the fact that he *had* killed somebody years ago in Berne, Switzerland, as Major Forell liked to remind him every so often.

He got up from the sofa and paced the living room, stroking his chin.

The telephone rang again.

"Eugene Boman."

"Mr. Boman, this is Herb. Could I come up and talk to you for a minute? It's pretty important."

"Where are you?"

"In the parking garage."

"What's this about?"

"Miss Campbell, sir."

Just then, the West Indian housekeeper, who'd arrived half an hour ago, lugged the vacuum cleaner down the hall and into the living room. Boman signaled her to remove the coffee cups that were still on the table from his meeting with the Japanese businessmen. "What *about* Miss Campbell?"

"Could I just come up and tell you?"

"All right," said Boman, and without another word, he replaced the phone in the cradle. While he waited for Dierickx—Deer-ick—he looked some more through his Disneyana catalog, jotting an X beside a Mickey Mouse one-sheet from "Society Dog Show," and a question mark beside a pair of Chip and Dale bookends.

But he couldn't get his mind off Major Forell's call.

Damn, he thought.

And then Herb Dierickx was there.

CHAPTER 5

JERE LEE MEETS DRACULA

O FTEN, JERE LEE WONdered if this was, like, *it; really* it. Would she freeze to death this winter? Get bronchitis, pneumonia? Get raped? Become an accident victim? A murder victim? A drunk?

Forget becoming a drunk: whatever else might happen, she wouldn't start drinking again, she was certain of that, determined. The same dented pride and recollected sorrow that made it virtually impossible for her to seek any kind of charity also kept her away from the booze. She hadn't had a drink, not so much as a beer, in almost a decade, and she wasn't about to start again now, bleak as things were and no matter how much comfort it might temporarily bring.

In the late seventies, immediately after her difficult marriage had broken up for the fourth and final time, Jere Lee had developed a serious alcohol problem. Her daughters were teenagers then, and Mom-in-her-cups had been rough on them both. Rough? Catastrophic. Alienating. Her loud, stumbling, self-pitying misbehavior had driven Annie from the house first, then Karen. And Jere Lee could never forgive herself for that, never.

Although she'd finally quit drinking (without any support group, of course: by sheer willpower), by then it was too late to reestablish the trust and easy affection she'd once shared with both her children. (They were grown, they were married, they were gone.) But at least she and the girls had gotten back on *fairly* friendly terms; at least they'd resumed exchanging birthday and Christmas cards.

Neither daughter, though, had visited her in the hospital last summer, or had invited her to come live with them— or even visit them—afterward. In October, Jere Lee had written to Karen and Annie to say that she could now be reached at a post office box; she hadn't told them that arson by a jilted lover (not hers) had deprived her of a rent-controlled apartment and that she was now living on the street, but she had strongly implied that everything was not going . . . well. That life had become difficult.

She checked her box every other day, and every other day she discovered it empty.

Occasionally, Jere Lee would fantasize that her daughters had contacted one another, and in a burst of filial concern and old sentiment, had decided to meet here in the city and search for their lost mother. She imagined them going to the police, and showing around her photograph (an old one, perhaps taken one happy Thanksgiving, pulled from a photo album); she imagined them both waiting anxiously at the Old Bergen branch of the post office for her to appear.

Wishful thinking. And about as likely a scenario as finding a wallet crammed full of thousand-dollar bills. And no identification. . . .

Today, she'd waked with congestion in her upper chest.

When she took a deep breath, a thick bubbling sounded behind her sternum. She felt a pang of terror. Illness was one of her biggest fears, a close second after physical violence. What would she *do* if she became seriously ill? If she ran a high fever, got shaky and weak? She couldn't allow it to happen; that's all, she couldn't.

Rousing herself and throwing off her blankets, Jere Lee crawled out of the lean-to. The ground was hard and stony, the patches of grass brown and dead, and there were snow flurries in the air. Every place she looked, she saw cardboard boxes with feet sticking out the open ends. No fires burning, no activity yet. Jere Lee suppressed a cough, then fetched from her coat a little mint-flavored breath spray—an extravagance, but she couldn't abide a stale mouth.

After she'd stuffed her blankets into the shopping cart, she remembered her flashlight, and crawled back inside the lean-to. For half a minute, she thumped and patted the ground with her gloved hands. Finally she knelt up with her fists planted on her hips.

Son of a bitch.

Geebo.

Coming outside again, she stood up and gazed across Big Lawn. On the steps of the band shell were a couple of figures. They were too far away, though, and the early daylight was still too poor, for Jere Lee to tell if one of them was Geebo.

The son of a bitch.

She set off for the band shell, rolling her cart in front of her, but then changed her mind abruptly, and stopped. She didn't want to see Geebo, he could keep the stupid flashlight. It was a piece of junk, anyway. To think about seeing Geebo now was mortifying. She couldn't face him again just yet.

Whatever had *possessed* her last night to kiss him? God. She was turning daft, going off the deep end—which was yet another thing, along with illness and violence, that she truly feared. She'd rather have croaked than started talking to herself.

It was *only* a kiss, she told herself. Only a kiss, for crying out loud.

And it's not like you're some *crone*, Jere Lee. You're forty-five years old. You haven't lost *all* your looks. You can't kiss a man if you feel like it? Sure you can.

Nevertheless, she wheeled her cart around and left the park by the path that skirted the playground. She'd decided she wanted the use of a toilet, a sink, and a mirror. But when she arrived at the bus station—it was already filled with street people who'd been locked out overnight—all the rest rooms were closed because the floors were being mopped. Jere Lee sat down on a bench and morosely waited. She listened to the departure announcements over the PA. Detroit, Boston, Miami. Platform nine, platform twelve, platform eight. On an impulse, she got up and went to the Greyhound window, and inquired about a ticket to Fort Lauderdale.

"One *way?*" she said, startled by how expensive it was. She'd had no idea. The man behind the counter looked her over disapprovingly.

"One way," he said. He had round eyeglasses and was very thin. Jere Lee glanced at his left hand, to see if he was married. He was.

She thanked him and went back to her bench, and had to chase away an old man who was trying to steal a blanket from her cart. She took out a library book, *Miracle at Philadel-*

phia, and sat reading, trying to ignore the growls and purls and oinks that came from her stomach.

Every half a minute, she checked on the rest rooms. It's deliberate cruelty, she thought, to mop those floors at nine o'clock in the morning. Deliberate cruelty.

After a while, she became aware of a very odd-looking man who was limping around the concourse. An extremely tall man dressed in a long black coat. No, it wasn't a coat, it was like a priest's cassock: shiny and collarless and with many buttons up the front. He was going along the walls, stopping every so often to peer at various men stretched out on pieces of flattened cardboard. He'd look, sometimes bending down to look, and then go on again.

He was bald, and his skin was so pale that it was almost blue. His eyes were heavily shadowed, his nose was long, a beak. To Jere Lee, he looked like a vampire. Years ago, she'd seen an old silent movie on public television, a German movie. A German Dracula movie called *Nosferatu.* This limping guy in the cassock looked just like that Dracula, except his ears weren't pointy.

He seemed to stagger now, but then steadied himself, and it suddenly registered with Jere Lee that he was bleeding. The hem of his cassock was sodden. He was leaving a spoor of big red drops.

He'd stopped again, this time beside a young man who was curled up on the floor under several layers of coats. Going down on one knee, he touched the man on the shoulder. (Jere Lee was rising, not sure why.) Then Dracula lost his balance, lurched backwards, flailing with both arms. The man who'd been sleeping under the coats came awake with a howl.

Jere Lee heard Dracula's head strike marble.

He lay on his back, stunned, and Jere Lee—saying, "You okay? Mister? You all right?"—hovered over him, appalled by the gauntness of his face, the fine trickle of blood down his chin. Jesus. Christ.

And when she touched his hand—saying, "Mister? Mister?"—it was like touching a block of ice.

CHAPTER 6

THE DEATH OF JOHNNY STILLBORN

FOR THE PAST SEVERAL weeks, Johnny Stillborn had been favoring a certain boyhood memory: of getting a haircut, then stealing an issue of *Action Comics* from the barber shop's magazine pile, and then tapping his stiff pompadour on the short walk home through a smoky October dusk. How old had he been at the time—eleven? twelve? Around that. Great memory. Johnny loved it, and could really get into it. He could almost relive it, it was that vivid. Whenever his cramps were bad, or his despair turned suicidal, Johnny Stillborn could get into that barber-shop memory, and time-trip. He could actually time-trip. Time-travel. It was so great. It was therapeutic.

This morning, he'd been dreaming of the buzz of electric clippers around his ears when he saw the world's most perfect girl.

He'd come into the mission at eleven o'clock for a cup of coffee. Sipped it alone, as usual, huddled on a bench against the wall. The church undercroft was crowded—a lot of quiet old people, mostly, who slurped when they drank—and the place had an unpleasant moldy smell. Better to think about the sweet scents of barber-shop tonics. Which is precisely what Johnny had done, at first. And then he'd fixed an image in his head of the barber himself. A short Italian guy named Vinny, a guy with dry stubby fingers. Johnny had recalled the satisfying, the *soothing* click of Vinny's scissors (he'd even taken out his own pair and, though his head was shaved, made believe he was trimming his hair with them), and then he'd moved on to the clippers: the wonderful chills they gave him down his spine, the insectile hum.

And then he'd looked up and there she was. The world's most perfect girl.

How could any girl *be* that beautiful? Look at her hair. Look at her *face!*

Johnny's heart was broken, instantly. He was a wreck, just a ruin, in and out of mental hospitals, in and out of jail. No ordinary girl would even look at him twice, but a girl *that* pretty probably wouldn't even *see* him if he stood in front of her. His heart was broken, and he had to control his temper. The girl made him angry about what he was, and what he wasn't.

And you know what was so terrible? It wasn't Johnny's fault. That he was a ruin, that he was a wreck. He was just *born* weird, like some people are born smart or stupid or mean. Really. Johnny knew it was true. Even as a little kid he'd been weird. His name, for instance. He'd started writing his name as Stillborn, instead of Stillman, on his homework and spelling tests *in the fourth grade.* That wasn't drugs. That was pure constitutional weirdness. The drugs came later.

And, of course, when they did, they didn't help any. Johnny would've been the first one to admit that. They just kind of *exaggerated* his natural tendencies. Made him, you know, *weirder*.

He watched the world's most perfect girl speak to one of the sisters in charge, a gray-haired nun in a brown pants suit. The nun shook her head, then passed a photograph back to the girl.

Johnny sighed, then wiped his nose and closed his eyes and remembered picking up that Superman comic book in the barber shop and very smoothly, *very* smoothly slipping it into his schoolbag. . . .

Pretty embarrassing, but it was the only picture of Peter Musik that Money had, a snapshot of him in his swim trunks on the beach at Scroon Lake, near Leesboro. Money had been in the picture, too (Herb Dierickx had taken it), but she'd torn herself out of it. She wasn't about to walk around the Bridge District asking people to look at a picture of her in a red bikini. Forget it.

She'd come out of the subway at Erie Street and walked east, but hadn't seen a single person washing windshields. Well, it was Saturday morning, and there wasn't much traffic. Hardly any. It was still early.

The first place she'd shown the picture was in a fish market, but nobody there recognized Peter. Next, she'd stopped a guy on the street, guy with a ponytail. She figured him for an artist—he had bad skin and was carrying a weekly tabloid newspaper under one arm. He looked at the picture and shook his head.

Then she came to a red-brick mission on the corner of

Avenue F. A number of hard-luck cases, a few on crutches, were milling on the steps out front. Money decided to go in.

The nun there was very nice, real friendly, but she didn't recognize Peter, either. Money talked to everybody in the mission who wasn't grumbling, but with no success, and she was about to take off when she noticed the skinhead. Sitting by himself with his elbows on his knees and his fingertips at his temples. Eyes closed. She almost didn't speak to him, he looked so . . . contemplative, but finally she decided what the hell. Unlike everybody else in the place, he was about Peter's age, he looked about thirty.

She excused herself, bent forward, and said, "Hello?"

His eyelids rolled back, like a ceramic doll's. He seemed shocked, and immediately glanced away. Nipped his elbows to his ribs.

"I'm sorry to bother you," said Money, "but—could I show you a picture? Could you tell me if you've ever seen this person?"

"He's got a beard now," said the skinhead.

"You know him?"

"Geebo," said the skinhead, and Money recoiled. *Geebo?* He was calling himself *Geebo?* My God.

"Do you know where he is?"

"Last night, he was up the corner."

"Which corner?"

"F and Erie." He was looking at her so intently that Money felt uncomfortable. Then he asked her if she knew Dustin Hoffman.

"Why should I know Dustin Hoffman?" she said. "I don't know Dustin Hoffman, no."

"Aren't you an actress?"

Not *that* again. God sakes. For the last three years of her life, that's all she'd been hearing, or variations on it. You on daytime TV? Do you model? Was that you in *Married to the Mob?* "No, I'm not an actress. Does . . . Geebo always use the same corner?"

"I seen him a few times in the park. You know Crane Park?"

"It's which way? East?"

The skinhead nodded. His eyes looked flat and distant again, and he was no longer staring at her, now he was staring at the baseboard. Money thanked him, and turned away.

Outside, she had to orient herself: which way was east? She was never any good at directions, she was always getting lost. East? Was that way.

She started walking, and noticed that the area was finally coming to life. There was some traffic now (but still no windshield-washers), and some of the delis and hardware stores had opened for business. She passed a mailman, and a thirteen- or fourteen-year-old girl carrying a tiny baby in a white crocheted blanket. On a sudden impulse, she stopped and looked behind her, and got a real start seeing the skinhead from the mission.

He was only a few lengths back, a smoking cigarette between his fingers.

"So who is this person in the picture?" he said. "Your brother?"

"No," said Money. "He's just a friend."

"What, like your boyfriend?"

Money got a warning tingle: something *really* wasn't right about this guy. Watch yourself, girl. She thought about stopping into a coffee shop. Was he following her? "He's just somebody that got in trouble," she said, quickening her step.

But the skinhead quickened his, too, and then he was walking beside her, on the street side.

"Were you ever in *Playboy?*"

Money laughed. Jesus. No, she said, she wasn't in *Playboy.*

"You could be."

"Listen, thanks. But I don't want to talk to you, all right?"

"Yeah, all right." He turned sulky then, and dropped behind. When Money looked back again, he'd just finished kicking a fire hydrant and was giving her the finger.

"Hey, I didn't mean to be nasty. That sounded nasty. I'm sorry," she said. "I'm just a little nervous, I didn't even know till last night that this guy was still alive."

"The guy in the picture?"

She nodded, then hurried up the street. Don't follow me, please. She didn't turn around again for several blocks. Waited till she'd come to the park, *then* looked back. The skinhead wasn't there. Thank God. He'd disappeared.

Timidly—since this was a pretty shabby place, this park —Money resumed her search for Peter Musik.

Out of his generous spirit, he'd let her go; he hadn't hassled her, or let himself get mad at her; he hadn't taken a snippet of her bright yellow hair, as he'd left the mission intending to do. He was one noble guy, Johnny was. At least he *felt* noble, watching the world's most perfect girl walk away from him. He'd let her go. He'd given her up, the only girl he'd ever loved. *Because* he loved her, he'd given her up.

He would've only brought her down.

Heaving a long sigh, Johnny Stillborn headed back to

the mission, for lunch. On the walk, he tried to get that barber-shop memory going again, but it just wouldn't spark, so he tried for another one. A Cub Scout meeting? No, he'd hated Cub Scouts, all those nitwit projects with glue, all those idiotic merit badges. So what about this: the first time he'd kissed a girl. Mary Ann Laurino, junior year in high school. Time-trip on that one for a while?

But then all of a sudden—hey! where'd *he* come from— some Korean guy was taking Johnny by the arm and dragging him across the sidewalk. Toward a fruit store. Some *Korean* guy, some *immigrant* Korean guy, some goddamn Korean *immigrant* with ten thousand relatives taking jobs from *real* Americans was dragging Johnny into a goddamn *fruit and vegetable store!* Johnny whipped himself sideways. "Lay off, what's *your* story, pal?"

"Look, look, you stupid," said the Korean. "Look, you stupid."

"Who you calling stupid? Huh? Friggen immigrant!"

But the guy was pointing, and Johnny Stillborn finally looked, but then he didn't know what the hell he was *seeing.* In the aisle—in the air!—between raked bins of onions and scallions and green peppers and red grapes, a jagged vertical line was . . . growing. It was like—man, it was like an Etch a Sketch, Johnny thought. An Etch a Sketch in real life! Whoa.

He gaped for half a minute, and the Korean guy, who'd run and armed himself with a baseball bat from under the counter, was babbling. "Hey," said Johnny, "shut up, will you?" Still thinking, Etch a Sketch. He'd describe it like that if somebody asked him about it later, like somebody from Channel 7 news. Cool. Unbelievably cool.

When the first—*whatever it was* squeezed through the

fissure, Johnny Stillborn started to laugh. Because it was like a Steven Spielberg movie.

It was like a Superman comic.

It was—

The animal sprang at Johnny, and clawed out his throat.

And for just a moment, his last moment, he saw himself again in that barber-shop mirror: a small round-faced beautiful boy. Placid and content. Then, with a silent howl of regret, he ended.

CHAPTER 7

HIS MAJESTY'S TRAMP

TOGETHER THEY'D GONE down to the riverside park and were sitting on a bench under the bridge, Geebo and the tramp. Jack. Geebo had started calling him Jack; he wasn't the tramp anymore, he was Jack, this guy that Geebo knew. This guy who was trying to tell him now about some crazy place called Lostwithal. Los-twithal. (Like, say, Los Alamos, only Twithal.) Geebo let him talk because it was interesting; hell, it was fascinating. Here was a guy claiming he'd come from another time and place ("a few Moments farther from Creation" was how he'd actually phrased it), a guy just going on and on about wizards and witches and a king named Agel who sat on his throne like a sack of potatoes and hardly twitched a muscle.

It was all very impressive, Jack was a talented bullshitter. Even though Geebo figured he was rehashing a bunch of four-ninety-five sword-and-sorcery novels he'd read at the men's shelter, this guy Jack was still one hell of a talented bullshitter.

A king named Agel.

A wasp called Lita.

"What," Geebo had interrupted a few minutes ago, "no unicorns?"

And Jack had shaken his head, insulted for half a second, then he'd bummed another menthol cigarette, and started talking again. Telling Geebo then about some crazy cult and its cruel high priest whose face, get *this,* was crawling with slugs. Yeah, sure.

Geebo listened, then said, "Hey, wait, Jack, could I ask you one more question?" Jack stopped, nodding his shaggy head, and Geebo said, "So how come you speak English? If you just got here from another world. Huh?"

Answer Geebo *that,* wise guy.

Jack had lifted one shoulder and both eyebrows, and smiled. "Talent. Stick me anyplace, I'll speak what's spoken. Nothing to it. Any Walker can."

Geebo saying, "Right. Sorry. Just thought I'd ask." Meanwhile thinking, He's a piece of work, all right.

But Geebo had to admit that he liked Jack's company. Even *needed* it, maybe. After three months of scuffling around all by himself on the street, washing windshields, scrounging bottles for the nickel deposits, and struggling to block the Headache, Geebo needed a friend, a pal, someone he could be easy with. And he was hoping that Jack Walker was the guy. Why *else* had he bought him breakfast? And cigarettes? And then gone racing after him?

There was definitely something very likable about Jack, something appealing; there was, but still, Geebo had heard enough nonsense about wizards and magic insects. More than enough. If Jack was serious, then he was nuts, and that was that: Geebo wouldn't—Geebo *couldn't*—stick around with him. But if he'd been having Geebo on, riffing for the sheer hell of it, then that was different. Hey, possibly Jack was some kind of street genius, the Robin Williams of the underclass. Okay, Geebo could dig that. Enjoy it, even. Only —only now it was time that Jack turned off the invention for a while and got real. If he could.

Geebo dropped his cigarette and ground it out in the gravel with his sneaker. Here goes, he thought, standing up and walking to the wrought-iron fence. About twenty yards away, a stocky man in a buff overcoat stood gazing up at the gray bridge, where morning traffic glinted. Gulls wheeled, dove, shrieked. A tug chuffed up the Cushing River, hauling a garbage scow. Across the water was a big soft-drink factory with a rooftop clock that read ten past ten.

"Come on, Jack, you think I'm some flake? You think I'm gonna believe all this crapola? Who the hell you think I am?"

Jack said, "I don't have any *idea* who you are. Which is pretty strange, like I told you. I should know *everything* about you."

"Oh yeah, right: on account of the bee sting."

"Wasp."

Geebo stared at the tramp for a long moment, then returned to the bench, picked up his shoulder bag, slung it on.

Time to go.

He tossed Jack the Salems. "Keep 'em," he said, then flinched when the wasp flew suddenly up, from Jack's sleeve.

"Oh man, we got to get some *trust* established here," said Jack, springing to his feet and sticking the pack into Geebo's pocket. "So just watch, okay?"

"What?"

"Just shut up and watch." He'd taken Geebo by an el-bow and half-turned him, so that Geebo was looking down the length of the iron fence, at the guy in the nice mohair coat.

Who yelped with pain ten seconds later and slapped at his neck.

Jack grunted. "Come on," he said and started walking. They approached the guy, seeing him slump, moaning, onto a bench. He looked about forty, had thin brown hair. Nice shoes. Nice coat, nice shoes.

There Geebo went again, noticing stupid things. Unim-portant details.

Maroon tie.

"You feel okay?" said Jack.

The guy, whose face had turned white as milk, looked up. Eyes bugged, moist. "Something bit me."

"Bit you?" said Jack. "No kidding. Want me take a look?" He sat on the bench.

"Christ," said the guy. "I feel . . ."

"What, like you're gonna be sick?"

"Dizzy."

"Right," said Jack, his voice low. Then, gently, he re-moved the guy's hand from his throat. Geebo bent forward, saw the red swelling there.

"What the hell bit me?"

"You sure you got bit? Maybe you got stung," said Jack. Then he said, "What's your name?"

"Alex."

"Mine's Jack. We meet by accident."

Alex made to touch the swelling again, but Jack caught his wrist and pushed his hand down onto his knee.

"You were thinking of going up there and jumping off the bridge, weren't you, Alex?"

Alex nodded, slowly. "I was thinking about it, yeah." When he started to glance away, Jack told him, "No, look at *me*, Alex. Don't look at the bridge, okay?" He winked at Geebo. "Guy'll tell me anything I ask him. Won't you, Alex?"

Alex said, "Yeah," blandly, and with no hesitation. But then he frowned and said, "What?"

"It's all right, man. It's okay. But you know what I want you to do? Forget about jumping. Forget that. Quit your job, Alex. It sucks. Take a vacation."

Under his breath, Geebo said, "Christ."

Jack said, "Do it, man. Just do it, Alex. Put it all on American Express."

Alex said, "Yeah?" and Jack nodded yeah, really: *do it.*

Then he laughed and said, "But before you do, hey Alex? Gimme your cash, would you? Whatever you got."

With his mouth open, Geebo watched Alex unbutton his overcoat, reach inside, take out a leather billfold. Again: no hesitation. God almighty.

Jack was saying, "Go home, take a shower, then forget all about me, okay?

"Yeah?" Alex stood up. "Yeah, okay."

"Then call up your girlfriend. She got black hair, right?"

Alex nodded.

"Right," said Jack. "Take her with you on vacation." Then to Geebo: "Where you think Alex should go on his vacation?"

Geebo shrugged, then said the first place that popped into his head. "Fort Lauderdale?"

"Fort Lauderdale," said Jack. "Got that, Alex?"

"Yes." He put out his hand and said, "I got it, sure. Fort Lauderdale," then he shook with Jack and walked off.

"So what's it come to?" Geebo asked. Looking eagerly at the money in Jack's right hand.

"You count it," said Jack, passing him the cash. "You *keep* it, all right? I don't handle money, I tell you that?"

Warily, Geebo shook his head. "This how you stay alive? You hypnotize people, they buy you breakfast, give you money?"

"Already told you, I don't handle money. And it's not hypnosis, man. Come on, it's a little more *artistic* than that. It's a very *spiritual* fast one," he said, grinning. Then he pushed a finger through his hair and produced the wasp, on his knuckle.

Geebo let out his breath. "Who the hell *are* you?"

"I been *telling* you for the past hour, you just haven't been listening. Think you're so smart, think I'm crazy. I'm Jack," he said. "A Walker. His Majesty's Tramp."

CHAPTER 8

BODIES

"**Y**OU KNOW WHAT I'M thinking?" said Tucker. "I'm thinking napalm. Remember?"

"Yeah," said Dokus, "but it's not."

"Oh yeah, I know. It's just—looking at this, I'm thinking of that."

Dokus nodded.

The two Homicide detectives peered down at the bodies in the alley, the big one sprawled under the fire escape, the other one—the guy with the gun, a Colt Super .38, still in his hand—splayed across some trash barrels.

Both of them were burnt up, crisped. You could still, for Christ's sake, smell the barbecue.

Which was why the cops were holding handkerchiefs to their noses.

"So what, then," said Tucker, "a *flamethrower?*"

"Anything's possible, this city." Dokus glanced up the alley, at a couple of techs from the Photo Unit waiting their turn. Then, stepping carefully to avoid the patches of ice on the ground (go figure *them*), he went over and took another look at the big man's corpse, face charred, eyes jellied, skull bone visible in a few places.

The ears were gone, which was too bad: Dokus had been hoping to find an earring, a little black earring in the shape of an atomic bomb, the kind of bomb Dokus remembered from editorial cartoons when he was a kid, back in the early sixties. That would've clinched it, that earring. But even so, he was pretty sure he knew who this guy was; used to be. A shit named Cruz. Nestor Cruz. Nestor *Crash*. And if that was so, then the other corpse was Billy Pollux. Who'd had long green-dyed hair, Dokus recalled. Hair that must've gone up like a torch. What the hell *happened* in here?

Crooking a finger at the techs, Dokus walked out to the sidewalk with Tucker. A tall man with brown hair and a pasty complexion was coming up the street. The Assistant Medical Examiner, guy named Mort Cherkas. He never seemed very healthy—always looked like he was either coming down with something or slowly recovering from surgery. He shook hands with Tucker and Dokus, then listened. "No gasoline?" he said.

"Pretty sure," said Dokus.

"When I heard, I figured—"

"Yeah," said Tucker, "us too. But it's not that. These guys weren't doused and set on fire. They weren't sleeping."

Cherkas went into the alley. Dokus grunted, folded his handkerchief, put it away. While his hand was still in his pocket, he deftly unwrapped a Hershey with Almonds, then broke a piece off and ate it. Candy bar at nine-thirty in the morning. Great eating habits. He stood on the curb and looked across the avenue, taking in the peep shows, a tiered parking garage, Al's Lunch, and the bus terminal on the corner.

Tucker was standing a few feet away with a couple of patrolmen. Dokus watched them all glance down at the trail of blood droplets that led across the sidewalk and into the street.

Inside the alley, strobes were flashing.

Dokus walked over to Tucker and the blues. Tucker made the introductions, saying, "George? These are the responding officers. This is Gleason. And Roman."

"Rom*ar*," said the second officer, a guy with squinty eyes and a baby-smooth face.

"Who found the bodies?" said Dokus.

"Hooker named Silvia Mendez. That's her in there."

Dokus glanced toward a blue-and-white patrol car, seeing a young woman with jet-black hair seated in the back. She was freshening her lipstick.

"What time'd you guys arrive?"

"Eight-fifty."

Some more techs were traipsing into the alley laden with equipment.

Dokus noticed the guy with the body bags.

Then he heard a siren and turned. An ambulance shot past the alley, made a left turn at the corner, and disappeared behind the bus station. Dokus looked at Tucker, who said, "These guys were just telling me something interesting."

Dokus raised an eyebrow.

"That we followed the blood," said Gleason. He pointed.

Dokus nodded for him to go on.

"It comes and goes, Lieutenant. But we picked it up again across the street. Then again on B. Around the back of the terminal." Gleason used his hands when he talked.

"Found a guy in there passed out. Leg bleeding." He smiled. "Somebody shot him."

"No fooling," said Dokus.

Gleason and Romar both nodded. "We left Officer Henkins with him. Weird-looking bald guy, about six-five. And dressed like a priest. I guess that's his ambulance now."

"Dressed like a priest?" said Dokus.

"You know, that black thing they wear?" said Romar.

"A cassock," said Gleason.

Dokus asked, "You talk to him?"

"Well . . ." said Romar. "We *tried* to, but he didn't respond."

Gleason snorted. "He responded all right, Lieutenant. Except when he talked? It came out like this incredible whistle. I don't know what friggen language *he's* talking."

Then Tucker said, "You fellows didn't happen to notice if the guy was carrying a flamethrower, did you?"

The four cops laughed.

CHAPTER 9

GOING OVER

Peⁿople DIDN'T GIVE TWO
shits about anyone but themselves, and it was just pitiful.
That's how Jere Lee saw it. It was just pitiful. Take the poor
man who'd fallen down and cracked his head, whose leg
was bleeding. The bald man with the cold hands. Who
looked so much like that German-movie Dracula. He needed
help, he needed a doctor, it was *urgent*, but was anybody at
the stupid bus terminal willing to *do* anything? No way.

Most of the street people loitering on the concourse
acted like nothing was doing, acted deaf as posts when Jere
Lee—after lifting the sodden hem of Dracula's cassock and
seeing the nasty hole in his right leg, the blood still flowing
—cried out for somebody to run, find a cop. A few of the
bigger burnouts wandered over, peered down casually at the
poor man for a few seconds, then wandered off again.

Jere Lee had always had a wicked temper, and she
nearly lost it again then and there, but managed somehow to
check herself. What earthly good would ranting do?

She got up from the floor—there was blood on her

shoes, blood on her slacks, blood on the puffy sleeves of her coat—and hurried down the concourse, hollering over and over, "There's an emergency, somebody's bleeding," all the while pointing behind her.

But it was zombie city. Really pitiful. Hardly anyone gave her more than an instant's wary glance. At the Information kiosk, she pounded on the counter. There, at least, the two women didn't treat her like she was rabid. They listened, even asked some questions. *Where? A man? Is he dead?* "No, he's not dead," said Jere Lee, "but he *might* be soon, if you don't call an ambulance."

"You need to find somebody in Security."

"Why do *I* need to? This isn't *my* bus station."

"Down the end of the hall, to the right, is Security," said one of the women (who was about Jere Lee's age: there but for fortune) and then answered the telephone, saying pleasantly, "Bus information. Good morning."

Jere Lee nearly gave her the finger, but instead just turned and ran farther down the concourse, and found Security.

Naturally, the place was locked.

Swearing under her breath, she ran back. Dracula had come around and was sitting up with his back to a pillar. His head was rolling from side to side. He'd clamped both hands around his right leg, above the knee. When Jere Lee hunkered beside him, he turned and looked at her. She tried comforting him with a smile.

His eyes widened, then narrowed, then he removed one hand from his leg, reached out and limply squeezed the tips of Jere Lee's fingers. The fingers of her left hand. She flinched, and for a moment felt lightheaded. Heard a whistling sound.

"You'll be okay, honey," she said. "I'm gonna call the cops myself."

But that was unnecessary.

As she was heading off again, this time toward a bank of pay phones near the rear entrance, Jere Lee spotted three uniformed policemen on their way in through revolving doors. "There's a man over there," she called, "needs an ambulance."

They looked past her, spotted Dracula. "Okay, ma'am," one of them said, "we'll take care of it."

Spread out and moving slowly, cautiously, the cops headed up the concourse. Jere Lee shook her head. Why the hell were they acting like that, for crying out loud—like the Earp brothers and Doc Holliday heading for the Okay Corral? Big bananas. What was the *matter* with those big bananas? It was just a poor guy bleeding to death.

A guy with—

Oh my God, she thought.

A poor old guy with a *hole* in his leg. A *bullet* hole? Why hadn't it dawned on her before: he'd been shot. Lord, Jere Lee, how can you still be such an innocent?

She covered her mouth with a hand and watched.

That was fifteen, twenty minutes ago.

The coming of the police brought the oglers from every level of the bus station. Pretty soon the whole concourse had filled up, everybody straining to see. Then the medics arrived with a stretcher, then still more cops. Finally, the old man (Jere Lee had decided not to call him Dracula anymore, it was unkind) had been wheeled out and put into an ambulance, and the ambulance had sped off.

Almost immediately, the crowd evaporated. Even most of the street people drifted away. Leaving Jere Lee alone again on the bench where she'd first sat down an hour ago. A janitor appeared with a wringer bucket and a filthy mop and cleaned up the blood.

Jere Lee felt drained, shaky. She had a brutal headache, and sat with her hands folded in her lap, figuring to stay a few more minutes, then go use the lavatory, wash her face, comb her hair. That'd make her feel better. Like a human being. And then she'd get a cup of coffee somewhere. She nodded to herself decisively, but then lowered her head and softly began to weep.

"Mrs. Vance?"

Only her eyes moved, cutting nervously to the right. Oh God, she thought, let me vanish. Please. It was so humiliating every time somebody recognized her, somebody she'd known . . . before. Somebody like her old mailman, whom she'd run into once at the Old Bergen post office; like her former neighbor, who'd suddenly hailed her one day last month in the park; or like the friend of her ex-husband who tried to give her a twenty-dollar bill—the bastard!—after chasing her for two solid blocks. Humiliating! Horrible.

It was just horrible to meet anyone who'd known her as Mrs. Vance.

Jere Lee hadn't used her real surname in months.

Even at Shop-Rite yesterday, filling out the job application, she'd put down Lee as her last name, Jeremia as her first.

Jere Lee was her real name, but it was her given name.

"Mrs. Vance? Hi. Remember me, Brian Tucker?"

Meekly, she looked up, saw a man in his late twenties with short blond hair. Wearing a dark overcoat, unbuttoned.

A gray vested suit. Another man, slightly older, stood behind him. Jere Lee puckered her forehead.

"You don't remember, do you?" said the blond man, smiling. "West Twenty-third Street? I used to go out with your daughter Karen. How's she doing? How're *you?*"

"Oh—Brian," she said, not really remembering him; well . . . maybe. He played . . . football? In high school? "Karen's just fine," she said.

"Married?"

Jere Lee nodded. "No kids yet, though. She's living in Denver."

"Denver!" said Tucker. "Well." His eyes flicked to the laden shopping cart. Then flicked away. "And your other daughter . . . ?"

"Anne Marie. She's fine, too. She's up in Maine." Jere Lee glanced at Tucker's companion and saw him take a Mars bar from his coat. He nodded at her with a guilty smile.

"Next time you see Karen, tell her I said hi, would you? And you can tell her I never finished law school." He laughed. "It won't surprise her. She always said I wouldn't."

"She did? Well, that wasn't very kind."

"But she was right."

Jere Lee had the feeling that Brian Tucker was hoping she'd ask him what he *was* doing, if he wasn't a lawyer. So she did.

And he said, "I'm a cop."

Jere Lee struggled for a pleasant smile.

"I work in the Homicide Division."

"I'll be sure to tell Karen," she said, then realized that he hadn't asked her what she was doing sitting alone in the bus station at ten o'clock on a Saturday morning. Hadn't asked her, going on a trip? Going away for the weekend? Of *course* he hadn't: he'd seen her cart, all the junk in it. He *knew.* Her cheeks flushed.

Brian Tucker was staring at her. Then he cocked his head toward the janitor, still pushing a mop around. "See all the excitement?"

"I was here," she said, "yes."

Tucker lifted his eyebrows interrogatively.

"The poor man fell down," said Jere Lee. "And I tried to get somebody to call the police, but nobody would. And that's it."

"Did you talk to him?"

"No. I *checked* on him."

Tucker said, "Of course."

"Did somebody shoot him?"

"Looks that way."

"What, did somebody rob him?"

"That we don't know."

"I thought he might be a priest," said Jere Lee. "But he didn't have the, what's that thing? The white collar."

"So you never talked to him."

"No. Where is he now?"

"St. Vincent's. That right, George? St. Vincent's?"

The second detective nodded.

"The poor man," said Jere Lee, then frowned. "But why're *you* here? You said you worked in the *Homicide* Division."

Tucker didn't reply. Just stood up, shook her hand, thanked her. "It was nice seeing you, Mrs. Vance." He seemed about to say something further, then didn't.

The two detectives walked away, up the concourse.

A minute later, though, as Jere Lee was wheeling her cart toward the restrooms, she felt a tap on her shoulder. It was Tucker again. Alone, and looking slightly ill-at-ease now.

"You'll remember to tell Karen you saw me?"

"I most certainly will."

"Talk to her often?"

She hesitated. "Not as often as I'd like."

"Sure," said Tucker. "I know all about that. My mom's in Florida now."

"Fort Lauderdale?"

"Tampa."

They stood looking at each other.

"Mrs. Vance . . ."

She straightened up, her grip tightening on the cart handle.

"I was wondering . . . do you have Karen's number? I'd love to talk to her again. I thought maybe I could call her myself."

"I'm sorry," said Jere Lee, tersely. "But I don't have it with me."

"Well . . . could I call *you,* then—maybe this evening? —and get it?"

She lowered her eyes.

"Mrs. Vance, excuse me, but is everything all right?" His gaze moved from her face to the shopping cart.

"Please," said Jere Lee. And didn't know what else to say, was *afraid* to say anything else.

Tucker took out his wallet, and from that extracted a white stiff card, which he passed to her. "You can reach me there. I'd really like Karen's number."

"All right," she said. "Of course."

Of course? The hell with of course! Give him Karen's

number—what, so he could phone her up and say your mother's a bag lady?

Jere Lee didn't have much anymore, just a lot of crummy old coats and blankets from the Goodwill, and that squeaky cart, and a few library books she'd never returned, and maybe twenty dollars stuffed in her bra. But she still had her pride. Yes, she did. Her pride.

What a joke.

God, it was good to eat. She hadn't realized just how famished she was. But go slow, she told herself. Take fussy bites, little sips, don't rush: stretch out the meal. Which consisted of a seeded roll and a large carton of sweetened coffee.

She was three blocks north of the bus terminal, in Norris Square, sitting on a bench. Usually whenever she ate, she tried to keep her mind blank; or rather, to concentrate only on the fact that she was taking nourishment, *fuel:* it was a way to convince herself that she *was* struggling to survive, that she *hadn't* given up. Gone over.

This morning, however, she kept thinking about the incident at the bus station. Kept seeing that man's strange face (that strange man's face) and remembering his touch, how cold it had been, snow-cold, and how weirdly . . . dizzy she'd felt when he'd feebly—gratefully—reached out and touched her fingertips.

She looked at her hand now, the hand that he'd touched, her left hand, and frowned. Then she finished the roll. And it was only then, as she was folding up the waxed paper to stick it away in her cart, that she noticed the pigeons.

There must've been thirty or forty of them, filthy

things, clustered in a ragged semi-circle on the pavement in front of her.

That'd be the day when Jere Lee fed pigeons. "Shoo!"

She picked up her coffee carton and drained it, tipping her head back and letting the sugar sludge drip slowly into her mouth.

SQUINTIK.

Jere Lee flinched, and glanced behind her, but there was no one there. The other benches were vacant, as were the chess tables. Nobody here but us pigeons, she thought, and smiled grimly. But she'd heard a voice, she'd definitely heard a voice: it was as though . . . someone had whispered directly into her ear. SQUINTIK.

Squintik?

No, she told herself. I didn't hear anything. I don't *hear* voices. She got up from the bench, expecting the pigeons to scatter, to clear a path.

But they didn't.

And as she stared at them, a tingling started at the base of her neck and moved rapidly down her spine.

A flock of pigeons—and not a cooing sound from *any* of them?

They collected around her ankles.

SQUINTIK. SQUINTIK. SQUINTIKSQUINTIKSQUIN-TIK. SQUINTIK.

Her eyes grew wide, her jaw dropped, and she clapped her hands suddenly to her ears.

But still she heard: SQUINTIKSQUINTIKSQUINTIK.

As in a nightmare, she tried to scream, but could not.

The pigeons brushed up against her, she felt their beating wings. She buried her face in her hands.

SQUINTIKSQUINTIKSQUINTIK SQUIN

Then, a burst of noise: the pigeons all taking flight at once.

When Jere Lee found the courage to let her hands fall, she discovered that all the birds were gone, and standing in their place was a filthy gray-and-orange tabby cat with one torn and droopy ear and a muzzle thickened with scar tissue.

Jere Lee's throat felt scalded, it was painful to swallow. Painful to breathe.

Her head was throbbing.

Blindly, she felt behind her, grabbed her cart and braced herself. Then, before her knees could give out, she sat back down on the slatted bench.

The cat regarded her, blandly.

It took a minute before Jere Lee's heart began to decelerate; two minutes before she could breathe again without gasping. Three, before her legs felt solid.

She tried laughing at herself. Oh, you're a great one, Jere Lee. Eyes tearing, nose running, hands shaking. Here you've been worried about muggers and rapists, and what happens, you go to pieces over a bunch of—pigeons. Thata girl, Jere Lee. Big banana. You silly big banana.

But it didn't work.

She looked at the cat, and shook her head.

And the cat nodded.

Then said, DON'T SCREAM, ALL RIGHT? 'CAUSE THIS IS PRETTY WEIRD FOR ME, TOO.

Jere Lee began to giggle. Well, why not?

DON'T, said the cat. OKAY? DON'T DO THAT. JUST GET UP AND FOLLOW ME.

Jere Lee steepled her fingers and pressed them against her lips.

I've snapped, she thought. Gone over.

And having gone over, having snapped, there was nothing else to do but rise shakily from the bench, rub her nose with her sleeve, tip back the cart—and follow the cat to the curb.

She wasn't afraid, or ashamed.

She'd tried. She'd tried her best.

And failed.

So now it was out of her hands.

For the first time in months, Jere Lee felt happy.

"Squintik," she said.

A man and a woman at the corner, waiting for the light to go green, looked at her sidelong.

Thinking, of course, that she was a crazy.

But Jere Lee couldn't have cared less.

"Squintik," she said again. "Squintik."

And laughing, she followed the vagabond cat across the wide avenue.

It was twenty-five minutes before eleven, by the clock on the Graetna Life and Casualty building.

CHAPTER 10

SATURDAY DRIVER

IT WAS ELEVEN-SEVENTEEN
by the dashboard clock, and Jack was saying no, he wasn't
on *vacation*, anything like that, although, yeah, he *had* been
here a few times before, to Kemolo. Basically for just a look-
see. A short Walk. You know where he'd been, those other
visits? Let's see. Wazirabad—that was in Pakistan. And a
place called Pistol River. In Oregon? And Kazan, which
wasn't too far from Moscow. Geebo nodded, then flipped up
the directional signal and made a right turn, taking it kind of
wide. Driving again. How about that.

"And this other place called Hobart," Jack said. "In
Tasmania."

"Tasmania?" said Geebo. Thinking, Christ. "What a
weird bunch of places."

Jack shrugged. "Yeah, but interesting. It's always interesting."

Geebo gave him a quizzical look. There was something
about the way Jack said *interesting* that gave Geebo the feeling he wasn't using the word in the vague, lazy way that

most people did. That's an interesting shape, that's an interesting color. Which meant what? Nothing. Jack saying it, though, somehow it sounded, well, precise; specific. "What do you mean, interesting?"

Jack thought awhile before answering: narrowing his eyes and staring through the windshield, up the street. Then he leaned against the passenger door. "Meeting you, for instance: that's interesting."

"Yeah? Glad you think so. Meeting you, man, is friggen *fascinating.*"

"No, I mean I had no idea I was *going* to meet you, but now I know I *had* to. That's interesting. I wasn't looking for you, but now that it's happened, it's . . . interesting. Important."

"How?"

"Light's green," said Jack, and Geebo touched the pedal. Instant acceleration. Nice car. Toyota Cressida. Last year's model. July inspection sticker on the window, vanilla deodorizer in the shape of a pine tree hanging from the rearview mirror, 7,635 miles on the odometer—four of those miles put on since Geebo and Jack "borrowed" the vehicle from a guy who was no doubt still standing back on Ninth Street right where they'd left him holding his bag of dry cleaning and nursing his swollen, envenomed left wrist. Whoopee!

"How's it important?" Geebo asked again.

"I don't know. Definitely it is, though. Might even turn out to be perfect."

There Jack went again, making a nebulous adjective sound positively unequivocal. *Perfect?* Interesting, important, maybe *perfect?* "What're you saying?" Geebo asked. "That nothing happens by accident, that what you're saying?"

"No, man, that's *not* what I'm saying. Listen to me. I'm saying just the opposite. *Everything* happens by accident, to guys like me. When I'm out on a Ramble and something happens? It's *always* useful."

Interesting.

Important.

Perfect.

Useful. Now here was *useful.*

"How?" asked Geebo. "How's it that? Who's it useful *to?*"

"I'm the King's Tramp."

"Right. So it's useful to the King, this guy Agel."

"This guy Agel," said Jack, shaking his head, meaning: Show a little respect, Geebo. "His *Majesty.*" Then, pale eyes studying Geebo, Jack expelled a long breath and said, "Sure, useful to His Majesty, the King."

"Oh, come on."

"You *asked.*"

"Yeah," said Geebo, "I did."

"You asked, I'm telling you," said Jack.

Geebo had been asking questions for the last hour, lots and lots of questions, and now that he believed (really! he did believe, he *did*) that Jack was who he claimed to be (this strange visitor from another—no! no more of *that* shit; no more kidding around, okay?), Geebo was paying keen attention to every word the guy said, taking it all in, filing it away, trying to make sense of the whole crazy business.

Even so, there were still a lot of holes. Swiss cheese, man. Swiss friggen cheese.

Jack had been very obliging, eager to tell Geebo anything he wanted to know, it was just . . . difficult for him to explain one thing without getting bogged down in other things chock full of screwy names and peculiar details; without veering off, becoming sidetracked.

Jack tried, though. He'd been trying his best to answer every question that Geebo put to him, and he'd been doing so with patience, with humor, even with buoyant spirits. He wanted Geebo to understand.

For some reason.

For some reason it seemed important to him that Geebo understand.

Questions and answers.

In a maroon Toyota cruising around the city, heading north: Bridge District to Bergen Hill to Greenville, then midtown, uptown. Jack talking without hand gestures, Geebo driving cautiously, creeping along, stopping at amber lights, slowing at every intersection (he didn't want to get stopped: no license) and enjoying the hell out of it all, happy to be at the wheel again. (How long *had* it been? Never mind. Don't think about *that*. Think about what Jack's saying.)

Jack saying now, "How'd I *get* here? The only way I *could* get here, the only way there *is*. Through a cut." (Geebo thinking, It probably should be capitalized, italicized: *Cut*, seeing as how Jack emphasized the word. Through a *Cut*.)

Jack saying, "I met this guy the other day and Lita stung him, and in his head I found this story he'd been reading to one of his kids. At bedtime. Story about this boy who wants to go to the circus, but he doesn't have any money. It's called *Toby Tyler's Big Top Adventure*—you know that book?" (Geebo laughing, saying no, man, he'd never read it; thinking, Toby *Tyler?* What's that got to do with the price of eggs?)

And Jack said, "So in this story, the kid takes a penknife and goes around to the back of a circus tent, and slices through it. And that's how he gets in. Through the cut. And that's how *I* got in. Only instead of a penknife, I used a ring. Has these sharp points. The Schoolteacher's Ring. There's more than one, there's three. Three Schoolteacher's Rings. Three kinds. I used the one for Kemolo. Actually *I* didn't use it, I *can't* use it—Squintik used it for me."

Geebo said whoa, back up. "I'm still at the circus. Schoolteacher's Ring? *Kemolo? Squintik?* You *cut* your way in?"

"Master Squintik made the Cut."

"Yeah, yeah," Geebo said, "okay. But I mean—you *cut* your way in?"

Jack took a breath, held it, expelled it, then finally said, "In Whole Creation there are three—*probably* three, but some people, like the Mage of Four, Mage of Luck, think there's another one—three or four Moments from the Source. There's Feerce . . . and Kemolo . . . and Iss. And maybe—just maybe—one called Bulcease."

Geebo frowning then, saying, "What about Lostwithal? You forgot Lostwithal."

And Jack said, "Lostwithal isn't a Moment. I'm talking *universe* here, Geebo, *universe*. Universe*s*—get me? Lostwithal is just a human world, in the Moment of Iss. Get it? In the universe named Iss. See? And you're in Kemolo. You call this sphere Earth, we call it something else, but Earth is just a human world, the *only* human world, in the Moment of Kemolo. Which is a few Moments closer to creation than Iss. And a few Moments later than Feerce."

Geebo thinking, Oh *brother*. And hoping there wouldn't be a quiz later.

They cruised for a while then in silence, through Olmstead Park, passing runners and cyclists and horse-drawn carriages; driving around the pond, the brown softball fields, the zoo. And finally Geebo asked, "How long've you been here?"

"Your time? Couple days. Day before yesterday."

"What've you been doing? Stinging people left and right?"

Jack's lips broke in a big smile (those yellow teeth; those sharp canines). "How else was I supposed to pick up the language again? Langua*ges*. There's more than one language that humans speak here, you know."

Geebo nodding, wryly: yeah, he was aware of that.

"How else was I supposed to find out about . . . everything?"

"*Every*thing? Nice trick."

"I know how to play poker," said Jack. "Could beat you, I bet. And I can tell you what's on television tomorrow night. And Meryl Streep is a good actress. And the Yankees play baseball. Three strikes, you're out. And people think about sexual intercourse more than anything else. Any time of day."

Geebo smiled and said, "Welcome to Kemolo."

"It's true," said Jack.

"I believe it. But so tell me about the wasp. She's your bread and butter?"

"I know that expression," Jack said, looking puzzled, "but—how do you mean it? My bread and butter: how?"

"I mean, you use her to get what you need? Money. Food."

"Food," said Jack. "Yes. But not money. A King's Tramp can never use money. If I sought wealth, I would be no better than a Finder."

Geebo wet his lips. A *Finder? Another* screwy name.

Man, how was he supposed to keep *track* of all this stuff? Talk about confusing.

Yeah, but it was fun, too.

Asking all these questions.

Doing my job.

Then he thought: *What?* Doing my what? My *what?*

And Jack said, "Hey!" when Geebo suddenly winced, and took one hand off the wheel to press the pain from the back of his neck. Jack asking, "You okay?"

And Geebo saying, "Yeah," meanwhile struggling to turn off the pain. Keep talking. Don't think.

About yourself.

Don't think about yourself, man. Just keep talking. Say: "So what's a Finder?"

But Jack didn't reply. First question he'd refused to answer. He just sat hitched around in his seat, staring at Geebo. "What happens to you, when you get like that?"

"Headache."

"Humans here take little capsules for that. Or little white pills. Why don't you?"

"Doesn't work."

"Why not?"

"I thought I was asking the questions."

"Why don't you have any memory? A full *self?*"

"Good question."

"Yes," said Jack. "It is." Then he turned in his seat, facing front again, and Geebo watched him fold back his cuff, exposing the bracelet and the wasp in repose. "Drive," said Jack.

But though he'd bested the Headache this time, Geebo still felt sick to his stomach, queasy; always happened. Always, always. His vision had turned watery. And the euphoria he'd felt for the past hour sitting behind the Toyota's wheel had dwindled and died. Been replaced by a case of the jitters. Christ, he'd *stolen* a car; kind of. He didn't have a driver's license. He could end up in jail. "Let me just park," he said. "I'll go down the next street and park, you don't mind."

"But I *do* mind," said Jack. "Keep driving."

Geebo felt a spasm of annoyance. Who the hell was Jack to order him around? Huh? "Wasp doesn't work on *me*, pal," he said. "Remember?"

"You bought menthol cigarettes. *Pal.* Remember?"

"One thing had nothing to do with the other."

"Just drive," said Jack.

And Geebo got the idea all of a sudden that he was missing something, something was going on, but he was missing it. Completely. Jack insisting, Drive the car, drive the car. Urgency in his attitude, in his voice. Shit, though. Geebo didn't *feel* like driving anymore, all right? It wasn't fun anymore, okay? Enough driving. He wanted to park now.

"Drive," Jack said again, then looked past Geebo, at the cars and buses and cabs streaming down Avenue C. "Drive."

And Geebo steered back into the heavy flow of traffic.

The moment he did, though, a long white Cadillac limousine (vanity plates: G BOMAN) suddenly braked, and the Toyota plowed into it. Metal crumpled. Headlights and taillights shattered.

Geebo's teeth clacked together.

"Run!" he said, hitting the seatbelt release.

But Jack violently grabbed hold of Geebo's right arm and held tight.

He was smiling.

CHAPTER 11

THE FIVE

ON A MOUND OF ICED shrimp in a bin at the rear of the little neighborhood grocery store on Avenue F: the glassy-eyed corpse of Johnny Stillborn.

Directly to the right of the front door: another body, the Korean's, face down on worn green linoleum. His baseball bat, gnawed around the hitting area, still clutched in his hand.

One of the small reddish-brown creatures had clambered onto a tall shelving unit and was sniffing box after box, clumsily knocking several down. Cheerios, Wheat Chex, Mueller's macaroni, saltine crackers. At last it found something it wanted—Tender Vittles cat food—and tore open the package, and fed.

It made a low, keening noise.

As did the four other creatures, two of them burrowing through a bin of cantaloupes, another stretched out languorously across the top of an antique cash register, the last perched on the shoulder of a small, round-faced man with a high forehead and weak, watery eyes.

A man whose columnar neck was speckled red with measleslike eruptions.

As were the backs, and the palms, of his hands.

And the insteps of his filthy bare feet.

He was dressed in a light-gray caftan splashed dark red in several places. His arms were bony, spindly, and the left one was crooked awkwardly at the elbow, and palsied from there down.

On the first finger of that hand: a gold ring set with three sharp prongs.

He sat on a stool by the plate window, his legs dangling three inches above the floor. The creature on his shoulder nuzzled his ear, and moaned, and the man nodded.

Across the street, a woman in her late thirties was unlocking the driver's door of a white Mitsubishi Mirage. She reached in and switched off the alarm, then backed out and called to a boy standing several yards away outside an Army-Navy store perusing cartons jumbled with canteens and hooded sweatshirts.

He was wearing a blue windbreaker, new dungarees, white sneakers.

Staring, his eyes tightly narrowed, the little man on the stool in the grocery store gave a soft grunt.

He watched the boy climb into the white car, the car pull into traffic.

He continued to watch the passing life outside.

Two women in beige raincoats dashed into the street for a taxi. An older, heavyset man—with both arms around a huge black-and-white stuffed animal, a panda—ran for the same cab, but from the opposite direction. There was an argument, the women both gesticulating broadly, the man shaking his head.

He was wearing a tweed overcoat, black trousers, black wingtip shoes.

The small man on the stool in the grocery store grunted again.

Several canataloupes tumbled from their bin.

Nearby, church bells tolled the Angelus. It was noon.

On the pavement directly in front of the grocery, an elderly woman had paused, and was scrutinizing grapefruits. She picked one up, checked it for blemishes, then replaced it and picked up another.

The small man watched her tear a plastic produce bag from a roll on a wooden spindle. He lifted his good hand, his right hand, to his mouth and tapped his lips.

She finally selected three grapefruits, then came around to the door.

When she tried to pull it open, the creature on the cash register slowly rose, baring its teeth.

"Hello?" she called, tapping on the glass. Then, puzzled, *"Hello?"*

And the small man pressed his eyes shut, wincing at the sound. It was painful to his ears, the language of these too-humans of Kemolo; painful and unintelligible. Once, he could've learned it—*absorbed* it—in a matter of seconds, that vile language. Absorbed it, then spoken it.

Once.

When he'd been a Walker.

"Hel-*lo!*" Clucking in annoyance, the old woman stepped back from the door. "You have a customer out here!

Hello? Why is this door locked?" She expelled a long, deflating breath, then irritably deposited her grapefruits back into their bin. This never happened when the Italians were here! With a final exclamation of disgust, accompanied by an edgy frown, the old woman turned away and crossed the street.

Inside the grocery store, a bag of corn meal dropped suddenly from a shelf and burst open on the floor.

The small man waited a few moments, then climbed down off the stool.

Now. At last he was ready to begin. Using his right arm as a fulcrum, he slowly raised his left hand to his mouth, then bit into his wrist.

The five reddish-brown creatures all squealed in pain.

Then gathered around the man's legs.

It was time to begin. To work.

To Find.

Down by the entrance to Stephen Crane Park, the old woman was speaking with a neighbor she'd met coming out of a pharmacy.

Oh, she couldn't kick, she said, she couldn't complain, she was feeling all right. That? On the bridge of her nose? Oh, *that*. Was where she'd had a jot of skin cancer removed last week. It was still sore, but what was the use of complaining? Eh? What was the use of kicking?

Her friend kept nodding, then mentioned that she'd spent four hours the other day waiting to see her doctor— her arthritis man? Four hours! Luckily she'd thought to bring a good book along with her.

The old woman was about to ask after her friend's husband when she was startled by something across the street.

A most homely-looking little man (but *very* smartly dressed: in a tweed overcoat, charcoal-gray suit pants and gleaming black wingtip shoes) stood on the corner surrounded by—his *sons,* she supposed. *That's* what startled her. Stupefied her, really. Them. The boys.

Five little boys with reddish-brown hair.

They *looked* nearly identical, and they were certainly *dressed* the same, in blue windbreakers, new dungarees, and white sneakers. Are they quints? the old woman thought.

She'd never actually *seen* quintuplets before. Except, of course, in magazine pictures.

And she'd never, *ever* seen five boys who looked so— what was the word she wanted? A word that came up every so often in her Sunday crossword puzzle. Not ferocious. (Though "ferocious" was often the *clue.* "Ferocious, in a wild state.")

Feral.

That was it. That was the word.

Feral.

Those five boys looked positively feral. Look at their eyes, their hunched shoulders. The way their arms . . . dangled. Dear God, look at their fingernails! She could see them from here, from all the way over here!

Those long fingernails.

When they all started across the street with the homely little man, she felt a shudder pass through her and quickly turned her back to them.

Her oblivious friend was saying now that her senior citizens group had taken a charter bus to a dinner theater out by Old Tappan, day before yesterday, and they'd seen a marvelous production of *Show Boat.* And she'd had shrimp scampi. It was delicious!

The old woman smiled, nodded absently, then couldn't resist one last peek at those—boys.

Who loped along like little animals, and entered the park behind their . . . father.

I

CHAPTER 12

BAND SHELL

IT WAS PURELY BY ACCIdent that Money Campbell discovered Geebo's water-heater carton.

For an hour, maybe longer—Money couldn't say exactly how long, since, like a real nincompoop, she'd left her watch at Eugene Boman's apartment—she'd wandered all around Crane Park showing the photograph.

Trying to show it.

Half the people she'd approached wouldn't even *look* at it; they just looked at *her*, sometimes lecherously, sometimes cantankerously, but *always* suspiciously, too.

The others, the ones who'd agreed to look, merely shrugged. Saying, No. Never seen him.

Money didn't know whether to believe them or not. They were so weird, so creepy. All of them. Jesus. These people actually lived in cardboard boxes and little shelters made of doors. They leaned against trees, against snow fences, and clustered around the backstop in the ball field. No kidding. And they sat on Hefty bags. In the freezing cold, they sat outside on Hefty bags, on spray-painted boulders, on vandalized bubblers. They muttered, and they smelled, and sometimes they bellowed for no reason at all except they were *nuts*.

Oh yeah, she *felt* for them, and all. She *guessed* she did. Shoot, who wouldn't?

But they were scary.

With a capital S.

Was Peter really living down here?

She wanted to go home.

And not back to Boman's place, either. *That* wasn't home. She wanted to go back to Old Tappan, to her poky off-campus apartment with its sink full of dishes and its unmade bed and its teeny bathroom with an old white tub on big claw-feet. Home. She wanted to go home. To *her* place. With boring textbooks scattered around, and audiotapes and clogged ashtrays, and the Tandy computer that Peter Musik had used three and four evenings a week, typing his notes onto a hard disk.

Jeez, she hadn't been home in, like, days. Not since . . . Tuesday. Man, it'd be nice to go home. Maybe rent some good new videos. Something with Bette Midler in it. Or Danny DeVito. Something silly and fast.

Heaving a long sigh, Money trudged across Big Lawn with the torn-in-half snapshot still in her hand.

" 'Scuse me. I'm looking for—"

" 'Scuse me? Would you happen to—"

" 'Scuse me—miss? You ever see the guy in this picture?"

" 'Scuse me."

" 'Scuse me."

'Scusing herself till she wanted to scream.

Maybe this was a bad idea.

Maybe Herb Dierickx had been mistaken.

Also that weird guy with the shaved head. Maybe *he'd* been mistaken, too. (Imagine asking her if she knew Dustin Hoffman! Right.)

Maybe Peter *wasn't* down here.

Maybe he was dead.

Like she'd figured all along—like she'd figured since last September. She hadn't believed Eugene Boman, not even for one second. What'd he take her for, an airhead? Feeding her that story about Peter Musik having some kind of nervous breakdown. Sure. Tell me another one, Gene.

Suddenly very tired, Money leaned against a little shelter with a peaked roof.

A band shell.

She tapped the snapshot against her chin.

Then she held it out at arm's length, staring at the image. Peter Musik in his swim trunks. He wasn't a very *hairy* guy, was he? A grassy beach sloping away behind him, you could see a bit of the dark-green lake.

Peter, she thought. don't be dead. Please?

Be here. Be close by. Be *somewhere*.

At a rasping sound, she turned suddenly toward the band shell and noticed a long cardboard carton swishing sideways across the floor in a gust of wind.

Money started to turn away again, but then checked herself.

Saying, "God," and getting goosebumps.

PRIVATE PROPERTY. DO NOT REMOVE OR INHABIT.

In green Magic Marker.

Hand-lettered on the side of the carton.

Peter.

Or maybe: "Peter."

Maybe she'd actually *spoken* his name, she wasn't sure, she'd gone all light-headed.

That was Peter Musik's printing. Absolutely. No doubt about it. Look at the D, the R, the B. See how they were so *swaybacked?* And the Os. Look at those funny little curlicues at the tops. And look at the H in INHABIT. Just *look* at that H. The second vertical line bent up sharply to make the cross-line. So instead of the cross-line being horizontal, it was, like, *diagonal*. That was Peter. Peter's printing. Oh yeah. *Oh* yeah. Definitely.

She'd seen a lot of Peter's quirky printing last spring and summer, on legal pads and stick-em memos affixed to mini-cassettes. The stuff he'd brought to her apartment and transcribed into the computer while she sat around drinking coffee, doing calisthenics. He'd got a special kick out of using her Tandy, since Eugene Boman had paid for it. Money remembered now, and smiled. Then she called his name again, first calling, "Peter?" Then frowning, thinking, Shit, right, and calling, "Geebo?"

Geebo.

The file name that he'd given to his notes. Hitting Control/Save, then typing G-E-E-B-O, then pressing Enter.

Geebo. Short for Gene Boman.

Money thinking, Oh *man*, calling louder now, "Geebo!" as she walked around to the steps. "Geebo?" She put a hand on the skinny bannister, which was full of carved initials and nicknames and sexual verbs. "Geebo? You *in* there?"

At last, she took a deep breath and went up on the porch and crouched down and peered into the carton.

Nobody home.

So *now* what?

With her arms folded, hugging herself tight, Money started walking around and around the porch, the wind picking up her yellow hair and blowing it. Every so often she stopped to gaze out over Big Lawn, hoping to see Peter (to see Geebo; *Geebo)* heading this way. Coming back.

But what if he didn't *come* back?

What if he'd moved to a different park? Or, like, found a better carton?

Better carton. Listen to her: what if he'd found a better carton. Wow, if this wasn't so awful, so *serious,* it'd be almost funny. DO NOT REMOVE OR INHABIT.

Eventually, and she didn't know *why* she did it (because it was cold? hey, it wasn't *that* cold; no, probably just because the sign said don't inhabit, and it was Moncy's nature to be contrary), she knelt down and crawled into the water-heater carton. Turning around so that she faced the opening, she sat hunched over with her knees drawn up and her head touching the top and her back braced against the closed end. She felt skeevy.

And wondered what was going to happen when Peter showed up. (When. Not if. *When.* 'Cause he *was* gonna show —right? Right?)

And then remembered a lot of stuff that she'd just as soon have forgotten.

That, in her heart of hearts, she wished had never happened.

Starting, she supposed, with going off to college. Like so many other things—like *most* things—she'd done in her life, Money had enrolled at Old Tappan not because she'd wanted to, but because it was the very *last* thing that people —her father, in particular—expected of her.

Monica? Go to college? What in heaven's name *for?* She's very sweet and all, but *college?* Be just a waste of time.

Her whole *family* saying that, not just her father, but her mother, too, and her older brothers, even her aunts and uncles; *everybody* saying it, including teachers and guidance counselors, even her girlfriends, because Money had been one of those high school kids who'd answered Russia when the question was who'd we fight in World War II. Who kind of thought that Portugal was in Central America. And that Korea was a planet.

Money? In college? It was—daffy. Better she went to work in some nice department store (she'd always made a very good appearance) or learned something about word processing or married a handsome lawyer. But all right, said her father, who owned the True Value hardware store in Beimdeck, Ohio; all right, if she was determined to go, then fine. He'd pay for it, but only if she went to a *local* college.

So, of course, she'd picked one six hundred miles away.

And not a cheap one, either.

Her father saying, "And how're you gonna afford *that,* Miss Alberta Einstein?"

Money saying, "I'll work."

She could've done some modeling part time—everybody, her old man included, said that, that she could've made good money as a model. A catalog model. A bathing-suit model.

So, of course, she wouldn't even *consider* it.

Modeling? Yuck. And she found instead some dreary office job, working mornings, at Boman Pharmaceuticals, corporate headquarters—you could walk there in no time from the Old Tappan campus, it was only a quarter-mile away, across Highway 9 and up a steep landscaped hill. . . .

Hunched inside the moldy old water-heater carton, Money grimaced, remembering that stupid job, typing letters and filing invoices, the middle-aged women all snippy, the nowhere men all tracking her with their beady eyes every time she moved, staring soulfully at her breasts, and if she bent over for something, trying to look down her dress or blouse or sweater.

What a stupid place.

And the hourly wage was pathetic.

But she'd put up with it.

Though she couldn't have said *why*. Working that crummy job with those dreadful people just so she could pay almost every cent she earned for a college education? Why?

She *hated* college.

Well, the *college* itself was all right, no complaints about the college *buildings*, the college *grounds*. It was a very pretty campus, with lots of pine trees and statues and stuff. Oh, the college itself was definitely all right, it was just the classes that she hated. If she hadn't learned so well back in high school how to cheat on exams without getting caught, man oh man, she *never* would've survived even the first semester.

But survive she did, and not only the first semester, but the second one, as well.

At the end of her freshman year, after having taken eleven dull courses and blown nine thousand dollars, not counting room and board, Money still had no idea—not so much as an inkling!—what she might eventually major in. Oh well. In time. No hurry.

That summer, the summer before last, she'd worked at Boman Pharmaceuticals full time. The only thing about the job she truly enjoyed was the free lunch in the cafeteria. And it was there, one afternoon in late July, that she noticed a fat, almost-bald man she'd never seen before watching her from the doorway of the executive dining room. Let him look. Free country. Money was used to men staring.

But this big fat one wasn't satisfied just to look, as she learned later that same day, when she received a phone call at her desk. "Miss Campbell? This is Eugene Boman. I wonder, um, if you'd be so kind as to, um, come upstairs when you get a chance. I'd, um, like a word with you." Money had been amazed by his hesitant manner, by those nerdy *ums*. So amazed that, at first, she'd honestly believed that somebody in the office was playing a joke on her. . . .

Inside the carton, Money began to squirm with discomfort. Her neck had a crick in it, and a charley horse was starting in her left calf. What was sort of interesting, though, she wasn't cold anymore; this baby was a good insulator, this box. No fooling. Her breath wasn't even coming out frosted. She unzipped her coat, pulled off her gloves, and leaned back. But the cardboard suddenly buckled, so she had to lean forward again.

Then she folded her hands in her lap, and just sat there, waiting.

And remembering: how startled she'd been when the super-rich big-shot owner of Boman Pharmaceuticals, the guy who'd called her on the telephone, turned out to be the fat, almost-bald guy she'd caught staring at her breasts in the cafeteria. Jeez. And then she was amused by how flustered he got the moment she walked into his office. Man, you look at "Dallas," you look at "Dynasty," shows like that, you figured rich guys were all suave and silky. Like John Forsythe, right? Patrick Duffy? Forget it. Would Patrick Duffy stammer and sweat like some high school dweeb? No, but Eugene Boman did. Would John Forsythe have a Mickey

Mouse telephone on his desk, a "Star Trek" poster on the wall? No, but Eugene Boman did. And that wasn't all. There were a couple of showcases, like you'd find in Woolworth's, and the shelves were crammed with little toys. Donald Ducks and Fred Flintstones, Bullwinkles and Deputy Dawgs, junky stuff like that. Very weird.

Boman asked her to sit down, then he asked her if she wanted something to drink—a Coke or a cup of coffee?—and then his eyes went sort of blank. He laughed nervously and suddenly blurted, "You're a very beautiful girl." And even though she figured this was going to cost her her summer job, Money smirked in his face. His big round cheeks turned bright red. This is so *weird,* she thought. This is just about the weirdest thing. But funny enough, she enjoyed it. It was great to see a guy so rich behave like any breast-fixated jerk on the street.

When he asked her if she'd consider, um, seeing him some evening, um, socially, she leaned forward on the sofa and asked him point-blank was he married. "You married?"

Yes, he was. He wanted to be, um, candid. Yes, he *was* married, *but.*

And Money laughed again. But. Always a but.

But he was, um, kind of hoping they could be friends, anyway.

Money looked at him and smiled. Friends. *Good* friends —right? She got up to leave, and that should've been the end of it, only it wasn't. Because instead of becoming angry or nasty, as she'd expected, Eugene Boman started to laugh. Like he realized himself how stupid this all sounded, and what a cliché it was. She liked that. She respected him for it, almost.

She sat down again, crossed one leg over the other, and

suddenly it was all make-believe, a goof. She thought, Why not? What the hell? Sean Young can play me in the miniseries. "So what do you have in mind?" said Money. "A nice restaurant might be good, but don't waste your money on the symphony orchestra, stuff like that. I hate stuff like that."

Eugene Boman said that he did, too, and they shook hands as though sealing a business contract, which of course they were, and his hand was soft and damp.

They saw each other one or two times a week after that. Their meetings were on the sly, but you could never have called them tawdry. The restaurants they went to were small and dark, but the entrees began at a hundred dollars and the wines were all vintage. (Kidding around, Money would say, "Oh, *another* dusty bottle?") He chartered a yacht, and she never saw the crew, but she did see Boman's American Express receipt, and was very impressed.

Couple times that first month he drove her (well, *he* didn't do the actual driving, his chauffeur did; Boman *took* her) to a chalet that he owned at Scroon Lake. There were no other houses, no other people, for miles around, just pine wilderness and small rivers the color of weak tea. He told her he'd paid cash for the house. Nobody else even knew about it. Just him, and now her. Money said, "No kidding."

The second time that he'd brought her there, he left suddenly after making a phone call. It was business, he said, and promised to return in a couple of hours. But then he didn't come back till the following morning. Boy, was he apologetic, and Money said, "Hey, it's all right. It's a great house. I used the sauna, I went swimming." (She could've said, "I didn't miss you at all," but didn't.)

She said, "But where'd you go?"

"Into Leesboro."

"Leesboro?" She was surprised because Leesboro was a one-street town with some old clapboard buildings. The kind of place that has one gas station with round-topped pumps.

"I wasn't *in* Leesboro," he said, "I was at . . . a farm *near* Leesboro."

She'd almost asked what kind of business did he have on a *farm*, but let it pass. He seemed uncomfortable talking about it, and besides she wasn't interested.

Naturally, one thing did lead to another, but not as quickly as Money had expected. For the longest time, Boman had seemed perfectly happy just to stare at her, to touch her lightly whenever she passed in front of him, to rub his hand in circles on the small of her back, to squeeze her fingers across a table. He complimented her on her good looks so often and so extravagantly that she finally asked him to please stop it. And he did, and after that's when they finally started sleeping together.

It didn't bother Money to have sex with a klutzy guy she wouldn't have looked at twice if he hadn't been so loaded. Maybe it should, she'd think, but it doesn't. It's all a goof. It's experience. And the spending money's great.

Nor did it bother her that Boman was married. He'd told her once, and only once, that his wife was an unpleasant, selfish woman, and maybe she was and maybe she wasn't, it didn't really matter. Edie Boman lived two hundred miles away, never came to the city, never called. She wasn't a factor.

What did bother Money, though, a little, was waking up in the dark sometimes to find that Eugene Boman had drawn back the top sheet and was propped on an elbow staring at her. He must've had cat eyes. *That* was creepy.

Even creepier were the times he'd lunge up from his sleep like a dead body with rigor mortis. Then he'd start gulping for breath, and he'd be completely covered in sweat, and Money would turn clammy just seeing him like that, hearing him sob, and she'd wonder how a guy with all his millions could have such nightmares. What the hell did *he* have to worry about?

He was such a drippy, dull man, a man without friends, it never dawned on her that he could have any, you know, *deep dark secrets.* Never dawned on her. Never.

Till Peter Musik had showed up.

And now, sitting in a stupid cardboard box in a stupid band shell in a stupid ugly park, Money Campbell thought, Peter—you bastard! This really is all your own fault. It was all a silly goof till you had to come along and spoil it. Bastard!

She was sitting in a stupid cardboard box. In a stupid band shell with stupid peeling paint in an ugly stupid park. Was this ridiculous, or what?

And she had a stupid charley horse in her stupid right calf, and *that* was Peter Musik's fault, too.

And on top of everything else, she was getting a stupid headache. Cooped up in there, she was probably breathing her own stupid carbon dioxide—or was it monoxide? Or was that from cars? Monoxide, dioxide, whatever the hell it was, it was giving her a stinking little headache, making her sick to her stomach, kind of woozy even.

It's all Peter Musik's fault, she thought. Big deal reporter. Big deal, my ass. Coming on to me like he was those newspaper guys that got Nixon. But Peter Musik wasn't *any*-thing like them. What'd *he* ever do that was so great? Nothing. Nothing nothing nothing. Writing stupid stories for idiotic supermarket tabloids. Asshole. Asshole! And you dressed from hunger. You really and truly dressed from hunger.

Money thinking, Peter, this is *not* my fault, this is all *your* fault, you brought this all on yourself. I hate you.

She realized then that she'd clenched her hands so tightly that her knuckles ached, and that she was crying. She wiped her eyes. Then her nose started running.

I didn't mean that, Peter. Honest to God, she thought. I'm sorry. You believe me?

Peter?

Be alive. Please be alive. Please?

And then she heard it: footsteps on the porch.

She listened and her heart raced. The way her neck was throbbing, it felt like her heart was in her throat.

Awkwardly, she went down on all fours and stuck her head through the opening and into the dreary afternoon light.

Leaning kind of nonchalant against one of the roof posts was a funny-looking little man in a nice tweed overcoat.

He was holding his left arm with his right hand, sort of cradling it.

Oh jeez, Money had to laugh at herself: what she must *look* like, her weepy face sticking out the end of a cardboard box.

Then she wasn't laughing anymore. She was frowning, seeing a bunch of redheaded little boys ranged along the slatted railing, *five* of them. And not only were they dressed alike, they *looked* alike. Like *identical*. Wasn't that *weird*?

They were staring at her.

Well, sure: girl comes crawling out of a cardboard box,

who wouldn't? Stare at her like she was from another planet or something.

Money said, "Hey, campers," which she was instantly proud of. Not bad for spur-of-the-moment wit. Only trouble was, the funny-looking little man didn't even crack a smile. Instead, he flinched like he'd just heard a truck backfire.

That did it. Enough weirdness. Money thinking, So long, mister. See ya, kids. And screw this park. I *hate* this place. Starting to her feet, then going rigid, spine prickling, a reedy "Huh?" coming from her throat.

When—jeez-*us!*—the boys all started to, like, *growl*.

CHAPTER 13

PANDA

Regarding his expertise, his created instincts, Eudrax understood next to nothing; nothing of how it was that he—formerly a Walker, formerly an Outrager—could, with unhesitating confidence, now pursue his master's enemies throughout all of Lostwithal; pursue them even, as he had done this day, into another Moment. Pursue them and find them without need of visible signs or the smallest scrap of information. It was a mystery, how he could *do* that, but he was content, he was *determined*, to have it so.

While he remained altogether ignorant of his Finder's nature, and of his significance in the Order of Things, and of why he'd been chosen for such a thirdwork, Eudrax, however, understood only too well his violent craving for bounty. Be it a bracelet set with odstones or a single bag of wormy rice, a common pair of sandals or the favors of a smooth-bellied woman on the Isle of Lace: whatever bounty his master, the great mage of Manse Seloc, chose to bestow upon him at Killing's End was fit and good. Fit and good!

Most excellent! Oh, *most* excellent! Desirable! Redemptive. Analgesic. Since it kept away the brainsickness, the frightening public convulsions, the taste of wet coal ash in his mouth.

For a time. . . .

Eudrax and his five claws had entered the park at twenty minutes past noon.

By twelve-thirty, the Finder had come upon the carton in the band shell.

He hadn't known that he was seeking such a thing till he'd spotted it.

And once he had, he studied it for a short while, and then, mysteriously, it became clear to him that he had found Jack, a Walker.

So be it.

He would take the Walker now, the Cold Mage later.

It made no difference to Eudrax who died first.

The claws had clambered onto the railing, were poised there, waiting for Eudrax to bite deeply into the slack flesh on his withered Hand of Favor.

Waiting for him to release them from *their* torment.

To give them *their* fit and good bounty.

Eudrax would enjoy seeing the Walker bleed.

It would be almost a bounty in itself.

Almost.

Eudrax leaned against a post, waiting. No need to rush. Let him crawl out.

Jack, he thought. A Fool. Then Eudrax shivered with pleasure, speculating upon what manner of bounty his master might bestow when he returned to Lostwithal with fresh blood on his hands. No doubt it would be a *special* one—the Mage of Four, Mage of Luck had even promised him that, leaning across the refectory table at Manse Seloc, then lacing his fingers together and making the Sign of the Cradle.

"But do not fail us, Eudrax," the great mage had said.

Of *course* he would not fail.

He stood in the band shell, serene.

But when suddenly the girl—not the Walker—appeared, Eudrax felt a blast of panic that nearly exhausted him, and he tasted, for the briefest moment, wet coal ash on his tongue.

His bland expression, however, remained unchanged.

Till the girl's language pierced him.

This girl. This . . . girl. Eudrax tried to discover the meaning of this *girl.*

But could not.

He understood nothing. Unless . . .

Suddenly tantalized (unusual, to be *that*), Eudrax stared across the band shell, and the girl stared back.

He smiled.

Unless she were the wasp—eh?

The Walker's Sting.

The witch Aculita.

Had she taken this . . . *form* here?

It *must* be that, Eudrax decided, she *must* be the witch. Why else had he found himself standing upon this board floor, in this green pavilion? Why else had he found *her?*

With his right arm, he lifted his withered Hand of Favor to his lips.

Growling, the five claws moved.

But then, abruptly, he let the Hand drop.

No need, thought Eudrax, to rush.

He would kill the witch later, in the presence of the Walker.

In that way, she could watch her beloved host suffer and die, and might know despair before the claws took her down.

And the Walker—the Walker could die with the knowledge that his wasp had not escaped. And bear the guilt for it, all the way into the Void.

Somehow, Eudrax was certain that *these* would be the better deaths, deaths that would give his master greater satisfaction, and earn him a finer bounty.

The girl screamed when he banished the too-human shadows he'd gathered.

She went limp at the sight of the claws.

Eudrax struck her anyway.

And then, taking her by an arm, he pulled her roughly down the steps. The claws scrambled behind.

Several of the homeless people milling on Big Lawn glanced away from their drum fires, saying, Holy Christ, would you look at *that*.

Five identical redheaded boys following a small, moon-faced man in a tweed topcoat who was dragging in tow a huge black-and-white stuffed animal, a panda.

CHAPTER 14

PATIENT

FOR SOME TIME NOW, MASter Squintik had felt as though his body were floating above the hospital bed, suspended in space. It was not unpleasant, the languor, but since it was artificial, wholly effected by medicines, the Cold Mage was offended, his conscience sorely troubled. With an effort of will, he tried taking back possession of his faculties and his limbs, but could not; finally, with a long, shuddering sigh, Squintik dropped once more into unconsciousness.

. . . and, in dream, returned to Lostwithal, to the chamber of Agel, where he waited on a bench in the cool dimness beyond the citrine light that bathed the royal seat. Waited his turn, an opportunity to speak, struggling to maintain respectful composure though he was half-mad with wicked impatience.

He watched as the Minister of Intemperate Seasons (who'd followed the Deputy of Public Health and Generation, who'd followed the Mage of Useful Numbers, who'd followed . . .) droningly reported upon anticipated rainfall, come Storm Time, in the northern province of Dael.

The old King, his eyes barely open and his lips shiny with the black salve that his youngest page, a boy of nine, had just applied to them, listened (or, possibly, did not), then nodded, then gestured feebly: the report was accepted, with gratitude.

The Minister of Intemperate Seasons bowed, and was excused.

Squintik watched him retake his seat.

Squintik leaned forward.

Squintik very nearly leaped from the bench.

But in good conscience he could not impose or interject himself, could not disrupt the harmony, the orderliness of state business, *he could not*. Though he had a crisis to report— the crisis which for several months the Cold Mage had anticipated, but which only a day earlier had been confirmed to him, with the sudden return of Jack, a Walker to the capital city—Squintik could not bring himself to interrupt the proceedings. So, trembling with impatience, he was compelled to sit and listen . . . to the Minister of Conflict and Redress . . . then to the Minister of Agriculture . . . the Minister of Secondwork Education . . . and to a delegation of regional sheriffs charged with the efficient collection of the Summer Tax; compelled to sit there in the chamber's deep gloom and to wait till he was called upon.

Because, above all else, the Order of Things must be maintained.

One by one, the ministers and deputies and mages reported, and the King nodded, accepting their reports with gratitude . . . gratitude . . . gratitude, and time crawled, and the citrine light that bathed His Majesty-Most-Still steadily waned.

Squintik felt ill, knowing that soon, too *soon* the light would gray to gloaming, and the Prime Minister would step forward to announce the end of the King's Attention, till the morrow. But what Squintik had to say could not *wait* till the morrow, and he clutched himself to check his trembling, his breathing became rapid, then halting, and so raspy that it drew notice from others sharing the long bench with him, old mages like himself, many accompanied by their yawning apprentices. His fellows rebuked Squintik with their eyes, and he pressed both palms against his forehead, cold as marble. Frustration racked his body.

And the citrine light passed, and the Prime Minister—Rampike, a Reciter—brought the proceedings brusquely to a close.

All rose and bowed to the King, who merely nodded, again, then drew a brown monkish hood over his head. As the chamber began to empty, several pages carried in a table laden with fruit. They set it down before the throne.

Squintik had not moved to leave. Fingers nervously pleating his cassock, he stared at the King, wanting to rush forward, to prostrate himself, to beg His Majesty's indulgence, and then to blurt of the great danger which threatened not only Lostwithal, but the very Moment of Iss, which threatened *all* the Moments of Whole Creation: to tell Sad Agel that the fabled infant was alive, yes, it *existed*, fashioned of straw and stony mud in the port city of Tiedek; that the Walker had found it, a Perfect Accident leading him to its cradle in the moons' light: the Epicene Whose Eyes Are Death, the Son-and-Daughter of Plenary Chaos.

But Squintik could not bring himself to speak so.

Because, above all else, Perfect Order must be maintained.

With a final bow in the direction of the throne (where the King, having rejected nourishment for the time being, had slumped over and appeared to be sleeping), Squintik humbly left the chamber.

Minutes later, passing through the castle gateway, in the glare and heat of noon, he was accosted by the Mage of Four, Mage of Luck. "A word, my old friend," he said, touching Squintik with the head of his crosier.

Reluctant, Squintik turned and looked upon the great mage of Manse Seloc, his black eyes narrowed, his cheeks writhing with fat slugs.

"A word concerning what matter?"

"The Walker."

Squintik drew his lips tight against his teeth, and waited.

"He has returned."

"Has he?"

"And you have seen him."

Squintik said nothing. Although his eyes never left the great mage's face, he was aware of Sister Card, the pythoness, standing behind him, her dry lips twitching. And he was aware, too, of several small children—three, possibly four—covertly watching from behind topiary in the Public Garden of Our History. They were pointing, whispering. Squintik could sense their excitement, their nervousness, and remembered a nursery rhyme that all mothers sang in Lostwithal:

A mage alone—say *please* and *sir*
He's apt to show you magic.

But a mage and his peer—say nothing, sweet dear
Or else your life be tragic.

"You have seen him," said the Mage of Four, Mage of
Luck, taking a step nearer to Squintik. "You have spoken
with him. I would know what he's told you. I would know
. . . when he intends to gladden His Majesty's heart with
the tales of his travels."

Squintik slowly shook his head, then turned to go, feeling that he must leave immediately, he must; otherwise, he
could no longer hold his tongue, control his wrath.

The monster would *not* goad him.

Nor frighten him.

But, it seemed, he *would* threaten him: "Be cautious,
Squintik, be meek," said the Mage of Four, Mage of Luck,
"and see that you bury yourself in your *own* affairs. Lest you
find yourself buried in the Manse Seloc. The Walker belongs
to me."

"Good digestion, my lord," said Squintik, choosing the
least generous (though by no means affrontive: that
would've been suicidal) of leave-taking expressions. Then he
walked unsteadily away, glowering at the dwarf, who
merely chuckled beneath her breath.

Skirting the garden, Squintik crossed the Avenue of Pa-
cific Order, and headed into the market square.

There, he stopped and looked back.

Head down, and with her hands clasped behind her,
Sister Card was following him.

Squintik smiled, then glanced around, noticing a large
black dog sleeping in a splotch of shade by a water pump.
The mage summoned to mind certain configurations, some
geometric, others ideographic. He sorted them, gave them

color. Then he moistened two fingers on his Hand of Favor, and pressed them to his brow.

Claimed, the black dog scrambled to its feet, and set off to summon the Walker.

Squintik watched it dash through the marketplace, then briefly smiled again.

Before leading the pythoness through a series of alleys that, eventually, would perplex her and leave her grim and sweating and lost, the Cold Mage glanced back once again at the Mage of Four, Mage of Luck—who had beckoned the small children from their place of concealment in the public gardens and was ruffling their silky hair, letting them pull slugs from his face, to keep.

Thought Squintik, We shall see who ends up buried. . . .

Opening his eyes, he was pleased to feel pain, both in his right calf and in the back of his skull, above his left ear. His tongue was parched. Closing his eyes, Squintik concentrated upon the mustering of some curvilinear shapes. Keeping those clear in his mind, he next computed sums. Water bubbled up gently from the palms of his hands and then froze.

He broke the skin of ice, and refreshed himself.

Then he gazed placidly at the ceiling, waiting for the kindly woman to arrive. . . .

CHAPTER 15

THE SPARK FADES

SHE'D FOLLOWED THE CAT for several blocks, just drifting along, pushing her cart, wearing a placid smile.

Not the least bit curious where she was going.

Where the cat was taking her.

Downtown? Fine. East? That was fine, too. It was all the same to Jere Lee. Nothing mattered, least of all direction—destination. A *cat* was leading her. Had *spoken* to her. Why should anything matter now? She'd gone over.

She was following a tabby cat.

Well, at least this was better than finding herself covered with fruitflies nobody else could see. Better than being absolutely convinced that every fire hydrant in the city was a neutron bomb in disguise. Living on the street, Jere Lee had met women with precisely those delusions; she'd met others with even wilder ones. So when you got right down to it, a cat that talked—well, not exactly a *talking* cat, a *telepathic* cat—wasn't so bad.

Kind of a *nice* cat, too, she thought. *Scruffy.* But nice.

But then, heading down Twenty-first Street and seeing the massive red-brick pile that was St. Vincent's Hospital loom ahead, Jere Lee stopped dead in her tracks.

Oh no, she said to herself. *Oh* no. No way, no sir.

I'm not going nuts *this* easy.

I got a slight fever, that's all.

That's all.

She wheeled her cart around and hurried back up the street, afraid to look behind her, afraid that the Squintik cat (was that different, ho-ho, from a Jellicle Cat?) might be coming right after her.

Breathless, she crossed Twenty-first Street on a diagonal, then slipped through a commercial arcade lined with camera stores and junk-jewelry shops. Came out on Twentieth, turned west, and found a drug store where she bought a small bottle of cherry-flavored Sudamax syrup for bronchial congestion.

She asked the pharmacist for a spoon. Please?

Calling her "lady" but making it sound rude and insulting, he told her that he didn't supply spoons—she wanted a spoon, try Woolworth's. But when she opened the box, took out the bottle and was about to fill its cap with syrup, he quickly produced one.

"This is for a fever too, right?" she asked.

"Read what it says," the pharmacist replied, curtly, then turned away and resumed hanging festively packaged condoms on a wire rack.

The cat was waiting when Jere Lee went back outside.

YOU GOT TO FOLLOW ME. IT'S WHAT YOU GOT TO DO.

She rolled her cart to the corner, looked both ways,

started crossing. I don't *got* to do anything, she thought. Except pull myself together.

And survive.

That's all I *got* to do.

YOU THINK THIS IS MY IDEA? I DON'T KNOW WHAT THIS IS ALL ABOUT, EITHER. BUT YOU GOT TO FOLLOW ME. AND I GOT TO—

Jere Lee thought, Jellicle Cats are black and white, Jellicle Cats are rather small, Jellicle Cats are merry and bright . . .

Behind her, she heard the tabby cat hiss.

She headed south at the next corner, walked two blocks, then turned west again. She went into a Burger King, where she sat nursing a cup of tea for almost forty minutes. From eleven thirty-five till a quarter past noon. She would've stayed there even longer, but the lady manager came over and said that her cart was "hindering mobility." And besides, she said, this was a restaurant, not an SRO.

Jere Lee said, "You call this a restaurant?"

Outside again, she was greatly relieved not to find the tabby cat.

Five minutes later, she arrived at the Old Bergen branch of the post office.

Before going in, she looked over a shoulder.

Still no cat.

Of course not.

Because the medicine had started to work.

In the post office lobby, to the left of the front door, was a wall of rental boxes. Jere Lee's box was number 118. Bending down, she closed one eye, peered through the tiny window, and smiled. There was mail! And it had to be from one of her daughters! Who *else* knew this address?

She ran through the combination eagerly—too eagerly: it took her three tries before she did it correctly. Reaching a hand in, she pulled out the stiff white envelope. Hallmark embossment on the flap. Christmas card. Bangor postmark. Annie's handwriting. Wow, Annie was really on top of things: imagine her getting out Christmas cards this early.

Well, she'd always been an organized kid. Why, Jere Lee could remember when Annie used to—

No. Jere Lee *could* remember, but felt it wiser *not* to.

She took the card over to a glass-topped table, and carefully tore it open.

She was hoping there'd be a note. Annie had never been a big one for letter-writing, but—just a brief note. Would be nice.

There wasn't any note.

The illustration on the card showed a horse-drawn sleigh, banks of creamy white snow, thick woods, a red farmhouse with a smoking chimney.

Season's Greetings From Our House To Yours.

Jere Lee's eyes began to itch.

From Our House To Yours.

She'd kind of been expecting a card that said Mother.

From Our House To Yours.

Love, Anne, Harold, Beth and Bear.

Bear was the dog, a German shepherd.

Beth was Jere Lee's granddaughter, aged seven. But she'd be turning eight in February. February third.

There was a photograph of Beth enclosed.

Well, *that* was thoughtful.

Beth in a white pilgrim's bonnet, on stage at her school's Thanksgiving pageant.

Oh, Beth looked *so* much like Annie when Annie was little. Same sweet smile. Same blue eyes. Same—

Christmas is the perfect time to tell you how special you are to us all thru the year.

Love Anne, Harold, Beth and Bear.

Pocketing the photograph, Jere Lee tossed the envelope and card into a wastebasket.

The door opened and a postman came in.

The gray-and-orange cat dashed in behind him, scooting through his legs before the door could swing closed again.

"Oh no you don't," he said, stooping to grab the cat by the scruff of its neck.

Jere Lee exclaimed, "No!" then blushed. "That's all right, she's . . . mine. I'm sorry."

The postman watched her scoop up the cat and put it in her cart, on top of all the coats and blankets.

"Now, you *know* you weren't supposed to come in here," she said. "Naughty cat. Bad Squintik."

"Squintik?" said the postman. He laughed.

Jere Lee smiled and lifted a shoulder. "My granddaughter named it," she said. "She lives in Maine. She's going to be eight in February."

After Jere Lee had wheeled the cart outside, the cat leaped to the pavement, glanced up at her, then led the way.

The hospital?

This was where the cat was taking her?

To St. Vincent's Hospital?

"And what am I supposed to do in there?" she asked,

bending down and speaking in a whisper. "Look for the psy-chiatric ward?"

The cat swiveled its head, gazed briefly at the old brick building, then raced off again, through the parking lot.

Heaving a sigh, Jere Lee followed.

As she was going around to the main entrance, a white stretch limousine passed in front of her, heading for the Emergency Room.

For a moment, she locked eyes with a man sitting up front in the passenger seat. Long tangly hair, blue eyes—familiar. Though she couldn't place him.

The cat was already at the front door, waiting.

An Hispanic couple came out of the hospital, the woman holding a newborn, all bundled up. Jere Lee smiled, feeling—what?—sweetly sad, she guessed. Nostalgic. Yeah, sure. Remembering. When she'd brought Karen home from the hospital. And then Annie. There'd been some good years. Honest to God. Some *very* good years. Happy ones. It hadn't always been—

The guy who'd taken Geebo's carton.

The guy in the limousine? Was the same guy who'd taken Geebo's carton, last night.

She looked behind her, frowning.

What the hell was *he* doing now in a stretch limo?

He win the lottery or something?

Shaking her head, she joined the cat at the hospital's front door, then muttered half-to-herself (and wasn't that just what she was *supposed* to do, a loony like her?), "So now what? Really and truly—what?"

HE'S WAITING FOR YOU.

"Who is?"

A guard standing just inside the hospital lobby glanced at her.

Jere Lee smiled at him pleasantly. He scowled back. Then, covering her mouth so he couldn't see her lips move, she whispered to the cat, "Who is?"

YOU DON'T HAVE TO TALK, WOMAN. JUST THINK.

"Just *think?*" she said, too loud.

THINK. DON'T TALK. I CAN HEAR YOU FINE, IF YOU JUST THINK.

Jere Lee thought, Really?

REALLY, came the cat's reply. NOW GO AHEAD, HE'S WAITING.

But who? Who do I know in St. Vincent's? I don't *know* anybody there.

Suddenly, though, she felt carbonated, head to foot.

Oh my lord, she thought. The man from the bus station?

HE'S WAITING.

I don't understand.

YOU THINK I DO? GET GOING.

You'll come with me? Please?

I CAN'T.

Why can't you?

And the tabby cat replied, BECAUSE IT'S FADING . . . ALREADY.

What is?

ALREADY!

What?

The tabby cocked its head and looked up at Jere Lee. Its soft purring sounded plaintive.

And then it ran away.

CHAPTER 16

BREAKING THE CONNECTION

HIS BODY WAS THRUM-
ming hard, he couldn't think straight, and his ears were
ringing. It was like when he was a dumb, bored teenaged
kid—other kids on the block used to call him Dix, Herbie
Dix, in those days—and for a cheap schoolyard thrill he'd
sprinkle some cleaning fluid, some Carbona, on a handkerchief then take a few good sniffs: head going wah . . . wah
. . . wah.

That's what it felt like now, moving down the long,
apple-green hospital corridor: like he'd sniffed Carbona and
had the wah-wahs.

Moving in that daze, that fog, and with that wicked
spin on, almost lurching, Herb Dierickx turned a corner and
kept going, past service elevators and curtained-off cubicles,
a restroom with an extra-wide door for wheelchairs, then a
flower shop. That was a good sign, that flower shop. It meant
he was probably headed in the right direction, after all. To-

ward the lobby. For a while, he'd been afraid he was lost, might end up in the X-Ray Department, someplace like that.

Back in the Emergency Room, he'd told a small, wiry male nurse that he needed a pay phone that wasn't just on the wall—you know? Was there a telephone *booth?* So he could shut the door, sit down, make a private call. And the male nurse said, yeah, the coffee shop. Saying go right, then go left, saying it was just off the main lobby, opposite the admitting office.

And here it was now, dinky place crowded as the city subway, every counter seat taken, the tables jammed with doctors, some of them in surgical gowns.

The clock on the wall above the cashier's station read twelve-forty.

After making sure that he had some change, Herb elbowed his way toward the pay phone in the rear. He closed the bifold door behind him, then emptied his pockets, separating and spreading coins on the narrow shelf below the phone. All right. So far, so good, he thought. After he'd deposited a quarter, though, he couldn't remember his telephone number. Oh come on. Jesus. Was it a 433 exchange or a 343?

Four-three-three. It was 433.

Mr. *Boman's* number was 343.

Herb dialed.

Be home, Margie. Just be home.

And she was, answered on the second ring, saying, Oh —Herb! Nice surprise. She wasn't expecting him, and it was lucky he'd called her right then; otherwise he would've missed her. Two minutes later, he would've missed her. She was on her way out to do the grocery shopping—did he want her to get him Cheerios again this week, or give them a rest and go with Kix for a change? Then saying, "Herb?" Saying, "Herbert?" Suddenly alarmed, and he hadn't even *told* her anything yet. Kind of thing that happens after thirty-three years married. *Almost* thirty-three. Saying, "Herb, whatsa matter? How come you're calling? You gonna be late? You're not taking his nibs down to Leesboro again, are you? Herb?"

Herb sagged a little, then said, "I'm in trouble, Marge. I think."

He could picture her in the living room, eye-level with that Japanese calendar that he hated so much, bamboo job with the watercolor volcano. And he knew the expression on her face: gray eyes widening, those tiny lines (he wouldn't call them *wrinkles)* appearing at the corners of her mouth. Jeez, he could just see her. She'd be turning pale just about . . . now. And now she was moistening her lips. "Tell me what's wrong," she said, cool as a cucumber.

Margie the brick.

Which is why he'd had to call *her.*

When maybe he should've been calling Mr. Boman.

"I had an accident. With the boss's car."

"You hurt?"

"I'm fine. Really."

"What kind of accident? Serious?"

"Not too. And it wasn't my fault. The other guy hit me."

"Was Mr. Boman with you?"

"No. I'd just dropped him off."

"Where'd it happen?"

"Midtown."

"And where are you now?"

"St. Vincent's."

"But you said—"

"*I'm* not hurt. Honest to God, Marge, I'm not. It's the other guy."

An electronic voice interrupted: "Please. Deposit. Twenty. Five. Cents. For three. Minutes."

"I'll call you right back," said Marge. Even at a time of crisis, Marge was thrifty. "What's your number there?"

He read it to her twice, hung up, then slumped backward against the wall. Thinking, It's the other guy. The other guy.

Come on, Marge—call me back, already.

Herb pushing dimes around on the counter with his fingertip, reading the long-distance dialing instructions, blotting his face with his shirt-sleeve.

Standing at a window-wall in Eugene Boman's apartment, peering down into Sixty-third Street, seeing a line of people get on a bus.

He'd come in looking sheepish, feeling sick to his stomach, and the boss said, "All right, so what is it, Herb, what's this about Miss Campbell, what's the problem?"

And Herb had said—blurted, "She went downtown to find Peter Musik, boss. And it's my fault. It's all my stupid fault."

At Peter's name, Eugene Boman flinched. But he quickly recovered his composure, even smiled. It was a thin, strained smile, but it was still a smile—right? That was good, right? Herb stuck his hands into his pockets, to keep them from shaking.

Then Boman said, "Your fault? How is it your fault?"

"I told her that I seen him. Yesterday."

"And did you?"

"I *think* I did."

"Where was this, where you *thought* you saw him?"

"Way downtown, Mr. Boman. In the Bridge District."

That raised Eugene Boman's eyebrows, sure enough. "Why don't you see if there's still some coffee in the kitchen, Herb? Fix yourself a cup and then we'll talk some more. Give me a minute."

Herb didn't want any coffee. As it was, he was feeling strung out. Caffeine, boy, would only make things worse.

But he went into the kitchen anyway.

Boss told him to drink some coffee, he'd damn-straight drink some coffee. Boss said to pour it on his *head*, he might've done that, too. Good chance.

He was making thirty-one thousand dollars a year driving a Cadillac automobile. Plus, the job came with medical benefits, which included dental. For him *and* Marge.

And every Christmas he got a cash bonus. Usually seven or eight percent of his annual salary.

And just last September—the week after Labor Day? Mr. Boman had presented Herb with two airplane tickets to Honolulu. He hadn't just paid for the tickets, either, he'd paid for the whole shebang—first-class hotel, rental car, spending money. Marge had been flummoxed, in seventh heaven. Hawaii! Where she'd always wanted to go, but who could afford? "But why, Herb?" she'd asked. "How come?"

And Herb had replied, "The boss likes me, what can I tell you? I'm a very dependable guy at the wheel." Which was bullshit, of course. The trip? Had been a kind of bribe. Go to Maui, go to Molokai, have fun, and forget you ever knew anybody named Peter Musik . . .

In the kitchen, he found a black promotional mug with "Aspirin-Free Sudamax Syrup" and the Boman logo lacquered on it, in bright red.

As he was taking the heavy cream from the refrigerator, he glanced through the doorway, saw Boman speaking with the cleaning woman, a tall, handsome Jamaican with broad shoulders like a pro basketball player.

Boman wrote her a check, helped her on with her coat.

Getting rid of her, Herb thought. So we can be alone. He fixed his coffee very light, it was more cream than coffee, then carried the mug into the living room, careful not to spill any.

The woman was gone, and Boman had taken a seat, ensconced himself on the leather sofa below a framed original "Peanuts" comic strip. "Now tell me what happened, and start from when you *think* you saw Peter Musik last night."

"Yesterday afternoon."

"So tell me."

And Herb did, saying how he'd gone downtown for a supply of secondhand paperbacks and was on his way back when he stopped at a light on Erie Street—Erie at Avenue F —and saw Peter washing car windshields, using a spray bottle and a squeegee.

"And did *he* see *you?*"

"No, sir."

"You didn't get out of the car."

"No."

"Why not?"

Herb lowered his eyes, took a sip of coffee.

"All right. Then what?"

"The light changed."

"And you drove away."

"That's what I did, yes."

Boman fell silent, staring at Herb with no expression. Then: "I just wonder why you didn't tell *me* about this. I mean yesterday. I mean before you told Miss Campbell."

"I didn't intend to tell *her*, either. It just happened."

"Oh?"

"I don't know why I did it. Soon as I did, though, I knew I'd made a big mistake. I'm sorry, Mr. Boman, I really and truly am."

"But why didn't you tell *me*, Herb? You still haven't answered that."

"Because I figured . . ."

"What? What did you 'figure'?"

"That if Peter . . . that if Peter was down there like a regular bum, it was because that's how you wanted it. And it was none of my business."

Boman's gaze dropped to the Disneyana catalog on the table. "You just assumed this was *my* doing? That somehow I was responsible? Herb?"

"Yes, sir, I did."

Boman laughed. Sort of laughed. "He tried to kill me—as I'm certain that you recall. You certainly remember the little incident with the fireplace shovel?"

"I remember."

"Peter Musik had a nervous breakdown and tried to kill me. He went to pieces, Herb. Fell apart." Boman hunched over the table. "Which is why I don't get it. How come you're so surprised that an unstable man like that is now living on the street. Is a bum. As you say."

Herb swallowed, then straightened in his chair. Then shrugged.

"Well? Why *were* you so surprised to see him? I don't—"

"Because I thought he was dead, sir. And so did Miss Campbell."

"Dead."

"We both thought so. Yes."

"Why would you think that?"

"Oh Jesus."

"Herb?"

"Mr. Boman, I mean this from the bottom of my heart: I'm sorry that I ever said *anything* to Miss Campbell. Believe me, I'm a very loyal person. I've always been a loyal person, whoever I worked for. And you've been good to me, and I don't make any judgments. I don't understand business too much, but I know it's complicated. And that sometimes, maybe *lots* of times, when business people like yourself run up against a problem you don't just go call the cops. Like ordinary people would, and that there's—"

He broke off and looked at his hands, kept his eyes fastened on his big knuckles.

"*Why* would you've thought that Peter Musik was dead?"

Herb shut his eyes for a moment. Opened them. His shoulders slumped. "I assumed," he said in a voice that was practically a whisper, "that you and Major Forell, that the Major and you . . ."

The color had drained completely out of Boman's face. He nodded: go on, go on, finish what you're saying.

". . . killed him."

The two men stared at one another across the coffee table.

At last, Boman leaned forward and picked up his catalog and flipped through it. His hands were shaking. "Is that what you thought?" There was a pause, then he said, "*Both* of you? You and Miss Campbell talked about this?"

"At first. But we haven't for a long time. Not for *months*, Mr. Boman. Swear to God."

"Makes me feel kind of funny, Herb. Here you are

thinking I'm a killer. You and Miss Campbell, both. You can't imagine how funny that makes me feel. What, you think I'm just like one of those rich bad guys you're always reading about in your secondhand books?" Herb was shaking his head. "You do, right?"

"No, sir, I really don't."

Boman thought awhile, then sighed. "The Major probably *should've* killed him," he said. Herb felt suddenly as though he'd fallen on a rock, had the wind knocked out of him. "God knows, that's what he *wanted* to do. But I wouldn't let him. I don't go in for that stuff, Herb. I honestly don't."

"I believe it." And his mind flashed on that scene in the lake house: Eugene Boman with blood on his face, Peter Musik out cold on the living-room floor. Money Campbell wandering around barefoot, moaning. That scary guy Major Forell talking on the telephone.

"Do you? You like me, Herb?"

"I do, Mr. Boman. I mean that. Bottom of my heart." And it was true: he *did* like Eugene Boman. Even though the man kept mispronouncing his last name. Saying Deer-ick. But so what?

"Herb?"

"Yes, sir?"

"I don't care whether you like me or not. It doesn't affect me, one way or the other. Okay?"

Dropping his head like some kid in the principal's office, Herb mumbled, "Yes, sir." Then he looked up again and asked—because, well, it was best to get this straight right now: "Am I still working for you, Mr. Boman? Because I'd understand it, if I wasn't."

"Herb? Herb, you're going to be working for me for the rest of your life. However long that may be."

Herb's vision furred.

"Yes, sir," he said. "Thank you."

The coinbox telephone was ringing.

It *had* been ringing for quite some time.

Herb Dierickx kept looking at the handset, the push buttons, the armored cord.

His skin gleamed with sweat—man, was it *hot* in that damn booth.

And now some long-faced lady in a beige waitress uniform started tapping on the door, tapping with her paste-on fingernails, scowling and pointing to the phone. Herb looked at her a moment, then he nodded and picked up the handset.

But then he put it right back down again, breaking the connection.

He squeezed his eyes shut, and a chill ran down his back, and . . . something was strange. Not *wrong*, exactly. Yeah, wrong, but not . . . scary. At least it didn't scare Herb: it *surprised* him, that he'd gone so numb, and wasn't in control.

That, once again, another mind was moving in on his. As it had done just after the accident, back on the midtown street.

It was all right, though.

It was all right.

Really.

Herb undoing his top two buttons, spreading his collar, jiggling his shirt a little, fanning himself.

Herb cringing when the telephone started ringing again.

Herb driving the white limo up the garage ramp, then checking for traffic before hanging a left turn into Sixty-third Street.

Saying to Mr. Boman, "I could take the East Side Drive, you want me to? We could get there quicker."

"That's fine, Herb," said Boman, sitting in back with the VCR going—an old "Gunsmoke" tape, judging from the bits of dialogue he was catching. "Go any way you choose. After you drop me at the Alexander Gallery."

"Mr. Boman?"

"Fifty-first and Third."

"I know where it is, sir. But—you're not coming with me?"

"Is there some reason that I should?"

"I just thought."

Boman said "Mmmm," and Herb looked up into the rearview, saw the man going through his gallery catalog again. "You remember 'Mod Squad,' Herb?"

"What, with Peggy Lipton? Sure."

"I understand there's a very nice 'Mod Squad' lunchbox available. With the original thermos. Mint condition. I thought I might take a look at it."

"You want to go to the Alexander Gallery *now?*"

"Something wrong with that, Herb?"

"No, sir, I just thought you'd want to go look for Miss Campbell."

"You can do that, Herb, can't you?"

"Well, sure."

"Then do it."

There was silence for a while, then Herb said, "Assuming that I find her—"

"Tell her I'd like to see her."

"Should I tell her—that I told you everything?"

"I think not."

Herb kept glancing into the rearview, his mind racing, until finally he said, "And what if she's with *him?*"

"Do you think that's likely? Is she a policeman, Herb? Is she a bloodhound? Was she on 'The Mod Squad'? I'd say her chances of finding Peter Musik are fairly slim, wouldn't you? A city this size. What do you figure the odds might be?"

Herb was shaking his head. "I don't know. Slim, like you say. But just—what if by some *chance* . . ."

Gene Boman switched off the VCR.

"Herb, do you know what I'm feeling right now?"

Pushing out his lips, producing a mirthless smile, Herb said, "I can guess, Mr. Boman. You're pretty pissed off, right? And I don't blame you—"

"I'm feeling at something of a loss. And do you know why? Because I'm not sure just how much you know about my business."

"Like I told you, I don't—"

"Or how far I can trust you."

Herb felt a tightening of his stomach muscles. He didn't say anything.

Then Gene Boman said, "The Pharmacy."

"Sir?"

"The Pharmacy."

"*Which* pharmacy?"

Then Boman said, "Blue Mark. What about Blue Mark, Herb?"

"I don't know what that means."

"Why should I believe you?"

"I'm not a nosy person, Mr. Boman. If I hear a few things, well, I really can't help that. You talk to people, and sometimes I happen to be there, and—well, you know." His eyes went to the mirror again. And met Gene Boman's. "But I don't know what Blue Mark is, sir." The truth. "Blue Mark?"

"Is a drug that never was. Ninety percent of drugs that're developed never come to market. You know that, Herb? They're rejected by the FDA. Or else they're just so . . . problematic that we never even bother submitting them."

"Is that a fact?" said Herb. "Ninety percent."

Boman said nothing.

"Blue Mark," said Herb, just to say something. "Kind of catchy name."

"It's a proofreader's expression. It means to cut something out of a text. Delete it. That's where the name comes from."

Boman was silent for half a minute, then: "Say that something really awful happens to a person. It could affect him the rest of his life. Ruin his life. Or hers. Something traumatic. Say a woman gets raped. This happens all the time, Herb, am I right? Or say you're on the street and you see somebody jump off a building. Okay, that's kind of extreme. Say you're in a liquor store and there's a robbery, and somebody gets shot. It could haunt you. This kind of thing, Herb, it happens."

"I know it does, Mr. Boman. And I know exactly what you're saying. Because my cousin in Westfield? Was there when some nut shot up the McDonald's with a machine gun. Nothing happened to my cousin, he dove for cover and all, but jeez. Since then? Nightmares, all that stuff. So I understand exactly what you're saying."

"This world, Herb, everyday people are traumatized left and right."

"That's the God's truth. It's awful. But so what were you saying?"

"Blue Mark, Herb, I was talking about Blue Mark."

And all of a sudden—bing!—Herb got the drift. Drift, schmift, he got the whole magilla in a bolt, thinking Holy Christ, really? Such a thing can be *done?* "You're talking about some . . . drug that makes people forget?"

"The bad things that happened to them, yes. So they can get on with their lives."

And Herb said, *"Just* the bad things?"

No reply.

At the next red light, Herb turned around in his seat and looked at Boman, whose face had gone pale, even waxy.

"I wouldn't allow the Major to—to do what he wished to do about Peter. As I've told you. I just wouldn't allow that. But obviously something had to be done. He lied to us all, Herb. He wasn't writing any newspaper story about 'celebrities and their hobbies.' He was trying to find out about Leesboro."

"Leesboro?"

"About The Pharmacy." He was frowning now, wringing his hands, speaking softly, almost as though he were talking to himself. Then he snapped out of it, smiled. "Obviously, something had to be done."

Behind the limousine, car horns were blowing. Herb glanced around, the light was green. He sped across the intersection.

And Eugene Boman was saying something about a

kinder, *gentler* punishment for Peter Musik, making a joke. "Blue Mark, Herb."

"So the bottom line, Mr. Boman, what you're telling me is that Peter Musik doesn't remember anything that happened? Nothing about him sneaking around and being kind of a spy and stuff? And nothing at *all* about the lake house?"

"Peter Musik doesn't remember anything about Peter Musik. Period. Is what I'm telling you."

Herb took one hand off the wheel to squeeze the back of his neck.

"I'm trusting you, remember," said Eugene Boman.

"But I still don't get how come it doesn't worry you much that Miss Campbell might find him. Say that she does —just *say* that she does—then what's to keep her from *reminding* Peter who he is? Or taking him to the hospital where they could—"

"There wouldn't be time for that, Herb."

"Mr. Boman?"

"He suddenly remembers that he's Peter Musik?"

"Yes, sir?"

"He'll get a headache."

"So?"

"A very *terrible* headache," said Eugene Boman. "And then he'll have a stroke."

"You can't be serious. Mr. Boman? Mr. Boman?"

"So you can see why Blue Mark could never be manufactured. Why we simply stopped testing it altogether, years ago. Why it's called an Idiot Drug."

"A stroke."

"A stroke, Herb. Now, of course, I pray that it never happens to Peter, I'd hate for it to happen. Which is why I'm hoping that Miss Campbell—"

"I'll find her," said Herb.

Boman sat back and sighed again, then he turned his face and gazed out the tinted window.

Herb thinking, Fat little monster with his ten zillion bucks.

Thinking, Jesus holy Christ, a *stroke?*

Sitting hunched in the telephone booth, Herb Dierickx felt vaguely nauseous—it was so damn *stuffy* in there, so *warm.* He should at least crack open the door, but no . . . just leave it alone, leave it be.

Everything was all right. It was okay.

Really.

The pay phone was ringing again, so once again Herb picked up the handset, then put it down.

Breaking the connection for the fifth or sixth time.

And thinking about when Mr. Boman got out of the Cadillac—

GO ON.

When Mr. Boman was shutting the door, he—

SAID SOMETHING? COME ON, HERB DIERICKX— WHAT? HE SAID SOMETHING? DID SOMETHING?

Herb folded his arms on the coin shelf, leaned on them, and blew out a long, quavering breath.

HERB DIERICKX, EVERYTHING IS ALL RIGHT.

EVERYTHING IS OKAY.

REALLY.

THIS MR. BOMAN? WHEN YOU DROPPED HIM OFF. HE SAID SOMETHING? DID SOMETHING?

Mr. Boman had *said* something. Mr. Boman had said, "I expect to find both you *and* Miss Campbell at my apartment later this afternoon. And then the three of us will take a drive down to Leesboro. And Herb? If she's gone a little . . . funny on us, you'll make sure, won't you, that she doesn't speak to anybody? About certain things?"

Herb had given him a nod.

SO THEN WHAT? WHAT HAPPENED NEXT?

Herb had continued driving downtown, that's what had happened next, and got stuck in Saturday traffic. He'd banged the wheel with both hands. What a mess! Look at what he'd done! Him and his big mouth. Christ, it was going to take him half an *hour*, at *least*, to make it down to the Bridge District. And when he finally got there? What the hell were his chances of finding that ditzy college girl, the girl with the great breasts? She'd disappeared into the subway over an hour ago. She could be anywhere.

It'd take a miracle to find her.

And yet he *had* to find her. Mr. Boman said.

Ah God, what a mess.

Stuck behind a bus, Herb reached out and switched on the radio. Went through the stations till he found some classical music. That stuff, so long as it wasn't opera, always kind of soothed him.

But then with a sharp pain in his stomach that nearly doubled him over, he remembered Mr. Boman saying, "You're going to be working for me the rest of your life. However long that might be."

That was a threat, right?

Way things were going, he really *would* end up someday in a true-crime book, wouldn't he? *Wouldn't* he?

One of the victims.

He wondered how he'd be described, what they'd say about him in that true-crime book.

A schmuck.

Herbert Leslie Dierickx, they'd write, was a great big schmuck.

He sat in traffic and his temples pulsed.

AND THEN WHAT? HERB DIERICKX?

And then—then traffic had started flowing again, and it seemed at last that he was going to make some progress getting downtown, and he gave the Caddy some gas, but then had to hit the brake, and the next thing he knew— wham! crunch!

Rear-ended by a goddamn Toyota.

He couldn't believe it. On top of everything else—an accident?

A goddamn lousy *accident?*

He pulled to the curb, switched off the ignition, jumped out of the car. Aggravated to hell, *really* peeved. Putting one hand on his hip, he surveyed the damage, the busted tail- light and the crumpled fender, the skinned-off paint. He swung his face around, lifted both arms and gestured with them: *Hey!*

Guy driving the Toyota? Hadn't budged.

Herb folded his arms and leaned against the limo. Body language saying, Hey you, jerk, I'm waiting, you wanna step out and see what you done?

But could you believe it? Guy *still* wasn't moving.

Well, Herb wasn't about to stand around for the rest of the afternoon. The rest of his *life*. Angrily pushing himself away from the Cadillac, he walked back to the Toyota, bent down at the driver's window, saying, "I'm not going away, pal, so whyn't you—"

He was looking at Peter Musik, who was looking back at him.

At first, Peter seemed more scared than anything else—all fish-eyed. But then his expression changed. Turned quizzical. He cocked his head, like a dog hearing cats meow on a television set. Lifted a hand and covered his mouth with it. Frowned.

Then winced.

And Herb kept staring, not knowing what to say, what to do.

This was impossible—right?

This *couldn't* be an accident, right? Or a coincidence. Right?

Right?

Herb said, "Peter? Man, it *is* you, it's you. *Peter?"*

And suddenly Peter Musik's eyes seemed as though they might pop right out of their sockets—like Herb had read always happened when they stuck you in the electric chair and pulled the switch.

His eyes bugged, and his head snapped back. Then he pressed his face between his hands, started shaking it from side to side.

Herb thinking—it just snapped into his mind, he couldn't help it—of that old Jimmy Cagney picture, *White Heat*, where Cagney's this very scary gunman who goes apeshit every twenty minutes, rolling on the floor, screaming about the pain, the buzzsaw.

The headache.

Herb staggered backward, away from the car door and nearly into the flow of traffic.

Thinking, Oh, Jesus.

A very terrible headache. And then he'll have a stroke. A stroke, Herb. A stroke, Herb. A stroke.

Peter had toppled over, was squirming around on the front seat.

And then the other guy—yeah, there *was* another guy besides Peter in the car, Herb had scarcely noticed him till then; long-faced and long-haired, filthy clothes, a tramp: got out the passenger door and stared at Herb across the roof.

He didn't seem particularly concerned by the turn of events.

He didn't seem concerned at all.

He even allowed himself a tiny smile.

One of his eyebrows crooked up, inquisitively. And he said, "We meet by accident."

What was he trying to be, funny? We meet by accident. Damn *straight* we meet by accident.

Herb's knees felt weak, rubbery.

Traffic going by, people walking past, nobody stopping. Whatever happened to bystanders? Good Samaritans? Gone, Herb thought, the way of the ten-cent Coke.

He stepped back to the car and peered in again, his chest so constricted he could scarcely breathe.

Peter was lying across the front seat, very still.

Herb leaned away, just as some kind of bee flew in front of his face. Landed on his wrist. He slapped at it, saying, "Shit!"

The long-haired tramp bent into the Toyota and lifted Peter Musik out in a fireman's carry. Held him like he weighed almost nothing, like he was a child.

Herb nursing the sore red lump on the back of his left hand, giving a nervous giggle, feeling slack, weirdly *calm,* then walking over to the Caddy and opening the rear curb-side door.

For the trampy guy and Peter Musik. . . .

Herb collected all of his change from the pay phone shelf, and put it back in his pocket.

Lifted the handset, mumbled, "It's okay, Marge, it's all right," then hung up again. Breaking the connection.

He swung around and pulled open the door.

Thinking, So *now* what?

NOW, said the voice that had followed him out of the Emergency Room and down the corridors, the voice he'd tried to escape but could not, the tramp's voice: COME BACK TO US.

Herb nodded meekly.

On his way out of the coffee shop—it was almost one, by the wall clock—he noticed several people looking at him kind of strangely.

But what did he care? They wanted to look at some beefy, almost-old guy in a crisp driver's uniform, his face shining with perspiration, his damp hair sticking to his head, kind of a glazed look in his eyes, and a goose-egg swelling on his left hand: well, so what, let 'em look.

It was okay with Herb Dierickx.

It was all right.

CHAPTER 17

CHANCE ACQUAINTANCE

IT WAS A PRETTY NICE place, the doctors' lounge: pale-blue walls, dark-blue carpeting, good sofa, three upholstered chairs, a table, clock radio, color TV, twin bed. Several cots were stored in one of the upright metal lockers; in the other lockers were street clothes on hangers, hospital greens on hooks. There was a little refrigerator, too, containing lunch meats, cheddar cheese, seeded Italian rolls, Gulden's mustard, and cans and cans of Coca-Cola. Classic and diet Coke. Cherry Coke. Diet cherry Coke. Caffeine Free Coke. Caffeine Free diet Coke. Jack, a Walker was frowning, he couldn't make up his mind. Talk about plenary chaos, man. How could there *be* so many different things *all* named Coca-Cola?

At last, he grabbed a can of Caffeine Free diet.

Trusting the partiality of Dr. Carmelo Lim, who sat tensely on the sofa, mouth drawn, eyes fixed on Jack.

Dr. Lim *always* chose Caffeine Free diet Coke, if he wanted a soft drink.

Jack knew it. He just did. For a fact. Same as he knew

that the doctor liked Amstel beer and Julio Iglesias records, had a pretty wife named Rowena whom he'd married in the Philippines, was the father of three small boys, specialized in sports medicine and orthopedic surgery, had a great fear of deep water, an even greater fear of an IRS audit. That he did his professional and financial thinking in English. But worried in Tagalog. That he owned some commercial real estate in the Greenville section of the city, had recently bought an Audi, red as blood, and usually spent Monday evenings in a studio apartment on West Seventy-third Street that belonged to a nurse by the name of Linda. Who had a lush, big-girl body but the smallest white hands . . .

Jack knew quite a lot about Dr. Carmelo Lim.

Everything, in fact.

He popped the tab on his can of Coke, sucked off the foam, then sat down in one of the upholstered chairs, a thoughtful look on his face. Guy on the radio saying, "For tomorrow, WKDH meteorologist Jessie Burns says to look for partly sunny skies, with—uh-oh—a chance of rain before evening. Currently, it's twenty-seven and cloudy, at twelve thirty-six. Shoppers, it's a fact that nobody beats Crafton's when it comes to fine furniture, and that's because Crafton's . . ."

Jack was tired, bone-weary. How many I's had he taken since this morning? Not counting Geebo—and Geebo didn't really count, since Jack hadn't taken very *much* of him— there were . . . three? four? Guy at the bridge, guy with the Toyota, guy in the uniform—that Herb-guy. And Dr. Lim. Jack was thinking now that he probably shouldn't have had him stung, the doctor, but he'd felt he might need some ally in the hospital.

So Dr. Lim made four. Four hosts.

Four spiritual fast ones.

Had drained Jack.

And on top of that, he hadn't slept well last night, cramped inside that moldy carton, dreaming over and over of the infant of mud and straw that he'd found on a rooftop in the port city of Tiedek.

Found by the purest chance, by sheer accident.

A Perfect Accident whose meaning was clear, but whose afterclap?

Was still anything but certain.

Jack crumpled his soda can and pitched it into the wastebasket, then turned his thoughts to the Accident named Geebo.

It was a true Accident, of that Jack had no doubt.

But its meaning?

Was unclear.

Its afterclap?

Undecipherable.

He wondered when his Sting would return. He'd sent her to keep watch on the Accident-named-Geebo, who'd been transferred to a gurney a short time ago, then hustled away into the bowels of the hospital.

Geebo. Whose self was clouded. Whose I was buried.

And who might well be dying.

Dr. Lim was staring at the swelling in the palm of his left hand.

Jack stretched his legs out, then let his I walk to another's.

Heard clearly in his mind, "I'm in trouble, Marge. I think."

Folding his hands behind his neck, Jack leaned back and looked at the ceiling.

"I had an accident. With the boss's car."

Jack smiled. Accident. Indeed. With the boss's car and His Majesty's Tramp.

What could be made of this Chance Acquaintance? he thought. This Chance Acquaintance named Dierickx.

Or of this Rumor named Eugene Boman? Now *that* seemed interesting. (. . . "I expect to find both you *and* Miss Campbell at my apartment later this afternoon. . . .") The Rumor named Boman.

Interesting.

But unclear.

Undecipherable.

The Chance Acquaintance named Dierickx was asking Jack, SO NOW WHAT?

And Jack, a Walker thought, Come back to us.

He was tired. Bone-weary.

It was, he thought then, quite possible that he might die there in Kemolo. Waiting for Master Squintik to beckon him home to Lostwithal for an audience with His Majesty. But how long would that be? The old King's Attention was short —it could be weeks before Sad Agel might agree to see his Walker and to hear of his travels, according to the Order of Things.

Jack was certain he couldn't *wait* several weeks.

That, somehow, the Mage of Four, Mage of Luck would learn of his flight, and send a Finder.

It was more than just *possible* that he might die there in Kemolo.

It was likely.

And the Walker was terrified of dying.

As a much younger man, he'd first worked as a printer's devil, and dreamed of travel.

Foolishly, he'd dreamed of nomadic travel. . . .

CHAPTER 18

PERFECT SHAPES AND
USEFUL NUMBERS

THEY CAME IN A FEW MINutes before one and stood at the foot of his bed, two men in dark-brown overcoats. They introduced themselves: Lieutenant Dokus and Detective Sergeant Tucker, of the Homicide Division. Immediately, Master Squintik was troubled, seeing in their faces the knowledge of wickedness and human chaos. They were stained, these men. Were they mad? He was sympathetic, but wary. He would listen to what they said, but would study their eyes carefully, and see how they swallowed, and he would keep his mind teeming with Perfect Shapes and Useful Numbers.

Where is the kindly woman? he thought. His Heart of Talent had told him: she has seen the Walker. She has seen the Walker. He had need of the kindly woman.

Tucker, a Detective Sergeant, whose hair was yellow, removed a chart from the foot of the bed. He looked at it, then he looked at Master Squintik. "Still no name?" he said.

"How about we start with that, sir? Could you give us your name?"

Squintik made no reply.

"What do you think, George—he doesn't understand English?"

Dokus, a Lieutenant, also called George, whose hair was black-flecked-with-gray, folded his arms and shrugged.

But Squintik understood English. And not only English, but Spanish and Vietnamese and Tagalog. He had touched, and been touched by, several too-humans—the kindly woman, the uniformed policemen at the bus terminal, the ambulance medics, several nurses, two doctors, and the technician who'd given him a CAT scan.

He understood English. Master Squintik understood. He simply chose not to reply.

He lay still, watching as Dokus and Tucker spoke to each other in low voices. Then Tucker left the room.

With a grunt, Dokus, a Lieutenant sat on a chair beside the bed. Squintik looked deeply into his eyes: so *much* knowledge there of wickedness and human chaos. More than enough, thought Squintik, to ensure madness.

"Detective Sergeant Tucker went to find somebody that speaks Spanish. We'll try that, eh?"

Squintik wet his lips, and began to add numbers. Columns and columns of numbers in his mind.

"But that's not really necessary, is it? You understand me, don't you?" said Dokus, a Lieutenant. "You do. I can tell."

Yes, thought Squintik, and curvilinear shapes spun and glowed in his mind, you can tell.

Dokus, a Lieutenant leaned forward, hands on his

knees. "How'd you do it?" he asked. "How'd you do it to them?"

Squintik concentrated, harder.

"If you ask me, friend, you did everybody a public service. All I want to know is how? How'd you do it?"

Curvilinear shapes, and numbers, and now the tiniest point of light . . .

"You were out walking," said Dokus, a Lieutenant. "All of a sudden here are these two guys, one has green hair, the other one's an ape. What'd they do first, ask you for a cigarette? Then bam, they're shoving you. Into an alley. Am I right so far? So far am I right? They get you in an alley, and the guy with the green hair pulls a gun. That about right?"

Curvilinear shapes, columns of numbers, and *two* points of light, one hovering, vibrating above the other . . .

Squintik had his sum, the lights had merged, the shapes had intersected. All that remained: to speak a word, the merest breath of a word, in Losplit.

For this man whose face bore the knowledge of wickedness and human chaos to catch fire suddenly and burn.

Just as the other two men, the men in the alley, had caught fire and burned.

A word. The merest breath.

"Just tell me how you did it. For that matter, pal, *teach* me," said Dokus, a Lieutenant. He began to smile, but then his jaw dropped and his forehead smoothed out.

He was staring at the frost that had crystallized on the fingers of Master Squintik's left hand.

"Who the hell *are* you?" he said, getting up.

Squintik's eyes had narrowed. Then suddenly they widened, and he glanced away from the policeman, to the door, which stood half-open. Then he looked toward the ceiling, then back to the door. His breathing became rapid. His left hand was completely covered in frost.

Dokus, a Lieutenant said, *"What* the hell are you?"

But the Cold Mage already had forgotten about the policeman. The policeman was of no importance. His eyes fixed upon the door, his two hearts racing, Master Squintik trembled.

Thinking, He is here! In this hospital. He is *here*. And the crisis is upon us!

CHAPTER 19

IN THE LOBBY

THE GUARD WAS A REAL creep, saying, "And where do you think *you're* going, huh?" Calling Jere Lee "sister," and telling her the free clinic wasn't open on Saturdays, come back Monday. She didn't like his tone. It was insulting. She replied that she wasn't *going* to any free clinic, thank you very much; she was there to see a patient. Saying she wasn't his sister, she was a human being with as much right as anybody else to visit a patient. If she felt like it.

Guard said, "You got to get a pass."

Jere Lee said, "Fine, so I'll get a pass."

Guard said, "Only it ain't visiting hours. Visiting hours don't start till one."

It was five to one, by the round clock on the wall.

"I think I can wait."

"And you can't bring that upstairs."

Pointing to the shopping cart.

Which, of course, was why he'd started giving her such

a hard time in the first place. That cart. Meant: Crazy lady. *Not* a human being. No matter *what* Jere Lee claimed.

"You make women check their handbags?"

"That's not a handbag, lady. Don't give me any civil rights crap, okay? That is *not* a handbag. And you can't take it in with you."

"Well, if I leave it someplace, will it be safe?"

The guard rolled his eyes, making her feel like two cents. "Lady—"

"Mrs. Vance!"

Jere Lee and the guard turned simultaneously.

But only Jere Lee smiled.

Well, *this* was new. Happy, for once, to be recognized as Mrs. Vance.

"Brian!" she said. "Hello again." She glanced smugly at the guard. "This is Brian Tucker," she said. "He's a homicide detective." Then, to Tucker: "I came to visit . . . you know. That poor man."

Tucker was staring at her intently. "You're here to *visit* him?"

"If he's well enough, yes."

"Why?"

"Why? Because I want to know how he is. Why *not?*"

The guard folded his arms across his chest, cocked his head. Waiting, eyes moving.

"I'm afraid you can't see him just yet, Mrs. Vance," said Tucker. "We still have some questions for him."

"But—"

"I'm sorry."

Jere Lee felt like *smashing* him. Detective or no detective. But then she grinned and said, "Has he *answered* any of your questions yet?"

"Well, ma'am, I don't think I can—"

"Has he told you his *name* yet? Because if he hasn't, his name is Mr. Squintik."

Tucker put his head to one side and looked at her quizzically. His expression changed, became less friendly. "How do you know that?" And his voice was different, too. Sharper. Professional. "Mrs. Vance?"

Jere Lee shrugged.

"You told us before that you hadn't spoken to him."

Jere Lee stood very still.

"Mrs. Vance . . . ?"

"Oh, why don't you just let me see him? He might talk to *me*."

"And why would he do that?"

"Because he wants to see me."

"He wants to see *you."*

Folding her hands on the cart handle, she smiled again.

Then the lobby guard said, "Officer, you want me to handle things? We get this kind of person in here all the time, I wouldn't—"

"Take a walk," said Tucker.

"Hey—"

They both glared at each other. But finally, the guard threw up his hands and went and leaned on the information desk. Bogart. He muttered something to a gray-haired woman. She glanced up, taking note of Jere Lee and the homicide detective.

Who was saying then, "So what's the real story, Mrs. Vance? *Do* you know this guy?"

"Brian? Whyn't you just take me to him? Would you do that?"

There was a long pause. Then "All right," he said. "I think we should talk some more anyway."

As she was pushing her cart into the elevator, Jere Lee said, "Oh Brian, I wanted to tell you. I remembered Karen's telephone number."

The elevator doors slid closed.

The guard, whose name was Kenneth Rodale, shook his head. Detective. Well, detect *this*, asshole. He fished out his pack of cigarettes and lit one—even though there were No Smoking signs posted. It'd serve the asshole detective right if that bag lady went nuts upstairs and killed somebody. Well, if she did, it wouldn't be on Ken Rodale's head. He'd tried to do his job. He always tried to do his job; he took it very seriously. You acted funny, you looked suspicious: you were going to have to deal with him. And he didn't take guff from anybody. And not just bag ladies. Anybody. *Everybody.*

Stunts people tried to pull in a hospital, you wouldn't believe.

Look at that stupid jerk just came in. For example. Guy lugging that dopey-looking stuffed animal. Walked straight to the elevator, didn't even pick up a visitor's pass. Infraction number one. Infraction number two? Infractions two through *six?*

Those five kids with him.

Nobody under twelve was allowed upstairs, unless they were patients.

So where'd that stupid jerk with his dopey stuffed panda think he was going with *five* little kids?

You know where he was going? Right back out the front *door*, that's where. Take his kids and his dopey-looking stuffed panda with him.

Ken Rodale would see to *that.* Right *now*, as a matter of

fact; saying, "Hey—you!" and crossing the lobby, the stupid jerk not paying him any mind, too busy watching some guy in a chauffeur's uniform who was coming out of the coffee shop. "Hey, *you!*"

Finally, getting his attention.

And the attention of those five redheaded infractions of hospital rules.

Ken Rodale thinking, *Jeez*-us, they're identical. Identical twins, except instead of two there's five.

Then saying—not to the kids, kids didn't count, you always dealt with a parent or guardian—saying to the stupid jerk with the panda bear, saying, "You can't bring these boys upstairs. They got to wait down here. And you got to get a pass, you can't just . . ."

The stupid jerk all of sudden looked like he'd just got a migraine headache or something.

". . . go upstairs without a pass. . . ."

The elevator doors opened.

The five redheaded boys ran straight in.

"Mister, you hear what I'm saying? *No kids.*"

The stupid jerk tossed the panda into the elevator.

Then, with his scrawny right hand, he grabbed Ken Rodale by his throat, lifted him off his feet, and carried him into the elevator.

The doors of which then . . . closed.

CHAPTER 20

GEEBO'S END

THERE WERE BEEPING
sounds and red lights that blinked, voices that murmured, grunted, but everything was so far away.

He was inside himself, deeply. Yet he was outside, too, and floating.

Inside and outside. Of himself.

That was funny. Outside, *in*side? Impossible. I can't be two places at once. I *can't* be.

I—

I?

And that was even funnier. Much funnier. *I?* Question mark? As if I didn't know? Of course I do. I remembered. In the car, the nice Toyota. I remembered. I'm—

Floating above himself, looking down at men and women in green, in drab-green hospital gowns, he remembered . . .

Turning his face to a glazed-brick wall, *green* brick, then being sick, then stumbling up a flight of steps. Coming into

158

bright daylight, humid heat, splinters of pain behind his eyes. And that's all: splinters of pain, but that was all.

Nothing else behind his eyes.

Except a word: Geebo.

And he remembered thinking, Me? Then rushing to a trash can, being sick into it, his body shuddering, and in the trash can was a newspaper, the date September fifth.

And now he was remembering a slim, pretty girl with large breasts and bright yellow hair. A beautiful girl on the beach. And a bald man. *Almost* bald. Someone I don't like. And *another* man, a man with a gun. A man with a gun and a syringe. And then—

He'd never felt such pain before.

In his head.

And now the beeping sounds were growing fainter, so much fainter, and the murmuring voices, too, and the lights were smeared, had become fuzzy. He was hovering above himself, moving higher, and someone in a green gown was saying, "It's a goddamn wasp, what's a goddamn *wasp* doing in here, get rid of it—now!"

He was going deeper into himself, falling *inside* himself, tunneling, and then he was sitting in a marina bar. In— Florida. It was in Florida. Naples, Florida. Through a picture window, houseboats bobbled in their slips, moonlight glinted on dark water. And a man was drinking with me, we'd only just met. The pair of us on a binge, drinking ourselves white and almost sick. Trower. The man's name. Trower. *Trower*. Who kept asking me over and over, "You ever pay for story ideas? Say a guy gives you a tip—a lead, like, about something big—you ever pay money for it?" Trower crushing out one cigarette, lighting another, fiddling with his matchbook, rubbing the back of a hand across his stubbly face, saying then, "What about two thousand—could you go that high?" And I smiled, I remember saying, "I'm just a freelance hack, chum. Specializing in Martians Stole My Baby. You got something big, go to the Miami *Herald.*" Trower shaking his head, saying no, saying, "Eight hundred?" And I really had to get up and go take a piss, but I stayed and said, "For *what?* Eight hundred bucks for what? You haven't told me anything yet." Trower leaning forward on his elbows, then saying he was a chemist, whispering it like he was telling me that he was a goddamn secret agent or something, it was funny, the way that he made being a chemist sound so dangerous, and I laughed, which he didn't like, and then he said, "Buy me a drink," and I said, "Sure, why not?" and then he said, "You ever hear of a man named Eugene Boman?" and—

Then somebody in green said, "We're losing him," and a violet fog swirled around him, and Trower was gone, and the bar, and the marina, and he was walking into a big college lecture hall, maybe a hundred students, everybody talking or doing homework or reading "Bloom County" in the campus daily.

I was wearing jeans and a gray T-shirt with a red Beer Nuts logo on the front, and she was real easy to spot even in a crowd that size, beautiful girl like her. I took a seat beside her, and she never even turned to look at me. I looked at her, though, I *studied* her, and she knew it but she never even blinked, and when the instructor came in and started lecturing she took a few notes, and her handwriting was even poorer than mine. I passed her a note, carefully printed. It said, *Take a walk?* She frowned, then crossed out the question mark, added an exclamation point, and tossed it back on my desk. She still wouldn't look at me. *Take a walk!* I laughed, hung around a little while longer, then got up. "I'll wait for you outside," I whispered and finally she did turn and look at me, and her expression said drop dead, but her face, God, what a gorgeous face, those sea-blue eyes. And later when she came out, I fell into step with her in the corridor, saying, "I'd like to talk to you," and she said, "Yeah? Well, I'm sorry, I got another class," and I said, "No, you don't. I know your schedule," and it was true, I did, I'd conned it out of the Registrar, nothing to it when you're a professional liar, Martians Stole My Baby, and I said, "You don't have any more classes today and you're not supposed to see Gene Boman till this evening. So—you're free. So let's have a cup of coffee or something."

And she looked suddenly startled, frightened, there I'd gone and mentioned Gene Boman and that was supposed to be a secret, which was a joke. Secret. Some secret. I'd been hanging around Boman Pharmaceuticals, I'd been following *him,* I'd seen *her,* I'd seen her lots of times, and she was saying then, "Do you—do you *know* Mr. Boman?" and I ignored her question and pushed open a door and held it, and she looked at me, very suspicious, and then she walked outside.

I nodded toward the parking lot, and she came with me, just came with me, didn't anybody ever tell her you shouldn't trust strangers, and I made small talk, pointing to some old brick buildings and saying they were nice, telling her I hadn't been around a college in a long time, then asking if she was hungry, saying it was little early for lunch, but if she was hungry, we could go to a diner. And she said, "How do you know Eugene Boman?" and I told her, "I don't —not personally," and I gave her a very soulful look, scaring the shit out of her. She figured me for a private detective, oh sure, hired by *Mrs.* Eugene Boman, and she was scared. When she saw my car, a seven-year-old Ford Escort, she turned immediately scornful. "Get in," I told her, and she said, "Like hell. What do you think you're pulling?" And I said, "I want to talk to you about your friend Eugene." Then she glared at me. "Mr. Boman isn't my friend," she said. "Who gave you that idea?" She tried to laugh. No go. And I said, "Hey, Money?" Her name was Money. Monica. Monica . . . something. I said, "Hey, Money? Cut it out."

She took a step back from the car, then walked away. I watched her. She stopped at the gate, one foot on the speed bump. Looked back. I sat in the car and waited. I only waited a minute. She pulled open the passenger door, brushed some juice boxes off the seat, got in. "What the hell is this?" And I said, "Your friend Eugene ever mention a guy named Forell? A place called The Pharmacy?" And she said, "Who *are* you?" And I said, "I'm—"

"—almost gone," someone in green was saying. "We're losing him," and the violet fog swirled up around him, and he was unwrapping gifts beneath a Christmas tree, a black-and-white cowboy suit, two guns, Bonanza stitched on the holsters, just what he wanted, Mom saying, "Merry Christmas, Petey." Etey. Etey. And someone in green said, "We're *losing* him!" Oozing him oozing him . . .

And the fog swirled in again, and there was sheeting rain, and then he was running from his car toward a steel-and-glass building with a fountain on the plaza, then he was in a mirrored lobby, marble and mirrors, then stepping into an elevator. Stepping out. Upon carpeting that closed around his wet shoes like mud. A secretary saying, "Oh yes, you're expected." Then: a fat man seated behind a desk with a Mickey Mouse telephone. Yeah, and a Batman coffee mug. A balding man, a—shy man. Very strange. Not what I expected, though she'd warned me that day in the car, after I'd told her about Trower and what Trower had told me, about Major Forell and Eugene Boman, Eugene Boman and The Pharmacy, The Pharmacy and the Idiot Drugs. The girl named Money . . . something, Money saying, "Maybe Eugene *is* a monster like you're telling me, but he's also very, very . . . shy."

The balding, fat, shy monster pointing to a sofa, saying, "Sit down, please." Saying, "As a rule, I never talk to gentlemen of your profession, not that I have anything *against* your profession, it's just . . ." Trailing off, waving a pudgy hand in small circles, smiling shyly. Saying, "But since our . . . mutual acquaintance says that you're a pretty nice fellow, and since you're not really interested in me, but in my little collection, well—I don't think there's any harm in our having a chat." He smiled again, and looked at his hands, saying, "But I must tell you, that compared to *some* people's collections, my . . . accumulations are rather modest. And nothing is really that old, you know. I only collect things from the sixties, early seventies. Hardly old things. And they're just things that I personally like." Then he got up and went over to a long glass showcase, slid open the door, reached in and took from one of the shelves a red beach pail and a shovel bearing decals of Huckleberry Hound. One of the richest men in the world stood there with a red beach pail and a shovel in his hand, and I kept a straight face and said, "I'll try not to be a nuisance." And Eugene Boman said, "Oh, I'm sure you won't be." Then he said something about . . . music? Something about music . . .

And the purple fog started swirling in again, and the fat man was fading, but he was still speaking, saying something about . . . music. Saying, "Is your name German?" And I said, "What?" and he said, "Is it German, your name—Musik with a k."

Merry Christmas, Petey. Peter. Musik. Musik with a k. Peter Musik. With a k. Yes, German. Musik with a k. My name? My name. Is Peter Musik.

Then someone in green said, "We lost him. He's gone."

Peter Musik with a K *yes* the name *is* German, you son of a bitch, and *you* did this to me, you fat bastard! *You* did this to me! Peter Musik crying, But oh Jesus! as the violet fog closed all around him, cold wet violet fog. Don't let me die!

I don't want to die!

WELL, THAT MAKES TWO OF US, GEEB.

Peter Musik thinking, *Jack?*

DOOR WAS OPEN—FINALLY—SO I THOUGHT I'D COME IN. THAT OKAY?

It's too late, Jack, too late, too late, I'm gone, I'm—

YOU'RE MINE, IS WHAT YOU ARE. AND YOU'RE NOT GOING ANYWHERE 'LESS I TELL YOU TO. ALL RIGHT? OKAY?

As the fog was scattering, somewhere, far away, the beeping sound kicked in . . .

CHAPTER 21

A PERFECT ACCIDENT

DURING HIS BRIEF STRUG-
gle, the too-human had accidentally punched a black button.
The elevator had risen swiftly through the hospital without
stopping, then opened directly into an empty corridor with
access to the roof.

Eudrax went outside and roamed around, but found no
one there.

With his right hand braced on the ledge, he looked up,
and noticed an air machine. The only time he'd been to
Kemolo before—when he'd come gathering soil for mud—
he had traveled in one of those, in an air machine. He remembered it fondly, the Pan Am. Little bits of food were
served, in clear bags or on foam plates. Wonderful! Eudrax
had enjoyed the experience.

As he watched the air machine dwindle to a dot, behind him the claws continued playing with the too-human's
dead body. Rolling it around, doing tumblesaults upon it.

One of them broke away suddenly from the others and
bounded across the roof, straight toward Eudrax's prisoner,

who was crawling on her stomach. Her clothing was torn, she was bleeding freely from her neck and face. Her hands were scraped raw. Her right arm stuck out at an awkward angle. The claw approached her, circling.

Eudrax waved it off.

Then sighed noisily.

His instincts had brought him here, to this place—but where were his quarries? The Cold Mage? The Walker? If not up here, then where?

Below his feet?

In this building?

He went and squatted by the girl-who-must-be-Aculita. When he touched her, she flinched, drew her knees up and tried to crawl again. But collapsed.

"Your host is near. Isn't he?" Eudrax stood. *"Isn't* he?" Speaking in a language called Losplit.

She whimpered.

Eudrax snatched hold of her arm again and dragged her back across the roof.

Herb Dierickx was sitting opposite this handsome Filipino guy with black wavy hair, skin the rich color of mahogany, and just about the whitest, straightest teeth outside of a Crest commercial. Guy with small hands and narrow wrists, and a trimmed, slender mustache that made him look dashing, a little frisky. The doctor. Herb was thinking that if things ever loosened up—like, for instance, if the trampy guy ever gave him back his free will and stuff (not that Herb was complaining, mind you; everything was all right, it was *okay)*, well then, he just might ask this Dr. Lim if there were some pills he could take for his bad shoulder, for his bursitis.

Which caused him a lot of grief every night of his life. But the pills had to be *safe*. No side effects, okay? (No . . . idiot drug. Herb thinking, Jesus. Idiot drugs . . .)

He was aware, somehow, that Dr. Lim specialized in that kind of stuff, bursitis, low back pain, trick knees. That he had a terrific practice. A pretty wife. A red Audi. A Range Rover. And a real nice boat, a Chris-Craft. A summer place in the mountains. And a mistress. Who called him Mel.

The longer that Herb Dierickx sat there facing the guy, the more he knew about him.

Which was pretty strange. Goddamn strange. Pretty goddamn strange.

He figured that, everything being equal, the doctor was very likely picking up some tidbits about him, too, which could be embarrassing, depending on *which* tidbits.

He smiled at Dr. Lim, who didn't smile back.

Herb felt like telling the guy, Oh, don't *worry*, Mel, everything's all right, it's *okay*.

For some reason, though, he couldn't bring himself to speak.

Same as he couldn't bring himself to hitch around in his chair and have another look at the trampy guy's girlfriend.

Herb was real curious about where *she'd* come from.

He'd walked in, maybe three, four minutes ago, guided there God-knows-how, like by remote control; door said Doctors' Lounge, he'd just walked in, radio on, announcer going, "The news at one is sponsored by Chad's, making perfect steaks since 1879," and there was Dr. Lim parked on the sofa, and there was the trampy guy slumped in a chair, and there was the tramp's girlfriend—what *else* could she be?—

standing behind him pushing her fingers through his snarled dark hair. And whistling. That's right, *whistling*. It wasn't a song or anything, there wasn't any *tune*, she was just . . . whistling.

Giving the tramp a vigorous scalp massage, and whistling.

Yeah, for sure Herb wanted to have a second look. At that. At *her*. She was worth it.

What she was *definitely* worth was a good long ogle.

The tramp's girlfriend? Had extremely short brown hair that looked soft as ash, and brown eyes tipped down at the ends—almost, but not quite, Japanese. Pale white skin and a dark-red mouth.

She was gorgeous.

So *what* if she was only, like, four feet tall.

Gorgeous was gorgeous.

And besides, she was very well proportioned.

Perfectly proportioned.

And naked.

Herb may've been a one-woman man, but he wasn't dead, and sitting in that chair where the trampy guy, without speaking a word, had *made* him sit, just sitting there facing the dapper little doctor, he wished like *hell* that he could bring himself to turn around, put his chin on his shoulder, and take another look at the girlfriend. A nice long one.

But he couldn't.

So he cocked his head and closed his eyes, catching snatches of the radio news and glimpses of Panther Lake as seen from the Lim family's vacation cottage, flashing on Mel's zoftig mistress painting her toenails sparkly beige, all the while hearing behind him the tramp mutter through clenched teeth and the beautiful midget whistle incessantly.

Wait'll he told Marge. . . .

All right, so he'd ill-treated her: okay, no argument. But he'd already apologized, hadn't he? Come on. How many times did Jack have to say he was sorry? A million? All right. Sorry. Better? Sorry. Sorry, Lita, my life. Now, come on, *really* come on. Lay off. And speak English. No, there was nothing wrong with Losplit, Losplit was fine, it was a beautiful language, Jack wasn't saying Losplit wasn't a beautiful language—when did he ever say that? It was just—they were *here* now, where the too-humans spoke English, so come on—come on, already. Speak it.

She dug her fingers into his scalp, and he winced.

Then, half-turning, looking up at her, Jack smiled; lifted one shoulder, a shrug, then apologized again.

In Losplit.

And Lita said, "Did you have to make me snatch every I that you met in the street? You want to *kill* me?"

Saying that in English.

"It wasn't *every* I," said Jack. "Hey."

"Practically."

"I think you're exaggerating. Don't you think you're exaggerating—a little?"

She sighed, then swung her head, still annoyed, and folded her arms below her small breasts.

Jack knelt up on the seat of his chair, looked at her for a moment, then kissed her on the forehead. "I think you should put on some clothes. *If* you're going to stay yourself. You want to stay yourself for a while?"

"You don't mind, yeah."

"Check out those lockers, you'll find something."

She went over, took a look, and found a green scrub shirt, matching trousers. She had to roll up the trousers. The shirt hung on her like a tent. Stepping into the bathroom, Lita examined herself at the sink mirror, and laughed. "I look like an Old Aunt," she called to Jack. "From Black Lake."

"Yeah? Well, you've looked worse. You've *worn* worse."

She stretched out on the twin bed, plumping a pillow and then folding her hands behind her neck. "You bet I have, Jack. It's been a true joy traveling with you."

He glanced at her, and they exchanged smiles, then Jack rolled his head, and sent his I walking, back to Geebo.

To *Peter*. He'd have to get used to calling him Peter.

Or maybe he wouldn't.

He preferred the name Geebo. He maybe even preferred the *guy* Geebo. It was funny.

Two doctors were staring at Geebo.

Who was perched on the side of a stainless steel table, hands moving up and down his bearded cheeks.

A nurse was rolling away a big machine.

The clock on the wall in the white-tiled room where Geebo was sitting said five minutes past one.

Then Lita said, "You saved him. How come?"

Jack shrugged. "I didn't *save* him. I just . . . told him he couldn't die. He did the rest."

"But why *bother?* He's only an Accident."

"Maybe a perfect one, though—and part of the Ramble."

"We're in Kemolo, my life. What connection could that too-human have with—"

"The infant?"

"The Epicene. What connection?"

Jack came out of his chair suddenly, and paced. He stopped, fists at his waist. *What* connection? What connection, indeed? He couldn't figure *any* of this.

But that didn't worry him, it was to be expected.

He *never* understood—till all the pieces collected, fell into place.

Which was the beauty of being a Walker.

All you had to do was move, and keep moving.

Stay alive and keep walking. And things just happened, Accidents happened, and signified.

Lita said, "Jack?"

He looked at her.

"I *still* don't know why you saved his life."

Jack nodded: yeah, well, neither did he. Except: "I may need him as Witness. He could be part of Ramble's End."

"How? We've only come here to hide."

Jack didn't like the sound of that: to *hide*. "To wait until I'm granted an audience with His Majesty," he said, correcting her. "And, *until* then, I'm still out Walking, aren't I? According to the Order of Things. I'm *still* on Squintik's Ramble till the King consents to hear of my travels."

Lita said, "Squintik," with an edge in her voice. "So where is he? Why hasn't he come for us?"

"He'll come."

"And if the Mage of Manse Seloc comes first?"

"How would he know where to look?"

"Jack, a Walker don't be a fool."

Jack nodded again, thinking, Yes, *don't*. Don't. He went and stood beside Dr. Lim, then touched him gently on the shoulder. The doctor blinked, smiled.

Then Jack turned to Herb Dierickx, who immediately glanced back at him with good-humored curiosity.

To Lita, Jack said, "Get up, my life. We're all going for a walk."

Because the trick, you see, was to move, and keep moving.

See what happened.

Instead of bringing Jere Lee upstairs, Brian Tucker had taken her to the hospital basement, where there were clerical and staff offices. She hadn't caught on immediately. She'd rolled her cart into the hall, then stood waiting for him to show her the way to Mr. Squintik's room. Instead, he pointed to a bench beside a soft-drink machine. "Have a seat."

"Why?" she asked. Somewhere, a high-speed printer was chattering.

"Because I want to get a few things straight. This *friend* you're so eager to see is very likely involved in a double homicide. I'd like to hear what you can tell me about that."

"Absolutely nothing, Brian. What double homicide? Oh, don't be ridiculous."

"He wants to *see* you. Is what you said. But, Mrs. Vance, how would you know that? Unless you spoke to him. But you tell me you didn't."

"Brian, why are you doing this to me? I don't know anything about any double homicide. And I never laid eyes on Mr. Squintik before I saw him at the bus station. I just got the *feeling* he'd like to see me again."

Tucker expelled his breath, then sat down beside her. "Mrs. Vance, I believe you."

"Then why—?"

"Maybe I'm really trying to talk to you about . . . something else."

"Such as?"

"You're living on the street."

"Is *that* what you think?" She looked at him sharply. But there was apprehension in her eyes, too. "Well, I'm not. I live at Ten West Ninth Street. In a rent-controlled apartment, thank you. And I work a job, I work at—Shop-Rite."

"I don't mean to embarrass you," said Tucker. "I'm sorry."

She went over and jabbed the elevator button several times.

Tucker stared at her from the bench, then smiled. "I remember you always had a temper."

"Oh, you do?"

"Yeah. I remember once. Bringing Karen home at three in the morning? I thought you were going to hit me with something."

"I should've."

"Mrs. Vance . . ."

"Are you going to let me see this gentleman or aren't you? Just tell me. Because if you're not, fine, then I'll just leave. I have things to do. I have chores. It's Saturday. I can't just waste my entire Saturday hanging around here talking to you."

He looked at his hands. "All right. We'll go up. Okay?"

When the elevator arrived, a few moments later, Brian Tucker noticed a long dent in the side wall that he didn't remember seeing there five minutes earlier.

He touched it, and his fingertip came away red. Wet.

"Which floor, Brian?"

"What?"

Wet blood.

"Which floor?"

"Two," he said, distracted. "Room 214."

And strands of hair.

Wet blood and strands of hair.

He didn't know what to do first.

A few possibilities came to mind, though.

Like, for instance, maybe he ought to just slip *out* of there. Go find Jack. And thank him.

Or find a telephone—yeah? First find a telephone?

Very interesting possibility.

He'd finally remembered Money's last name: Campbell. And now he'd even remembered her phone number, area code and all.

Call Money up, and when she answered, he could say, "Know who this is?"

See if she fainted or something, started shouting for joy. See if she hung up.

Or you know what else he could do? Be even better? Forget about calling Money, at least for now. What'd be better?

Call Gene Boman.

"Gene?" Say, "Gene? How you doing? It's Peter. Yeah, it's the Music Man. 'Member how you liked to fool around, call me the Music Man? Hey, so what've you been up to, pal? How's your father-in-law?"

Sitting hunched on the edge of the stainless-steel table, Peter Musik grinned down at the floor. He lifted his eyes.

One-oh-seven, by the electric wall clock. Bulova clock. Details, details.

Thinking he could say, "How's the Major? What's doing at the farm?"

Then thinking, No, that's too slick. I don't want slick. I don't want clever. September, October, November. Three months. After three lost months, all the shit I've been through, I don't want slick, I don't want clever.

I want revenge.

Call Gene. Go, "Gene? I'm coming for you."

Something like that.

But then Peter thought, Why *tell* him?

Just *do* it.

Then he looked up, seeing doctors peer in at him from the doorway.

He recognized the one with the long, thin face and the grooved forehead. Dr. Watson. No kidding. Like in Sherlock Holmes.

He'd been there when Peter died, for want of a better word, and still there when Peter came back to life, snapping his eyes wide open, startling the hell out of everybody.

Dr. Watson came in now with his two colleagues, saying, "This is Dr. Lamar and this is Dr. Howard." They surrounded Peter, staring with grave, pensive expressions. And Peter said, "So why the long faces? Afraid I don't have Blue Cross? Well, gentlemen, you're right."

Dr. Watson allowed himself a brief smile. "We'll let you worry about that. Later. Right now, we'd like to ask you a few questions. If you're feeling up to it."

"I'm feeling fine."

"Happy to hear it. But frankly, you shouldn't be."

"It wasn't my time, was all."

"Oh? Are you a religious man, Mr. . . ."

"Musik. With a k. And no, not especially. It just . . . it just wasn't my time. This happens, doesn't it? I mean, I've read a few articles about people dying, coming back after a couple minutes."

In fact, Peter Musik could now recall having written one such article, himself. For a newspaper Sunday supplement.

"Sure, it happens. But normally the patient's recovery is not quite so—remarkable. So complete. You had a stroke, Mr. Musik. Are you aware of that?"

"I'm lucky." And said to himself, Lucky? Never thought I'd call myself *lucky*. But it's true. I am. I *am* lucky.

Starting now.

The doctors were leaning forward intently, studying his face. The one who was short and stocky, and who seemed to be the oldest, the doctor named Lamar, said, "We need to get your medical history, if you'd be so kind. And then, of course, we'd like to have you undergo a series of tests."

Peter pulled a face and shrugged, then Jack was in his head again, saying, NO TIME FOR THAT. GOTTA KEEP MOVING, GEEB, KEEP MOVING. AND HERE WE . . . COME!

A small, wiry, brown-skinned doctor briskly entered the room pushing a wheelchair. "We've found a bed for Mr. . . . Musik."

The other doctors all blinked in surprise.

"Mel?" said Dr. Watson. "What're you doing here?"

Dr. Lim paused before replying. "I'm taking the patient to his room."

"We're not nearly finished with him yet," said Lamar.

He sounded a bit sniffy. "And when we are, I'm quite certain we can find an orderly."

Dr. Lim seemed to slump.

And Peter, who'd noticed the red swelling on the Filipino's hand (details, details; a good journalist pays close attention to the smallest details), slid from the table. "I tell you what," he said. "I'd really like to put this off till later. Could we?" He plopped down in the wheelchair. "A bed sounds good, you know?"

The three doctors went and stood in the corridor, watching Dr. Lim roll away their mystery patient.

Peter glanced left and right, ogling young nurses. Then tapping his hands, doing a little be-bop, on the arms of the chair, he asked Dr. Lim, "So where's our friend?"

Dr. Lim wouldn't reply. Or maybe couldn't.

At the far end of the corridor was a dayroom, a solarium, frail men and women in bathrobes playing cards, reading paperback novels, staring wistfully out the casement windows. That seemed to be where Dr. Lim was headed. Then, oh yeah: definitely. Definitely where he was going. Peter spotted Herb Dierickx first, then Jack, Jack standing with his arm around a tiny woman's shoulder, a woman wearing hospital greens.

Peter thought, Now who the hell is *she?* Then grinned when Jack gave him a thumbs-up sign.

"Hey, doc, I'll walk the rest of the way." He jumped from the wheelchair.

It was about twenty yards to the solarium. Peter took it slow, walking with a smart-aleck bounce. Hey, why not? Back from the dead. Literally and figuratively. A young nurse glanced up from her station, first smiling, then scowling. Peter winked at her, then turned his head and peeked into a room, where a fat teen-aged boy was lying in a cranked-up bed watching TV. Then he glanced into another room, noticing a guy in a brown topcoat speaking with an old man who was bald as a melon.

He was going past the elevator when the doors opened and Jere Lee came out rolling her shopping cart.

"*Geebo!*" She gave a little gasp. "What're *you* doing here?" Saying, "Geebo!" over and over, and he was far too surprised to say anything back. He just gawped at her.

Jere Lee? What the hell was *she* doing there? He glanced helplessly up the corridor, at Jack, who met his eyes, and shrugged.

A tall blonde man had followed Jere Lee off the elevator, just before the doors closed again. And now she was turning to him, saying, "Brian? This is my good friend Geebo. Geebo, this is Brian Tucker. Brian's a policeman."

Peter's head fizzed a little as the plainclothes cop scrutinized him, checking out his bedraggled sweatshirt, his crusty jeans and filthy sneakers. Pegging him as a low-life. Christ, maybe even noticing the lump in his flak jacket, where the sap was.

Jere Lee suddenly reached for Peter's arm, but he pulled it away. She blushed, and he thought, What'd I do *that* for? She looked at her hand, then dropped it and managed to smile. "Are you okay? Geebo? You're not sick, are you? You a patient?"

He shook his head, said no, he was fine. Then he glanced at Dr. Lim standing like a park statue behind the wheelchair. "I just had a little dizzy spell," he told Jere Lee. "But it's nothing. I'm okay. But so what about you? *You* okay?"

"Oh sure. I'm just here to visit a friend of mine." She

smiled at the plainclothes cop. "A friend of *ours,* in Room 214. Mr. Squintik."

Peter's face turned chalk white.

Squintik?

He whirled around to face Jack, who was grinning from ear to ear as he walked quickly down the corridor, the tiny woman in the hospital greens trotting along close behind him. Herb Dierickx in back of *her.* Little parade.

Jack calling to Peter, saying, "I had this *feeling* you were perfect—perfect!"

Jere Lee saying, "Hey, you're the guy that stole Geebo's box!"

Brian Tucker unbuttoning his coat, spreading it open, giving himself clear access to his hip holster.

Seeing: two bums. Thinking: Here to avenge two *other* bums? Named Crash and Pollux?

A bell dinged. The elevator opened.

And into the corridor burst five small redheaded boys.

CHAPTER 22

AFTERCLAP

ON HIS LAST RAMBLE through port Tiedek in Lostwithal: by chance, Jack had seen two shadowed claws, at a seamen's masque.

Most revelers at the Maritime Hall that evening (it was the Feast of the Most Temperate Season) wore costumes that satirized nobles: mage robes sewn from coarse wool blankets, pytheness habits stitched together from jute sacks, art-princekin formal jackets fashioned from burlap, chips of broken glass substituted for splendent jewels. There were countless Agels, of course, feigning exhaustion and perched on shipping crates and wooden barrels. Some Agels were even part of *tableaux vivant*, with ministers of state, pages, attendants, a naked fool.

Dressed in a soiled purple cape with a raveled hem (Hill Barons fancied purple), Jack had gone alone, Lita having traveled ahead the previous morning to her home-lake for Childling Days.

The crowd was thick-pressed and giddy, and he'd wandered through it with his ears tuned, pausing only whenever he failed to recognize a name. Or was intrigued by some fragment of drunken conversation. Eavesdropping. Nothing of much interest, though—till very late in the evening, as the revel wound down. Jack was taking yet another turn around the hall when he'd glanced up to the balcony and spied two russet claws pressed against the railing.

To everyone else, they were tall, stoop-shouldered mariners, wearing tattered versions of courtiers' clothing.

But Jack could scarcely see those auras, the shadows they'd borrowed.

It was one of the few privileges that came with being a tramp in the service of His Majesty. You had a certain . . . vision; an extra-sight. It would take a great mage, indeed, to cast the shadow that could fool even a first-degree Walker.

Jack wondered idly for whom they'd come, the two claws; he had not heard of any intriguers during his brief stay in Tiedek. And he wondered also if their Finder were near at hand. He knew all the Finders up and down the Major Coast, and most of those practicing elsewhere; had he looked, he surely could've recognized whichever one had brought the claws. But why bother? The Finder might've recognized *him*, too, and Jack, a Walker wasn't keen on speaking to someone of *that* ilk. *All* Finders were his social and professional inferiors.

It hadn't crossed his mind that the claws might be there for *him*.

After spotting them both, he'd lost interest, and passed the remainder of the evening cadging drinks at the bar. Several times he was offered vapors, but declined. He spoke and flirted with a shy pretty girl who'd come to the masquerade dressed as the Throne Widow, King Agel's Queen. Then, around three in the morning, he stumbled from the Maritime Hall, by himself. (The girl had been far too shy to agree to what he'd suggested they do.) Both of heaven's moons were bright. Almost immediately Jack became aware of scuffling noises behind him.

He started to turn when something slammed into the side of his head and knocked him off the pavement. When he hit the street, he rolled, and the claw struck a cobblestone just inches to his left with such velocity that it cracked a forefoot, then tumbled six or seven times, shrieking with pain.

Jack scrambled up and ran—through empty, winding streets and slender alleys and courtyards-leading-into-courtyards. At last, just before he collapsed with exhaustion, he stopped and leaned against the mortar wall of an old tenement house. His lungs felt scalded, his breath came in sobs, and his legs quivered.

Claws? After him?

But *why?*

Why *him?*

Then he heard them again, and a nerve in his neck pulsed violently. He tried the tenement door. It was locked, but he threw himself against it, leading with his shoulder, and it flew open. Inside, it was too dark to see. There was a keenly sweet odor of rot. Vermin scrambled and chittered as Jack moved forward cautiously, feeling his way. He came to a flight of stairs. Climbing through the house, his vision adapted gradually to the gloom. Every door in the house, save the door to the roof, stood open; every room was empty. He paused on the top landing and listened. Heard nothing. Wondered if he'd managed to lose the claws. Then shoved open the roof door and stepped outside.

The flat roof looked milky under the twin moons' clear

light. Just beyond the chimney pot—between the chimney
and the low parapet—was a peculiar dome-shaped hut. Jack
had never seen anything quite like it. It was very small and
made of dung and thatch, but it glistened, as though viscous.
There was a round opening in its top, and three narrow
vertical fissures in the side closest to Jack.

This seemed—Interesting.

After pulling the door shut behind him, he moved
slowly across the roof. With every step, though, it became
more difficult for him to draw a breath, and the air turned
warmer, more heavily saturated with moisture. Alarm tightened in his chest. By the time he'd reached the chimney
pots, his face was streaming and his scalp was itching horri-
bly. He wanted to flee, to leap across the alley to the next
roof, and the next, and the next, but he was a Walker, and
he was on a Ramble, and this was . . . Interesting.

He blinked sweat from his eyelids, and peered down
into the hut through its top hole, which boiled with gnats
and barn flies.

The small, wet, yellow-brown thing within had two
arms and two legs, a torso and a head, and it writhed in a
cradle of braided straw, on a cushion of fat pallid slugs.

Jack knew at once what it was, and groaned, then
stumbled backwards, and turned to run.

A Finder named Heywix stood framed in the rooftop
door. Lifting his Hand of Favor to his lips, he said, "I bless
you for the bounty you'll bring, and shall whistle your soul
to the Void, poor Walker." Then he bit himself, and drew
blood. Howling, a tawny claw loped across the roof. Jack
spun away and headed for the parapet. He jumped, fell
through space, landed hard on another roof. Ran, and then
jumped again. Ran, jumped. And then kept dropping, till he

crashed through heavy canvas and into a fishmonger's empty stall. Pain shot in jagged lines through his shoulders and back. He rolled to the ground, and clenching his teeth, moved swiftly as he could along the pavement.

Soon, he was back at the waterfront. He crawled under one of the piers and sat down in the darkness with his back against a piling. Heywix, he thought. Heywix. Who was indentured, he knew, to the Great Mage of Manse Seloc. Which meant that it was the Mage of Four, Mage of Luck who wanted Jack dead. And now he could understand why. Oh yes. *Now* he knew. Heywix had been sent to kill him lest he discover the infant of mud and straw while on his Ramble through Tiedek. But the irony—and it was a beautiful irony, an irony that Jack could fully appreciate, no matter his pain and distress—was that the Finder himself had *caused* the discovery—had precipitated the Accident. It would never have occurred without Heywix. If the claws had not attacked him outside the Maritime Hall, he would never have run in *that* direction, broken into *that* tenement, climbed to *that* roof.

Wonderful irony. Perfect Accident.

Something splashed out in the harbor, and Jack flinched.

But then he smiled.

He decided to leave port Tiedek immediately. He would go collect Lita in the north country then return with her to the capital. To Master Squintik.

With news of the Epicene.

Before he could act upon his decision, though, he was knocked senseless, from behind.

The claws had not found him, a spice agent had, and

several hours later, he'd revived aboard a cargo ship bound for the Southern Isles. Rats scrambling over his stomach.

For twelve days he'd done sailoring, then jumped ship at Bethix Horn and tramped his way back north. It took nearly two weeks to make the capital. Arriving one rainy late afternoon, he'd avoided the city gates, not wishing to announce his presence. And went straight to Lita's quarters, near the market.

She was there, dressed in a gray mourning tunic. The Walker was flattered, and touched.

She flew into a rage, though, after he'd told her of his adventure on the spice ship: ranting at him as though it were his own fault he'd been shanghaied. He was astounded by her temper.

But she quieted abruptly when he told her about the claws.

And about the Epicene. "The great mage," he said, "has done what Master Squintik most feared. Created it."

"Jack, a Walker," she said, "I don't think I'm going to take off these mourning clothes just yet."

But he'd finally convinced her.

To take off the tunic, and everything else, as well.

Upon waking the next morning in Lita's bed, he'd thought, Precious little good having extra-sight did me at the Maritime Hall. . . .

Nevertheless, there in the corridor of St. Vincent's Hospital, in the Moment of Kemolo, he was glad that he had it.

When these other claws—five of them, a regular pack, shadowed as little boys—appeared suddenly in front of him, he saw their true shapes at once.

And it gave him the advantage.

He recognized them, and Eudrax, a second before they recognized him.

Long enough.

He plunged a hand through one of the "boys," reached straight down through the illusion and seized the claw by its neck, then snapped it. Immediately, the shadow vanished, and Jack was standing there with a small, short-haired dead mammal in his fist. Disgusted, he flung it. Against a corner of the nurses' station, where it split open and sprayed blood.

In the meantime, Jack had gone for Eudrax.

Propelling himself into the elevator, he kneed the Finder, then grappled with him, intent on breaking his right arm. If he could incapacitate it, Eudrax would have no way of lifting the Hand of Favor to his lips. No bites, no tricky stuff. Simple as that. Jack gripped the arm, above the elbow and at the wrist. But since he'd pinned Eudrax to the elevator wall, he couldn't twist it, couldn't wrench it backward. (A phrase that he'd picked up from Herb Dierickx: Oh great. Just great.)

When he tried to pull Eudrax away from the wall, he tripped over something—some*body*—and, splay-legged as a clown, crashed to the elevator floor.

Eudrax leapt upon his chest, grinning.

The doors had closed, and the car was going up.

Jack was more disgusted than frightened. *A Finder was kneeling on top of him! Breathing in his face! The lowest of the low, a piece of greedy filth, violating a fifth-degree Walker!* Jack became *so* disgusted, so *indignant* that he bellowed, and flailed out with both arms, clipping Eudrax high on his cheek and opening a two-inch gash.

As the elevator doors opened again—Third Floor: Maternity—Jack wheeled over. He threw off the Finder, and hoisted himself into a wrestler's crouch. Feeling dizzy. Eudrax shoved off from the back wall, driving his head into Jack's belly. Together, they shot into a corridor and crashed against a steel kitchen cart stacked with dishes. Over it went. Young women in bathrobes—new mothers—ran in all directions.

Whimpering, a blonde girl crawled from the elevator car. One of the nurses darted behind Jack and dragged her away by the collar of her shredded leather jacket.

Jack's mouth was full of salty blood, and he held three teeth upon his tongue. He was determined not to swallow them (bad luck), but he was also determined not to just spit them out as a common street brawler would do. He curled his tongue around them, protectively, and then stabbed at Eudrax with a shard of broken glass. It caught and tore the Finder's right arm, but not before Eudrax had pressed it into service, had lifted the Hand of Favor to his mouth.

He nibbled at the palsied wrist, and willed himself into flames; suffered but was not consumed.

Scuttling backwards on his heels, Jack levered himself upright and ran.

Eudrax moved after him, charring the floor, blistering walls, melting plastic chairs.

Jack bumped heavily against plate glass. Behind it was the nursery, about a dozen cribs, newborns in diapers and T-shirts and plastic ID bracelets. Most of them were bald. Some looked purple.

Fiery Eudrax kept coming

Then all of a sudden it was raining, a downpour—ceiling sprinklers letting go. Steam hissing. The Finder roaring in amazement, his flames pelted, drenched, weakening, but then licking back into red life again.

Jack was quickly approaching the end of the corridor, end of the line, dead end, no place to go after that, unless he turned around and charged Eudrax—tried to get past him. Odds? Worthless. So he ducked into a room and slammed the door. There were two beds, both unoccupied, congratulatory floral arrangements on the tables and on the windowsill, a couple of chairs, and a television mounted on high wall brackets. The set was on. A cooking lesson in progress. A woman deftly slicing mushrooms.

The metal door was glowing, buckling.

Jack picked up a chair and flung it through the window, then leaped onto the sill. Looked down. To the sidewalk. Odds? Not even worth calculating. If he jumped, he'd break every bone in his body.

Eudrax was in the room.

The television cable melted, the back of the set blew out.

Jack tried grabbing up a mattress, as a kind of shield, but then an arm of flame lashed out, catching him across his shoulder. His jacket went up, and his hair. And then he was covered with foam, spitting it out (and spitting out with it his three lost teeth) as he went tumbling through space. And came down on his back, hard.

Saw: a buxom black nurse with snow-white hair brandishing the horn on a heavy steel cannister. Another blast of foam. And Eudrax, on his knees, face and hands blistered, right arm bleeding, tiny flames twitching on the hem and sleeves of his garment. He was smothered in sticky foam.

The big nurse turned the horn again on Jack, defensively, when he sprang to his feet. Then she screamed. He grabbed the Finder by the front of his caftan and plucked him up.

Looking Eudrax in the face, he smiled. "Final reward," Jack said, in Losplit, and thrust him backwards. Through the broken window. The Finder's heel snagged between a jagged V of glass. The nurse dislodged it with a final burst of foam.

Grudgingly, Jack blessed him and whistled his soul to the Void.

As he turned to leave the room, the nurse dropped the fire extinguisher and fled. The cylinder rolled. Jack stopped it with his foot. And thought, in English, Handy things.

Sad Agel will enjoy hearing of them.

If I ever make it back to Lostwithal.

Coming along the corridor, he passed the nursery, where all the babies were squalling in unison.

The blonde girl was sitting huddled, clutching herself, on the wet carpet in the nurses' station.

Jack hunkered beside her. "Money Campbell," he said. "I know you."

She blinked several times to focus, then stared at Jack.

Who bent over, licking at some of the cuts and plum-dark bruises on her forehead.

Money pulled a disgusted face. "Hey, don't do that, that's gross."

Then she got a bad case of the shakes, began laughing and crying at the same time.

Jack scooped her into his arms, and the nurses and doctors and new mothers and visiting husbands all fell back and let him pass. Move unimpeded down the corridor. There was smoke in the air. An inch of water on the floor. Walking, Jack made a splashing sound.

He went directly out through the fire door, then took

the concrete stairs, down. Money saying, "He dragged me across town, and there were some people asked him where he got me, what store, and how much I cost! How much I *cost!*"

And then she was crying and laughing, all over again.

As soon as the elevator had closed, the redheaded boys went totally berserk, hurling themselves against the doors with mad ferocity.

For some reason, that sight was more terrifying to Jere Lee than the fact that one of them had apparently—had apparently what?

Vanished?

It all happened so quickly, but yeah, one of them had simply . . . vanished.

Jere Lee telling herself, You're crazy: there wasn't five of them, only four. You miscounted, you—

No. Five, I counted *five*, and one of them *vanished*.

Hold on. Wait a second. That kind of stuff, a disappearing kid? Only could happen in a fifty-million-dollar summer movie. Not in real life. (Not in *my* life!) And what was that bloody mess down the hall? Talk about weird stuff. God, it looked like road kill, a small dog or a poor raccoon. What the hell was *that?* First, one of the little boys suddenly disappears, and the next thing you know, some limp *thing* goes flying past your head. Bursts open. And then . . . then that scruffy bum who stole Geebo's carton last night jumps into the elevator, the doors close, and—

The four little redheads go . . . totally berserk.

Hurling themselves against the doors.

And howling.

Perfectly okay in a hit movie. Totally wrong in real life.
(In *my* life!)

Jere Lee wanted to scream.

But couldn't.

Her eyes were open so wide they stung. She was a camera, taking in the wild boys, who were actually hammering
dents into the elevator doors. Taking in a candy striper, hysterical, arms flung out. Taking in Geebo, with a six-inch slab
of rubber-sheathed lead clutched in his hand.

Then Brian Tucker roughly pushed her, up the corridor.

And her camera eye focused on the man in the chauffeur's uniform who was slumped against a wall, one hand
covering his mouth.

Then on Geebo again, Geebo staring down at a green
scrub shirt and pair of pants lying on the floor.

Jere Lee felt a spasm of fear. A fleeting wave of dread.
Hey, come on. Can't be. That little snippet of a woman:
Gone? Vanished? Like the redheaded boy? *Both* of them?

Maybe this really *wasn't* happening. Maybe—maybe
she *had* wigged out, gone over; maybe—

All around her, people were shouting; an alarm bell
sounded, a maddening jangle.

Jere Lee's eyes darted back to the four boys, just as they
began to shimmer and fade.

She watched Brian Tucker moving toward them. He
tried to grab one, but his hand plunged straight through the
child's body, as though passing into a beam of light, a movie
projection.

Finally, Jere Lee did scream.

As Tucker was flung backward, violently, his cheek
slashed open and spraying a fine red jet.

He spun around, struck the wall, then dropped to his knees.

There were no longer four little redheaded boys in the corridor.

Instead, there were four small reddish-brown animals, their lips drawn back, their teeth bared. Their teeth were curved and bony; more like—like hooks, like *claws* than like goddamn teeth.

One of them drew itself up on its hind legs, then sprang. And hit Jere Lee with such force that she was slammed backward into her cart. Which crashed over, dumping out coats and blankets, unreturned library books, and a small teak box containing her daughters' birth certificates, first teeth, and grammar-school report cards.

Jere Lee raised herself on an elbow. She was bleeding, but couldn't tell where from, or how badly. The front of her coat was bright red.

The animal that looked like a mink (but was clearly not) stood perhaps two yards from her face, poised to strike again.

Panting. Flanks moving in and out.

She stared into its eyes: moist black buttons.

Dear God. Jere Lee thinking, And I was worried about pneumonia. What a joke. My whole life's been a joke. My whole life is *over*.

Thinking, I'll never see my girls again. I'll never—

The animal left the ground.

But never reached her.

Brian Tucker fired his revolver from a kneeling position, and it flipped over backward in midair with a hole through its neck the size of an old-fashioned watch face.

Herb slumped against the wall, stifling a groan. Hey Marge. Margie. I'm scared.

One of those . . . things is looking at me.

Hail Mary, full of grace—

It caught him just under the heart, scooping out a chunk of flab. Herb doubled over, landed on his knees. He clutched at the wound, holding it closed, and stared in horror at the blood that was leaking through his fingers.

. . . the lord is with thee, blessed art thou amongst women . . .

Then a violent pain erupted in his head, and he was looking out through somebody else's eyes, seeing a pillar of fire—no, a person *on* fire—scorching everything black. He heard babies crying. And the trampy guy's voice:

ROOM 214. THE OLD MAN. PROTECT HIS LIFE.

And Herb thought, What about *my* life?

THE OLD MAN. PROTECT HIM.

And then he was back in his own head. He shut his eyes against the pain, and refused to look at his wound. (I'm not hurt bad I'm not hurt bad I'm not hurt bad.) In agony, and with his shoes slipping in his own blood, Herb drew himself up the wall.

When he finally opened his eyes, he saw the Filipino doctor trying to fight off one of those . . . things (friggen weasels! Or something) with a folded-up wheelchair. Like he was Gunther Gebel-Williams, for Christ's sake. But go, Mel: do it! Look at him club that sucker like it was a big golf ball.

But a moment later, it was on the doctor's face.

Herb thinking, Oh Jesus Jesus no Jesus! as he went lumbering down the corridor, one hand pressed to his side, the other stretched out with the fingers curled . . . just so.

JUST SO.

Herb thinking, I'm supposed to break its *neck?*

YOU KNOW HOW TO DO IT.

Yeah, but—

DO IT.

Herb stooped and lunged, then clenched his fingers— just so; big clumsy fingers not clumsy now—and snapped the thing's brittle neck.

The animal's death shudder passed through Herb like an electric shock.

Then it fell away from Dr. Lim, who toppled.

Seeing Eudrax and his despicable claws, Lita had expected to die with her host.

And was unafraid.

She'd grown up in the north country of Lostwithal among the Women of Mist: thus she believed there was conscious life, another *corporal* life (for most) beyond the Void. And to die with a trusted friend was the best of all possible deaths: it meant eternal companionship.

Lita didn't *want* to die, but she was not afraid.

Reflexively, instantly she'd made the loathsome transformation to wasp, and—suddenly deaf, her vision suddenly prismatic, a thousand shards of information—she'd followed Jack, a Walker into the elevator.

She buried herself in the tangle of Jack's hair, her sting in his scalp. Her life in his.

Expecting to die. . . .

When she did not—when her host snatched up the

Finder like a scarecrow and pitched him through a broken window—Lita felt giddy, intoxicated, and whirled briefly in the memory of her violent birth, her mother's blood. She felt buoyant.

But she felt, too, the smallest draft of disappointment.

It would've been a fine death, death in the company of Jack, a Walker. Her life.

She removed her sting from his scalp, and flew free.

Then watched the Walker, in slivers and fragments, turn from the window, regard a steel cannister that was lying on the floor (memorizing it, of course, to describe later for Their-Majesty-Most-Still), and then finally stumble from the room.

She followed again, sought out the groove in his wrist bracelet, and lodged herself there.

With her host, her life.

Peter Musik had seen the man on fire, same as Herb Dierickx. (And same as Dr. Lim.) He'd been staring in horror at one of the animals as it flung itself at Jere Lee—and then he was behind Jack's eyes. *With* Jack. *In* Jack. Seeing baskets of flowers, and "The Saturday Gourmet" on a TV set. Jack tossed a chair through the window. The television exploded. PROTECT MASTER SQUINTIK.

"What *are* they?" Peter said, seeing through his own eyes again, seeing the gunflash, watching one of those—animals—flip over and hit the floor with a loud smack. *"What?"*

PROTECT HIM.

Then Jack was no longer with him, he was no longer with Jack: he was running.

It didn't seem to Peter, though, that Master Squintik
needed his protection.

He came slamming into the room, Room 214, like the
hero in the next-to-the-last scene of a psycho thriller, and
there was Jack's boss (or *whatever* he was) shooting balls of
green fire, from his fingertips, at that—thing. Animal? Ferret? Whatever: it was now in flames.

There was another man in the room, who from the look
of him just *had* to be another cop, and his eyes were bugged
and he was saying, "Holy Christ, so *that's* how you did it."

When Squintik lowered his left hand, Peter followed it
down with his eyes. There was a thick, spiked ring on the
first finger. The hand was blue and rimed with a white frost.
And so was Squintik's other hand. And throat. And face. The
old man looked . . . frozen.

Peter whipped around at a scuffling noise behind him.
Dr. Lim blocking the doorway, brandishing a folded wheelchair. Then: a sharp crack. And the doctor pitched forward,
into the corridor.

Stepping toward the bed, Peter said to Master Squintik,
"The Walker is near."

The plainclothes cop had his gun out. But pointed at the
floor. "Who the hell are *you?*" he said.

Saying that just as the last—ferret, weasel, fox, monster
—sprang out from under the bed? a chair? the table? from
*some*place and tore out the cop's stomach. Then leapt away.
Onto the bed, going for Squintik's left hand.

Instantly, Peter was there, crooking back his forearm
and driving his fist down, hard, doing that over and over, till
the sap was slick red and he heard the crisp snapping of
bone.

Then he pried the animal's jaws from around Squintik's hand.

Blood mixing with the frost, making a pink slush.

Nice detail, thought Peter. Disgusting, but . . . nice.

He rolled the dead animal off the far side of the bed.

When Jack appeared, moments later, Peter scarcely recognized him. His head was blistered and covered with ash, his clothes were all singed. He looked ready for the burn unit, but didn't seem to be suffering any pain.

He stopped, stretched out both arms like Moses at the Red Sea, then touched his bracelet. "I have rambled for you, dear master," he said, "and would now, with your—"

Squintik shook his head violently, almost contemptuously, and Peter got the feeling that the old bald guy couldn't be bothered now with formal ceremony. He nodded toward his legs. And said to Jack, "I remember hearing you once tell His Majesty about guns. You described them well."

"Somebody *shot* you?"

"We meet by accident," said Squintik, permitting himself a smile.

Jack bowed his head, his expression a curious mixture of pride and self-reproach.

Peter glanced from Jack to the magician—the *mage*—and then to the doorway, seeing Herb Dierickx step into the room. God almighty, bleeding like a pig. But he carried himself stoically, his chin jutted like an army cadet's.

Behind him stood Money Campbell.

Red raw scratches on her face, her yellow hair in disarray. Her blue eyes round and scared as a lost child's.

Peter groaned, appalled at the way she looked and vastly glad to see her again.

But what was she *doing* here? How—?

Goddamn, thought Peter, god*damn,* and moved toward her.

She flinched, giggled explosively, said, "Hey! That beard. Changes your whole face." Then she saw the dead policeman crumpled on the floor and threw herself against Peter, sobbing uncontrollably.

Holding her as tightly as he dared—she seemed so fragile, not like the old Money—he told her it was okay, everything was okay, and as he whispered, his lips touching her hair, he squeezed his eyes open and shut, open and shut. Seeing the big wall clock out in the corridor, above the nurses' station: nineteen minutes past one. Seeing flecked blackness. Seeing Jere Lee limp toward him. Seeing flecked blackness. Seeing his own breath, frosty as though he were outdoors.

Enclosed in his arms, Money Campbell shuddered.

Peter saying, "You're safe, you're all right now, it's over, it's over."

Meanwhile telling himself, Liar. *Liar.*

The entire door wall was sheeted with ice.

Broken and bleeding and nearly blind with pain, Eudrax struggled on his back, trying—like a beetle—to turn himself over. But he couldn't. He lay on the pavement, dying. His mind raced, teeming with the memories of bounties he'd earned, taken some pleasure from. His mouth felt—clotted: with coal dust. From the corner of his left eye, he saw the twitching fingers of the Hand of Favor.

Which had been severed from its puny wrist when the Finder had plunged through the high window—lopped cleanly off by a prong of sharp glass.

The fingers scrabbled, the long nails ticking cement.

There was a collective gasp from the small crowd of too-humans that surrounded Eudrax; blanched faces staring down in fascination and horror.

The hand moved across the pavement, and up the Finder's chest.

And now there were police sirens, and the squeal of tires, panicky voices, ringing bells, and Eudrax heard it all as so many distant explosions, and winced, and ground his teeth, and strained to see past the haze, and dimly saw the hand, no larger than a child's, dripping blood, leap from his shoulder to his throat. Felt its thumb digging into his neck, its fingers crushing his windpipe.

He was released.

The Hand of Favor let go its grip, then scuttled like a crab down the length of the Finder's body and across the pavement. It stopped, reared itself up, then plunged forward, the ring on its second finger making a wound in the air, through which it vanished. . . .

CHAPTER 23

RAMBLE'S END

THE FOUR WALLS AND THE ceiling (but not the carpet) of Room 214, St. Vincent's Hospital, were slabbed with glistening blue-green ice. Everyone's breath, except Master Squintik's, came out in long, ragged plumes. Beyond the impenetrable doorway: muffled voices, indistinct faces, smeary color, glimpsed movement. The corridor might just as well have been the moon. On the nightstand, the telephone was ringing. The Cold Mage gestured toward it with his left hand, and the instrument suddenly frosted over.

Then he looked at Jere Lee, and beckoned her.

She crossed the floor, stopped at his bedside.

High sums and manifold shapes streaming through his mind, the mage reached with both arms outstretched. She bent, accepting his embrace.

When he released her, she stepped away. Crystals of ice glistened on the back of her coat.

"I give thanks to you, who gave me comfort in my hour

of suffering." Slowly, with scrupulous respect, the mage bowed his head.

Jere Lee nodded hers, dubiously. "I'm gonna wake up any second in the park, aren't I? Me still in my lean-to. This is all a dream—isn't it?"

Squintik smiled, and glanced away, at Peter Musik and Money Campbell, at Herb Dierickx, all of them watching him with half-expectant, half-stupefied expressions. Then he locked his gaze on Jack, a Walker.

Who stepped promptly forward. And touching the wasp on his wrist bracelet, addressed Master Squintik with rigid formality (again): "I have rambled for you, dear master, and would now, with your willing permission, have Our Majesty-Most-Still hear of my long season's travels. This tired Walker has been to many places of interest and has chanced upon sights he must humbly leave to the great wisdom of his King and patron to interpret, according to the Order of Things."

After a moment's silence, Squintik said, "I rejoice that your wanderings have led you back to me, who bade you farewell when all the world was wet." The Cold Mage pressed his lips together. "But why are we speaking English?"

"For them," said Jack, nodding at the others. "It is the language they speak. And they are my Witnesses, if this be Ramble's End." He drew an anxious breath, held it. Then repeated, *"If* this be Ramble's End."

Squintik's face remained impassive, ceremonial. Then quietly, in English, he said, "I would have you know, faithful Walker, that Our Majesty-Most-Still bids you . . . come."

Jack slumped in relief. "Sad Agel will hear of my travels? You've arranged an audience?"

"It was done within hours of your flight to Kemolo. Much to the displeasure of the Great Mage of Manse Seloc."

"To the Void with his displeasure," said Jack. "To the Void with *him!*" (And to the Void, obviously, with protocol: he brusquely rubbed a hand across his mouth.) "I'm to see the King—at once?"

"According to the Order of Things."

"But how *soon?*"

"Soon, Jack, a Walker."

Jack's eyes flashed, then darted to the spiky ring on the mage's left hand. "We're to return—now?"

Squintik nodded.

The Walker's lips split into a broad grin.

So did Herb Dierickx's.

And Peter Musik's.

Automatically.

Frowning, Money Campbell put both palms firmly against Peter's chest and shoved. None too gently. "What the hell are *you* so happy about? There's somebody dead on the floor! We're inside a goddamn iceberg! The telephone is frozen! What the hell *is* this? How come they're talking like the Old Testament? Are we on *drugs,* or something?"

Gently, Peter touched three fingers to her lips. "Wait."

She batted his hand away.

"Wait! Wait yourself. I wanna go home! Go to sleep! Wake *up!*"

"You and me both, dear," said Jere Lee. "Only I don't think we're dreaming. We dreaming, Geebo?"

Peter shook his head.

"Drugs, then," said Money. "Gotta be drugs. Idiot drugs!" She spun around and began chopping at the sheeted ice with the edge of her hand—then flinched when she felt real pain. She hadn't expected that. "This is only, like, happening in our heads, right? Or maybe just in *my* head. The rest of you aren't here. Not really. None of you. It's Gene Boman. Gene Boman! Gene Boman did this! I'm a guinea pig. I'm in The Pharmacy and everybody's laughing—right? Taking notes. Making a video." Pushing her fingers through her hair, she frantically shook her head up and down, then from side to side. Hysterical again. Saying, "Right? Right?"

With a grimace, the mage had thrown off his bedsheet, and now, using Jack as a crutch, he stood.

Peter thinking, VIP from another universe—in a faded blue hospital gown with a black laundry stencil on the sleeve.

Beautiful.

Drawing himself up to his full height, Squintik, once again, looked slowly from Peter to Money (still muttering, "Right? *Right?*") and then to Herb Dierickx. "I give thanks to you," he said, "who kept company with this Walker and brought him safely to me, that he might tell his King and patron of sights he has chanced upon, according to the Order of Things. Dear hosts and Witnesses! I bid you come listen to the tale that he tells."

And with a violent downstroke of his left arm, he made the Cut.

Peter thinking, *Toby Tyler's Big Top Adventure.* He almost laughed. Then remembered traveling through central Mexico once, on a magazine assignment. Coming to some poor little village. Where there was a holy man, a sorcerer. A *so-*

called sorcerer. Who levitated himself briefly from a grass pallet. Peter remembered being totally—amazed. But compared to *this?* That was nothing. A cheap trick.

This, he thought, is *really* happening. Really.

Thinking, Into the Big Top.

Then thinking, *All* of us? No! *Why?*

"Because," said Jack, staring at him, "you've brought me to Ramble's End. You're a Witness. You're all Witnesses. It's an honor, Geeb, trust me." His voice had risen an octave, turned street-cocky again. "You get to watch me entertain the King. You *got* to watch me entertain the King."

Taking a step backward, Peter shook his head.

"I'm not going."

"No choice," said Jack. "Soon as that door opened in your head, I went in." He pressed his lips tightly together.

AND I'M STILL HERE, GEEB.

"Peter."

"I like Geebo better," said Jack. "Now, come." An edge in his voice.

On a live-wire edge, Peter resisted—and it was Herb Dierickx who went first, who went quickly, almost eagerly, through the Cut.

Thinking, Wait'll I tell Marge.

His hand still squeezing his side.

The moment he was gone, Money started slapping and kicking at the ice. Then, despairing, she slid to the floor.

"Enough!" said Jere Lee, tense and angry and looking the mage dead in the eye. "Either I'm going to wake up— right now!—or you're going to leave us in peace! Right now! Right . . . oh *damn!*"

Squintik extended an arm toward her. His left.

Jack slipped out from beneath his right.

And Jere Lee, who'd started to grin, took the Walker's place.

Became the mage's crutch, because he needed her.

She escorted him . . . away.

Leaving Jack and Peter Musik. Both staring down at Money Campbell, huddled against the ice. Staring at her with identically sad expressions.

"Leave us," said Peter.

"To your revenge?"

Peter stooped beside Money, then glanced back up at Jack: *"Our* revenge. Hers, too."

"There'll be time for that later. First share in mine."

"Not interested. I want—"

"I know what you want. I know *who* you want. But, Geebo: later. According to the Order of Things."

"Now."

"Come."

"No!"

"With a little . . . push, I can make you. And I will."

Peter laughed. Said, "Jesus." Said, "Christ." Said, "Yesterday I was Mr. X living in a cardboard box." Said, "Ignorance ain't so bad, when you think about it."

"Well, think about *this,* Geebo. You're going someplace *else. Truly* someplace else. There are two moons in the sky."

Money had stopped shivering. With her head slightly turned, and her chin on her shoulder, she looked at Jack. Sniffled once. "Really? Two *moons?"*

The Walker stooped. "Two. Count 'em." And winked at Peter.

But she turned away again.

Through the ice, on the other side of the doorway: commotion. Bleared faces trying to peer in.

Jack's hand tightened on Money's arm. "They're waiting for us."

He drew her to her feet.

"She's not going," said Peter, still in a crouch (then standing). *"We're* not going."

"Trust me, Geeb, I'll bring you back."

"This place," says Money, "is it, like, superscientific? With monorails and stuff?"

"Come see for yourself."

"Yeah?" The color was returning to her cheeks. "Hey, wait a second. How do they treat women?"

With his right hand, Jack separated the Cut. As though parting a theatre curtain.

Peter glanced behind him, then to his left, then toward the window wall.

Jack was waiting. One eyebrow cocked. That wise-guy smile. Those sharp, faintly yellow teeth.

Peter thinking, A bum that I met in the park. Yeah, right.

"Geebo?"

Peter thinking, There's a dead cop lying on the floor and a dead doctor outside and over there are two hunks of meat that five minutes ago were monsters from a monster movie, and this is all turning into the friggen Wizard of Oz. Thinking, No! Thinking, I'm in a *hospital* room, a very ordinary hospital room, there's the bed, there's the table, there's the chair, the TV, the toilet, the oxygen, the call-button; an ordinary everyday hospital room, yeah right, except it's also a glacier and in the air there's a long quivering slit, a *Cut*, through which three people have vanished. Thinking, No!

Thinking, No! No. But then, leaning toward Jack in resignation, he thought, I'll be back, Eugene, I'll be back.

Leave a light burning.

Then he went.

CHAPTER 24

THE MISSING

BRIAN TUCKER WANDERED the hospital roof. He'd gone up there forty minutes ago, not really expecting to find anything new, and he hadn't. Earlier, immediately after the security guard's body was discovered, the roof had been thoroughly searched, vacuumed and photographed. Still, Tucker had wanted one final look before he took off. Also: he'd wanted a quiet, empty place where he could throw up, which he'd done, twice. George Dokus was dead. His partner—his goddamn best friend!—was dead. Gutted. Like a, like a—

Oh Jesus. He felt his gorge rising again, but this time nothing came up. He just retched, bent over, till his knees felt weak. Then, listless, he prowled some more. Under the surgical dressing, his face still throbbed.

It was going on five o'clock, and dark.

A TV-news helicopter passed overhead, circled around and swung back.

Down below, a couple hundred people milled in front of the hospital.

The roof door opened and a uniformed cop came out. "Sergeant? You're wanted on the phone. Medical Examiner's Office." Tucker nodded, went inside, rode the elevator down to Two.

The corridor was still thronged with police officers and techs. The patients and hospital staff had been removed to another ward. For now they were all being kept in isolation. Tucker pushed through the crowd. He noticed Jere Lee Vance's shopping cart standing flush against a wall. He stopped and looked at it for a moment, then walked into the head nurse's office and took the call. Saying, "Tucker" while perching on the side of the desk.

"Brian? Mort Cherkas. Didn't actually expect to get you."

"Yeah, well, I'm still here."

"I'm real sorry about George. It's—"

"Thanks. What do you have?"

"The little guy in the caftan? That went out the window? Was strangled to death. *Afterward,* not before." Cherkas paused, clearly expecting Tucker to say something. But Tucker didn't. "Brian?"

"I heard you. What about the burns on his body? How extensive were they?"

"What burns? There *are* none, Bry. How come everybody wants to know that? This guy definitely wasn't burned. Was *not.*"

"Okay."

"What do you mean, 'Okay'? How come everybody thinks he burned to death?"

Tucker said nothing.

"Brian? You know there's some people from Washington been in here looking at the body?"

"That was quick."

"Brian? This guy? Who was strangled, not burned? I opened him up. Everything's normal inside except for one small thing. He's got two hearts."

"I'm not surprised."

"What?"

Tucker glanced across the office as a tall, sandy-haired man stepped inside and closed the door. "Anything else, Mort?"

"Not at the moment."

"You going to be there awhile?"

"Looks like it," said Cherkas. Then, lowering his voice, he said, "Brian? Come on. What *is* this? You wouldn't believe the rumors."

Tucker said, "Yeah, I would." Then he said, "Call you later," and hung up, turning toward the man who'd come in and was now standing with his back to the door. He was a little stooped, and thick around the middle, with a full, ruddy face, alert brown eyes, and a chin pitted with old acne scars. Tucker put him in his late forties. He was dressed in a charcoal-gray suit, the knot in his maroon tie no bigger than a pretzel nugget. He said, "Detective Tucker? I'm Blaine." Then he produced his ID.

Tucker's eyebrows rose. "Why?"

"Am *I* here? Hey, who you gonna call? It was either us or Ghostbusters. And we're cheaper, I would think."

Tucker merely stared at him. Watched him take out a pack of unfiltered cigarettes, shake two up.

"You smoke?"

Tucker shook his head.

"Mind?" He was already lighting one as he asked that. "Some people do, these days. Mind."

"I was just talking to the Assistant M. E. He said you guys had already been around to see him."

"Well, you hear about a hospital room that turns into an igloo . . ."

"Is *that* what happened?"

Cocking his head, Blaine regarded Tucker for several seconds, then shrugged. "Maybe not, huh?"

"I'm just asking. It's been almost four hours and so far as I can see, there hasn't been a single reporter upstairs. Just outside."

"Exactly. Only story they got is some guy falling out a window. With a bit of added fun about his hand running away. Unconfirmed, of course."

"Won't work, Blaine. Must be a hundred people saw what happened up here."

Blaine exhaled a plume of smoke, then rubbed out his cigarette. "Yeah, I know. It *won't*. But what the hell. Everybody's seen *Gremlins*, nobody gives a shit anymore. Monsters in the hospital? Big deal—what's tomorrow's weather? I don't think we have to worry too much about panic in the street."

"Who's worrying?"

Smiling, Blaine pulled the chair away from the gray metal desk and sat down. He folded his hands behind his neck, leaned back. Then he leaned forward again and said, "I know this is going to sound funny—what with everything that happened and all, but you know what's driving me nuts the most? Where's the toy panda?"

"Where's the *hand?*"

"Yeah. That, too. But the panda. All those people in the lobby saying they saw the guy with the five kids walk by dragging a stuffed panda. It went into that elevator. Where'd it go?"

Tucker shook his head. "You know about the blonde girl?"

"Sure. What happened to the panda, and where the hell did *she* come from? Crawling out into the maternity ward." He reached for another cigarette, but changed his mind. "Speaking of that girl. I understand you saw her."

"Yeah, I did."

"With the guy that everybody describes as 'the bum.'"

"Yeah."

"And she went into Room 214, with the others. Just before—"

"The door froze over." Tucker seemed to wince.

"At that time—when you saw her—you were where, exactly?"

"About ten feet away, flat on my ass."

"This was before or after you shot one of the . . . animals?"

"After. I think. Yeah, it was after."

Blaine was staring at him, not unsympathetically. "And by then you'd already been sliced across the face."

"You're thinking *I* should've gone into that goddamn room. Well, you're right. I should've." He'd clenched both hands, but when he noticed Blaine staring at them, he opened them.

"The situation was pretty chaotic, no?"

"I'm a cop."

"You did your job. I'm just trying to get the picture, believe me. I'm not making any judgments, Brian."

"I should've been in that room."

Blaine stood up. "And if you had been? Where would you be now? Think about that?"

Tucker frowned at his open hands. The palms looked anemic.

"Seven people," said Blaine. "That's the general consensus? Seven people in 214? Brian? Detective Tucker?"

"Yeah," he replied distractedly. "Seven."

"The blonde girl and the bum. Names unknown. And George Dokus. And your old neighbor Mrs. Vance. Four. Who came to pay a visit to the patient, whom she referred to as Mr. —"

"Squintik."

"Mr. Squintik. That makes five."

"And Geebo makes six," said Tucker.

"That's what the Vance woman called him?"

"Yes. Geebo."

"And this Geebo was apparently the same man who was brought into the hospital sometime earlier. Who'd suffered a stroke."

"Jesus," said Tucker. "But yeah—apparently. That's how it looks."

"Except that this Geebo told three doctors that his name was Peter Musik." Blaine slipped a hand inside his jacket and came out with a small spiral notepad. Flipped it open. "I just got off the phone before I came in. Computer check on Peter Musik, with a k, turned up somebody that looks right. You said he was how old?"

"Late twenties. Early thirties."

Blaine nodded. "We got a guy named Peter John Musik, aged thirty-one, sort of a journalist. Freelance. Did a couple of movie-star biographies. A quickie book about the Hunt

Brothers. Lotta magazine stuff. Junk newspapers. *Enquirer,
National Star.* Last known address, Naples, Florida."

"This character looked more down and out than his pal.
Definitely a street person."

"So you said. And I guess you know what the doctors
said."

"Yeah. That he died. But then suddenly *wasn't* dead."

Blaine grunted, snapping the notepad closed. He put it
away. "What about number seven, this guy in the uniform?"

"Livery."

"Yeah? You got some people, I understand, swear it was
a soldier's uniform."

"Christ, no. I saw him. Guy was a doorman, a driver,
delivery man, something like that."

"What about the little girl in the scrub clothes?"

"I'm not even sure there *was* such a person. I didn't see
her."

"Several people did."

Tucker lifted a shoulder.

There was a long silence.

Then Blaine twisted his lips sideways, and threw up his
hands. "You know what? I think I'm going to suggest we let
the news guys come in. Show 'em the room, show 'em
where the ice used to be. Let nature take its course."

Tucker looked at him.

"Because, frankly, Brian, I don't know what the hell
else to do."

"What about the animals?"

"What *about* them?"

"Where are they now?"

"Tell the truth, I'm not sure myself. But they're probably in the same place where we've been hiding all the dead

aliens that've crashed their UFOs since World War II." He smiled at Tucker's blank expression. "I'm making a joke, Brian."

"Yeah? Well, sorry, but I don't have much of a sense of humor today."

Blaine walked to the door. "You should go home."

"Soon."

"I'm sure we'll talk again." With a nod, Blaine left, and Brian Tucker pushed himself away from the desk. He walked to the window and looked down. The parking lot was jammed with vehicles, and he wished to God it had been cordoned off hours ago. At least some of the people who'd vanished from Room 214 must've come to the hospital by car—but *which* car, which *cars?* No way to tell. Not yet. And probably not till tomorrow morning, at least.

I *should've* gone into that room, he thought.

But like Blaine said: if I had, where would I be now?

Jesus: where?

Where *were* they?

Six people—vanished.

And one butchered.

He pressed his hot face against the cold window, and wept.

CHAPTER 25

WHITE LIMOUSINE

BY FIVE THAT AFTERNOON, Eugene Boman had spent nearly twelve thousand dollars at the Alexander Gallery on Disney posters, Hanna-Barbera animation cels, a Mod Squad lunch box, and a horse bridle used in several episodes of "Mr. Ed" during the 1965–66 television season. He felt ebullient—till he'd written a check and collected his goods. Then he felt depressed. But that wasn't unusual: he always did, afterward. A bit silly, too, and vaguely guilty. He'd look at the stuff that he'd coveted and think, What the hell do I want with this crap? What's the *matter* with me? It seemed to Boman that, with all of his money, he should be collecting grander things. Like islands, for instance. Some billionaire *he* was. His grandfather had endowed Old Tappan University, his father, a couple of children's hospitals in the Midwest. And here he was, glomming pieces of acetate with Lippy the Lion and Wally Gator painted on them. Thing was, though, he *liked* cartoon stuff, old movie stuff, TV memorabilia.

Because, he supposed, they reminded him of his brief

childhood. Of those few—but long and pampered—years before he'd turned his full attention to the family business. He'd gone—overnight, it always seemed—from Saturday matinees, Zorro capes, and Matchbox cars to marketing seminars, dark suits, and financial reports. By the age of fourteen, he was part of it. In the company. One generation following the other, according to the order of things.

Clutching his packages (Mr. Ed's bridle in a huge manila envelope, the cels and folded posters between two pieces of taped-together cardboard, the lunch box jammed under his arm), Eugene Boman stepped outside. It was dark by then, and cold. The temperature had dropped twenty degrees since noon. A sidewalk Santa Claus—the first he'd noticed this season—was vigorously ringing a bell over his black collection pot. Boman glanced around, expecting to see the Cadillac. Didn't, and swore under his breath. Deer-ick! Where the hell is Deer-ick?

Then he remembered.

Thinking, Christ, how could I've forgotten?

That he'd sent Herb Deer-ick to fetch Money Campbell —who'd gone off (the dizzy thing!) looking for Peter Musik. Fetch her, bring her back to Boman's apartment, and make damn certain she stayed put. Which, of course, was why there was no limo to collect him now. In many ways, Deer-ick was an oaf, but he was dependable. Boman had no doubt that he'd found Money, and that she was uptown waiting for him. But what the hell was it going to be like when he arrived? Confronted her? Ah jeez.

He'd hoped that the whole Peter Musik fiasco was behind him; thought that Money Campbell had finally come to believe what he'd told her back in early September: that Peter Musik had had a nervous breakdown, and that he,

Boman, instead of calling the cops and having the crazy man thrown in jail for assault (not to mention for theft of documents, invasion of privacy!) had taken pity on him, given him a handsome sum of money, advised him to use it for psychological counseling, then put him on an airplane back to Florida, where he'd come from.

But thanks to Dierickx, Eugene Boman had now been exposed as a liar. And worse. Much worse.

Which made him feel pretty damn . . . funny. Make that sick to his stomach.

Here were these two people—one driving him around every day, the other sleeping with him almost every night—and both of them now considered him to be one ruthless son of a bitch. A bad guy. Who'd crushed some down-on-his-luck journalist and thrown him to the dogs. Yeah? Well, there were two sides to every story, and Boman just didn't see himself as a bad guy. No way. He'd tried to reason with Peter Musik; what he'd *really* tried to do, that day at Scroon Lake, was buy him off. And what had Boman gotten for his trouble? A bleeding head. The madman had struck him with a fireplace shovel!

Okay. So maybe it *was* pretty horrible, drugging Peter the way that he finally had, pumping him so full of Blue Mark that not a speck of his memory—not a mote of his sleazy identity—remained. No argument there, it *was* grotesque. But if you looked at it from Boman's point of view, it was a rather *tempered* (even compassionate!) response.

After all, Major Forell had wanted to *kill* the guy.

When you got right down to it, this was *all* the Major's fault. Absolutely.

There's your ruthless son of a bitch, he thought. Not me.

All that Boman had ever wanted to do with his life was

to make sure the family business wasn't ruined under his stewardship (because that would've been embarrassing) and to spend a few grand every month buying collectibles. Junk.

That was the *real* Eugene Boman.

No matter *what* Peter Musik had thought.

Or what Herb Dierickx and Money Campbell still *did* think.

The truth about the mysterious Boy Billionaire? He was more boy than billionaire. And always had been. Except for one momentary lapse in Switzerland.

Boman thinking again, as he hailed a cab, *There's* your ruthless son of a bitch. My goddamn father-in-law. The goddamn blackmailer.

Riding the elevator to his apartment, twenty minutes later, Boman kept trying to figure what he might say to Money Campbell—how he could play the scene. Earlier in the day, he'd been well satisfied with how he'd handled his chauffeur: friendly, then tough, then intimidating. That bit about *You'll be working for me the rest of your life, no matter how long that is.* Inspired! (He'd learned a few things from the Major, hadn't he? Yeah, well—unavoidable.) Should he try the same tack with Money Campbell? Maybe. He'd first have to see what kind of state she was in. But if she wouldn't listen to reason, or quail under his threats? *Then* what?

As he was unlocking his door, he felt a spasm in his chest.

What if—what if he walked inside to discover not only Money Campbell and Herb Dierickx, but Peter Musik, as well?

What if by some crazy accident, she'd actually found him?

You're not thinking straight, Gene, he told himself.

Peter Musik *couldn't* be here. Because if she *had* found him (unlikely as that was), the poor guy would be a vegetable right now, or dead.

Nevertheless, Boman entered his apartment light-headed with anxiety.

Finding it dark, he panicked, and fumbled for the wall switch.

He called Dierickx's name, saying, "Deer-ick?" and waited. No response. His mouth was dry. Throwing his overcoat and collectibles on the couch, he went quickly from room to room—Jesus, what'd he think, they might be hiding, waiting to spring out at him? At last, he returned to the living room, and stood there with his hands on his hips. Then he glanced at the telephone, saw the message light blinking on his answering machine.

He'd had two calls, the first from Major Forell, just checking to make sure that Boman was coming down to Leesboro. "I hope you're already on your way, Eugene, but if not and you get this message, don't bother phoning me, just come. Come immediately. We have a definite . . . situation here."

The second call was from Boman's wife. "Eugene? Daddy tells me you're coming down this way this evening. If you plan to stay with us overnight, I'd appreciate your letting us know. Just—let us know. Thank you." There was a pause, then: "Eugene? When *you* spoke to Daddy, did he, did he sound a little . . . did you think he sounded—? Oh never mind. Forget it. If you're planning to stay with us tonight, please call first." Click.

Gene Boman stared at the machine, listening to the whir of the tape as it rewound.

God, he thought, Edie's a bitch. *Please call first.* How'd I ever—?

He threw himself on the couch, rubbed a hand across his face. What did Forell mean, a "definite situation?" What the hell did *that* mean? Had somebody died? Again? Another guinea pig? Another "testee"? Jesus Christ, why didn't that man just leave him alone? Boman wasn't interested. He'd given Forell all the Idiot Drugs there were, all the formulae —why didn't the bastard just play with them to his heart's content and leave Boman out of it? Lord. Well, he'd have to go, no choice, he wasn't a free man. He'd have to drive downstate and see about this "definite situation." But how could he leave now, with this *other* crazy business still up in the air? Where's Deer-ick? Where's Money? Why aren't they here?

Boman checked his wristwatch: it was almost five-thirty. Five-thirty, and he wasn't even hungry yet. Not only was he not hungry, his stomach was sour, tied up in knots.

He kicked off his shoes and stretched his legs. Then he stood up again and went and got one of the parcels from the gallery and carried it back to the sofa. Seating himself again, he dumped the horse bridle into his lap, ran a finger over the crownpiece, down the cheekstrap, across the noseband. Then he almost laughed out loud. God, he really *was* the world's dullest billionaire. What was Donald Trump doing right now? He sure as hell wasn't sitting alone in his apartment feeling up Mr. Ed's bridle.

Boman thought, I don't know how to do this, do I?

I don't *deserve* to be rich.

I'm such a—

Tossing the bridle away, he straightened up, refusing to let himself indulge in yet another attack of the unworthies, which he'd suffered from nearly all his life. Well, since adolescence.

But damn, a guy with his kind of money, he ought to have a butler, a cook—there should be a fabulous meal waiting. But all that stuff just made him uncomfortable, self-conscious.

And then he was thinking of Edie. And of the big house ten miles from Scroon Lake and seven miles from the Major's farm, the house that Boman owned but never considered *his*. Or *theirs*. Just hers. That monstrosity of a place had a butler, all right, and servants galore. A cook with three assistants. And Boman hated every minute that he had to spend there. No, that wasn't entirely true. He did enjoy seeing his two kids, the boys. He briefly considered calling them now. Then decided against it. He'd have to speak to his wife, and didn't want to. Don't worry, Edie, I won't drop in on you. Won't spend the night with you, God forbid.

Pressing his fingertips against his temples, he shut his eyes. His stomach was in turmoil, a fire burning in the pit. He decided to go get a couple of Digestabs. That was a chewable antacid marketed by Boman Pharmaceuticals. On his way across the living room, he stopped. Deciding that it was too damn quiet in the apartment, he found the remote and switched on the television.

The local news was on, an Hispanic reporter with a glossy mustache delivering his report in a deadly serious staccato. Another calamity in the big city. But that was to be expected, every day there were dozens. Fires, crane accidents, crack-related slaughters. Boman hardly ever paid attention to that junk; how could anybody, after a while? No, it wasn't the reporter's tone of voice or grim expression that made him flinch, and then go walleyed, staring at the projection screen. It was what he glimpsed *behind* the reporter, who was broadcasting live from a parking lot at the scene of the—whatever.

It *couldn't* be. But it *was.* A white Cadillac limo. Vanity plates: G Boman.

He clutched his stomach.

The taxi driver was saying, "Maybe you wanna go to the Medical Center, instead? There's some kind of police activity at St. Vincent's. That's what it said on the radio."

Eugene Boman said, "I'm not *sick.* I'm not *going* to the hospital. I'm going to St. *Vincent's* Hospital."

"You got it, pal."

"Thank you." Boman sat back and sighed. Then he belched. Then he fished out a little tin of Digestabs from his coat pocket and chewed another one. His fourth—or fifth—since he'd turned off the TV set fifteen minutes ago.

His Cadillac was parked at St. Vincent's Hospital—what did that *mean?*

It *couldn't* mean . . . Peter, *could* it? She couldn't've found Peter Musik. *Could* she? No. Relax. It could mean anything.

What, for instance?

Another gas bubble dissolved in his stomach, and he belched again. "Excuse me."

"You're excused." The driver laughed.

In the East Twenties, traffic became congested, and rather than sit there in the cab, Boman decided to get out and walk the rest of the way to the hospital. From the television, he'd gotten only the vaguest idea of what was supposed to have happened there. Some man had fallen, or jumped, from a window. Apparently he'd been on fire. Possibly he'd *set* a fire, in one of the wards. God knows what the real story was. TV news, he thought. *Another* idiot drug.

Eugene Boman was terrified by the thought that the crazy man who'd jumped out the hospital window might've been Peter Musik.

No, he said to himself. No. She didn't find him, and he didn't remember who he was. Didn't, didn't, didn't. And besides, when you have a stroke you don't go jumping out windows. You just . . . have a stroke. Keel over. Turn to celery.

Yeah, but. But what if Peter had a slightly *different* reaction to Blue Mark than both of Major Forell's . . . *other* testees? That was possible, wasn't it? After all, the drug *was* a goddamn wild card. A goddamn horrendous wild card.

No, he thought. No. She didn't find him, and he didn't remember who he was, and there's a perfectly good explanation why that goddamn limousine is parked in that goddamn parking lot.

He stepped out of the wind and into the doorway of a small gay-and-lesbian bookstore, took his Digestabs from his pocket and chewed yet another one. His stomach was burning out of control. A man on *fire?* he thought. Then, with the taste of chalk in his mouth, he walked the rest of the way to the hospital.

There was quite a crowd out front, most of it comprised of teenaged boys gesticulating and grinning as they moved from one television camera to another. Boman spotted the same reporter he'd seen earlier, but he was no longer in the parking lot, he was on the hospital steps now, thrusting his microphone at a young blonde man with a large bandage on his face who'd just stepped through the front door. "Detective Tucker? Sergeant Tucker? Luis Velez, WTDR 'Eyewitness News.' We understand that you were personally acquainted with one of the women who disappeared?"

The detective wouldn't comment. He pushed his way through the crowd, passing within a foot of Eugene Boman, who was thinking, Disappeared? *What* women? I thought somebody jumped out a window.

Then he thought, What am I *doing* here?

He stood on his toes, peering left and right, trying to discover where the lot was where he'd seen his limo parked. Thinking, Jeez, maybe—maybe that stupid girl Money got herself mugged, walking around the Bridge District alone. Maybe *that's* how come the car is here. Herb took her for stitches, maybe. Maybe she *did* get mugged. It'd serve her right. Maybe she got mugged, that's all, maybe—

He felt a hand clamp his arm.

Whirling around, he confronted a short, thick-bodied woman in a blue parka. "Mr. Boman? Is Herbert with you? Is everything all right?"

He stared at her.

"I'm Herb's wife," she said. "We've met a couple times, you don't remember."

"Oh! Of course I remember, I just didn't expect to—how *are* you, Mrs. Deer-ick?"

"*Dierickx,*" she said. "Marge. And I'm not so good, Mr. Boman."

She still hadn't released Boman's arm.

"I've been going crazy ever since Herb called me. Did he call you, too?"

"Call? He *called* you?"

"From the hospital. This afternoon. Hours ago. About the accident."

Boman's heart fluttered. He had to swallow before he could speak. "What accident?"

"He didn't tell you?"

"I haven't heard from him since—noontime."

"Then what're you doing here?"

He shook his head. *"What* accident?"

"Oh, Mr. Boman, why won't they let me into the hospital? What *is* all this?" she said, quickly turning her head, indicating the crowd.

"What accident?"

"With the car. With *your* car. But he said it wasn't serious, *he* wasn't hurt, just the other man. The other man was hurt."

Eugene Boman's face was throbbing. And his tongue seemed slathered with mucilage. The rest of him had gone numb.

"Mr. Boman, he *really* didn't call you?"

He shook his head.

"I tried to ask him some questions, but he sounded so funny. Then I told him to hang up and I'd call him back, it was a pay phone, and I did, I called him back, but he just kept picking up the receiver and putting it down. I must've called him ten times. And then he said everything was all right—and then he didn't answer anymore. It took me an hour to get down here, I don't drive, and when I did—they wouldn't let me in, and look at all these police and all these cameras, and all these people, and I don't know *what* to think. I don't know what to *think.* I'm usually good in a crisis, I usually am, *really,* but—Mr. Boman? Mr. Boman!"

He'd pulled away from her and was walking quickly up the street, pushing through the crowd, a hand pressed to his stomach. Other man. *Other* man.

He was trying to remember his lawyer's phone number, but couldn't even remember his lawyer's name. Kurtzman. No, Kurtzman died. Klein? Is it Klein . . . ?

Other man. Other man. *Other* man.

It was Peter Musik. He knew it was Peter Musik. Who *else* could it be?

It could be *anybody* else. Anybody in the world.

No. It was Peter Musik. They found him.

And then? They'd brought him to the hospital? And then? He jumped out the window?

What accident? What accident with the car?

Boman couldn't think, couldn't think straight, he was in a panic, same as he'd been that night in Berne, in that hotel room that awful night years ago in Berne, Switzerland when the man, nothing but a pimp, blackmailing German pimp, came in with photographs, demanding thousands of dollars—how many thousands, who could remember now, and what did it matter, the man was dead. Had rotten teeth, spoke bad English. Was dead. Was Peter? Was *Peter* dead?

There was the parking lot. And there was the limo.

All out of breath, dots wheeling in his vision, Boman jogged to it and tried to open the driver's door. It was locked. But he had his own key. Of course he did, it was *his* car. You don't own a car and not have the key. You don't own anything and not have the key. Christ, he even had the key to the big house downstate. *Her* house. But he *owned* it. You don't own something and not—

"Mr. Boman! What're you doing here if Herbert didn't call you? Did the police call you? Mr. Boman!"

When he started to get in under the wheel, Marge Dierickx grabbed his coat sleeve.

"Mr. Boman! Why're you behaving this way?"

Eyes wide, he gaped at her. Why *was* he behaving this way? Inappropriate behavior. *Insane* behavior. He was—he was a rich man. Rich men don't act like this. No. But what about rich *boys?* Rich babies? Rich—

He pulled himself together. Best as he could. He'd handled Herb just *fine* this afternoon. He could handle this woman. He was a rich man. "Your husband," he said, "failed to return this car to me. As far as I'm concerned—as far as I'm concerned he stole it. And then just abandoned it. Here. I'm taking it back. Remove your hand. Your husband . . . is no longer working for me. Kindly remove your hand. Thank you." He slammed the door. Where's the ignition? Where the hell is the goddamn ignition?

She was banging on the window. "What's the *matter* with you? Are you crazy or something? There was an accident! He didn't *abandon* your car!"

Boman tried to fit the key into the cigarette lighter.

He finally found the ignition and started the engine.

The driver's door opened. Boman swung his red face around. "Mrs. Dierickx," he said, his voice suddenly as high as an acolyte's, "I'm warning you!"

But it wasn't Mrs. Dierickx. It was a blonde man with a bandage on his face. Boman recognized him. *We understand that you were personally acquainted with one of the women who disappeared?* Sergeant Something. Detective Something. "Having a problem?" he asked, leaning in. Then, before Boman could answer, he said, "Your car?"

"Yes, of course it's my car." He tried to put on the headlights and managed instead to turn on the wipers.

And then Marge Dierickx was saying, "My husband is this crazy man's driver, and he's in the hospital and nobody will let me in. Who are *you?*"

The blonde man with the bandage—Sergeant Something, *Detective* Something—looked at her. "Your husband is a chauffeur?"

"Was," said Boman, squirting the windshield with fluid.

"*Your* chauffeur, sir?"

"*Former* chauffeur."

"Does he wear a uniform?"

"Yes," said Marge. Then, "What's the matter? Is he all right? Do you work here? Why won't they let me in?"

"About fifty years old?"

"Fifty-six," said Marge, her voice suddenly toneless, full of dread.

"I can get you into the hospital," said the man with the bandage. "And I think that *both* of you should come along."

"Why?" said Boman.

"Please."

Boman snatched the door and yanked it closed. That time he locked it.

"Sir?"

Boman pressed his foot down on the accelerator and the car roared. But the transmission was still in Park.

"Sir. I'm a policeman. I think you should come on out."

"If you have any questions for me," said Eugene Boman, "you'll have to speak to my lawyer. His name is Kurtzman. I mean *Klein.*"

He put the limo in Drive, and drove.

He was covered in sweat. Just covered in sweat. Same as he'd been that night in Berne, in that hotel room—afterward, after he'd . . .

And same as he'd been that afternoon last September in the house at Scroon Lake, when that son of a bitch Peter Musik came in and told him, "Screw your Huckleberry

Hound sand pail, tell me about the Idiot Drugs and you'd better tell the truth, Eugene, I know most of it already," and Boman said "How much do you want?" and Musik said, "You bastard," then hit him, "you *bastard,* how many people are dead, how many *testees?"* and Boman started to whimper, same as he'd done in Berne, whimpering and sweating, and Peter just stood there over him with a fireplace shovel in his fist, saying, "Tell me the truth, Eugene, tell me about the Major," and Money Campbell ran out of the room, and then Herb Dierickx came *into* the room—with the Major, and the Major had a gun.

The Major.

Hunched over the steering wheel, not sure whether or not he'd just turned up a one-way street going the wrong way, Eugene Boman thought, The Major will know what to do, he'll know what to do, and *this* time, this time I *promise* I won't give him a hard time, whatever he wants to do is fine, whatever he decides to do will be fine, just fine, will be fine with me.

And then, one hand on the wheel, the other in his coat pocket searching for the Digestabs, he made a sharp turn into Avenue B, steering the limo toward the Bridge District, toward the Cushing River, toward Leesboro, toward The Pharmacy.

At least he *hoped* he was steering it in that direction.

South, right? The bridge is south?

Right?

CHAPTER 26

SOMEPLACE ELSE

IT WAS NOT AT ALL A COMparable situation, but even so, Herb Dierickx kept thinking of the only time he'd been to Chicago. Marge's favorite cousin Billy, a buyer with Sears, had been transferred there and kept pestering them to come visit. This was ten, eleven years ago, long before Herb starting driving for Eugene Boman, back when he was still doing heavy construction. Before he had that fall and decided to find some less dangerous way to make a buck. Anyway. Marge had never been farther west than Philadelphia and wanted very badly to make the trip. So why not go? It wouldn't cost them much, just plane fare and spending money. But what happened? Two hours after they arrived in Chicago, Herb became violently ill with some monster flu. Spent three days in bed. And the rest of the week? He was so rocky and weak that he hadn't truly enjoyed one touristy thing he'd done. Chicago? Was a blur. He'd been there, yeah, but he'd missed it. Woozy memories were all that he'd brought home. All that he had.

And he was afraid the same damn thing was going to spoil *this* trip.

Here he was, *wherever* it was, sitting on the dirt floor of a dim, low-ceilinged wooden building, not much more than a shack, and he was feeling so flat-out lousy, so feverish and miserably sore that getting up to investigate his new surroundings was simply out of the question. He was afraid to move. The slightest shift in position caused a breathtaking twinge in his left side, under the makeshift bandage. He remembered the agony he'd gone through in '79 following his gall bladder surgery; *this* pain was like *that* pain, though perhaps—just perhaps—not *quite* as bad.

And then he wondered how come he kept trying to connect what was happening now to other experiences. That weren't at *all* comparable. Going to Chicago. Having his gall bladder out. Maybe so this wouldn't feel so scarily strange? Yeah, maybe. That made sense, didn't it? Sort of?

It was ten past two, according to his watch. That would be two in the afternoon, home time. But that didn't jibe with the time of day here. Here, it seemed to be early morning. A weak pink light, full of dust motes, was coming through the open doorway. Outside, the ground sloped away, was grassy, the grass tall, anemic green. Herb thought that if he had to describe that particular green, he'd say it was the color of lima beans. Yeah, he'd compare it to lima beans. That would be the comparison he'd make. . . .

He drew a long breath, which only made him clack his teeth and grind them. Whoa. Then he shut his eyes and tried to nap; did. And dreamed he was racing up the front steps of his little house with the beige vinyl siding, and there was Marge excited to see him, and he said, "Wait'll I tell you where *I've* been! You won't believe it!" But she wasn't smiling, she was very cross, saying, "If you were going to drive Mr. Boman to Leesboro, why didn't you *tell* me at least?" And Herb said, "Leesboro! Hey Marge, I've been to another *planet!*" and then she looked stricken, reaching out and touching his forehead with a cool hand, saying, "You still have a fever, but it's definitely gone down."

Only it wasn't *Margie's* voice, and Herb said, "What?"

Squatted close by, the woman with the lined, haggard face asked him, "Are you feeling any better?"

Herb blinked, shaking away the dream, coming awake. "Yeah. I think." He moved gingerly, trying to sit up. The soreness had diminished, a fraction, but his head suddenly buzzed.

"You should probably try to walk around a little bit, Mr. Dierickx. *Herb.* It's the best thing."

"Not . . . yet. Okay?"

Nodding, she got up. "But soon." Then she went and stood in the open doorway.

Herb inclined his head, trying to see past her. "What's going on?"

When she turned around, she was smiling. "What a question!" Then she laughed. "You're asking *me?*"

They looked at one another for a long moment. "Where is everybody?" Herb said.

"Down by the lake."

"There's a lake?"

"Yes. Quite a big one. The water is black."

"No!"

"Black as oil."

"I gotta see that."

"Yes. Why don't you get up right now and see it?"

"Later, okay?" He touched his bandage, and only then

realized what it was: a scrap of the shirt the trampy looking guy had been wearing. Jack's shirt. Jack. The tramp's name was Jack. Yeah, right. He remembered, now . . . coming through that slit in the air; stumbling, light-headed. Then passing right out. Here. Waking to see the tramp hunkered beside him. Then passing out again. Waking. Passing out. Waking. Napping . . . "Hey, miss? I'm really gonna be all right?"

"Oh sure. And please: not *miss*. My name is Jere Lee."

"No infection—you don't think? Jere Lee?"

"You're going to be fine."

"Man," said Herb. "I sure hope so."

"You thirsty? There's a well. I can get you some water."

"Is it black?"

"Gee, I don't know. Shall I go and find out?"

"No," he said quickly. "That's . . . all right. Don't leave me. Okay?"

"I'll be back."

"Hey—Jere? Where's everybody else?"

"On the beach." She glanced that way.

"Doing what?"

"Just standing around. I think we're all—waiting. For something."

Herb opened his mouth to speak again, but changed his mind. He pressed his lips together until they were white. A shudder ran through him. How come—how come he no longer felt that everything was all right, okay? How come? He looked at his left hand, where the wasp had stung him. The swelling had gone down. It wasn't red anymore, and it wasn't tender. He lay there on his back, breathing heavily.

· · ·

From the little wooden shack, Jere Lee followed the edge of the grassy hill that rose from the beach and then walked past a corral where there was plenty of fly-caked dung but no animals. The well stood about twenty yards beyond, near woods. It looked like an old-fashioned wishing well—the big round fieldstones, the peaked roof, the hand crank, the wooden bucket dangling from a thick rope; it actually looked like the wishing well in *Snow White and the Seven Dwarfs,* she thought, which seemed kind of appropriate.

Letting the bucket down, she leaned against the wall and watched Jack pull up clumps of grass from the hillside. Once his arms were filled, he carried them down to the cove. Then he dug a pit in the beach sand and tossed them in. Then Master Squintik, still dressed in his backless hospital gown, pointed both index fingers and the grass caught fire and burned with a bright green flame, its smoke drifting across the lake and toward the distant city that was just becoming visible in the early-morning sun.

Early morning. Well, it *felt* like high noon—like high noon in high summer. Although she'd taken off her coat and watch cap and a couple of ratty sweaters, Jere Lee was still uncomfortably warm. *Hot.* It must've been ninety degrees, at least. And the humidity was brutal, so bad that her hair had turned frizzy. And the midges! Were infuriating. There were clouds and clouds of them, whirling everywhere. Midges and flies and mosquitos. Delightful place.

She drew the bucket from the well, and although the water wasn't black, like the lake, it did look a little . . . funny. Cloudy. Dark-gray. But what the hell. It was cold. She splashed her face and wrists, and drank liberally. Then, hearing footsteps behind her, she turned, and there was

Geebo, Geebo and the young blonde girl, whose pretty face was now all puffy and purple. A mess. The poor thing. Was her name *really* Money? What kind of parents would call their child *Money?*

Though she knew it was a dumb question to ask at a time like this, nevertheless Jere Lee said, "Is Money your real name?"

"Monica," said the girl, smiling. " 'Cept I used to say it *Mun*-ica, when I was a baby and stuff. Then everybody started calling me that, I guess it was cute. You know? Then it got to be Munny. But I'm the one started spelling it m-o-n-e-y. In high school." She smiled again. "It's kind of a dopey name, yeah? But it fits," she said, then snorted through her nose. "Ohh, that water looks gross. You didn't *drink* it, did you?"

"What," said Jere Lee, with a mild flutter in her stomach, "you don't think I should've?" She glanced at Geebo, but he merely shrugged. He seemed preoccupied—had since they'd all arrived. Jere Lee tried speaking to him earlier, but all he'd say was, "My name isn't Geebo, it's Peter." Peter? How'd he get to be Peter all of a sudden?

"Could I call you Monica?" said Jere Lee. "Would you mind?"

"No. I *guess* not. Hey no, if you *want* to." Then she said, "Were you named after Jerry Lee Lewis?"

"Hardly. I'm afraid I predate Jerry Lee Lewis. *My* name is really Jeremia."

"No kidding. What, like Jeremiah? Only -mia? Hey, that's cool. That's cool. That's *nice.*"

Then she looked at Jere Lee and narrowed her eyes and said, "Are you real?" and Jere Lee, with a rush of pity for this poor, sweet, damaged girl, replied, "I *think* so, dear, yes."

Geebo—Peter—was staring down at the fire on the beach, which seemed at last to be dying out. Staring, too, at Squintik and Jack, a Walker, who'd gone to the water's edge. He pulled on his bottom lip, meditatively, then flicked his gaze to the low white city in the distance.

"Well," said Jere Lee, "it's not Fort Lauderdale, but at least we're not freezing."

Geebo (Peter! *Peter*) rubbed his chin, then turned to her. "Lostwithal," he said.

"What?"

"The name of this place. Lostwithal."

She frowned. "Lostwithal?"

"No," he said. "Not *lost. Los.* Rhymes with *dose.*"

Her eyebrows shot up, and simultaneously she and the girl began to laugh. And they went right on laughing, the tears springing from their eyes and running down their cheeks—laughing till, suddenly, Peter (Geebo; *Peter*) said, "For Christ's *sake*, shut up!"

Jere Lee and Money Campbell fell instantly quiet.

"What's the matter with you two?" he said. "Get serious."

"We *are* serious," said Jere Lee, bristling. "We're seriously coping—aren't we, Monica?"

The girl looked puzzled for a moment, but then nodded vigorously. Yeah. Seriously coping. *Yeah.*

Jere Lee unknotted the well bucket, turned to go.

"I'm . . . sorry," said Geebo. Said *Peter.* Oh, forget it, thought Jere Lee: she liked Geebo better. Which was peculiar, since she'd always *loved* the name Peter. If she'd had a boy, she would've called him Peter. Peter Vance. Good solid name. Not that she had any regrets that both her children were girls. Regrets she had by the truckload, but none that her children were daughters.

When she returned to the tiny flat-roofed shack, Jere Lee discovered that Herb Dierickx had pulled himself to his feet and was taking some tentative baby steps.

"Well, good!" she said. Then, lifting the bucket: "And here's your reward."

Herb's eyes suddenly widened, bulged, and he stared at her. "What? *What* did you say?"

She pulled a face. "I said, here's your water. I brought you some water. Ignore the color, it's delicious."

His white face paled further. He took a step backward, toward the wall. *"What? What are you saying?"*

Jere Lee set down the bucket on the dirt floor. "Herb? Do you have a fever again?"

"Jesus!" he said and pushed a hand through his damp hair. "You're whistling! Like *them!"*

"Like *who?* What are you talking about?" He was giving her the creeps, this crazy behavior, the way he was staring. In distress, she touched several fingers to her lips, and found them pursed as an old drawstring bag. Pursed as though to—whistle. "Herb?" she said, and realized that her tongue was flat on the floor of her mouth, that her lips had stayed bunched.

Herb continued to stare as though she'd gone crazy.

Then, carefully, after having drawn her lips against her teeth, she said, "Herb? *Herb?"*

"Yes?"

And she slumped, tingling with relief. "You can . . . understand me?"

"Yes—now."

"God," she said.

"*What?*"

Then, enunciating like some old-time diction teacher, she said, "God, what is going *on?*"

"I don't know," said Herb. "But you came in here—whistling."

"I was *talking* to you."

"Whistling."

She dropped her eyes to the bucket. Then looked up and met Herb's steady gaze. "It's the water," she said, laughing. "It's the water! Boy, could I've used some in junior high school. I flunked Spanish twice."

And Herb, blinking, said, "*What?*"

Peter Musik sat down on a hummocky mound of dark sand. He'd taken off his flak jacket and sneakers and socks and rolled up his jeans. Leaning forward, he crossed his arms on his knees. Man, it *was* hot. As Naples, Florida, in July.

Money was wandering up and down the cove, every so often stopping to collect stones and pebbles, which she'd fling violently into the black lake.

Seriously coping? Maybe Jere Lee is, Peter thought, but I don't know about *her.*

She was still moving in and out of a daze, muttering to herself, even—and this gave him chills in the moist heat—singing old Beatles songs in a low, uninflected, almost *dead* voice. "Hey Jude." "Baby, You Can Drive My Car." He'd been trying to talk to her for almost an hour, but every time he mentioned Eugene Boman, any of *that* stuff, she just went blank, or stiff, or laughed too loud. Way too loud.

"Hey, Pete?" she called to him now. "Pete! Is this really happening? Come on, tell the truth."

He sighed, then stood up and brushed sand from the seat of his jeans. "It's happening," he called. "Really."

"You sure? Maybe we should pinch each other." She laughed again, that scary laugh, and stared down the beach, at Jack, who'd drenched the fire ash with lake water and was stirring it with a twig, as Master Squintik looked somberly on. "You wanna come pinch me?"

"Sure," said Peter.

"Don't you *touch* me, you bastard! Don't come *near* me!"

He went to her anyway. But not too close. "Money . . ."

"You know, I got final *exams* in two weeks. What am I gonna do—blow a whole semester? Fifteen credits? Don't smile. Don't you *dare* smile. I swear to God, Peter, I'll rip your eyes out if you smile. It's not funny!"

"I'm sorry. It's *not* funny."

"I mean, *look* at this place. Would you look at this *place*? I'll say it's not Fort Lauderdale! Who *is* that woman, anyway? Is *she* real?"

"Money . . ."

"Where *are* we? And don't give me any los-rhymes-with-dose crap. Where *are* we?"

"Someplace else."

"Oh, thanks! You're such a smart guy. I guess that's how come I was so, you know, *attracted* to you. That, plus I was scared shitless you were gonna put me in the *National Enquirer*. Me and Fawn Hall, me and Jessica Hahn, me and—"

"Stop it." He reached and grabbed both her wrists. She didn't try to fling herself free, as he'd expected. Instead, she just looked at him, then lowered her eyes. "We're going to be all right," he said. "And then we're going home and take care of everything. Everything. Money?"

"I don't believe this. I don't care if you do, 'cause I don't. That guy I met in the park, when I was in your cardboard box—"

"What?"

"—he didn't put any magic spell on me, I don't believe in that shit, he was from Eugene, he was from that Major guy, and it wasn't any magic spell, he stuck me with a *needle* —he stuck me with a needle, that's what he did. That's what happened. We're not in any los-rhymes-with-dose *Princess Bride* baloney place—we're in The Pharmacy. Or *I* am. I don't know about you!" She sneered. Then, ignoring Peter, looking past his shoulder, toward the lake, she hollered, "You there, Gene? You watching? What was it? Some floperoo arthritis drug? Epilepsy drug? Leukemia? Mono? Some *mono* drug? Huh? Oops! Doesn't cure mono, but it'll give Money Campbell one hell of a psychedelic trip. Asshole! Can't even make drugs that work. That do what they're supposed to! Idiot! *You're* an idiot, Gene! With your Idiot Drugs. And you can't fool me! I know where *I* am!"

Peter was shaking her roughly.

"But so what're you gonna do now, Gene? *Eu*-gene? What a dumb name. *Eugene.* I *hate* that name. And I hate you! What're you gonna do now, *Eugene?* Huh? You can't get rid of me easy as you got rid of Peter. Nobody cared about Peter. Peter didn't have any family, Peter didn't have anybody that cared. You could just put *him* on the street and that's that. Who'd come looking? Nobody! Except me."

Peter let go of her wrists. His complexion had turned

white, his vision bleary. He said, "No." He said, "Money." He said, *"Listen* to me."

She continued to ignore him. And why not—he wasn't there. He simply . . . wasn't there.

"But you can't do that with me, *Eu*-gene. *I* got family, *I* got friends, I go to *college*—people are gonna miss *me!* And *you're* gonna get caught. Think you're not? Bullshit! You are, too! Are, too! You and that horrible Major For—"

She broke off with a gasp. Her eyes widened.

Staring at a flat barge that was coming down the black lake, toward the cove.

They were speaking losplit.

"The Keepsake," said Jack.

"It was this size, and no bigger?"

Squintik had cracked a limb from a dead tree and was leaning upon it, his long face drawn and tired. At his feet in the sand was the small crude figure that Jack, a Walker had shaped from sodden ash and pebbles and leaves of beach grass. "Just this size?"

"I didn't measure it, good mage. Considering the circumstances. But I would say it was this size, yes."

"Weeks have passed."

"But surely it's still an infant—still helpless."

"If what you saw in Tiedek is truly the Epicene of Our Schoolteacher's Saga, then it can never be helpless." He stared again at the wet doll, then exhaled. "Let it dry in the sun."

Jack nodded, the vaguest trace of a smile passing between his lips. Master Squintik noticed and craned an eyebrow. "His Majesty," said Jack, "will be . . . distressed to receive *this* Keepsake of my season's Ramble."

"And that is amusing to you?"

"No! No, I was just thinking of another gift I might have given him, for Keepsake. That would've *pleased* him."

Squintik was waiting.

"A fire extinguisher," said Jack with a grin. And lapsing into English.

"This, I believe, is more appropriate."

Jack said, "Indeed. Indeed. You are surely right." Then, chastened, he turned from Squintik and strode up the beach, to speak with Peter Musik.

"Well," said Peter, "nice of you to drop by. What's new in the walking business?"

Jack frowned, shook his head, spread his hands.

"I'm being sarcastic. You bring us all here to your very lovely garden spot, then just dump us? Be nice if you could spare a few minutes for us dopey Kemolons. Maybe explain a few things? Like *that*, for instance?" He pointed toward the barge, moving rapidly into the cove without sail, engine, oars, or poles. "I mean, are we being attacked, or what? I count twenty heads."

"Twenty-*one*."

"Twenty."

"Well, all right, Geeb. The twenty-first head *is* kind of tiny, I give you that." Jack put his thumb and first finger together, then separated them just the slightest bit.

"What's that supposed to mean?"

"Lita."

"The bee?"

"Christ, Geebo, it's a wasp, a *wasp*. Don't you know anything?"

"Don't *you?* Geebo was the bum that had a stroke. I'm Peter."

Jack rolled his eyes, as though the distinction were simply too silly even to talk about. "We are not being attacked," he said. "Those are friends. Lita's people."

"Oh sure," said Money Campbell, springing up suddenly from a motionless crouch on the sand. "Absolutely! And I love their robes! Doesn't *everybody* wear monk robes in Hobbit movies? Gimme a break! Hey, Gene? Gimme a break!"

Jack looked at her with a gloomy expression.

And Peter said, "Maybe you should sting *her*—might calm her down. Hey Jack? What do you think?"

"I think," he said, "that I liked Geebo better." Then he turned abruptly and walked up the beach to meet the barge.

They were telling each other all about themselves, in Losplit, but every few minutes they'd just crack up laughing, saying—whistling!—hey, would you *listen* to us, we sound like a pair of intelligent tea kettles! It was so *funny.* Herb said it was better than swallowing helium, and Jere Lee said, oh yeah, *much* better. "Have another drink?" she said.

"I don't know. Think we should?"

"Why not?"

"Right! Why the hell not!" And he tipped the bucket to his mouth, took a swallow, passed the bucket over to Jere Lee, then said—whistled—"We *tried* having kids, we would've *loved* it, we always *wanted* them, but we just weren't blessed. But we have our bowling to keep us busy, we're in a league, Marge and me, and we like going around to garage sales. I like to collect old clocks and old typewriters." He said "garage sales" and "typewriters" in English, and they both laughed. "And I collect the covers from old paperback books. But you said you had kids, right? How many?"

"Two," said Jere Lee. "Two girls. They're both grown."

"Any grandchildren?"

"One. A little girl. She's going to be eight."

"That's wonderful," said Herb.

And Jere Lee nodded. "Some more water?"

He held up a hand. "Not for me. Otherwise I'm gonna need a bathroom."

He said "bathroom" in English.

"Uh oh."

"What?" said Jere Lee.

"They mustn't have any bathrooms here."

And then they both started laughing again, Jere Lee saying, "No toilet paper?"

Saying "toilet paper" in English.

And then they were really laughing, which ultimately wasn't all that much fun for Herb, since it made his wound smart anew.

A few minutes later, after they'd both calmed down again and while Jere Lee was explaining the circumstances that had led up to her life on the city street, and Herb was saying, oh no, oh *no*, oh *jeez* (saying *jeez* in English), Master Squintik appeared in the doorway.

He was startled to find them conversing in Losplit, and they were startled to see him dressed now in a long black cassock with many buttons.

"How'd you get your clothes back?" said Jere Lee, but the mage didn't reply. He stepped slowly into the shack, then grunted when he saw the water bucket. "How's your leg? How's your head? Are you feeling better now, Mister Squintik?"

But she didn't say *mister*, she said *master*, she realized; she said *master*, in Losplit.

"I am well," said the Cold Mage. He was beginning to smile now, his glance skipping from the bucket to Jere Lee, to Herb, then back to the bucket.

"Hey," said Herb, "it's all right that we drank that, isn't it? It's not poison, is it?"

"How much did you have?" Squintik asked.

"A . . . bit," said Jere Lee. "Why?"

The mage shook his head. "Oh dear. I'm afraid you're going to turn into pigs," he said.

"Pigs!" said Herb.

But Jere Lee was smiling, at Squintik, who smiled back.

"Forget it, Herb," she said. "He's joking. He's joking! I like you, Master Squintik, you're okay. I'm glad we met."

"Yes," said the Cold Mage, "I too am glad." Then all vestige of amusement left his face, and his expression became somber again. "You must come down to the cove now. It is time we set off for Beybix."

"Beybix?" said Herb, "What's Beybix?"

"Our capital city."

"Can you see it from the beach?" said Jere Lee. "Is it *that* city?"

"It is that city."

"Well, that's not far."

"A day's travel."

"A day," said Herb. "Is a day . . . a *day?* Here? I mean —is it twenty-four hours?"

"You will find it no different."

"Well, *that's* a relief."

"Bring the bucket," said Master Squintik. "We shall have need of it." He went out.

"Beybix," said Herb. "Weird." Then he said, "Hey, Jere, you ever see those Conan movies? With Schwarzenegger?"

She smiled. "You carry the bucket and I'll carry you."

"I don't have to be carried."

"Just lean, then."

CHAPTER 27

THE MAJOR

BEFORE MAJOR FORELL had purchased it with money generously given to him by his son-in-law, the place had been a training farm for thoroughbreds with a solid, even celebrated, reputation in racing circles. Two legendary triple-crown champions had come from its stables. In fact, it was an amalgam of *their* names—Man o' the Hour and Lancelot—that had given the farm *its* name: Mancelot. Mancelot Farms. The name, in fancy gold-leaf script, was still posted on the front gate, but there wasn't a blood horse in any of its seven red barns.

Here was The Pharmacy.

At twenty minutes past ten, Eugene Boman arrived after having driven nonstop from the city with his shoulders hunched and his fists clamped tightly around the limo's padded wheel. Awkwardly, he rolled out of the car and approached the floodlit gate. There were two surveillance cameras mounted on poles. "Richard?" And there was a heavy-duty grilled speaker-box affixed to the gate itself. "Richard?" Usually, there was somebody standing guard—one of Richard's three cronies from the service. Gorman or Teasdale or Luks. But not tonight. "Richard?"

Boman felt yet another twinge of anxiety.

A definite situation, Forell had said. A definite situation.

"Richard?"

He flinched at the splat of static. "I'm in the main barn, Eugene. Come ahead."

Boman nodded and turned to go back to the car.

"Eugene? Walk in. The chauffeur can wait for you there."

"He's not with me. I'm alone."

There was a long pause before the Major's voice came again: "Then you may as well drive."

Thank you so *much,* Boman thought, climbing into the limousine. He waited for the gate to swing open. When it did, he gave the gas pedal some pressure. Nothing happened. Oh shit, he thought, I'm still in Park. Stupid car.

As occurred every time he was on his way to see the Major, Eugene Boman's stomach was gripped by cramps that took his breath. Some billionaire *he* was. Afraid of his own father-in-law. Some father-in-law!

Although the road to the barns was blacktopped, brilliantly lit, and not at all winding, Boman drove as if it were unpaved, unlighted, and treacherously twisty. He was stalling. Stalling, and thinking. Of how different his life would've been had he never gone to Berne as a callow eighteen-year-old and tried to act like a worldly-wise grownup. Grownup rich businessmen—Gene Boman's father excluded —always enjoyed the company of prostitutes on a business trip, didn't they? Well, *didn't* they? Yes, of course—of course! So he'd found one his second night, a blonde Italian girl with large breasts. Or rather she'd found him. Oh yes, *she'd found him*.

And to this day, *to this very day*, he couldn't figure out how those pictures had been taken. For God's sake—where was the camera? Where had the weasly little German shit been hiding? That son-of-a-bitch weasly German *shit*. Showing up at his room the next evening, spoiling everything. Asking for thousands of dollars. Saying in thickly accented English, "Your father would be very angry, you think?" Angry? Yes, the founder of the American Decency League and a lifelong railer against prostitution, pornography, abortion, even contraception, even the *bikini*—would be very angry; very angry, indeed. Frighteningly—ferociously—angry.

That son-of-a-bitch blackmailing German *shit*.

Boman thinking, I didn't *mean* to kill him. Then thinking, Yes. Yes, I did. I just—didn't think it would be so easy. Who'd imagine you could kill somebody, actually *kill* a man, with a Swiss-made, unavailable-in-the-United States Yogi Bear ceramic figurine? Jesus Christ.

Boman thinking, as he saw the main barn loom ahead, But you're scared, you're terrified of your father, you're only eighteen, you make a mistake, you should be able to put all it behind you. Especially if you—if you're *rich*.

And then he was remembering those terrible hours spent in custody of the Swiss police. But ultimately they were nice to him, considerate—once his father's lawyer had arrived from the States. *Very* considerate, very *gracious*. And it was a shame, they said, that such a despicable thug should break into young Boman's room—looking for valuables, of course. Certainly, Mr. Boman was justified in defending himself. But Mr. Boman, they said, please don't hold this against the Swiss. Eugene Boman said that he surely *wouldn't.* The man, after all, was *German.* And since the police hadn't found the photographs—Boman had torn them up and flushed them away—that was the end of it.

For many years.

Until Richard Forell came into his life. At that auction. Bidding against him. Introducing him to his daughter, afterward. Buying him a drink. Inviting him to lunch the following week. Telling him that Edie had found him . . . charming.

Boman could scarcely believe that. She'd found *him* charming? Indeed. Richard Forell saying, "Indeed she did. She *does."* And why, of *course* she'd be glad if he called her sometime. She'd be delighted. Delighted! Richard Forell saying, two months later, "I'm so delighted!" Then embracing Boman at news of the engagement. "I'm delighted!"

Eugene Boman parked the car and switched off the ignition, but didn't move to get out. He leaned over the wheel, staring bleakly at the huge barn, still thinking. Still thinking. But thinking now of the day, just a month after the wedding, when Richard Forell had come to see him at Boman corporate headquarters.

He was in his crisp military uniform, was carrying a manila envelope, and no, he said, nothing to drink, thanks. Then "Eugene," he said, "do you remember a chemist that used to work for you, named Trower?"

Boman said no, but then he scarcely knew *all* of his employees. Forell saying, "Naturally not, naturally not. But this fellow Trower works for us now—in development. And the reason I mention him is because of something that he happened to bring up recently in conversation. I thought it was fascinating."

Forell smiling, leaning forward, saying, "Trower was

telling us about what you people here refer to as—Idiot Drugs."

Boman had rolled his eyes, waved a dismissive hand. And said, "Our expensive failures."

"That's a relative term, isn't it?"

"*What* is—'expensive' or 'failures'?"

Forell smiling again, saying, "Failures."

Boman sat in the car, knowing that he should get out, that the Major would be annoyed at his dawdling, knowing that and not caring; thinking. . . .

At first, he'd assumed the Major was talking just to talk, asking about the Idiot Drugs simply because they were, as he'd put it, fascinating. Fascinating failures. Drugs with wild-card side effects. How could I've been so dumb? Stupid!

The Major had asked Boman to tell him about Aldo-phine, about Dorbitussen, about Tappedrin, about Aceto-phren. A few of the Idiot Drugs that Trower had mentioned.

Boman saying, "Made with the best intentions, Major."

Forell raising an eyebrow, Boman smiling ruefully, then saying, "A mouth-sore ointment, a nasal decongestant, a children's liquid cold medicine. Heart pills. Expensive failures. Dangerous stuff. But thank God we realized it in time."

The Major had sat back on the sofa, nodding, and Boman suddenly felt strangely . . . uncomfortable. He became positively unnerved when Forell started in again about that Trower man, the chemist. Who, apparently, had told his new employers *everything* about the Idiot Drugs from Boman laboratories. Forell saying, And does *this* one actually cause obesity? And *that* one persistent hiccups? Merrily ticking off side effects. Incontinence. Gastric inflammation. Impotence. Miscarriage. Fetal deformation. Deafness. Loss of smell. Of taste. Of hair. Exhaustion. Depression. Severe Psychosis.

Boman, dry-mouthed by then, nodded reluctantly—yes, yes, impotence, yes, deafness, loss of smell, yes, depression, yes, psychosis, yes; *yes.* "But this is all very confidential, of course, Major. You realize that. They'll never see the light of day, I can assure you of that. And I must say that I'm shocked at this man Trower's breach of confidentiality. Of ethics."

Forell had merely smiled, but then he'd jumped to his feet, clearly excited. Pacing Boman's office, he'd suddenly, and bizarrely, started rattling on and on about certain freedom fighters in various parts of the world—in the Middle East, in Africa, in Central America. Brave men, he said, courageous patriots fighting against tyrannical left-wing governments, giving their all for democracy, but financially strapped because the goddamn U. S. Congress, the *treasonous* U. S. Congress refused to fund them adequately. To fund them at all, in many cases. Heroes, Forell kept saying. Heroes. Heroes left high and dry.

Boman listened quietly, but he'd never been interested in politics, and he certainly wasn't interested in "freedom fighters" and at last he said, "Richard? What on earth are you talking about?"

And Forell had said, "Oh—about nasal decongestants, mouth-sore ointments. Heart pills."

And Gene Boman said, "Don't be foolish—no."

He remembered this, he would *always* remember this: The first thing he'd said was, "No."

Regardless of what he'd done later, he'd first said, "No."

"No," he said, but Major Forell simply ignored him.

"Think about the wars of liberation we could win. With a cold tablet."

Forell saying "We."

Boman saying, "No." Saying, "That's ridiculous. And illegal."

But suddenly Forell's face had changed expression, become scornful. "Don't say that, Eugene. Don't say illegal. Don't say that to me as if you were the unblemished *emblem* of lawfulness. Don't say that, Eugene. Just . . . don't," and he'd touched a finger to Boman's lips, smiled cruelly, then dumped several photographs from his manila envelope. Newly developed photographs made from rather old negatives.

And the craziest thing was, Boman's initial reaction was this: How could he have let me marry Edie if he'd known about . . . these. About that. About . . . the German.

Boman was speechless. Forell wasn't. He'd talked on and on, about there being no statute of limitations on murder, *even in Switzerland,* and about how he was certain that the Berne police would be interested, *even after all this time,* in the *real* story of what happened that evening in 1979 in a very rich American's lovely hotel room.

Boman remembered asking, in a high, constrained voice, "How did you get these?"

Forell laughed. "Eugene, Eugene, I'm a professional. You're an amateur."

And Boman, feeling as though he were sinking, just nodded.

"I'm a man, Eugene. And you, I'm afraid, are still a boy. So! Shall we discuss when you might possibly have our chewable cold tablets—*et cetera*—ready for delivery?"

Boman nodded. Sinking, sinking. . . .

"Eugene!"

The Major rapped harshly on the driver's window. "Eugene, what the hell!"

Boman flinched, then managed a smile. "Hello, Richard," he said, then opened the door.

The Major was a thick-bodied—burly—man of fifty-six with short, iron-gray hair, an unlined face, and Hollywood-blue eyes. He was wearing a plaid hunter's jacket, dark corduroy trousers, and heavy boots. He was also, Boman noticed, wearing just one glove, a yellow work glove, on his left hand.

"I was surprised that no one was at the gate," said Boman. He'd always thought that was stupid and unnecessary—a round-the-clock sentry—but the Major still liked to play soldier. And his cronies humored him. Well, why not—they were being paid enough. As Boman knew, since he was, via some artful bookkeeping dodges, their paymaster. "You've made some changes?"

The Major scowled, then gripped Boman by the elbow and started leading him toward the barn. "Teasdale and Gorman are no longer with me."

"Why?"

"And Luks is . . . away."

"Richard. What's going on?"

"If you'll come the hell inside, I'll show you." He chuckled low in his throat, and Boman was suddenly terrified. When should he tell him about Peter Musik? *Should* he tell him about Peter Musik? Well, of course, he *had* to, he simply had to, but . . .

Later.

Stepping into the barn after the Major, Boman took a deep breath and held it. He hated this place, he *loathed* it. Even more than he loathed the house where Edie lived. In

Edie's house he'd wince at the mingled smells of pool chlorine and stale cigarette smoke and French cooking, but here, Christ Almighty, *here* he'd practically gag on the infinitely more vivid odors of human fear and misery, illness, despair. It was a horror, and he was part of it.

No. No, he was not! Was *not!* He only footed the bills, provided the formulae and the drugs, the syringes and the alcohol, the encephalographs and the electrocardiographs—but he did nothing else. Not one thing else. He was a victim, he *was*—as much a victim as any of the Major's testees strapped to their beds in those white-tiled chambers, below. He *was!*

Forell lugged up the heavy iron door that opened to stairs leading to the barn cellar.

"Do we have to—go down?"

The Major laughed through his nose. "Yes, we have to go down. But relax, Eugene, we're alone tonight. Everyone else is . . . gone."

"Gone? I don't understand. Gone where?"

"I wouldn't worry about that if I were you. Gone. Excused." And then he smiled his cool, bright-eyed, confident, and utterly contemptuous, smile. A smile that had been so familiar, four years ago, to members of a Senate investigating committee, and to millions of rapt television viewers. During the so-called "Patriot-gate Scandal."

That smile.

"No, sir," he'd say—he'd lie—"I don't recall that particular gentleman. If you tell me that he's an armaments dealer, then I'll take your word for it, Senator. But I'm afraid that I just don't know him." And then he'd smile.

And, "Yes, sir," he'd say—he'd lie—"I most certainly *do*

cherish the Constitution of the United States of America. But can you say the same thing, Senator?" And then he'd smile.

"Do I believe that I have the right to contravene the express wishes of Congress simply because I happen to believe that your *august body* is crippling the efforts of freedom-loving patriots elsewhere in the world? Do I believe that an American military officer should operate covert missions without authorization from his President? Of course I don't, Senator," he'd say—he'd lie. "Of *course* I don't." And then he'd smile that smile.

It had taken Eugene Boman quite a long time—years—to see that smile for what it truly was: the rictus of a madman.

A madman.

Whom Eugene Boman now followed down a short flight of stairs and into a long narrow corridor.

It was eerily quiet. No groans, no sudden screams, no outbursts of vile language coming from any of the small white rooms, the doors of which not only were unlocked, but stood open. The beds were all stripped. "Richard? Are you shutting down your . . . operation?"

"That would be a relief, wouldn't it? For you?"

Boman didn't reply. But yes, he thought, oh dear God *yes!* A relief! An answered prayer! Nearly every night for the past several years, he'd waked up bathed in a cold sweat, having dreamed of the inevitable . . . revelation. Of being arrested and led, absolutely naked, in front of hot television lights, where angry men screamed "Monster!" into his face. He'd shield his eyes and start to weep, to apologize, to blame Major Forell. "Those drugs were never meant to be used, *never!* It was *his* idea, not mine. The man thinks he's a goddamn hero, but he's crazy!" Then he'd bolt up in bed, gasping.

He'd lived in sheer terror of the revelation, and knew in his heart that it would come some day, that it had to. This couldn't go on.

When the Patriot-gate Scandal had broken in the press and Major Forell was hauled in front of Congress to explain his involvement in a certain guerrilla war in the People's Republic of San Isabel, Eugene Boman suffered a complete nervous collapse. Stayed in his bed for a month and a half, waiting, just waiting. Watching the Major smile that smile on television, and dreading the first mention of Idiot Drugs. But miraculously it hadn't come.

There was testimony about secret war materiel and millions of dollars of laundered cocaine money, shredded documents and forged letters, but nothing about the Idiots. There were heated exchanges about loyalty and Americanism, soldiers of fortune and Pentagon secretaries, but nothing about the Idiots. There was much discussion and quite a lot of speculation regarding two suicides and one cerebral hemorrhage, which ultimately had abbreviated the hearings, but nothing, nothing at all, about the Idiots. Nothing public.

In private, Major Forrel had spoken to Boman about them at some length. He'd come to Boman's apartment one evening soon after the hearings were completed. "You can open your eyes now, Eugene," he'd said, dripping scorn. "You can get out of bed and put on your clothes and get the hell on with your wonderful life." And Boman kept saying, "But how? How, Richard?"

How had he kept those drugs a secret? When everything else had come to light. *How?*

"By using them," Forell had said. "By using them, of course."

"The suicides?"

"Hydropadim," said Forell. A nasal decongestant.

"The cerebral hemorrhage?"

"Blue Mark. Naturally."

"You can't go *on* like this," Boman had said.

"No, I agree. Those bastards haven't proved a thing about any of my activities, but they *have* managed to wreck my career. It's over, Eugene. And I'll tell you the truth, I'm glad. I am! I've devoted my entire life to this country, fighting for democracy, for decency—and look what they've done! Held me up to ridicule. Calling me a loose cannon, a renegade. Impugning my honor. When they goddamn ought to be calling me a hero. To hell with them! It's about time I stopped working my butt raw for ingrates. And started working for myself."

Boman had run a hand across his dry lips. "Doing . . . what, Richard?"

"Well. I *have* become very interested in pharmaceuticals, as you know. So why not pursue that? Only this time with a *commercial* motive."

"You can't sell those drugs! Are you—?" He'd almost said *mad*. But wisely shut his mouth before the word could escape. "You can't sell them."

"In your markets, no. But I have certain other markets in mind. Institutions and individuals that people like yourself aren't aware even exist. Oh, I'm not worrying about markets, Eugene. When the time comes for selling our product, the markets will be there. I can assure you. But why even *speak* of markets now? At this stage of the game we should speak of . . . research. Further research." He'd smiled that cold smile, then tossed a real-estate prospectus in Boman's lap. "Have a look, see what you think. *I* think it's perfect."

Mancelot Farms.

Where Eugene Boman was now about to watch a videotape.

CHAPTER 28

TESTEES

THEY WERE IN THE LARG-
est of The Pharmacy's test chambers, where there was an
elaborate setup of consoles, cameras, and monitors. A shelving unit ran the length of the rear wall, and was filled with
cassettes, each one dated. Forell had taken down two. The
dates: November 23 and November 30. Last week, and yesterday. He inserted the first cassette into a VCR and switched
on a monitor. Then, with his yellow-gloved hand, he gestured Boman, who was still standing, into a chair.

"Eugene," he said, leaning against a console, folding his
arms. "You recall Batch LS-TW?"

Boman nodded. "We had high hopes for that one."

"Yes."

"Hodgkin's Disease."

"Yes." The Major was smiling.

"But . . ."

"Yes," said the Major, *"but.* It had an unfortunate side
effect. Paranoia, your people said."

"Hallucinations."

261

"Vivid hallucinations. Of a very peculiar nature. Do you recall?"

"Not really," said Boman. "LS-TW was a long time ago. Peculiar *how?*"

"They were consistent. The hallucinations were remarkably consistent, from patient to patient. Everyone involved in the testing of Batch LS-TW ended up seeing almost exactly the same things."

Boman opened his mouth, then nodded. "Oh—yes."

"You remember now?"

"Yes. They were convinced they were . . . someplace else. In fairyland."

Forell grinned. "For want of a better term."

"With castles and such."

"Exactly."

"Peculiar," said Boman. "But there was—wasn't there something else? *Another* problem?"

"Physical."

"Physical? Was it?"

"It was," said Forell, and held up his left hand. Then smiling, he drew off the yellow glove.

His fingernails were as thick as bones, as *talons:* they curved and ended in sharp points.

They were also bluish gray.

"Richard! For God's sake!" He was on his feet now, and gawking. "Do you want to kill yourself? You can't just—"

He'd broken off when the Major suddenly gripped him by his shoulder and pushed him into his chair.

"Just . . . sit. Sit." Forell touched one of the talons to Boman's lips. "And be still." Then he regarded his hand, palm and back.

Boman leaned forward, about to speak again. Forell

shook his head. "I just wanted to ask," Boman said anyway.
"It's only . . . the left hand?"

"Only the left. It seems to be the favored one." He
smiled. That smile.

"But Richard, why? Why would you . . . ?"

The Major turned and walked across the room, pressed
the Play button on the VCR. On the screen: furious gray
snow, then a sudden image—of a small, emaciated, grizzled
man splayed on a hard bed, struggling against his straps. The
nails on his left hand thick and curving and bluish-gray.
"This is Dean," said Forell.

Boman stood up, came closer. Thinking, Dean. And remembering other names, other testees: Bill. Ed. Mark. Mary.
Joe. June. First-names only, simple names only. Anony-
mous. Nobodies. Plucked from city streets up and down the
state, cajoled from charity wards, SROs, bus stations.
Gorman saying, How'd you like to make a hundred bucks—
Bill? Teasdale saying, Easy money, Ed. Luks saying, Nothing
to it, Mary. Nothing to it, June. Nothing to it, Joe. Dean.

"Richard . . . ?"

"Watch, dammit. And listen."

And Boman did; he watched intently, his temples
pounding. And listened: to the man on the bed mumbling
and muttering, then whimpering and then . . . whistling,
or *trying* to whistle. Puckering his lips, blowing and blowing,
and then someone off-camera—not Forell, possibly Luks, or
maybe Gorman—asked, "Tell me what you see. Come on.
Dean? Try."

Boman said, "Richard . . ."

"Watch!"

The off-camera voice said, "Dean, what do you *see* . . .
there?"

"A city . . ."

"What kind of city? A big city?"

"Not big. Stone. White stones. A wall."

"Good."

"And a lake. It's black."

"Go on."

"I want to come home!" He began writhing again, and blowing.

"A black lake," said the off-camera voice. "And what else, Dean?"

"There's a . . . castle."

"In the city?"

"No. In a forest."

"Do you want to go inside, Dean? Go ahead, Dean. Go inside."

"I don't want to."

"Do it anyway. Go in. Go into your castle."

"It's not *my* castle. It's—I want to come home! I'm afraid."

"Nothing to be afraid *of.* It's only a dream."

"No—not a dream. I'm there! I'm here!"

"In the castle?"

"Yes! And there's—oh please, let me come back!"

"There's what, Dean, *what?* What do you see?"

"Men on fire. Men burning and not-burning. They're burning but they're not burning *up!*"

Fascinated, yet repulsed, Boman stared at the wriggling, tormented man on the videoscreen.

"He's coming!"

"Who is?" said the off-camera voice.

"He's coming! No! Please let me home. Let me home!"

"Who's coming?"

"It's his . . . this is his . . ."

"Dean. What are you seeing?"

"Things on his face! *Things on his face!* Bugs. Worms! Things on his face!"

With a howl, Dean lunged forward and broke his restraints, then began scrabbling wildly at the air.

"Richard, for Christ sake!"

"Watch!" said Forell. "Watch *this,* Eugene!"

"My . . . God."

"You see it?"

"Yes. But—"

"You *see* it? He tore a hole in nothing! In *nothing!* And look!" Reaching out, Forell froze the picture. "Look, Eugene —you can see something *through* it. There's something on the other side. There's someplace else!"

"No."

"What do you mean, no? You *see* it. It's there. He tore a hole in nothing—with his left hand. With *this* hand!" Forell raised his fingers in front of his face, and smiled. "And there's something on the other side."

"What?"

Forell looked at him, then shook his head. Then he ejected the tape.

"What happened to Dean?"

"He was excused."

"Excused," said Boman dully. And remembered saying to the Major last September, speaking about Peter Musik, "What do we do with him?" and the Major had replied, "Oh, I'm afraid we're going to have to *excuse* him."

Boman thinking now, I still haven't mentioned Peter. I have to tell him. I can't just—

Later. Thinking, Later. Tell him later.

And saying, "This hole . . . in nothing. What is it? Did you see?"

"Only what you saw. Then it closed. But there was something there."

"Yes." Boman sat down again, squeezing his face between his hands. "And so that's why you injected yourself? Richard, this is madness."

"This is extraordinary! Do you realize what we've discovered?"

"No, I do *not*. And neither do you. You've got to stop this!"

Forell drew his lips into a tight line. "You sound like Gorman and Teasdale. That's what *they* said. I rejected their suggestion, Eugene. And excused them."

"And everyone else here? What about everyone else? The Joes and the Bills and the Marys. Where are they?"

"Eugene." He came and stood in front of Boman. "I've terminated all other research. I think we should concentrate on this, exclusively on this. Don't you?"

"We?" said Boman. "*We* should concentrate?"

"We, yes."

Boman shook his head, slowly.

"We're about to become the most famous people who've ever lived. Heroes. We've discovered a new world, Eugene."

"You don't know *what* you've discovered. And I haven't done *anything*, and I don't intend to."

Thinking, Tell him about Peter, tell him now. Tell him it's all going to come apart. *Tell* him.

But all he said was, "Luks. What's happened to Luks? Did you excuse him, too?"

"Luks," said Forell, slamming the second tape, the one

dated yesterday, into the VCR. "See for yourself what happened to Luks."

The man on the monitor screen was tall, several inches over six-foot and powerfully muscled—broad-shouldered, small-waisted; his arms and legs were almost freakishly thick. His face was squarish, and he wore—incongruously, Boman thought; had *always* thought—round tortoise-shell glasses. College-boy glasses. Luks was anything but a college boy. He was in his late thirties, and his expression was dour, almost malevolent. When he smiled, he revealed one gold eyetooth. He was smiling now, on the screen.

"You see anything?" said the off-camera voice, Forell's voice this time. "In your head?"

"I don't . . . know," said Luks. "Maybe."

"Be a little more specific, will you, Frank?"

"Well, I don't *know* if I see anything, all right?" He'd been standing close to the camera; now he stepped away from it, and Boman could see his left hand: the gray talons. And the gun strapped to his waist, a military-issue automatic.

Luks sat down on the side of the bed and closed his eyes.

"Frank?"

"Whyn't I just *do* it, Major? Just *go?*"

"You're going, Frank. A little patience. Anything yet? Frank?"

"No. Yeah. Wait. *Yeah.* Dean said a lake: I see it, too. Man, it looks like *oil.* Maybe it *is* oil." He stood up, rolled his head on his shoulders. "Major? Now I see a castle. Weird."

"Describe it, Frank."

"Well, this is gonna sound disgusting. It's—made of stone. But hey, Major? The stone looks—slimy. Friggen place got sticky stuff dripping from the walls. Like, like *ooze*, or something. Major?" His eyes snapped open, looked directly into the camera. "I wanna go now. I don't wanna get too near that place. I wanna go *now.*"

"You feel ready?"

"Oh yeah—I'm ready, all right." He grinned. Then lifted his hand beside his head, and struck it downward.

Boman let out his breath in a long, quavering hiss.

Another tear. In nothing.

Luks regarded it with amazement, delight. "Hey, Major? One small step for mankind—right? I'm going in the history books."

"What's he doing? Richard, what's he doing?"

"He's going . . . there," said Forell.

On the screen, Luks said, "Hey, Major. I get the credit, right? For being first?"

"It's all here on tape, Frank. You're the first."

Luks smiled. "Major? When you're ready, get the castle fixed in your head and just come. I'll be waiting."

The off-camera voice said, "God bless, Frank."

And Luks, halfway through the slit, said, "Huh?" Then he was gone.

The Major stopped the tape.

Boman continued to stare at the monitor, moving his lips, shaking his head from side to side. He flinched when Forell put a hand on his shoulder. Even though it was only the right hand, he flinched badly.

"He hasn't . . . returned?"

"I didn't expect him to," said the Major. "He's waiting."

"Waiting! The man is probably dead. You don't have the slightest inkling of what this is all about."

"Perhaps not, Eugene. But we will. We soon will."

We.

Boman cut his eyes to the Major's clenched left hand, looked quickly away, then rose to his feet. "I think . . . I think you should destroy those tapes. I think you should destroy *all* your tapes."

Forell craned an eyebrow. "Eugene. I can see it." He pressed a knuckle to his forehead. "I can see the lake. The black lake. The city. And the castle." Pursing his lips, he softly blew. Whistled. And took a step nearer to Boman. "It's time you became a man, Eugene. Time at last. I'll show you how it's done."

"What're you talking about?"

"Shall we go? Luks is waiting. Our *luck* is waiting."

"You're out of your mind. You're crazy! You're absolutely mad." There. Christ, *there:* he'd finally said it, he'd said it to the man's face. Called him mad.

Forell's reaction?

That smile.

And when the Major tore a slit through the air? Boman's reaction?

He opened his mouth and wailed. Like a little boy.

CHAPTER 29

HEY MARGE

THERE HAD BEEN A TIME, some fifteen or twenty years ago, when it seemed to Herb and Marge Dierickx that practically all of their married friends were getting divorced. Herb used to say, "What is it, something in the water?" and Marge would respond, "Water! They've never talked to each other. Not really. Not like you and me. That's the secret. Talk. About anything. About everything." Sometimes Herb would kid her, saying, "Hey Marge, you sound like an article in *McCall's,*" but mostly he'd just nod his head.

They were great talkers, it was true. Over the course of their long marriage, they'd developed the habit. Herb would come home in the evening, and they'd sit down and talk over the events of the day, Herb telling Marge that he'd had a tuna steak for lunch, Marge telling Herb that she'd done two loads of laundry and *still* couldn't find the match to his good blue sock—oh, and that some Jehovah's Witnesses had come by around eleven, trying to give her *The Watchtower.* He'd tell her about driving the boss out to company headquarters, about seeing a couple of hot-air balloons and a Fuji blimp, then mention that he'd finished reading his book about the JFK assassination being a Mafia hit. Marge would tell him she'd paid the phone bill, the cable-TV bill, and maybe show him the new Lillian Vernon catalog, say that she kind of liked the bird feeder on page 34—did he?

In the morning, they'd tell each other their dreams, even the naughty ones, and at night, before going to bed, they'd let each other know if they were tired and just wanted to sleep, or if they were in the mood for a bit of fooling around.

Talk. Talk Saves. Marge firmly believed that, and so did Herb. Everything—from their fears about growing old to their brand preferences when it came to canned soups and American cheese—was brought out and discussed. Well, *almost* everything.

Herb didn't know whether there was anything that Marge had ever held back, but there were two things that he'd never told her: about her crazy younger sister once trying to seduce him at a christening party, and about Peter Musik's sudden . . . disappearance.

He'd told Marge all about Peter when he'd first come along, saying, "Hey Marge? There's this reporter guy doing a story about the boss's goofy collection. And Mr. Boman really likes him—he even took him out to dinner the other night." Every few days he'd mention Peter again. "Mr. Boman's started calling him the Music Man. You know, like that musical? It's kind of funny, the guy sticking around so much. You'd think he was writing a *book* instead of some dinky little article."

And then, late last August: "Hey Marge? I'm taking the boss and Money Campbell and that Music Man guy down to the lake this weekend. I got to stick around, I guess, so that means you're gonna have to go to the Matetskys' barbecue without me. Don't be mad, okay? It's not my idea, Marge. Mr. Boman wants to show Peter the posters and stuff that he got at the lake house."

That was the last time he'd ever mentioned Peter. Several weeks later, though, Marge had asked him, "Whatever happened to the man who was writing the article?" and Herb, trying to keep his voice steady, had replied, "Oh, he's all done. He's finished. And gone."

It bothered Herb a great deal that he'd kept secret something so *important*, but what could he do? He *couldn't* tell Marge. She was so *moral* that she'd probably have said to call the cops. And forget that. Herb wasn't about to end up in any true-crime book, not if *he* could help it.

Funny thing, though, ever since the brouhaha at the lake house—upon which Herb had chosen not to eavesdrop; he'd just telephoned Major Forell, as the boss had instructed him, then made himself scarce—he'd become kind of a blabbermouth at home, burying almost every anecdote beneath an avalanche of picayune details. He figured it had something to do with guilt, and even though Marge would sometimes look at him quizzically, sometimes *yawn*, he couldn't edit himself. Which *was* kind of dopey when all he was telling her about was how he'd changed a flat tire. On the other hand, his new passion for accuracy could make a really interesting event—like, for instance, the time he'd spotted Gene Hackman filming a movie on Fifteenth Street— sound positively epic. Couple times, Marge had told Herb that he was just as good a storyteller as Charles Kuralt. And she meant it.

And now, in Lostwithal, Herb Dierickx—the Charles

Kuralt of interdimensional travel—was concentrating hard, intent on memorizing every little thing that happened, so he could tell Marge about it, actually make her *see* it, when he finally got home. Whenever that might be.

Marge? he would say. *Honey, let's make some coffee and get comfortable. You're gonna* love *this. . . .*

Hey Marge? Marge? he'd say. *The grass there is the color of lima beans.*

It's real hot, and the air is full of bugs.

They got mice same as we got, only their mice are blue. They got blue mice.

Hey Marge? he'd say. *Marge . . . ?*

. . . after that magician guy came into the shack and told us to go down to the beach, me and Jere Lee grabbed the bucket of crazy water—we'd started calling it Berlitz Water, as a joke—and went outside. And the first thing that we noticed? Was a barge, like something you'd see on the Cushing River. It was beached in the lake cove and all these . . . people had got off the barge and were standing around a hole in the sand where there'd been a bonfire. But guess what? These people? These barge *people? Were all women. Every single one, Margie, was a real tiny woman. And I mean* real *tiny. Midget-tiny. And they had on these robes with hoods—just like that guy in* Star Wars*, what's his name? That English guy. Alec Guinness. Remember old Ben, in* Star Wars*? Dressed like him. A whole bunch of tiny women, carrying food hampers. And hampers full of clothes.*

Well (Herb would say), *I was hungry by then, but I got to tell you, Marge, I wasn't thrilled when I saw what the chow looked like. The meat? Was lumpy and black, like a piece of coal, only soft —or like something you might've shish-kebabbed a week ago and had sitting around in the fridge. And the bread was flat, like that middle-eastern stuff you tried foisting on me last year: flat and* green. *That's right, Marge, green. I thought it was moldy, but it wasn't. It was just green bread.*

So everybody gets a ball of coal-kebab and a loaf of green bread and we're supposed to eat.

I didn't know if I could, but I gave it a try. And it wasn't half-bad, especially the bread, the bread was good, almost a little . . . sweet? Yeah, sweet. I had a second loaf.

No (he'd say), *nobody was talking, just eating. The little women in the brown robes, the old guy Squintik, the trampy guy Jack, and me, and Jere Lee. Oh! And Jack's girlfriend. 'Member I told you about her, about seeing her in the hospital, but then she'd disappeared? Well, she was back again. I don't know where she'd gone, but now she was back. And dressed just like the other women. In a robe.*

So. There was the little women . . . Jack's girlfriend . . . Jack . . . the guy Squintik . . . Jere Lee, and me. Eating weird food.

But the girl with the great breasts? Money? Money Campbell? She wouldn't touch a thing. She was still out of her head. Saying over and over that none of us were real.

And Peter (he'd say), *Peter kept trying to calm her down . . .*

Here, though, as Herb Dierickx mentally rehearsed his story, he ran into a snag. Thinking, Oh boy, I'm gonna have to watch that. No calling the guy "Peter Musik." That'd just open a whole can of worms. Marge would say, "Wasn't that the same man who'd . . . ?" Et cetera.

No, he'd really have to watch that, when he got home and talked to Marge. The guy wasn't Peter Musik, he was just . . . the guy who'd rammed his car into Mr. Boman's limo. Right: just some guy. Don't call him Peter, call him . . . Geebo.

And Geebo (Herb would tell Marge) *kept trying to calm Money down, but it wasn't doing much good.*

So we finished eating, and then that magician guy, Squintik? Takes the bucket of Berlitz Water and gives it to Pe—to Geebo and Geebo has a drink, and the next thing you know, he's whistling "Dixie" like the rest of us. Yeah, but he's making perfect sense, too. He says, "Now what?" not in English but in that whistling-"Dixie" language, and the trampy guy Jack says, "Sit." Meaning we should all sit, not just Geebo.

So we do. The whole bunch of us. We all sit down.

Well, everybody except Money. She's still tottering around the beach, white-faced and mumbling. It's so weird that she didn't believe in us, but I could sympathize with her. Hey Marge, I mean: here we were, someplace else. Someplace else.

Hey Marge (he'd say), *really and* truly. *I'm not making any of this up.* You *believe me, don't you?*

Well, it's true (he'd say), *it happened. And* this (he'd say) *is what happened next:*

Jack turned his hands over, palms up, and put one hand on top of the other, then he touched his thumbs together and made kind of a sign-language divining rod. He pointed the make-believe divining rod at the little women, then bowed his head. I guess he was being polite, showing respect. Then he thanked them—calling them Women of the Mist—for bringing us such good food to eat. And for bringing us clothes to wear. Then he said he was really glad that he'd chosen his Sting from such a noble and generous clan.

I'll tell you, Marge (he'd say), *I didn't know what he was talking about. What Sting? But then I happened to look over at his girlfriend, the tramp's girlfriend, and I still didn't know what a Sting was, but for sure I knew he was talking about* her. *She had this proud, shining face.*

Hey Marge (he'd say), *you remember that expression of my* mother's? 'Member how when Mom would see some young couple holding hands on the street, she'd say, "Brother, I can feel their love buzzing all the way over here"? 'Member her saying that? Well: I could feel the love buzzing right off Jack's little girlfriend. Buzzing right at him. But hey Marge: he didn't seem to notice. He just went right on thanking and complimenting those teenie-weenies, till finally one of them, a real pioneer-type old lady with a wrinkled face, raised her right hand, and he stopped.

I got the impression that she didn't much care for Jack. There was something about her eyes, how she looked at him. It was like— it was like how your mother used to look at me, when we first started going out. It was that same you're-not-good-enough-for-my-little-girl kind of look. 'Least that's my impression.

Anyhow, she cut him off. So then Squintik stood up and walked over and hugged her. Not with any real affection—you know how you'll see on TV that Gorbachev guy hug some other Communist guy at the airport? Squintik hugged the old lady like that. It was, like, an official hug. Then she kissed his left hand, and walked straight back to the barge. The other women in robes— everybody except Jack's girlfriend, whose name I should've told you before is Lita—waited for about ten seconds, then followed her.

And there went the barge, Marge (he'd say, and smile). Barge-Marge. There went the barge, floating off the sand, plopping into the lake, sailing away. And then . . .

And then (Herb would say, scratching his scalp) . . .

Jack picked up this ugly doll that he'd made out of ashes. And then . . .

While that crazy Money Campbell walked off by herself, saying, "You're not really whistling, you can't kid me, it's all drugs," Jack explained to us guys from Earth, us three Earthling guys, me and Jere and Geebo, just what the hell this was all about.

And jeez, Marge (he'd say) it's really . . .

It's . . .

I'll tell you something, honey, it scared the living shit out of me. Pardon my French.

Herb would say to Marge, when he got home.

If he got home.

CHAPTER 30

THE OLD STORY

MASTER SQUINTIK STOOD apart from the too-humans and carefully watched their faces, their expressions in constant flux, moving from placid curiosity to vigorous attention, to alarm, to denial, and finally to wondrous dread. The mage was well-satisfied, and immensely impressed, by the Walker's narrative skill—he was, thought Squintik, a credit to his kind and truly deserving of his fifth-degree rank. Oh yes, he knew precisely which things to tell these Witnesses from Kemolo, and which to omit. He had abridged—simplified—the Old Story, retelling it in a manner which they could most readily grasp; perhaps later—but then, perhaps not—these Witnesses would have need of a larger, deeper understanding of the Schoolteacher and his First Pupil, but for now the Walker's rudimentary explanation would suffice.

Tightening his grip on the branch-crutch, Master Squintik leaned forward and glanced down at the three discrete circles that the Walker had sketched with a finger into the sand, to illustrate that in Whole Creation there are three known Moments. Three distinct universes. And that in each Moment there exists a human world.

Excellent, thought Squintik. They have found that comprehensible. Even . . . charming.

Then Squintik cut his eyes to the fourth circle, which Jack had drawn somewhat apart from the other three. And within which he'd sketched a punctuation symbol familiar to the Witnesses. A question mark.

A fourth Moment, with a fourth human world, Jack had told them, is . . . a possibility. An idea long debated, he'd said, among scholars and mages in Lostwithal.

Debated, thought Squintik. A wise choice of word. No need for these Witnesses to know that this long-debated "idea" had led to the waging of a hundred bloody wars. No need for them to know that the resultant chaos had finally, after a millennium, been quelled only by the rise of the House of Agel, with Perfect Order as its metaphysics and its polity. No need for them to understand the system or logic of Perfect Order; for now, it was enough that they understood that its destruction would mean the destruction not only of Lostwithal, but of all the human worlds.

And now that they did understand, somewhat, thanks to the Walker's suppleness of speech, their faces had gone pale and their eyes were fixed on the Keepsake—the figure of the Epicene Whose Eyes Are Death.

Squintik sighed deeply, waiting for them to break their silence.

They were, after all, humans too. They would have many questions.

The man called Geebo-Peter was first to speak, and he insisted upon speaking in English. Which Squintik realized was quite an effort of will. He said, "This is the second time that I'm hearing about this three-worlds, four-worlds stuff. All right, no problem. But I'm still not sure who this guy the Schoolteacher was. Are you saying he was, like, Adam? Or are you saying he was, like, Columbus? Who *was* he?"

"Who *is* he, you mean," said Jack. And Squintik winced, not because the Walker had also reverted to English, but because the mage felt it unwise of him to mention that the Schoolteacher still lived. That would only *complicate* matters.

"You mean he's still . . . around?" said Geebo-Peter.

"Perhaps," said Jack. "Perhaps. The Old Story does not mention his death, only that he is . . . resting."

"Hey, like King Arthur!" said the kindly woman, Jere Lee, speaking in Losplit, but saying the name "Arthur" in English. She turned to Geebo-Peter and said, "It's just like King Arthur, Peter. It's like a legend. Maybe he's alive, maybe he's not, what's it matter . . . it's just a legend. See?"

Geebo-Peter pushed out his lips, but finally shrugged.

And Squintik smiled. His fondness for the kindly woman kept swelling in his breast and two hearts.

"All right," said Geebo-Peter, "we'll let that go for now. But you still haven't answered my first question."

"The Schoolteacher was not the first man, but a great magician who discovered the existence of human worlds in Feerce and Kemolo," said Jack, playing the Simplifier again, much to Squintik's satisfaction.

"So that's how come all you guys here are magicians."

"But we're not!"

"What I mean is, that's how come you guys all use magic. I mean, instead of science. He was a *teacher,* and what he taught was *magic*—right?"

Jack frowned, and Squintik thought, Tell him yes, just tell him yes.

"Yes," said Jack. "Right."

And Squintik let out his breath.

The kindly woman had been staring at the sand circles, and now she asked Jack, "If this Schoolteacher found only three, as you say, *human* worlds, how come there's been all this . . . debate about a fourth one? I mean . . ."

"Because of his First Pupil," said Jack.

Squintik thought, Careful now, careful. Keep it simple . . .

"According to the Old Story," said Jack, "the Schoolteacher's First Pupil, who was also called the Mage of Luck, became convinced that a fourth, and final, human world *had* to exist."

"How'd he become 'convinced' of that?" said Geebo-Peter.

"Mathematics," replied Jack, grinning. "He was adept at Useful Numbers."

And now Squintik watched the man called Herb Dierickx throw his hands up in despair. "Hey, I'm completely lost. Is this really *necessary?* All *I* want to know is what our chances are of getting out of here alive. I'm married, you know. I got a wife, you know. You scare us half to death with some mumbo jumbo about the Last Humans and the end of everything and stuff like that—and now you're talking about *mathematics?* Come on. Come *on!* Are we gonna die? Or what?"

Jack, wisely, didn't answer *that* question. Instead, he laid a hand on Herb's shoulder and said, "The First Pupil, and the first Mage of Luck, was a very arrogant young man. When he became convinced that a fourth world existed, he went to the Schoolteacher and mocked him. He said, 'I know more than you do.' "

"Hey," said Herb, "this *is* an old story."

Jack smiled.

And Master Squintik smiled.

And Herb Dierickx smiled, then said, "So let me guess what happened next. This Schoolteacher guy told his wise-guy pupil to get lost. Take a hike. And threw him out of school."

Jack was nodding.

"Yeah? I guessed right? So, like, after he gets thrown out of school, he's real angry so he tries to, um—hey, Jack, you take it from here."

"The Schoolteacher *did* send him away," said Jack, "and he *was* angry—very good, Herb. Very good. And what he did next was seek a way into the fourth Moment, which he'd named Bulcease. He knew the secret of the Schoolteacher's Rings, but no matter how hard he tried or long he labored, the First Pupil could not find entrance to the fourth Moment. And then," said Jack, glancing toward Squintik, "he had a dream."

"Right!" said Jere Lee, the kindly woman. "What's an old folk tale without a good dream?"

"Exactly," said Jack. "And in this dream—which may've been true or it may've been false: here's the origin of the great debate—a monster appeared to the First Pupil, a monstrous human. That called itself the Epicene. And it said, 'The fourth Moment you seek is indeed real, as is the fourth human world. And that is the *final* human world, where live the Last Humans.' "

Jack had hunched over, and the Witnesses from Kemolo were leaning toward him now, and Squintik couldn't help but feel amused. They resembled small children attending a ghost story.

Herb Dierickx said, "Yeah? And *then* what?"

"And then," said Jack, "the Epicene told the First Pupil exactly what he must do to enter into that final human world."

"So *how?*" said Geebo-Peter.

Jack hesitated, glanced again to Squintik, then finally replied, "The Old Story never said."

"Oh great!" cried Herb Dierickx.

"The Story merely recounts to us that the First Pupil did as the Epicene had instructed him, and then concludes with his death at the hands of the Schoolteacher."

"The Schoolteacher killed his own pupil?" said Geebo-Peter. "Was he *that* jealous?"

"Jealousy," said Jack, "had nothing to do with it. The Schoolteacher was afraid. He'd come to believe that the fourth Moment—if it truly existed—must never be entered. That the Last Humans—if *they* truly existed—were evil beyond measure. That an entrance *into* Bulcease would also mean an exit *from* Bulcease. That the Epicene was, in fact, the Bringer of Plenary Chaos. And that if the Last Humans were ever to find their way into the human worlds of Iss and Feerce and Kemolo, they would destroy them."

Geebo-Peter said, "So he *did* believe in a fourth Moment. The Schoolteacher."

"Possibly," said Jack. "The Old Story is . . . vague."

"Well, he *had* to believe. Otherwise, why would he try to stop his First Pupil? Right?"

Jack shrugged. "This has all been . . . debated. And debated. And debated."

"Okay," said Herb Dierickx, "it's been debated. Fine.

Great. What happened, though? What's the end of the story?"

"It concludes in the little fishing village of Tiedek, with the Schoolteacher confronting his former pupil, who was by then calling himself the Mage of Four, Mage of Luck. The Schoolteacher forbade the pride-lofty mage to continue with his efforts to breach the fourth human world."

"And that mage guy probably just laughed right in his face," said Herb Dierickx.

"Indeed," said Jack.

"And the Schoolteacher—killed him?" said Jere Lee.

"Yes."

"So that's the end of the Story, capital s, but it's not the end of the *story,*" said Geebo-Peter. "From what you told us before . . ."

"Correct," said Jack. "Since that ancient time, many great mages have sought to learn if the dream of the Epicene was real. And if real, to discover what instructions the Epicene had given to the First Pupil. There have been countless tales and legends, and many attempts to enter Bulcease. Many vain men who've called themselves Mage of Four, Mage of Luck. But none, since the first, as vain or as wicked as the one who calls himself by that name today. It is he who sent the Finder to kill me, and it is he I am bound to denounce and expose to His Majesty-Most-Still."

"And it's him—*he,*" said Geebo-Peter, "who's found out, *after all this time,* just how the hell you really *do* get into the fourth Moment?"

Jack nodded.

"How? How'd he find out?"

Squintik pursed his lips around the Losplit word for *dream,* and Jack said, "He dreamed it."

"And what, the little dream-monster gave *him* the instructions, too, just like he'd given to the first Mage of Four?"

"Yes."

"A little too neat, Jack, don't you think?"

Jack looked at Geebo-Peter, but said nothing.

"All right. So he knows how to do it. Okay. How *do* you do it? Or don't *you* know?"

"I know. But only because Master Squintik has told me," said Jack, with another glance, an uncertain one that time, toward the Cold Mage.

"So what's the deal? Tell *us.*"

Once again, Jack said nothing.

—Till Squintik limped forward several paces, struck the sand with his crutch, and declared, "Walker, with my permission, you may tell your Witnesses what they would know."

"So *tell,*" said Geebo-Peter. "How *does* a guy go about getting into Bulcease?"

And Jack said, "By gathering grass from the human world of Feerce, soil from the human world of Kemolo, to mix with water from the human world of Iss. Black water from Lostwithal."

The three Witnesses blinked.

"And once you have made the mud," said Jack, "you fashion an image of the Epicene and set it out under the twin moons, at the site of the Schoolteacher's final confrontation with his First Pupil. Which is now the great port city of Tiedek. And the mud babe takes life. And rapidly grows. Until it is full grown and can tear its way into the world of the Last Humans. That is how it *may* be done. That is how it is *being* done. The babe is alive. I saw it. And must now tell

my King, so that it might be destroyed, along with its cre-
ator."

"When did you see this thing?" Jere Lee asked.

"Some weeks ago."

Geebo-Peter shook his head, as if to clear it. "And you
haven't told the King about it *yet?*"

"I could not. I could say nothing till he had granted me
an audience. But before I could even petition for one, I had
to flee for my life."

"But why didn't you tell somebody *else* about what you
saw?"

"I did. Master Squintik knows."

"So why didn't *he* tell the King?"

Jack frowned. "He . . . could not. It would be a violation of Perfect Order."

"What are you guys, nuts? Standing on ceremony when
the sky is falling?"

Jack said, "I *told* you this was someplace else," and
smiled.

"So let me get this straight," said Herb Dierickx, "there's
a little mud monster growing somewhere and, if you don't
tell the King about it pronto, it's gonna grow up real quick,
open the door to another world and let out a whole bunch of
—of what?"

"Last Humans," said Jere Lee. Then, to Jack: "But who
are *they?*"

And Jack said, "We'd rather not know, I think."

He looked toward Squintik, who nodded.

"Yes," said Jack, "we'd rather not know."

"Holy mother of God," said Herb, slapping his cheeks
with both hands. "So when do you go talk to the King?"

"We leave shortly. And I speak to King Agel this evening."

"Well, that sounds pretty good. Doesn't that sound pretty good to you guys?" said Herb, turning to Jere Lee and Geebo-Peter. "Hey, if everything goes all right, we could be home by breakfast—yeah?"

Squintik shook his head and limped slowly up the hill toward the corral.

CHAPTER 31

BONES TO POWDER

"I'M LOOKING FOR THE barn door," said Money Campbell, and laughed, then kicked at a tree stump. "That's what this place is, *I* know, Eugene. An old barn. An old horse barn. Peter told me. He found it. Did you know that he found it, Eugene? Did you know he took pictures? He knows where it is, Eugene. Or he did. I guess he doesn't anymore. 'Cause that's not Peter out there, is it? Not really. So I'm looking for the barn door, Eugene. Am I getting warm? Will you tell me if I'm getting warm?"

Lita stood listening, her almond eyes widened with amazement and pity. She'd followed Money, according to Jack's wishes, down the beach and around the cove and into a stand of trees. But now what? Should she make the transformation again to wasp, and snatch the mad girl's I? Possibly she might be forced to, but for now she would . . . wait. And listen.

"I'm not warm?" said Money. "Or you just won't tell me? Which is it, Eugene?"

"My name is not Eugene," said Lita, speaking English.

"Well, I'm not talking to *you*. You're not *anything*. You're not real. But Eugene is around here somewhere. Aren't you? Aren't you, Gene?"

"You are in Lostwithal."

"Who dreamed up *that* dumb name?"

Lita sighed.

"Is that the name of the Idiot Drug that you got me on —is it? Lostwithal? Daytime cold medicine from the makers of Blue Mark? Contains four highly effective medicines to provide temporary relief of cold and flulike symptoms? Sounds about right." She laughed again, stood up, and resumed walking, deeper into the woods.

Lita reluctantly followed.

"You know," said Money, "I've been thinking. I probably deserve just what I'm getting, Eugene. I was a twit ever to get hooked up with you, but that's not what I'm talking about. No—you know how come *really* I deserve this? Because I'm a coward. I stayed with you after what you did to Peter. I mean, I didn't know what you'd *really* done, but I always knew it was bad. But still I didn't run away. Or call the cops. Or do *anything*. I hung around and went to school. 'Cause I was scared. What a jerk I am. What a coward and a jerk! I hate myself. I hate myself even more than I hate you! And that's saying something, *Eu*-gene!"

She was practically shouting now, and her eyes were swiveling left, right, up, down—searching everywhere for . . . Eugene.

Lita finally said, "We've gone far enough. It's time we went back to the others."

"Get lost," said Money. "You're not even an *interesting*

hallucination. You look like a stupid Hobbit. I mean, the black lake: that's pretty cool, I admit. But everything else? Strictly from hunger. Hey, Eugene, maybe you should increase the dosage!" Then she laughed again, and pushed on.

Lita was thinking that, loath as she was to do it again, she was going to have to make the transformation, and soon.

She'd briefly lost sight of Money, and when she came up behind her again, she froze, and her jaw dropped.

Money was saying, "Now *that's* pretty neat. That's a pretty good one, Eugene. Creepy—but *real* vivid."

Lita said, "Don't move."

A grayish-green fog hovered between two clumps of brush; suddenly it began to roil, as though stirred, and then you could see—almost see—a steady pink orb and something . . . *twitching.*

"Boy," said Money Campbell, planting her fists on her hips, "this is absolutely the last time that *I* eat acetaminophen before bed." Then she laughed and said, "How do you like *that,* Eugene? Did I pronounce it right? And you always thought that I was such a ditz, well I—"

Lita grabbed her by the shoulder and spun her around just as the ground pall leapt from its camouflage. Its head was the size of a peach stone, its neck a spindly stalk, its round body practically nothing more than a huge pink mouth and a small, squat propulsion coil.

"Run!" cried Lita. "Run, you idiot!"

But Money just stood there, blinking, bewildered, saying, "Why? Oh come on, it's not . . ."

Then she screamed, when the pall sank its teeth into her ankle.

Swearing to herself—in Losplit—Lita sucked in her

cheeks, collecting saliva, which she then spat into her left hand. She winced, recollecting the Useful Numbers she'd learned as a child but so rarely used, had scarcely needed, ever since, much to her mother's chagrin. (You were born to be a witch, my girl, *not* a Walker's Sting.)

She held up her hand, and averted her face.

And the ground pall fell away, dead, from Money Campbell's leg.

"*That,*" said Lita, "was real. Real." She strode angrily across the clearing. "Real. Real. *Real.*"

Money stared at the blood on her jeans.

"And if you laugh again, I'll turn *your* bones to powder!"

"Bones?"

"To powder," said Lita.

"Is *that* what you did?"

"Can you walk?" She lifted Money's arm and put it around her shoulder.

"You turned its bones to . . . powder? *Really?*"

"How's your leg? Does it hurt?"

"Yeah. A little."

"Good! So now you know."

"Know what?"

"That I'm real. And you're here."

"Yeah, but . . ."

"To *powder!* I'm warning you."

"I'm . . . *here?* No fooling? And Gene's not?"

Lita's eyelids dropped and she sighed deeply. Then, as she helped Money walk back across the clearing, she said, "What's a Hobbit, anyway?"

And Money might've laughed, except she was afraid

that this bona fide witch in this bona fide place might suddenly make good on her threat. . . .

Powder? she thought. Really?

Really.

CHAPTER 32

MANSE SELOC

THE CASTLE—A BIZARRE puzzle of ingenuous stone walls, battlements, turrets, causeways, and towers—stood roughly a quarter-mile distant from where Major Forell and Eugene Boman had concealed themselves on a slope of black, damp soil, behind trees that resembled, perhaps even were, sweet gums. Boman was groaning about the humidity, slapping at gnats, sweating profusely. The Major was using binoculars. He'd come through the Cut armed with an assault rifle, an automatic pistol, and a hunting knife. "We'll wait till it's dark," he said.

"And *then* what?"

"We go looking for Frank."

Boman sighed, then blotted his face with his shirtsleeve. "It must be a hundred degrees."

"Don't think about it."

"Oh sure. Right."

The Major grunted his disdain. Lifted the binoculars back to his eyes.

"You see anybody?"

"No."

"You think there's nobody *there?*"

"I wish you wouldn't talk so much, Eugene."

Boman looked at the assault rifle leaning against the sweet gum *(maybe* it was a sweet gum) tree, then glanced quickly back at Major Forell—at the long curved nails on the Major's left hand. And thought, I could shoot him. I could. Tear off his fingernail, use it, go home. Then: Come off it, Gene, he told himself. You wouldn't know how to *fire* the stupid rifle. You're losing your mind. I am? *I* am? Look at him! Thinks he's Rambo in Afghanistan. Insane. Always has been. But worse now. Much. Something in his eyes. Something new. The drug? Of course—what else? "Richard? What's that? Do you hear it?"

"Yes."

"What is it?"

Forell shook his head.

"Richard? It's coming from the castle."

"Sssh!"

"Oh Jesus, Richard, it's somebody screaming. It is! Please, let's go back, now! *Please?*"

The Major turned on Boman, drawing his right arm swiftly back to cuff him. Before he could lash out, though, something dropped from the tree and struck him on his cheek. Something moist, that clung. Boman's eyes opened wide with revulsion. "God*damn,*" said Major Forell, plucking the thing from his face and flinging it at his candy-assed son-in-law. "Goddamn it, Eugene, it's only a goddamn slug."

Shivering violently, Boman gaped at it, watching it creep across the toe of his shoe, leaving a silver stain.

And then he heard the screams again, coming from inside the greasy castle walls.

The left hand of Eudrax, a Finder chased a golden cock-roach down the length of a long wooden table in the oubli-ette of Manse Seloc. It pounced, clenched its fingers, then opened them and reared back on its wrist. The cockroach, only partly crushed, its antennae wriggling furiously, tried to crawl away. The Hand of Favor squashed it flat.

Across the gloomy chamber, a naked man dangled from heavy chains. His flesh was bright pink, his eyelids fluttered, and he was moaning, weakly. Every few moments he would start to lift his head, but the effort would prove too great and it would drop, chin striking chest.

When the tiny flames suddenly erupted from a hun-dred thousand pores, he screamed. Again. Burned, but was not consumed. Again. The fire licked him for several sec-onds, then blew out. And as soon as it did, Sister Card rose from her stool, reached into a metal bucket of yellow fluid, took out a thick sponge, carried it across the chamber, climbed a stepladder, then reached over, and squeezed out the sponge over the too-human's head.

Half-a-minute later, the flames erupted again from a hundred thousand pores.

This had been going on for nearly a full day, and the pythoness was growing weary.

She desired his death, but the decision to kill was not hers to make. But why keep the too-human alive? She was convinced he knew nothing about either the Cold Mage of Dwindling Street or the King's Tramp. That another Kemolon should appear in Lostwithal at such a time as this was certainly strange and curious, but Sister Card felt it was nothing *more* than that. Merely strange and curious. Her

Great Mage, however, did not share that opinion, and so the torture continued.

Wearily, she said, "Where is the Walker now?"

The too-human muttered.

"Where?"

"Don't know . . . any Walker," said the too-human, in Losplit—having drunk from a cup of gray water last evening. "Don't . . . know."

Then he screamed again, as the flames flew over his skin.

Sister Card rolled her shoulders.

On the long table, Eudrax's hand had drawn the too-human's pistol from its holster, and was now caressing it—grip, slide, safety lever, front sight—with small white fingers. When they accidentally released the cartridge clip, the hand flinched, and tumbled backwards. But it finally returned, and after cautiously pressing the clip back in, it hefted the pistol, raised it, then slipped a finger through the trigger guard.

The gun discharged, and the pythoness flung herself onto the stone floor.

The too-human scarcely blinked.

Picking herself up, Sister Card strode across the chamber, her face blanched with fury.

The left hand of Eudrax had dropped the gun and hastily retreated; it cowered at the far edge of the table, fingers tightly compressed, thumb tucked.

Narrowing her eyes, Sister Card glared at the hand, till —one by one, ultimately a dozen—soft, lozenge-shaped blisters sprouted on the knuckles. Then, with a great groan of disgust, she snatched up the pistol and stuck it away in her skirts. Hand of Favor! Hand of Treason! She could not under-

stand why the Mage of Four, Mage of Luck had not destroyed that gruesome . . . extremity immediately upon its
return, in disgrace. The arrival of the Finder's Hand of Favor,
and the story it had written with pen on parchment, had
thrown the Great Mage into a great frenzy.

Which had become even greater, and more deeply malevolent, when—mere hours later—Sister Card had spied
this too-human from Kemolo skulking behind the ridge line
that ran above the manse.

This too-human whose name—he'd revealed under torture—was Frank Luks.

Sister Card climbed the stepladder, again, and squeezed
out the sponge, again, and looked into the too-human's haggard face, again, and asked him, again, yet again, "Where is
the Walker now?"

She didn't even wait for his reply, simply went back
down the ladder and rolled her eyes when the flames rekin-
dled, and he screamed. Again.

The Hand of Favor, like some albino rat, was now racing up and down in front of the oubliette's iron door, stopping every so often to try to squeeze its fingers underneath.

"You want to go," said the pythoness, "go." She unlocked the door, opened it, and as the hand moved to dash
around her, she viciously kicked it—out, far out, into the
corridor.

Then, closing and locking the door, she went and sat
back down on her stool, elbows on her knees, chin on her
folded hands.

The Great Mage of Manse Seloc sat in pitch darkness.
Slugs crept over his face and forehead and through his long

gray hair and down the back of his head and around his throat and up his chin. They avoided his lips. His mouth. Though they would all end up there, eventually.

He was staring at one of the tall narrow windows in the turret room. When, at last, came the first pale shaft of moons' light, he rose from his chair and went swiftly to a child's cot in the center of the floor.

The youth of stony mud and grass lay curled on its side, sleeping, gathering strength. Its breathing sounded thick and bubbly. Another two or three nights and it would be of a size to sleep in the Great Mage's own canopied bed. In a week—perhaps less—it would be full grown, and then . . .

With trembling hands, the Mage of Four, Mage of Luck gently pushed the cot toward the window.

The youth stirred, and the mage averted his face.

Once the cot was in position, bathed in the cold light of the twin moons, the youth lifted its hands to its face, and its lips parted with a sloughy, sucking noise. The Great Mage quickly stepped back.

"You are safe here," he said. "Another night. Another long night." Then catching two slugs from his throat, he dropped them onto the cot, and withdrew.

A few minutes later, he was pacing the bulwark, searching the night sky. From up there he could see the walls and buildings of the capital city, and the castle of Sad Agel, just seven miles to the northeast. The audience which the Cold Mage had arranged for the tramp was to be this evening. This very evening! Was it possible that Squintik and the Walker had reached the city without his knowledge? No, he was quite certain they had not. He had spies there, of all species; he would've been told. But where were they, then?

It was almost certain that they had returned to Lostwithal by now—where would Squintik have chosen to enter?

He slammed his fist against a crenel, and swore so violently that cinders flew from his mouth in a spray of bile.

He would not be thwarted by a vagabond spy and a minor wizard! Would not! For more than a thousand years, great mages before him had sought entrance to the fourth Moment, and failed. But he, the greatest of all the great mages, would succeed. With the Epicene as herald, he would pierce the veil to Bulcease, seize the final Moment, and grasp the mystery of the Last Humans. And if, in doing so, he were destroyed? And destroyed worlds? Worlds upon worlds? Even Whole Creation? So be it.

So be it.

A large brown dog-faced bat swooped overhead, spiraled down, and came to rest on a bartizan.

GREAT MAGE, it said, I HAVE FOUND THEM. THEY ARE TAKING THE SOUTH ROAD TO THE CAPITAL, AROUND BLACK LAKE. SQUINTIK AND THE WALKER AND THE WITCH ACULITA. AND FOUR TOO-HUMANS.

"Four?"

FOUR, MY LORD.

"They have come from the Preserve, then?"

FROM THE PRESERVE, MY LORD.

"Only the seven? No Women of the Mist?"

ONLY THE WITCH ACULITA.

Nodding, the Mage of Four, Mage of Luck reached out and stroked the chittering mammal. "Since you have found them, I give you the honor of stopping them before they've come another mile."

YES, GREAT MAGE. WITH . . . PLEASURE.

The creature flew off into the darkness. Scarcely a minute later, from the trees and the caves in the surrounding forest land, ten thousand bats took wing simultaneously, eclipsing the moons.

Below, the Epicene Whose Eyes Are Death cried out in distress.

"Another night," said the Great Mage, more to himself than to the youth of stony mud and grass. "Another night. You are safe here, with me."

Then he moved to go back inside. But stopped suddenly. Had—something caught his eye, below? A light? A movement? He leaned forward, scowling.

And saw them.

Two figures.

Moving down a shaley slope, ducking behind trees, and coming toward the Manse Seloc.

Let them come, thought the Mage of Four, Mage of Luck, with a slow smile. Let them come. . . .

CHAPTER 33

TRAVELERS

THEY WERE SPEAKING EN-glish again, just for kicks.

"I haven't ridden a horse," said Jere Lee, "since I was thirteen."

And Herb said, "You call this a *horse?*"

"Well, it *looks* like a horse."

"It's *green.*"

"So? It's a *green* horse."

"All right, all right," he said, and gave the . . . horse a slight nudge with his heels.

They'd been traveling several hours already, Jack and Lita and Peter Musik on foot, Jere Lee, Herb, Money Campbell, and Master Squintik on horseback—or, rather, "Beast-back," since in Losplit, these huge, hoofed, slightly ir-ridescent green mammals with black manes and tails were called, simply, Beasts. The four Beasts had come cantering across the meadow behind the shack just after the question-and-answer session on the beach. Another gift—in addition to the food and the fresh Lostwithalian clothing—from the Women of the Mist. Lita's people.

South Road followed the contour of the vast lake, and as the group journeyed toward the capital city, the black water was to their right, while to their left was a boggy forest of spruce and white cedar—or reasonable facsimiles thereof. Occasionally, they'd glimpse, beyond the trees, a slitting mill, or a pig-iron furnace in blast, a sprinkling of tiny red-roofed cottages. Once, they'd seen a woman out priming a hand pump, a charcoal maker covering a mound of burning cordwood with chunks of sandy turf.

"Wow, is this ever primitive," Money had said. "It's a little like Epcot Center."

She was back to her old self again, pretty much.

As the sky darkened, the moons—"Two of 'em!" exclaimed Herb. "This is better than any planetarium, huh, Jer? Wait'll I tell Marge!"—rose slowly and shone brightly.

"Amazing!" said Jere Lee. "Beautiful!" She was feeling fine, just fine. So maybe this wouldn't be any picnic once they'd got to where they were going, and she certainly wasn't forgetting yesterday's (or was it earlier today's?) horror, that savagery in the hospital, young Brian Tucker with his pretty face slashed—but even so, she was almost giddy, optimistic for the first time in years, savoring every moment, enjoying every sight, marking every new scent. What an experience! Here she was on a green horse! A *green horse.* Suddenly, she laughed out loud.

Master Squintik, riding slightly ahead and to her left, turned quickly and looked at her.

"How're you doing, Master Squintik?" she said, in English. His eyebrows rose. So she switched to Losplit. "I said, how are you, Master Squintik?"

He nodded, then fixed her with a stare of such dramatic intensity that she felt her cheeks go toasty. "Master Squintik? Is something the matter?"

And he blinked. Shook his head vigorously. Then looked discomfited, and slightly bewildered. He glanced away, and urged on his horse.

Jere Lee cocked her head, shrugged.

"Hey," said Herb, who'd been watching, "I think the old guy's sweet on you."

"And I think," said Jere Lee, "that you've had too much of that water."

A minute later, though, she leaned over and whispered to Herb, asking him how old he figured Master Squintik was, and they both broke into giggles. God, she liked this man Herb. Her friend Herb.

Jack, a Walker had preceded the group from the time they'd left the cove. In fact, he'd immediately put several hundred yards between himself and everybody else, except Lita, and then assiduously maintained the gap. Lita walked along with him, but kept to the lake side of the road, while Jack stayed to the wood side.

Peter Musik had attempted, at first, to walk along with them, but Jack said no. No explanation, just—no. And Peter, more than a little burned, had dropped behind, but not all the way back to the others. So it was Jack and Lita, followed at some distance by Peter Musik, followed by the four on horseback.

After moons' rise, though, Peter decided to catch up with the Walker and his witch. He'd enjoyed the solitude of the past few hours, the opportunity to think in peace, but now he wanted company. But not *only* that, he had some things he needed to say.

As he quickened his pace, he caught snatches of talk, Jack talking, and as he came even closer, he saw that the Walker was gesturing fluidly, waving one arm, then the other, and it all reminded Peter of some ham actor doing one-man Shakespeare.

Abruptly, Peter halted in the road. Jesus, he thought, that's exactly what Jack *is* doing—kind of. Rehearsing. Preparing to entertain the King with tales of his travels. God. Peter felt . . . funny. Tingly. So much stuff had gone down since yesterday, but he'd never genuinely felt the *strangeness* of it all, till now, till this very moment, seeing and hearing Jack prepare for his gig at the castle. Rehearsing what he'd say to his King. His *King.* Peter thought, This is a *kingdom.* This is Lostwithal, and Lostwithal is a kingdom where magic works, and he's . . .

A Walker.

Peter clamped a hand to his mouth. Astonished.

—As Jack said something about a costume ball. ". . . a seamen's masque, Your Royal Highness, which I did attend . . ."

Your Royal Highness.

Jeez, Peter thought. *Jeez.*

He walked quickly up the road.

Jack saying something then about claws. ". . . with borrowed shadows . . ."

Peter cleared his throat.

And Lita said, "You must not interrupt my host." Speaking English.

"Sorry. I apologize," said Peter, in Losplit, "but—"

"What do you want, Geeb?" From Jack, in English. Sounding only a little cross, and—maybe?—a little anxious. "What is it?"

"Couple things. I been thinking over what you told us—"

"Geebo, this can wait."

"Just let me run it by you, quick. How come if the Old Story says this Mage of Four is such bad news—how come you've had the modern-day version running around loose and nobody stopped him?"

"He is a noble and a scholar. If he wants to speculate about a fourth Moment, that is his right. It's only—"

"If he tries to *get* there, *then* it's a crime."

"A violation of the Order of Things, yes."

"Right. Okay."

"Is that . . . it?"

"Not really."

"Geebo . . ."

"You're gonna keep calling me that, aren't you?"

"Is *that* your next question?"

"No. Am I still . . . is the sting on my wrist still—working?"

Jack smiled. "If it were, Geebo, you'd be twenty yards behind us right now."

"Really?"

NOT REALLY, NO.

"So we *are* still hooked up."

"For a time. But it's fading."

"You could always do it again, though."

"I could. Is *that* all?"

"Where do I get some paper? I got to write this stuff down."

Jack hesitated before answering. "You can find plenty of paper and pens and ink in the city. I'll find you some myself. Tomorrow. *Afterward."* Then he turned and walked rapidly ahead.

Peter moved to follow, but Lita placed her hand against his chest. "You must leave him alone now."

But he ignored her and called, "Jack! You said something to me about first *your* revenge, *then* mine. We should talk about that. I was thinking of some ways you could *help* me."

"Tomorrow," said Jack; then, not to Peter but to the night air, he said something about a tenement building, a darkened hallway, a flight of stairs. ". . . all the doors were open throughout the house, but all the rooms were empty . . ."

Lita walked on. Peter stayed behind, standing perfectly still in the road. Something startled him, flying overhead—a bird, or a bat. There was a rustling in some brush. Then: hooves, directly behind him.

Glancing around, he saw Herb Dierickx on his mount, the man's face, and troubled expression, clearly illumined by the twin moons' light. "I, uh, wanted to talk to you."

Peter said nothing, and began to walk.

"I want to apologize, I guess."

"Sure. Sure you do."

"I was never—I never really knew what was going on with Mr. Boman."

"Right. You only drove the car."

"Until yesterday, Peter, I didn't know anything about those . . . drugs. I'd never *heard* of Idiot Drugs. When you and Mr. Boman had that big blowout at the lake house, I figured you were trying to nail him for—for what newspaper guys are always nailing rich guys for. I don't know. Income tax evasion. Something like that. I mean . . ."

"What *do* you mean, Herb?"

"I mean: we get back, Peter, it's probably gonna be real nasty for me. You go to the cops—they'll find something to charge me with. But what I'm saying, Peter, I'm saying that's okay. I can deal with it. And I'll help you."

"You'll help me."

"Whatever you want, whatever I know."

"Hey, that's mighty nice of you, Herb. *Mighty* nice."

"You're being sarcastic."

"Me? *No!*"

"I can understand how you feel about me, Peter. And I should've gone to the cops, maybe. But I want you to realize: I never seen Mr. Boman and Major Forell give you any drugs. And I wasn't the one that dumped you on the street. That night? They made me drive Money back to the city. Mr. Boman and Major Forell did . . . any dumping."

"You know what strikes me funny right now, Herb? You keep calling them *Mr.* Boman and *Major* Forell. Showing respect. That's the kind of guy you are."

"I guess."

"Mr. Boman."

"Peter? Let me tell you something else. I'm not defending the man. How could I, now I know the story? But he's not . . . he's kind of a sad guy. He's kind of pathetic. All that money and he acts like the kid on your street that wears white socks with dress shoes and his pants way too short."

"Jesus. You feel sorry for him."

"Yeah? I suppose I do. I can't help it."

"You're just a nice guy."

Herb said nothing.

Finally, Peter stopped walking. Then he reached up and

stroked the horse's neck. "Herb? I really appreciate your apology."

"No you don't, you're still angry. But I understand."

"Hey. That's *nice* of you. That's *real* nice. But then you're a *real nice guy*. But I gotta tell *you* something, Herb. Relax. Don't *worry*. You're worried about after we get back, I'm gonna call the cops, they'll charge you with this or with that? Forget it, Herb, won't happen."

"But I *want* to tell the police what I know. Now I *do*. See?"

"Yeah, only it won't be necessary. Because, Herb? I'm gonna settle up with *Mr.* Boman and *Major* Forell . . . privately. No fuss, no bother, no cops, no charges. You'll have to find another rich guy to drive for, of course, but I'm sure you'll manage. A nice man like yourself."

"Privately. You're gonna settle . . . privately?"

"That's what I said."

"I won't help you with *that*, Peter."

"Absolutely not! And I wouldn't *expect* you to—a guy with your deep-rooted sense of ethics."

"I apologized, Peter. And I meant it."

"Good. Good! Now, do you mind just turning your hobbyhorse around and getting the hell away from me? Could you do that, please?"

"Yeah," said Herb. "Sure."

When he was alone again in the road, Peter spat out the word "bastard," first in English, then in Losplit.

But wasn't quite sure who the hell he was talking about.

• • •

Some distance on, they left the main road and followed an old sand trail for about thirty yards into pinelands, and came to an abandoned iron furnace. There, they stopped to water the horses and take refreshment. Jack still kept his distance from the others, wandering up and down, rehearsing his tale, beneath the old trestle bridge that had once been used to convey ore, flux, and charcoal to the furnace stack. Lita paced with him, in deep silence.

Money Campbell put herself in charge of distributing the food, which was just more of the same meat and flat bread from the morning. When she came to Peter, who'd stretched out on his back with his hands folded behind his neck, she squatted beside him. He raised his head slightly. "Hungry?" she asked.

"Not very." He put his head back down.

"So what's the matter with you? You mad at *me*, too?"

Rolling onto his side, he said, "You, *too?*"

"I was talking to Herb."

"Oh."

"He said you sounded real bitter. I said, oh that's how you always sounded. Bitter you weren't famous, bitter you weren't rich . . ."

"Bitter that some bastards stuck me with a needle and turned me into a goddamn neurotic panhandler. Hey, excuse me. You're right. Nothing I should feel bitter about."

"Jere says you were a pretty nice panhandler. All in all. I don't think she thinks you were neurotic."

Peter snorted.

"She liked Geebo a lot."

"Yeah?"

"Yeah."

"Money? What happened to all my notes? Diskettes? You still got them?"

"Sure."

He rolled onto his back and let out his breath.

"What, you thought I'd, like, *burnt* them?"

"Where are they?"

"Right where you left them."

Peter bolted upright. "In your apartment?"

"What's wrong with that?"

"Jesus. What's *wrong?* Well, for one thing, they're probably *gone* by now."

"Yeah? Maybe. Since Herb kind of spilt the milk, huh? But why should you care? I thought you'd decided to settle this thing privately. What Herb says you said. I mean, you go and kill Gene Boman, I doubt you're gonna write up the story afterward."

"Who says that *I* intend to kill Gene? Herb? He's drawing his own inferences."

"Inferences. What language is that? Talk English. Or Losplit," she said, and laughed. She'd had quite a few swigs of Berlitz Water since hitting the road.

"What I mean is, Herb's got it wrong."

"Yeah, I know what you *meant.* I was kidding. You never did have much of a sense of humor, Peter."

"I was thinking that *we* should . . . pay Gene back. That's what I meant. Pay him back. Not kill him. Pay him back *in kind.* The both of us. Together."

Money pushed her lips out, drew them in. Then stood up.

"Hey . . ."

"I gotta go see if anybody else wants some more bread. You try it? It's good, isn't it?"

"Money. I find it hard to believe you don't harbor some
. . . desire to square things away."

"Maybe. Maybe I do."

"So?"

"So, Peter? Drop dead, would you? I'm really sick to
death of that whole business. It's a million miles away.
Maybe a trillion. Maybe a *zillion.*"

"We're going back, eventually."

"Well, I sure *hope* so. Otherwise I read *The House of Mirth*
for nothing!"

"After Jack has his revenge, we're going back and have
ours."

"Jack's having his revenge? *That's* what he's doing? Gee,
and I thought he was saving the universe. Like Flash
Gordon. Hey, can't you even *smile?*"

"We'll talk again."

"Yeah, Peter, sure."

She found Herb Dierickx sitting on the side of a spill-
way, staring morosely at the scummy water of a dammed-up
river that was dotted with tree stumps. "Still hungry?"

"Nah. But you know what I'd like right now? A
cigarette."

"You don't smoke, Herb."

"Yeah, I know, but it'd be nice."

"I wonder if they even *have* cigarettes here. I bet they
don't. We could ask Mr. Squintik. Want to?"

"No."

"Hey, don't look so glum. I heard you before, laughing
and stuff with that lady. I should tell your wife."

"You're a good kid, Money."

"Uh, oh."

"No, that's it. That's all I want to say. You're a real good kid. It was good, what you did yesterday. Going off by your-self looking for Peter. I should've gone, too."

"You did, we wouldn't be here now."

"Like I say, I should've gone." His shoulders heaved. "I feel like a shit. I *belong* in a true-crime book, Money."

"Well, if you do, so do I."

"Nah."

"More than you."

"Well okay, but you gotta be the second hero. You helped *him.*"

"Yeah, but who says he's the *first* hero? Who says Peter's the good guy?"

"Come on, he *is.*"

"This isn't a book, Herb. Yet."

He smiled. Then snorted. Then sighed.

There was a long silence.

Then Herb said, "I bet you they *do* have cigarettes here. Or something *like* cigarettes."

"All right, I bet you they don't. Let's go see Mr. Squin-tik, and settle this once and for all."

"I wouldn't bother them right now."

"Them?"

He pointed, down toward the river bank, where Jere Lee and the Cold Mage sat talking.

"Hey, romance."

"I tell you," said Herb. "Before you came over here? I'm kind of watching them, and Jere Lee's swatting away all these bugs and stuff? So what's Squintik do? Some magic—and the insects all freeze, turn into little ice balls. Ice skee-ters. I could see them floating away."

"No *kidding.*"

"Yeah," said Herb. "It was neat."

Then they just sat there staring down at the river, Money saying, hey, was that sorghum growing over there, like you get at the florist's? Herb saying it sure *looked* like sorghum, then saying, you know, this wasn't so different from home, after all. Money saying, "Now let's not lose our heads, Mr. D.," and she pressed his hand, and he nodded and then went on nodding.

From where Jere Lee sat with Mister, uh, *Master* (Mister/Master, Mister/Master) Squintik, she could see Jack, a Walker traipsing back and forth beneath the trestle, his hands moving in spirals. And the girl. She could see the tiny girl, following him. "Lita," she said, and surprised herself that she'd actually spoken the name out loud. In Losplit.

"What?" said Squintik.

"I was just thinking. About Lita. She's really *devoted* to your pal Jack, isn't she? Are they married?"

The Cold Mage was astounded. "Of *course* not! He is her life-host. She is bound to accompany him on his rambles, to ease his way, to protect him."

Jere Lee shook her head. "Sounds like a marriage to *me*," she said, more harshly than she'd intended. Maybe.

"They are not married, no."

"But you people here *do* get married, don't you? What about life-*mates?*"

"Some people do marry, yes."

"What about yourself? Are you . . . ?"

Smiling, he turned and faced her. "No, I am afraid that I am not."

"Well—maybe *some*day, huh?"

"No," he replied. "I *am* not and I *can* not."

"Oh," she said. Then, after a pause: *"Why* can't you?"

"We should be leaving," he said, getting slowly to his feet.

"Let me help you. Your leg . . ."

But he was emphatic about walking now without her assistance, and made his way back to the others using only his crutch.

Oh well, thought Jere Lee, who'd want to marry a bald magician anyway?

God, she *did* feel good this evening, didn't she?

Even the six or seven bats that she'd suddenly noticed flapping and swooping over the river couldn't skeeve her, and ordinarily she just *hated* bats, despised them with a passion.

CHAPTER 34

THE BATS

IT WAS CUSTOMARY AMONG Walkers to appear before the King in raggedy clothes—and new black walking shoes. And wearing a fine sword in a lavishly ornamented scabbard. Jack owned three swords, one a gift from his teacher, the others bestowed upon him by His Grateful Majesty. Those, however, were back in his quarters in the northern city of Sett. Nevertheless, he carried with him that evening a most handsome sword in a very pleasing scabbard—on loan, as were his tattered blouse and soiled peasant's trousers, and his new shoes of soft black leather, from the good Women of the Mist.

When he'd strapped it on, back in the Preserve, the thought had crossed his mind that perhaps, for the first time in his career, he might actually have to unsheathe the weapon, and use it.

And six miles from the city gates, he did.

Herb Dierickx shouted the warning, but he'd completely misreckoned the danger. He thought he'd heard hoofbeats. "Riders coming!" he hollered. "Fast!"

But it wasn't hoofbeats, it was beating wings: not riders, bats; and as he twisted around in his saddle, looking behind him, four of them slammed into him, and toppled him from his mount. He crashed down onto his shoulder with a grunt. The wind was knocked out of him. He tried to lever himself up, but could not. Teeth nipped at him, tiny fingers snatched at his shirt, his hair. With a suddenness that turned his stomach, he was plucked from the ground and carried skyward, his legs pedaling and flailing. His head struck a branch, an arm stripped leaves, he lost one shoe. Then he was lofted higher still, thinking wildly, This isn't *possible*, this isn't *happening*, bats can't—

A screeching filled his ears, and he opened his eyes, and the lake was far below, a mile below.

And he thought of his wife, in another world, and loved her across the abyss. . . .

When Money Campbell had seen Herb borne off by a couple dozen enormous bats, she'd actually made a leap after him, from her saddle, but fell short. And hard. She rolled across the ground as if her clothing were on fire, keeping her hands to her face—then became so disoriented she didn't know whether she was rolling *toward* the lake or *away* from it. She only realized her direction when she picked up speed, toppled down a slope and splashed into the water. Touched mucky bottom, kicked off, broke the surface, gulped breath, and plunged back under again. Something snatched at her hair, and she slapped at it, frantically.

But *it* was Peter. She saw him only for a moment, though. Bats on his arms and chest like shingles. Then she dove under again.

When she came up again for air, he was gone.

The Beasts had reared and bolted, trampling into the

woods, their backs leathery and undulant with mammalian wings.

The bats kept swooping.

And Jack, a Walker, with his sword's hilt clutched in both hands, swung viciously—and kept missing. Missing! Kept . . . missing! It was impossible to strike any of them; they just veered away, uncannily, alerted to the sword by their complex ears and senses.

But still he kept swinging, and would till they overcame him.

Lita! he thought. I'm sorry.

Though she'd felt revulsion at leaving her host's side, the witch knew that her only chance to save Jack's life would require magic—her rusty magic!—and that to effect a bedevilment, she would need a few moments' respite, to summon numbers, collect saliva, envision the act. She scrambled into the underbrush, and huddled there, sucking and sucking at her cheeks, but her mouth was dry as sand. And the Useful Numbers—useless! They just flew harum-scarum through her clangorous mind, and would not calculate. Wretched, she burst into tears.

—Then wiped her tears with a knuckle, and streaked them across her forehead.

And somehow found the sums she required.

Still in a crouch, she flung herself back through the brush and onto the road. Instantly, a hundred bats were upon her.

Then were not.

They dropped from her like dry husks, their bones turned to powder. Their organs to stone. She extended her left arm toward the Walker, her host, her life. Blue light flashed from her fingers to Jack, engulfing him.

Protecting him.

Lita fell to her knees, pressing the heels of both hands to her forehead. She felt nauseous, exhausted, on the brink of a swoon. No! She would not falter or pass out, she would not, would *not*.

But finally she did, and the auras she'd created both failed.

No matter.

The bats began plummeting, by the hundreds and thousands, their wings and long bodies encrusted in ice. They dropped in the woods, in the road, in the lake, and kept dropping till finally the travelers found themselves in yet another kind of jeopardy—in danger of being buried alive under a sudden mountain, sudden *mountains*, of flash-frozen brown bats.

Jack sheathed his sword, scooped Lita into his arms and staggered forward, up the road, in a continuous downpour.

Money dragged Peter Musik, half-drowned, out of the lake and along the embankment.

And Jere Lee, keening softly, her legs buckling and locking, buckling and locking, slogged over the ever-swelling mounds of winged mammals, the Cold Mage upon her back.

"He's dead," she kept saying, "he's dead . . ."

Then she collapsed.

When she revived, some minutes later, Jere Lee was lying by the side of the road and staring into Money Campbell's face, which hovered just inches from hers.

"I knew . . . ," said Jere Lee.

"What?"

"That I shouldn't've felt so good. It never lasts."

Money touched her cheek, very gently.

"He's dead. He just turned so—bright. His whole body turned so bright *red,* and all those horrible . . . things just fell. It was too much for him. There were too many."

"Too many, for sure too many bats. But Jere? Squintik's not dead. He's not."

Jere Lee tried to sit up.

"Hey, just sit for a second, okay?"

Then Jere Lee asked, "What about Herb?"

And the girl's smile faded. "He's . . . gone."

They hugged each other and rocked slowly, there on the road to Agel's Castle. . . .

"The Great Mage of Manse Seloc always claimed that I was a minor magician," said Squintik. He was still resting where Jack, a Walker had placed him, with his back against a white oak and his long legs straight out in front of him. His face was ghostly pale, his eyelids drooped. Capillaries had popped all across his cheeks and on the tip of his nose.

"You are the greatest magician in Lostwithal," said Jack, hunkered close by.

"Compliment His Majesty, Jack, don't waste it on me. I burst something inside doing that last . . . trick." Then he tried to sit up, but couldn't. "I'm useless and I'm spent. And the hour is getting late."

Reluctantly, the Walker stood. "I'll carry you the rest of the way."

"No—you must leave me here. Take your Witnesses and go."

"I've lost one of them," said Jack.

"You've lost *two* of them," said Jere Lee. She came and stood at the mage's feet. "I'm staying here."

Squintik's lips moved.

"No need to thank me," she said.

"I didn't thank you, woman. I said no. You go with the others."

"Baloney," she said—in English. "I'm staying, that's all there is to it. And besides I already *know* Jack's story. I don't have to hear him tell it again."

"Master," said the Walker, "two Witnesses are enough. The woman will stay with you till we return." Then he knelt, kissed the mage's Hand of Favor, and withdrew.

"Go ahead," said Jere Lee, shooing away Money and Peter and Lita, "go ahead, go ahead."

And when all had gone, and Jere Lee was stooped by Squintik and holding his chill hand in hers, she said, "If my memory serves me right, we did this once before. Remember?"

Then she leaned forward, buried her face in Squintik's breast, and cried tears for Herb Dierickx.

CHAPTER 35

▲

IN THE GARDEN

WHEN THEY ARRIVED AT the city gates, Jack, a Walker signed the tally book. Seeing written Losplit, Peter Musik was reminded of plane geometry, from his high school days. No fooling—Jack writing with a long skinny pen, the kind that you dip? You'd think he was sketching out a parallelogram, an isosceles triangle, a rectangle, a square. Weird. Peter leaned over and whispered, "So which one is my name, the triangle or the square?" Jack frowned, and handed the pen back to the gatekeeper, a tall, robust young woman with short-cropped black hair and a startling gun-metal gray complexion.

She wore a pale yellow tunic belted at the waist, and there was a small tattoo above each of her nostrils; each tattoo was identical, and, if Peter wasn't mistaken, they were supposed to be flies. Like, *pest flies.* Common *house*flies. More weirdness, he thought. Well, what do you *expect?* We're . . . here.

The gatekeeper glanced at the tally book, then peered intently at the Walker. She seemed hardly to notice his companions. Which Peter thought—again—was kind of weird, especially since they all looked a mess, scratched up, roughed-up, black-and-blue.

"Come," said Jack.

On the road to the city, they'd seen very few citizens of Lostwithal, but that changed once they'd passed through the high gate and were in Beybix. There was an enormous plaza with several alabaster fountains and marble statuary on an heroic scale (the predominating figures were horses, or Beasts), but Peter had to force himself to look at that stuff because what immediately caught his journalist's eye, and imagination, were the people.

His first impression? That both the men and the women were boring dressers—loose blouses and billowy trousers. Not a whole lot of color. Grays and browns and blacks, and several shades of blue. Children of both sexes wore caftans—the majority of them. Footwear? Sandals or boots. But quite a lot of bare feet, too.

An inordinate amount (Peter thought so, at least) of the men were bald. Interesting. No beards. No mustaches.

No jewelry on anyone, either, not so much as a ring.

A lot of facial tattooing.

A number of distinct racial groups. And quite a lot of racial blends, too.

But only one language. And—

"*Come*," said Jack, hooking Peter by the arm.

"But this is—"

"Kind of like Florence," said Money. "Don't you think? A *little* bit?" She gave a shrug when Peter looked at her in amazement. "Florence, *Italy*," she said. "I went there when I was a junior in high school. I mean, Florence is old, too. This is an old place, right?"

Lita smiled. "Very old."

"This hardly looks like Italy," said Peter.

"Oh, you're such a drip. I don't mean *exactly*. I mean, the general idea. Only where are the churches?"

They'd left the plaza and were following a narrow and winding cobbled street. "Look," Money went on, "the houses come right to the sidewalk, almost. You got your whitewash, you got your flat roofs. You even got your pigeons." She was swinging in and out of Losplit and English. She said "pigeons" in English. "Florence is the only foreign place I ever was."

"Well, there you go," said Peter smugly, and she stuck out her tongue at him.

They turned a corner and were then in a street of market stalls and small food shops. Everything was torchlit, the black smoke thick and greasy. Money kept stopping, checking things out—finger cakes drenched in blue syrup, stuff that resembled giant sunflowers only it was obviously something baked—a bread, maybe. Cured meats that smelled *awful!* And, "Hey, look!" she said, "they got bananas here. Hey, you guys got bananas, too!" She smiled at a merchant, who was staring at her with more than just mild curiosity. Holding up one finger—wait a second—she ran off after the others, already halfway up the street. "Who can loan me some money?"

"Jack doesn't handle the stuff," said Peter.

"What?" She frowned, then shrugged, resolving not to look at any more food, it would only make her crazy. Even so, she had a sudden craving for a hamburger. And wondered if they had *cows* in this country. This world. This . . . whatever.

After walking for what seemed like miles (Peter thinking every so often, yeah, he *could* see, kind of, what Money meant about a resemblance to Florence, and thinking, Where *are* the churches?), they crossed yet another (the third? fourth?) broad plaza, which led them, finally, to a long boulevard lined with trees *(plane* trees, thought Peter. Just like in Italy, thought Peter; she's not as dizzy as she . . . , thought Peter).

"Oh *man,"* said Money. "This is it? Where we're going? That's the castle, right?"

The castle. Directly ahead.

"It looks just like it's *supposed* to!"

And Peter smiled. It does, he thought, it really does.

"Turrets and everything! A drawbridge!"

Turrets and everything. And a drawbridge.

Peter reached for Money's hand and squeezed it.

"Yesterday," she said, "you were sleeping in the park. Today you're going to the castle."

Wrong thing to say. Instantly, the smile was gone from Peter's face. He let go of her hand.

As they neared the castle walls, Jack, a Walker visibly tensed, and his pace slackened, till finally, when they reached the public garden directly opposite the portcullis, he stopped. Cupping his mouth with both hands, he hailed one of the guards posted on the barbican and identified himself.

"Your flag is orange," the guard called, then pointed upward.

The flag snapping at the top of a high wooden pole was green.

"We must wait," Jack told his companions.

"Well, at least you're not late," said Money.

"Yes," said Jack with a fleeting grin, "at least I'm not late." Then he led them through a gate and into the garden, where there were plain stone benches set among braziers and dramatic topiary.

Seating himself, the Walker expelled a long breath. In the flickering light, his face looked gaunt, his features craggy. "So you've made it," said Peter, sitting down on the bench opposite.

"I am not in his presence yet."

Lita walked around behind him. When she began to knead Jack's shoulders, Money's eyebrows shot up. Then she went and took a seat beside Peter.

It was extremely, extraordinarily quiet.

At least it was till Peter started in talking again.

"I think it's time you told us what to . . . expect. What does a Witness *do?*"

"Nothing." Jack raised his eyes, met Peter's. "You merely sit—in perfect silence, *please*—and listen to my story. His Majesty will look toward you when I'm finished. You'll nod."

"Nod," said Peter.

"Gee," said Money, "this is even easier than being a sponsor at somebody's Confirmation."

"And what happens to *you,* once you've finished?"

"To *me?*" Jack lifted one shoulder, in a kind of half-shrug. "I'll rest till the season changes. Then go on another Ramble."

"You know," said Peter, standing up, "I'm still not sure I understand exactly what you *do.* You've been telling us you're the *King's* Tramp . . . but the way I've been reading things, this last walk of yours? That got you in so much hot water? Was all Squintik's idea."

"It was."

"So then you're not the *King's* tramp, you're—"

"Please." Jack held up a hand. "This is not the time."

"Tomorrow?"

Wearily, Jack said, "Yes, tomorrow."

"So," Peter went on, "at the end of the . . . story, we just nod. And then you take a little rest, rest your weary feet a little. But what happens to the Mage of Four?"

Jack stared out past the firelight into the darkness, then replied, "He'll be seized and the Epicene destroyed."

"*If* the King believes your story."

"There is no question of that. Agel will believe."

"Some reputation you must have."

"I am fifth-degree."

"Fifth-degree?"

"Tomorrow," said Jack.

"Right," said Peter. "Tomorrow."

Lita walked to the gate, opened it, slipped out, was gone briefly, then returned and said, "The green flag still flies." She seemed to hesitate for a moment, checking an impulse to go back around behind Jack, then finally slid onto the bench beside him. "My life," she whispered, and rested her forehead against his shoulder.

"Mine," he said, then put an arm around her. His chin sank, his head lolled to one side.

And Peter, watching them both with fascinated interest, thought that they made a wonderful . . . image. He wouldn't mind having a picture of that—but of course, here he was with no goddamn camera. But he could memorize it, to describe later. When he finally wrote everything down. He'd write about how the fire shadows made all the wrinkles and folds in the Walker's torn blouse seem to writhe, and about how the tiny young woman in the coarse brown

robe had the milkiest skin he'd ever seen. He'd write about
how the two of them could've been mistaken for lovers.

He smiled, satisfied, and eager—for the first time in
how long, how long?—to get hold of a pen and a sheet of
paper. Then he glanced sidelong, to say something to
Money, but she wasn't there.

She'd gotten up and was now wandering around the
huge and fantastically shaped topiaries.

"Look at this one," she said, when Peter came and
joined her. "Is it a whale? It looks like a whale. And that
looks like a wave. And I think that's a boat. If that's the curl
of a wave"—she pointed, even tapped the shrubbery—
"then that's the boat, see?"

She walked to another garden work. "This guy's a giant,
right? Sure he is, because see there? That's somebody else,
and see how small *he* is? So there's a giant and there's a
regular guy. Hey, wouldn't it be something if they had the
same stories here that we have back home? Like, what if this
is supposed to be David and Goliath. Or, like, Jack and the
Beanstalk. And that one, back there? Be cool if it was, like,
Pinocchio. Remember the big whale in Pinocchio? Be cool,
wouldn't it? Same stories and stuff?"

"Hmmm," said Peter.

She frowned, moved on to another. This one she regarded from close range, then stepped backwards and folded
her arms. "Boy, can you imagine having to take *care* of these
things? *I* wouldn't want to be the gardener."

"Money . . ."

"You see what *this* one is? Looks like a witch's coven.
Hey, know what? I bet these are supposed to be those
women who came on the barge—with the food?"

"Money . . ."

"What?" Suddenly annoyed, she turned swiftly, and faced him. "What? *What?*"

"Hey, come on, I just want to talk."

"Well, *I* was talking, that doesn't count?"

He waited a moment, then: "I was thinking. Don't you find it strange that Jack seems so . . . anxious? This is supposed to be the easy part, way he makes it sound. Just go inside and talk to the King, he's done it lots of times before, nothing to it. Yeah? So how come he's so . . . tight?"

"What're you talking about? Lawrence Olivier got butterflies all his *life*, what *I* read. So he's nervous, so what? I'm always nervous when I take a test, even if I have all the answers right up my sleeve."

Peter frowned.

"Oh for God's sake, *smile.*"

So he forced one.

"Great." She began to stroll away, but he caught her by the wrist.

"Money, listen."

"Now what?"

"This is important."

"Sure. Everything *you* say is *always* important." She wouldn't look at him now. She glanced away, toward one of the walking paths, where a pearly ground mist was moving slowly, slipping out of the maze of hedges and across the open lawn. Well yeah, she thought. The temperature must've dropped thirty degrees in the last few hours. It was almost chilly. "So what's so important?"

"I'm going to ask Jack to come back with us. Tomorrow."

She finally looked at him again, puzzled.

"We've done him a favor, he should do us one."

"I thought he already did you one. Like, save your life. That's what Herb—" She broke off and bit her lip. Herb. Jeez. *Herb*. "That's what Herb said. And you want *another* favor? But that's typical of you, Peter. I remember when you were always asking me for one more favor. One more favor. Just get me Gene's telephone bills, that's all. Oh, and let me see his checkbook while you're at it. And can you get me his appointment calendar? But that's all. That's the very last favor I'll ever ask you, Money. The *very* last. Yeah, right. Till the next one."

Peter had waited—very patiently, he thought—till she was all finished. "I'm going to ask Jack to help us snag Boman and the Major."

"Snag. Help *us* snag."

"With a little assist from Lita. She'll do whatever he says."

Money folded her arms, hugging herself. It really *had* gotten chilly. "I'm waiting."

"I don't intend to take any chances—why should we? We don't have to go anywhere *near* those two, to make them pay. We let the witch do the job for us. Nothing to it. She stings them, Jack controls them, and *we* tell Jack exactly what we'd like done."

"We," said Money.

"I was thinking—what'd be *perfect?* We have Eugene and his father-in-law start injecting each other with every single one of their goddamn Idiot Drugs, and then—"

"Jesus Christ."

"What?"

"And Herb thought you were the hero."

"Herb."

"Yeah, *Herb*. Herb! Well, he's gone—does that give you

some satisfaction? It must. You got a *taste* of your revenge, at least."

"I held nothing against—"

"The *hell* you didn't."

"Money . . ."

"Jack liked Geebo better. Isn't that what he said? He liked Geebo better?"

Peter opened his mouth, said nothing.

"And Jere. *She* liked Geebo better. And know what? I never met the guy, but I bet you anything *I* would've liked Geebo better, too."

"Don't be—"

"Stupid? You were gonna say stupid. Hey, sorry, I just can't help it."

Once again she moved to leave, and once again Peter grabbed her wrist. This time, though, she violently flung him off.

She started away, back toward Jack and Lita, but half-a-dozen feet from the bench, she came to an abrupt stop.

And pressed her eyes shut, opened them, narrowed them. Then stiffened, with a sharp sinking feeling in the pit of her stomach.

The Walker and his witch were completely enveloped in the pearly-gray mist, and as immobile as any of the garden topiaries. Their eyes were open wide, fixed. Blank.

Money pivoted, *her* eyes flashing, following the mist back to its source, at the mouth of the hedge maze.

Where a dwarfish old woman stood, smiling.

"Welcome," she said, "to Lostwithal. I am called Sister Card. And you are called—?"

Money's hands had flown to her face. She felt light-headed, and tottered. Her gaze cut, instinctively, from the old woman's face to . . . something small on the ground beside her. A scuttling human hand, dragging a—

She was supposed to scream now. This, finally, was the last straw, the ultimate horror, and Money Campbell, schoolgirl and ditz, was supposed to scream.

At the sight of a human hand dragging an automatic pistol.

But she didn't.

Instead, she took a step toward the old woman, forced saliva into her mouth, and said, "I am called Monica."

Sister Card lifted an arm, pointed to a spot a few yards to her left. "Come and stand here . . . Monica."

Nodding, Money began to walk toward the pythoness, her legs heavy, her mind awhirl. The ground mist broke against her, dissipated.

The white hand was closed around the grip of the pistol now, and the barrel was lifting, and Money's eyes widened, and Sister Card said, "You are a Kemolon—I shall let you die by Kemolon magic."

Money flung herself behind one of the enormous sculptured hedges just as the gun discharged. Mist burning her eyes, she scrambled madly on hands and knees, then propelled herself with all her strength against the old woman, squeezing her hands around Sister Card's throat.

The old woman's breath scalded her cheek.

Money's hands let go, were forced to let go, but somehow she managed to bend her knee and then to drive it up hard, into the old woman's soft belly.

When the gun fired again, Money spun away, stumbled, went down. Opened her eyes to see, in the grass beside her head, a pulpy mass of fingers and blood.

The hand, blown apart.

Roughly, she was plucked to her feet.

Peter.

Holding her by an arm.

Aiming the pistol at Sister Card, whose eyes were ablaze and whose hands were rubbing a talisman that hung by a thin ribbon around her neck.

A new mist, not pearly but tan, began to form at her feet.

Peter fired.

A small red hole appeared in the old woman's chest.

But still her fingers worked the talisman.

She fell to her knees, and cut a geometric figure in the air with the blade of her hand.

The mist darkened.

And Peter fired again.

This time, the pythoness shuddered, her eyes rolled in her head, and she pitched forward, dispelling the mist.

Peter kept squeezing the trigger, but the clip was empty.

He dropped the pistol and slumped against Money.

"What?" she said. He'd muttered something. "What?"

"Kemolon magic," he said, then twisted sideways and was sick on the grass.

Then there were armed men, palace guards, everywhere.

And Jack, a Walker, clutching Lita, rose unsteadily from the stone bench.

"Well, Peter," said Money, her voice sounding harsh and louder than necessary, "I guess he *does* owe you another favor. Now. Which I'm *sure* you'll collect."

But Peter turned his eyes away when Jack's gaze fell upon him.

CHAPTER 36

THRONE ROOM

SOME JOURNALIST. RE-
mind me never to cover peace talks or a disarmament con-
ference, he thought. Christ, here he was now, seated in a
gallery of the huge throne room of the royal castle in a
magic kingdom, nobility gathered, honor guard at attention,
pages scrambling, a trumpet's blast, pomp and ceremony,
and no matter how hard Peter Musik tried to concentrate, to
absorb things, to catalog the major images and the tiniest
details, he could not. His mind kept wandering, his eyes kept
closing. Some journalist. Some goddamn journalist *I* am.

The King was a small, unimpressive man, his raiment
was drab, and he seemed preternaturally . . . still. Yes, all
right, Peter thought. There's something. The King is motionless. I'll remember that . . . and then his mind wandered
again and he was remembering something that Money had
said, when she was out of her skull and convinced she was
drugged; something about . . . nobody looking for Peter
Musik after he'd been dumped on the street. Nobody even
missed him. Nobody missed him. He could've stayed on the

street forever, nobody missed a down-at-his-heels trash-tab journalist. Nobody.

Except Money Campbell.

Who suddenly jabbed him in the ribs, and when he flinched, put a finger to his lips, then cocked her head toward the throne, where Jack, a Walker, who'd drawn the doll of ash from a small string bag, was now speaking, gesturing, saying something about a masquerade party.

". . . the seamen's masque, Your Royal Highness, which I did attend . . ."

Peter tried to concentrate, to focus on the Walker, and did, for a short time, watching him move up and down in front of the throne, pausing occasionally, dramatically, then continuing; and Peter studied King Agel's expression, only it never changed, and he glanced toward the noble's gallery and saw frowning faces there, and craned and looked back toward a gallery of old men in black cassocks and saw *angry* faces there. And then he looked around, and spotted Lita standing to the side of the throne with a tall, ferocious-looking man in a military tunic, whose complexion was sallow.

Sallow. He'd describe that man as "sallow-faced," later, when he wrote about all this.

Later.

But now, now he was thinking about . . . other things again.

Jack liked Geebo better.

And Jere Lee. She liked Geebo better, too.

And Herb thought you were the hero . . .

Peter leaned forward, burying his face in his hands.

He was tired, so tired.

And know what? I never met the guy, but I bet you anything I would've liked Geebo better, too.

Money nudged him again, hard.

Whispered, "Nod, stupid. *Nod.*"

And he looked up, blinking, to see the King of Lostwithal staring at him. Peter caught his breath, then, mustering as much dignity as a callous, sorry-for-himself, vengeance-seeking, trash-tab hack journalist was capable of, he nodded his head, once.

And then felt a little . . . *glow.*

His hand fumbled for Money's on the bench beside him.

Suddenly, the throne room exploded in a roar of excited voices, noblemen raising their right arms, mages extending their left hands, till finally with a single loud clap, the room, just as suddenly, fell quiet again.

I think I missed something, thought Peter.

Some journalist.

The sallow-faced military man was down on one knee before the King. Jack, a Walker was standing with Lita, to one side of the throne.

". . . with all swiftness," the King was saying, "to the Manse Seloc. According to the Order of Things."

The sallow-man bowed, and retired.

Then, both nobility and mages rose from their benches simultaneously, and looking toward King Agel, they nodded. In utter silence, they filed from the throne room.

Pages carried bowls of fruit to His Majesty.

Money leaned over and said, "I think we were *great* Witnesses, don't you?"

Peter looked at her, at her scratched and puffy face, at all the bruises and weals and sweaty grime, and something seemed to . . . burst in his chest, and he opened his arms.

And she said, "Hey," accepting his embrace.

"That's all there is to it?" Money was saying now, as they left the castle. "That's *it?*"

Jack nodded. "Almost." With his chin, he gestured at the royal troops mounting Beasts in the inner bailey. As Jack and Lita and Peter and Money stood watching, the soldiers made formation, and then, upon a signal, moved toward the portcullis, hooves clattering noisily on cobbles.

Peter said, "Don't you . . . ?"

Jack turned to him. "Don't I what?"

"Want to see it through to the end?"

"I am merely a Walker."

"Yeah, but what about . . . revenge?"

Jack studied Peter's face, sadly, but said nothing. When he started across the inner bailey, and Peter followed him, Money called, "Hey, no!"

Lita reached and touched her lightly, on the left hand.

A few minutes later, after they'd mounted, Jack smiled. "All of this simply because I slept in your cardboard box."

"Accidents will happen."

"Come, Peter, we'll see about this revenge you talk so much about."

"You called me Peter."

"It's your name."

"Yes," he said, glancing back at Money, who looked away. "It is, isn't it?"

CHAPTER 37

LAST ACCIDENT

EUGENE BOMAN, THE BOY Billionaire, was hopelessly lost in the gloomy corridors of the Manse Seloc.

He'd been running and stumbling, wheezing and coughing for what seemed like hours. He couldn't stop, though, he had to find some way out. But once he did—*if* he did—what good would that do? He was still here, trapped here, in this . . . this godforsaken *someplace else*. Without Major Forell, there was no going home, no way back . . . and the Major—

Was gone.

Boman came to the end of yet another corridor, and paused. Which way? What did it matter? He turned left, and his foot crunched something, and then he sprawled forward onto his face, scattering bones.

More bones.

There were bones, and bone meal, in nearly every passageway.

And iron doors, which he refused to open.

Gulping breath, he managed to pick himself up, and stagger on. His temples pounded, his heart felt as if it would explode.

In despair, he leaned against a moist wall, and slid to the floor.

The Major, he thought. The Major. And though he tried to push the image from his mind, he failed, and then was seeing that . . . man again, that whistling man with the writhing face.

Boman had *told* Forell it was madness to just walk into such a place, but what was Boman supposed to do—stay behind? And so he'd followed him into this hellhole, expecting at any moment to be seized by guards. But there were no guards. The place seemed absolutely empty. Like in *Dracula,* he'd thought. That guy goes to Transylvania? the real estate guy? He goes into the castle, and there's nobody there. Just a meal waiting. Well, there wasn't any meal waiting *here.* There was *nothing* here, except cavernous space and . . . bones on the floor.

He kept tugging on the Major's sleeve, begging him to turn back, and finally the Major had struck him. "For once in your life, be a man."

"Man," said Boman, summoning nerve, somehow, out of sheer panic. "I *am* one. A foolish, stupid, weak, and very guilty man, but a man nevertheless. You, though, you're a *monster.* Always calling yourself a hero. You're no hero. You're a goddamn *monster!*"

That's when Forell had struck him with the rifle barrel.

—Moments before the master of the house appeared, from nowhere.

He came forward several paces, a man dressed in black robes, a tall man whose cheeks seemed to be wriggling. And then he spoke. Spoke? He *whistled*, it was a high-pitched, quavering, piercing *whistle*, and Boman screamed, and his scream jerked him sharply backward. And—

Remembering the scene now, he shook his head, trying to deny it, but it happened, it *had* happened, it made no sense, but it had happened. He'd seen it. He *saw* it.

Saw Major Forell smile. That smile.

And saw an *identical* smile appear on the lips of the whistling man.

The identical smile!

It was as if, as if they *recognized* one another.

The whistling man turned abruptly and started up a flight of stairs; he paused, waiting for the Major to follow.

"Richard! Are you insane? Don't go!"

Boman had snatched at him, tried to pull him back, but it was useless. The Major was determined, and the Major was smiling.

He'd climbed the stairs behind the whistling man, and Boman had stared after them in horror. "Don't leave me!" he'd screamed, and his voice returned to him in echoes. . . . eave me, eave me . . .

Once the Major was out of sight, Boman tore at his hair, but then raced for the staircase. He couldn't lose him, *couldn't*, if he lost the Major, *he* was lost.

The stairs seemed to go on forever, and Boman was panting, clutching his chest long before he'd groped his way to the top. He saw Major Forell down a long corridor. "Richard!"

No response, not even a glance. It was as if Eugene Boman, so far as the Major was now concerned, no longer existed.

The whistling man opened an iron door, and Major Forell stepped into a room with curving walls.

And then Boman had started running—back to the stairs, but somehow he'd run past them, and when he'd tried to find them again, he couldn't, and wherever he'd turned, there was another corridor, and another, and another, and bones, and bone meal. . . .

And now, huddled in darkness, Boman let out an anguished cry.

His head jerked, at the sound of trampling feet.

He stood up, flattened himself against the wall.

Glanced to his left: the sounds were coming from *that* direction.

He thought, but for just a moment, of fleeing in the opposite direction. But then decided, no. He would go *toward* the sounds, try to find them, no matter what it meant. And it probably meant his death. But all right, all *right*. If it meant that, all right. It was better than running forever up and down endless corridors like a rat in a maze.

Or a man in a drug frenzy.

If his death were in that direction, he would go to it, not seeking it, but willing to accept it, if it came. To accept it, calmly. Like a man.

The sounds of trampling feet became louder, clearer, until finally Boman turned a corner, and froze, gaping at a dozen men, followed immediately by more and still more men, all of them racing up the wide central staircase—the lost staircase—all of them dressed in red military tunics and armed with heavy swords.

Unable to move from where he stood, forgetting even to breathe, Eugene Boman watched as the soldiers flung themselves at the iron door through which Major Forell had disappeared with the whistling man.

The noise was clangorous, bright sparks were struck, and hinges screamed.

And then: a deafening explosion sent the attackers hurtling back down the corridor and blew the turret room, in a cascade of flame and wood and masonry, out into the black starry night.

The room was simply . . . gone.

In the corridor, men were groaning, picking themselves up, talking excitedly in that strange skirling whistle-language.

Eugene Boman stood rooted, watching the smoke clear, and the chaos in the corridor sort itself out, till at last, it was clear that the explosion would be reckoned *a good thing* (most of the armed men were grinning) and not a debacle.

Eugene Boman understood absolutely nothing of what had happened, except that it had ended well. That it was a good thing.

For who, though?

For *them,* he thought.

But who are *they?*

He retreated four steps.

By then he'd been noticed.

Boman spread his hands, hoping they'd take it as a friendly, helpless gesture.

He wiped a hand slowly across his mouth.

Shut his eyes, swallowed, opened his eyes.

And started walking toward the soldiers.

But then stopped, seeing two figures, neither of them dressed as the others were dressed—who were dressed, in fact, in tatters—suddenly top the stairs. Two men.

One of whom turned and looked directly at Boman.

"Peter?" cried Boman, incredulous. *"Peter!"*

And Peter Musik, who'd frowned at his name, stepped forward, laughed softly, and said, "We meet by accident."

ABOUT THE AUTHOR

Tom De Haven has published six previous novels: *Freaks' Amour* (William Morrow, 1979/Penguin, 1986), *Jersey Luck* (Harper & Row, 1980), *Funny Papers* (Viking, 1985/Penguin, 1986), *U.S.S.A.* (Avon, 1987), *Sunburn Lake* (Viking, 1988/Penguin, 1990), and *Joe Gosh* (Walker & Company, 1988). He has produced the script for a graphic novel based on William Gibson's *Neuromancer*, published by Epic, and has written extensively for newspapers and magazines, including *The Village Voice, Goodlife, New Jersey Monthly*, and the *Philadelphia Inquirer*. He is a regular contributor to *RAW*, and has written episodes for *The Adventures of the Galaxy Rangers*, a syndicated animated television show (1986–87 season). Mr. De Haven is a recipient of two National Endowment for the Arts Creative Writing Fellowships (1979–80; 1986–87) and a New Jersey State Council on the Arts Writing Fellowship (1980–81). From 1981 to 1987 he taught Creative Writing at Hofstra University and is currently an Assistant Professor of American Studies at Rutgers University. He received a B.A. from Rutgers-Newark and an M.F.A. from Bowling Green State University. He lives with his wife Santa and their two daughters, Jessie and Kate, in Jersey City.

The Order of Things has been fulfilled. Jack, the King's Tramp, has returned to Lostwithal and warned the King about the coming Epicene. Action can now be taken to stop chaos from overwhelming the universes.

Or can they? The Mage of Four, Mage of Luck is determined to carry out his plan to unleash the Last Humans. If he cannot be found and stopped, the Epicene will fulfill the awful purpose for which it was born.

The End-of-Everything Man, Book 2 in the Chronicles of the King's Tramp, is available now in hardcover and trade paperback from Doubleday Foundation. Here is an excerpt in which we catch our first glimpse of the dread Epicene:

Well, there it is, she thought. Manse Seloc. And, shaking her head, Didge remembered she'd been here before.

It must've been, what, more than a hundred seasons ago—on a daytrip with her father, and her mother, and her mother's husband, and her father's brother Jix (her own brother hadn't yet been born; she herself was no more than eight or nine: her hair was straight then, it was yellow, golden yellow, and she wore it proudly in a long gleaming horsetail), and, and . . .

Didge remembering: as a treat, Uncle Jix had brought them all to the capital, to Beybix (he'd had some business there, perhaps a tax to pay), and one afternoon near the end of their visit (after they'd seen Agel's castle and filed through the Schoolteacher's Museum and prowled the market squares and wandered through the labyrinthine Public Garden of Our History) they'd rented (Uncle *Jix* had rented) a horse and small wagon, and they'd gone out of the city and into the pitch-pine barrens, following the old Sand Road, for a picnic.

And in the late afternoon Didge had wandered off alone, not far, not lost, just . . . alone, following a switchback trail (and there was fetterbush . . . and turkeybread . . . and a sweet bay magnolia: Didge proud that she could identify every shrub, every tree, and flowering plant; she was a smart little girl, was Didge, *everybody* said so), and finally she'd come to a bluff, looked down, and *seen* it: the small black castle. At once, she'd known what it was.

Manse Seloc.

(Where lived the End-of-Everything Man.)

(Don't be foolish, children, he's just a mage, like a thousand others.)

And Didge had stood there, transfixed and trembling, on that bright, hot Low Summer afternoon, till her uncle (with his bald sunburned pate) had come along and found her. And then *he'd* stood transfixed (and maybe trembling, too, Didge couldn't really tell).

At last, she'd said (murmured), "The End-of-Everything Man."

And Uncle Jix had said, "Time to go home, child."

"Time to go home," he'd said.

Not: don't be foolish.

That was years and years ago. Fifteen or sixteen.

More than a hundred seasons.

A bright, hot day, in Low Summer. And now, on a cold, dark night of torrential rains in Late Blaze, Didge sat with her nose pressed to the coach window, transfixed once again by the ancient (and greasy) black walls and towers of Manse Seloc, where torchlight jiggled in several slitted windows. Her head began to buzz. And—small hands clenched, both hearts pounding—she trembled.

The End-of-Everything Man.

She flinched when the mage's hand dropped upon her knee, and tightened there.

"Master . . . ?"

"Come along, woman, don't *worry* so."

Cloth cap plastered to his skull, the coachman pulled open the door and held out a hand to assist Didge to the ground, where she promptly sank into mud past her ankles.

When Amabeel had joined her, they slogged across the courtyard, their heads bent against sleet and rain, the surly wind blowing their hair pell-mell, his cassock whipping around his knees, her cloak snapping behind her. Didge felt a rush of excitement (and of dread, and of misgiving).

What am I expected to *do*?

The mage rapped upon the great iron door. Almost immediately it swung back with a grating sound, and there stood a tall—some six-and-a-half-feet-tall—grim-faced soldier in the gaudy red tunic and white crossbelt of a King's

Guardsman. A captain of the Guard. (On the dorsum of his nose was a spider tattoo, emblem of valor.) After he'd rattled off the fitting, and tiresome, words of welcome, according to the Order of Things, he made a slow, grave bow, to Amabeel.

But then he merely glanced (with perplexity? or was that just her imagination?) at Didge.

Who moved impulsively forward and dropped a curtsy, which she ought *not* to have done, but . . . well, she was flustered.

The Guard captain led them through an arched passage (chimneyed lamps burning in wall brackets) and into a cavernous, beam-ceilinged octagonal hall. There, a score (at least) of other soldiers stood warming themselves by the hearth's log fire, or were squatted at gambling, or sat morosely on the bottom steps of a broad winding staircase.

A number of the men's tunics were torn and scorched black.

There were six long windows hung with bloodred draperies, but no furniture.

And the floor (Didge recoiled with a sinking, then a spinning, sensation)—the stone floor was strewn with animal bones, and with chips and flinders of bone, and with bone powder that wet boots had tramped into gummy white paste.

"Come along," said Amabeel, vehemently, "we've services to perform."

She drew a deep breath, to still her trembling. Then, half-running, she crossed the hall, passing the mage (which, again, she ought not to have done), and started up the stairs behind the Guardsman. Whose sword hilt clinked softly as it bounced in its scabbard.

Suddenly Didge's hands felt very cold. Something was wrong. She glanced upward, and then saw him—a man. In shadow at the top of the stairs. Leaning against the balustrade. Arms folded. Clearly waiting.

The—

—End-of-Everything Man?

* * *

Brother, what Peter Musik wouldn't give right this second for a piece of paper and something to write with. It was driving him nuts, all these weird people traipsing around, and him not able to make notes. Just his luck, to pop into some alternate universe without so much as a Bic pen in his pocket!

He wouldn't have trouble remembering the first-graf stuff, so to speak—all the major *incidents*; it was the picayune things, the telling *details*, the choice bits of business he was afraid he'd forget if he didn't write them down now.

For example: this small, cute woman with the orange hair and pale-gray skin? Peter would *try* to remember that she had a slight limp on her right leg and a jeweled brooch, shape of a cat, pinned to her cloak, but he'd *definitely* remember how she reacted seeing Jack at the top of the stairs. She was shocked. So badly it seemed possible that her legs might buckle.

He'd remember, too, that Jack, seeing *her*, seemed taken equally by surprise—and that he'd reached out and grabbed her, drawing her up the last two steps, into the gallery, and that he'd called her Didge.

Peter the pro, the working journalist, stood five feet away, taking everything in: seeing Jack smile, Didge frown, start to cry. Peter watching, nodding, not knowing what the hell was *up*, but certain it was juicy, and then—

Then a very tall, white-haired geezer, a magician-type in a soggy brown cassock, came hobbling off the staircase, puffing and blowing, and suddenly Peter Musik (Your Correspondent in Lostwithal) was faced with a serious dilemma.

Should he stick around, see what happened between Jack and this Didge person—

(whose toenails were filed to points)

—or should he follow the old magician?

(who had a scuffed leather bag slung over his shoulder, and carried a pair of tongs)

Peter thinking, What would Jimmy Breslin do?

He glanced at Jack (still talking low, speaking Losplit, saying to the woman, ". . . your brother?"), then made a hasty decision, hoping it was the right one: he moved briskly along the gallery, trailing after the geezer.

Jack said, "Bladen? Is at the castle?"

Didge said yes, hadn't she just *told* him that? Bladen was at the royal castle. Doing his firstwork. Didge sounding cross, adding, "You want to talk about my brother, fine, we'll talk about him later. Right now I'm supposed to perform a service. You want to show me what it is?"

Jack didn't move. He just stood there with his back pressed to a bulky stone pillar, his eyes fastened on Didge.

He'd never expected to see her again.

No, change that: a fifth-degree Walker didn't think in terms of "expect" or "not expect."

He'd never *wanted* to see her again.

And what was most unsettling about this? Wasn't so much *seeing* Didge here as being startled by her sudden appearance.

A Walker wasn't supposed to *be* startled. By anything.

Jack saying finally, "I'll take you down to the cellar," then led the way, his mind drifting back, much against his will, to that *other* time she'd surprised him; remembering a humid, High Summer day when he'd woken in his bed, in his cottage in Sett, and there she was, spooned against him, naked and beautiful; the morning she'd ruined her life, and very nearly had ruined his. . . .

Wind-driven rain blowing in, slanted. through a big hole in the turret's stone wall, pouring down through gaps in the conical roof, bouncing on and puddling what remained of the floor—further drenching Master Amabeel as he crawled about on hands and knees, examining rubble.

Occasionally, he'd use the tongs to pick something up—a splinter, a singed clod of plaster, a chunk of iron, a chip of glass—and drop it into his gunnybag.

Peter Musik stood in the doorway, one hand braced on the sooty jamb, watching, seeing the Court Mage unsnap a little pouch-pocket in his cassock, and take out a small white tablet—it resembled, no kidding, a piece of

Chiclet gum—and then stick it on his thumb, the tip of his left thumb.

This called for a closer look.

Taking it slow, moving carefully—there were places, *rifts,* in the so-called floor where you could look straight down to a gallery twenty feet below—Peter stepped into the turret room and crouched.

The better to see Amabeel press the tablet to a splotch of mud that clung to a rocker on what looked like—

—a baby's cradle?

Peter took another step, easing forward slowly, saying to himself, Yeah, an old-fashioned wooden cradle.

There was a blinding flash—of blue—and Peter stumbled backwards (thinking, I'm gonna fall!), and the blue light, dense and glossy, began to pulse, strobing like crazy all around Master Amabeel, whose body shook and twitched, and whose face burst suddenly into flames.

The prisoner is burning!

What am *I* supposed to do about it?

Put out the fire, that's what.

Perform your service.

Dispell.

When her hands started to shake, Didge made fists.

The burning prisoner, a powerfully built man with dark red hair and bushy eyebrows, hung shackled to a greasy wall in the cellar, thousands of bright, tiny, hissing flames rippling upon—but not consuming—his naked body.

Abruptly, they all died, blew out, leaving his flesh dazzlingly red.

His chest rose and fell.

And the flames blossomed again.

He never made a sound.

But Didge groaned, recognizing the spell, and knowing how difficult it could be to break, that a pythoness had cast it, and—

And if Jack, a Walker hadn't been standing right there, she would've thrown up her hands, pleaded inexperience, turned around, and fled. Faced the consequences later.

Consequences. What was the worst thing they could do to her? Take away her documents? Stain her Heart of Talent? Say, Didge of Drawl, you're unfit to be a Dispeller—now go home?

Would that be so awful? It would be a relief!

Except that . . . discharged from her thirdwork, she'd have no other life-choice but to find a host, someone to support her, and that might get a little unpleasant. Lead to all sorts of complications. Like what happened to her mother—abstinently married to one man and producing children, as though they were fruit pies, for another.

Yes, well, the whole thing was moot, because she wasn't *going* to throw up her hands, plead inexperience, and run.

Not with Jack standing there, she wasn't.

She might *fail*, that was a real possibility, but she wouldn't fail without first giving it a try.

Not that she had to *prove* anything to Jack—to the Void with him!—it was simply that . . .

He was looking at her.

And she knew exactly what he was thinking. She did! She *knew*! He was thinking, Didge isn't worthy of a Talent, it's wasted on her.

Isn't *that* what he was thinking?

"You can go now."

Jack said, "Go? What're you talking about?"

"And take this man with you." Gesturing at the big red-faced soldier, a posted guard. "I prefer," she said, "to be left alone."

"Didge. We have no idea who this prisoner is, he could—"

She flared and drew back her shoulders. "Don't interfere! I've been formally summoned." (Formally summoned, indeed: by a Castle Dog that had scratched at the door of the visitors' hostel. MAKE HASTE! MAKE HASTE . . .)

Jack looked at her for what seemed to Didge a long time, his eyes piercing blue, then he nodded at the soldier, and they both went out.

The flames had died again on the prisoner. Whose eyes stood open, were glazed, and seemed sightless. And whose lefthand fingernails curled like talons.

Didge's gaze moved from the prisoner to the door. Then to a trestle table, to a water pail in a far corner, to a slug line that glistened across the stone floor. Stalling. That's what she was doing, she was stalling. Just *do* it, she told herself. Do it now.

You don't need . . . anything.

But she did. Oh but, 'Teacher, she did!

She couldn't *do* this without—

Reinforcement.

Turning her back to the prisoner, Didge shoved up a sleeve, exposed a wristlet of braided rag. Loosened one of the braids, spread it, and pinched out a winged beetle nestled in a twist of cloth.

Pinched it out, finickally, then squeezed it till it popped, and licked the ooze.

Half a minute later, when she turned again to face the burning man, her lips had gone flaccid, but her eyes were keen and bright.

Crooking two fingers, she worked them down beneath her collar, fished out a string pouch from around her neck.

Salt.

Removing the brooch from her cloak, she pricked her thumb with its post.

Blood.

Her mind was sluggish now, a faraway planet. She was moving erratically, unsteady on her feet, but . . .

But given just a few moments longer, she felt certain she could . . . that she would . . . that she'd even *want* to recall the Twenty-first Injunction, the Coda, the Relent, and the Low Paradox.

Words.

Just give her a few moments. A few moments, Schoolteacher.

First comes pleasure, *then* comes service.

To Didge, a Dispeller, that seemed only fair.

*   *   *

Now Didge came to the part she hated, that she'd always hated, where she had to rub her face till it stung with mineral salt, then roll her eyes, and get down on the ground and wriggle. All that stuff was so . . . *primitive*. Made her feel like a savage. It was stupid, a complete waste of time. Waste of motion. Her considered opinion.

Back at the Craft, she'd got into a lot of trouble for expressing those views to her Third Masters; they'd called her self-conscious and vain, accused her of being squeamish and lazy, a troublemaker. But they didn't understand: she was just practical. Modern. Look, everybody *knew* it wasn't salt that reversed a spell of magic, and it wasn't a lot of jigging around, either. Why pretend? Words did the trick—actually, their *vibrations* did. The rhythmic and modulated *sounds*. It didn't even matter what the words *meant*. It was all in the vibrations.

The rest of it was a lot of antique nonsense. Superstition.

But for saying that, for saying what everyone already knew, Didge had nearly been expelled from the Craft, nearly Stained, on two separate occasions. Once she'd even had her bags packed.

Finally, she'd learned to keep her big mouth shut.

That didn't mean, though, that she'd ever *accepted* all the rigmarole.

But she *had* taken an oath, and so . . .

She knelt down, stretched out full length on the cellar floor, and writhed.

As she began to utter the Relent, her mind was still hazy from the beetle sap, but her voice was clear and strong. She did, however, stumble over a word or two. But just a word or two.

When she was finished, Didge stood again, feeling slightly dizzy, and brushed off her cloak and trousers.

The prisoner was watching her.

Didge met his gaze, then looked away the moment his chest (but *only* his chest this time) darkened again with the red glow of fire.

His body strained against shackles, and his head jerked back. He grunted in pain.

It was the first sound of any kind that Didge had heard him make.

He grunted again as she raised cupped hands to her lips and began to articulate the Low Paradox, her thumbs moving deftly in and out of her mouth, pressing front teeth, side teeth, back teeth, manipulating her tongue.

A Paradox was to be uttered without hesitation (at the Craft she'd spent more than half a Wet Season just learning to breathe correctly), but now, midway through it, Didge drew a complete blank. Suddenly she couldn't remember what to say next, and in a panic she murmured three or four words from a stanza of the *Child's* Paradox. She broke off, in horror . . . shook her head to clear it . . . then went on, stammering, and finished.

She was afraid to look at the prisoner.

She was certain she'd botched it. The entire service.

If the prisoner were still in flames, what then?

Then what?

The sweat stood out in beads on her forehead.

Slowly, she raised her eyes.

His body glowed. He moistened his lips. Then clicked his teeth together. Didge could sense him bracing for more fire.

She held her breath.

But nothing happened.

Nothing!

She rubbed a hand across salty lips and sagged with relief.

The prisoner cleared his throat. Seemed about to speak, but then didn't.

His eyes followed Didge, though, as she moved confidently across the room, unlocked the door, and pulled it open.

"I'm finished, Walker," she said. "It's done."

It had been more than twenty minutes since Peter Musik had seen Master Amabeel go up in flames. And still he couldn't stop trembling. Thinking, Jeez, the guy's *head*! The guy's whole *body*!

He stood in the gallery now, opposite the turret room. Propped against a low balustrade. His mouth sandpaper-dry.

The Guard captain in the bloodred tunic was staring at him with his lips pressed tight together.

Peter straightened, rolled his shoulders, assumed—or at least *tried* to assume—a professional, inquisitorial demeanor. Brows knitted, head cocked, a hand on his hip. Then: "What happened in there?"

Which only made the Guard captain laugh.

Ever since Peter Musik was a kid, that had been the one sure thing to set him off, make him crazy, start him swinging. Being laughed at. He took a step toward the Guardsman, then stopped. His heart pounding. "What's so funny?"

"You're speaking the liquid language."

"The *what*?"

"You can always tell somebody who's learned Losplit from a cup of cold water."

Saying "learned" with a sarcastic, insolent edge.

Peter had learned—acquired the facility to speak—Losplit from quite a *few* cups of cold water, as a matter of fact: cold, cloudy water drawn from a well at a place Jack called The Preserve.

"What if I did? So what? You understand me. Now do you think you could answer my question? *What happened in there?* The old man was on *fire*." Yes, and then he wasn't. Just as suddenly as the flames had started, they'd ceased, and the mage, without so much as a blister, had calmly resumed canvasing the room. He was still at it now. "What's he looking for?" said Peter. "What's he doing? What'd I see?"

What, what, what, what, what.

Narrowing his eyes shrewdly, the Guard captain crossed the gallery. Then pressed his left palm flat against Peter's chest. The right side.

"You have only one heart," he said. There was a pause. A long one. "You are . . . too-human?"

Peter nearly made a wisecrack, but wasn't sure it would translate well into Losplit—into *liquid* Losplit, at that—so he just nodded. Feeling a slight glow, a tiny buzz, like a TV personality who's been recognized.

Immediately, the Guard captain drew his sword.

*   *   *

Jack was thinking he should maybe tell Didge she'd done a good job. That might smooth things over. But on second thought? It was a bad idea. She'd take it the wrong way, figure he was just patronizing her. He knew Didge, all too well. So he said nothing. Merely reached out and touched the prisoner's chest.

The right side.

Didge behind Jack now, saying, "What?"

"He's a Kemolon."

"He *is*? But how—"

"Did he get here?" said Jack. "No idea. Maybe he'll tell us." Then to the prisoner: "Care to?"

The prisoner blinked.

Didge saying, "If he's from Kemolo, he doesn't understand—"

Jack saying, "I think he does," then pointing at a pail of cloudy water. "You do, don't you? Who was it gave you a drink, the little witch? Sister Card?"

Still, the prisoner refused to speak.

So Jack switched to English: "I can help you. But first you have to talk to us. All right? Just tell us your name, how you got here. Don't be an asshole."

The corners of the prisoner's mouth tightly crimped.

"What, you don't like being called an asshole?"

"I'm not talking to anybody," said the prisoner, "so long as I'm hanging here. You let me down, then we'll see."

"First your name."

Jack had reverted to Losplit.

"No, first the iron comes off." Now the prisoner was speaking Losplit, too—the liquid dialect—though Jack figured the guy probably didn't even realize it. "First the iron."

"Oh, let him down," said Didge. "If the Mage of Four hung him up, then he *has* to be all right."

Jack, over his shoulder: "Oh? Really?"

Her eyes flashed, and her face turned two shades grayer.

Jack, to the soldier: "We'll leave him there, for now."

"No—wait!" The prisoner. In English. "My name's Frank Luks."

"All right," said Jack—in Losplit—then he turned again to the fat soldier. "You have a key?"

"Key? What key?"

"To unlock the manacles."

"What do you think," said the soldier, "I live here?"

"Hurry it up and get me down," said Frank Luks. In English. And: "Come on, come on, come *on!*" In Losplit.